WHERE THE CREEK BENDS

LINDA LAEL MILLER

WHERE THE CREEK BENDS

CANARY STREET PRESS

**CANARY
STREET
PRESS™**

Recycling programs
for this product may
not exist in your area.

ISBN-13: 978-1-335-00639-4

Where the Creek Bends

Canary Street Press
22 Adelaide St. West, 41st Floor
Toronto, Ontario M5H 4E3, Canada
CanaryStPress.com

Printed in U.S.A.

For Jenni and Dustin Gebhardt, with love and thanks.
When the going got tough, the tough got going.

1

She burst—no, *erupted*—through a shimmering splash of sunshine, like a human bullet, or an angel busting in from a neighboring realm, where magic was the rule rather than the rare exception.

Half-blinded by the glare—it was mid-July, the Montana sky was sugar-bowl blue, and he was sweating in his town marshal getup—Liam McKettrick squinted hard, sure he was seeing things.

Too much stress, too little sleep.

But she was real.

A bride, in full regalia, veil billowing, lacy skirts and snow-white train trailing in the dry dust of Bitter Gulch's Main Street, heading straight for the Hard Luck Saloon.

Liam, standing on the balcony outside the make-believe brothel above the very authentic—and currently empty—establishment below, bolted for the back stairs.

Whatever was going on here, he damn well wasn't about to miss it.

He'd just entered the saloon and established himself behind the long bar, idly wiping out a glass with a piece of cloth, when she arrived.

She pushed back the swinging doors with both palms, then swept across the sawdust floor to the bar.

After hoisting herself onto a stool, she folded back her veil, blew a strand of brown-gold hair off her forehead with a long, resigned breath, and rested one hand on the polished surface between them.

"Set 'em up, bartender," she said.

Liam was doing his damnedest not to grin.

The situation was wild.

And way more fun than he'd ever expected to have on an ordinary day in the "town" of Bitter Gulch—an oasis of fantasy, a place where men, women and children came to escape the modern world for a while and experience the Old West.

Standing at the southern edge of Painted Pony Creek, Montana, Bitter Gulch was Liam's brainchild; he'd designed it. Hired his younger brother, Jesse, to oversee the construction phase.

Liam swallowed, unable to look away from the bride, especially now that she was up close and very personal. Just across the bar.

She smelled of dust, subtle perfume and something sugary.

"What'll it be?" he asked, his voice slightly hoarse. He didn't use it much, his voice, as a general rule, and it was only eleven o'clock in the morning, according to the huge antique wall clock on the opposite wall.

So his social skills were still resurfacing.

She paused to ponder the question, looking solemn. She had wide hazel eyes, heavily lashed, and full of—something. Indignation, clearly, and confusion.

Pain, too, though she was doing a fairly good job of hiding that.

Liam's heart, usually heavily defended, like an isolated cavalry fort in those thrilling days of yesteryear, besieged by furious warriors riding painted ponies, hitched, and hitched hard.

"Whiskey," the woman decided.

"What kind?" Whiskey was whiskey, and he could have poured a shot without asking another question, but he wanted to extend this encounter.

It was amazing.

She was amazing, with those expressive eyes. Her skin was flawless, her lips full, and her shining brown hair, now slightly out of kilter under the exquisitely made veil, a lacy affair that might have been assembled from starlight and spider webs, in some strange and secret place beyond the tattered edges of the ordinary world.

"Any kind," she responded.

Liam nodded, put his hand out and introduced himself. "Liam McKettrick," he said.

They shook. Her hand felt dainty, but strong, too.

"Madison Bettencourt," she replied, straightening her spine and lifting her chin a little. Tears rose along her lower lashes and smudged her mascara when she brushed them away with the back of one hand. "By now, I would have been Madison *Sterne*," she told him. "But I bolted."

Liam poured two fingers of Maker's Mark into a clean glass, listening not just with his ears, but with the whole of his being.

It was an unusual thing, the way his senses seemed to be revving up, as if he were a race car instead of a man.

He'd never felt anything quite like this before.

"Ice?" he asked. He pushed the glass toward her—slid it, more like. He wasn't planning on making any sudden moves, lest she dissolve into sparkling particles and disappear. "Maybe some cola?"

Madison glanced back at the double doors, looking a little uneasy. "Ice," she said resolutely. "Otherwise, I'll take it straight."

Again, Liam wanted to laugh, but he knew that would be a mistake.

He filled a paper cup at the ice machine, brought it to Madison without another word.

"Is this place real?" she asked after dumping the ice unceremoniously into her glass, causing some of it to splash over the rim and stand melting on the scarred wooden surface of the bar.

"What do you mean, is it real?" Liam asked, amused, and not completely able to hide it, try though he did.

"It's like going back in time or something," Madison responded, after a long sip of whiskey. "One minute, I was at *my wedding*, across the road, finding out I'd just said 'I do' to a total pushover of a mama's boy, and the next—" She paused, raised and lowered her shoulders in a semi-shrug, and gazed sadly down into her drink.

A moment later, the lovely shoulders slumped slightly, and the sight gave Liam a twinge, deep in his chest. If he'd known her for more than five minutes, he would have put his arms around her right then and there, held her close. Reassured her somehow.

Yet another bad idea.

A few seconds of silence stumbled by. Then she looked up, met his eyes, and finished with, "The next minute, I was here, in the Old West. In a real saloon." Another sigh. "You know what I wish, Liam McKettrick the bartender? I wish I really could go back in time. Be somebody else. Live a different life— an entirely different life."

Madison took another swig of her whiskey. At this rate, she was going to be disastrously drunk, and soon.

Liam moved the bottle out of sight and leaned against the bar, bracing himself with his forearms.

She looked him over, taking in his collarless white cotton shirt, the black waistcoat he always wore when he spent time in Bitter Gulch. Along with his tall, scuffed boots, suspenders and itchy woolen trousers—not to mention the shiny silver star pinned to his coat—the outfit added to the ambience.

And Bitter Gulch was all *about* ambience.

That was the point of the exercise.

Tourists came from all over the world to don costumes, live the Old West experience. Movies were filmed there, on occasion, along with TV series for all the major players in the streaming game.

Liam knew most of the visitors wouldn't have lasted a day in the *real* Old West, but then, that didn't matter. They were paying to pretend, not to teleport themselves back to a previous century, when most of the amenities they were used to had yet to exist. Hot and cold running water had been a rarity in communities like Painted Pony Creek, electricity a fledgling science, and Wi-Fi—well, nonexistent, of course.

He pictured his kids, Keely, nine, and Cavan, seven, riding in wagons or on horseback everywhere they went, stripped of their cell phones, their tablets, the huge flat-screen TV in their grandparents' family room, and smiled.

God, he missed them.

"You wouldn't like it," he responded, at some length. He'd gotten lost in those lovely eyes of hers, along with his own thoughts.

"I wouldn't like what?" she asked, still putting on a brave front.

"Life in the past," he replied. "There are reasons why we're advised to live in the present, you know."

She let the remark pass.

"Are you really a lawman?" Madison inquired, having drained her glass while Liam was pondering the situation and, as always, wishing Keely and Cavan were with him instead of far away, staying with their grandparents in Seattle.

Liam allowed himself a minimal grin, really just an uptick

at one corner of his mouth, hardly noticeable to the casual ob-
server. "No," he replied. "I'm an architect."

Madison frowned, musing again. She was getting tipsy, and
Liam wondered how much champagne she'd had before deciding to ditch the mama's boy.

What a numbskull that guy must be.

"You don't look like an architect," she responded solemnly.

"What does an architect look like?" he asked.

"I don't know," Madison answered, still as serious as the proverbial heart attack. "But I'd have pegged you for an actor,
with your dark hair and those indigo-blue eyes and—well," she
paused, gestured with both hands, indicating their surroundings.
"When I picture an architect, I guess I see someone more—
ordinary. Like an accountant."

"An accountant," Liam echoed, hiding another grin.

"Whatever," Madison said, and now she sounded cheerier,
although the word got tangled up in her tongue before she
turned it loose.

Resolutely, she slapped the bar again. "More whiskey."

"Look," Liam reasoned. "Maybe it isn't the best idea—"

"Are you cutting me off?" she interrupted, though calmly.
Her beautifully shaped eyebrows drew together for a moment.

"No," Liam replied. "I'm just suggesting that, after what happened today, you might want to pace yourself a bit. That's all."

"Do you want to know, Liam McKettrick, architect and bar-
keep, just what *did* happen? I mean, bartenders are supposed to
be good listeners, right?"

"I'd say I'm a pretty fair listener," Liam allowed. Then, knowing he'd already lost the argument, unspoken though it was, he
picked up the bottle he'd set aside moments before, twisted off
the cap, and poured her a double.

"I could use one of those right about now," Madison replied,
after another healthy swig of liquor. "A good listener, I mean."

"Okay, shoot," Liam said. He'd done a lot of listening in his life, largely because he was a man, as the saying goes, of few words. So many people were uncomfortable with silence, felt a need to speak into it. "What happened?"

Madison mirrored his earlier posture, leaning on her forearms, all but hidden by puffy sleeves, and said in a confidential tone, "You won't believe it."

"Try me," Liam urged. Standing back a little, to give the runaway bride some space. No sense crowding her.

She seemed solid, but magical, too, which meant she could be a figment of his imagination, not a regular woman.

"I really thought Jeffrey was the man for me," she began, shaking her head, apparently reflecting upon her previous choices. "He ticked all the right boxes. He was handsome, employed, and he said he wanted kids."

Liam raised one eyebrow, though he was pretty sure she didn't notice that. She was too involved in the story she was telling.

"Your *first* husband?" he prompted casually, picking up the cloth, wiping down the spotless surface of the bar, glancing at the clock again. In less than an hour, Bitter Gulch would be open for business, bustling with appropriately costumed employees and the usual horde of families on summer vacation.

This delightful interlude would be over.

And how many times could something like this happen in one man's life?

"Yes," she began. "His name was—is—Tom Wainwright. He's an airline pilot, very good-looking and very macho. We were married for three years."

Liam thought of his own marital history. Reminded himself he was in no position to judge, given that he'd gone into that crap show of a marriage with both eyes wide-open.

His late wife, Waverly, a model and sometime actress, had been beautiful, with her fit, slender body, her gleaming dark hair, her stunning green eyes.

She'd also been a walking red flag, vindictive when she was

angry, which was often, jealous of just about everybody, and prone to straying, although Liam hadn't known that until he was in way over his head, with two children to think about.

Inwardly, he sighed. "Go on," he said.

Madison's fascinating, chameleon eyes seemed to be fixed on another place and time. "He promised," she said.

Liam waited.

"Tom knew I wanted children more than anything, and he promised we would start a family as soon as he got promoted, after we moved, that kind of thing. And, like a fool, I believed him." Madison paused, looked down at her drink. Her left hand, shimmering with a doorknob of a diamond and an impressive wedding band to match, trembled slightly. "Turns out, he never wanted children. He was just stringing me along, waiting for my grandmother to die, so he could raid my inheritance. And if all that wasn't bad enough, he got another woman pregnant. I divorced him."

"Understandable," Liam said, not wanting to break the flow. He felt honored, somehow, receiving her confidences in that quiet and otherwise empty saloon.

And very sympathetic. After all, he could identify. He would have divorced Waverly a lot sooner, for similar reasons, if she hadn't gotten sick. She'd died only six months after she'd been diagnosed with an aggressive form of leukemia.

Everything he'd felt for her had dried up and blown away like so much dust, once he finally admitted to himself that she'd been unfaithful, not just once or twice, but dozens of times.

But she'd been so desperately ill.

And she *was* the mother of his children.

He'd had to stand by her, whether he wanted to or not.

And stand by her he had, until the end, though even as she was dying, Waverly had been distant with him, cold.

If it weren't for you and these kids, she'd said once, lying skeletal in her hospital bed, breathless and bitter, while machines beeped and wheezed around her, *I would have been famous. I would have been somebody special.*

The memory, brief as it was, caused Liam to shut his eyes for a moment.

When he opened them again, Madison was throwing back more whiskey.

She teetered a little on the stool in the process, so that Liam reached for her, caught himself just short of grabbing her fore-arm to keep her from falling right into the sawdust.

"Steady there," he said.

"I definitely dodged a bullet today," she confided, though wistfully. "I need to rethink my entire life."

She fell silent again. Staring down at her drink, probably fighting back tears.

Liam had never longed to put his arms around a woman the way he did then, but that was a risk he didn't want to take.

She might vanish.

Anyway, somebody was bound to come looking for her soon—the erstwhile groom, for example, or maybe her mother, if she had one. It was a wonder no one had tracked her down yet, in fact, since Brynne Garrett's fancy wedding venue was just on the other side of the road.

He'd noticed the crowd gathered around the flower-draped gazebo earlier, though it wasn't an unusual sight, since Brynne and her business partner, David Fielding, did a land office busi-ness throwing lavish weddings, many of them complete with fireworks, strange costumes and paid extras.

Now he imagined the drama and chaos that must have started when the bride turned her "I do" into an "I don't," and fled the scene in a fist-clenching fury.

Again, he allowed himself the faintest of grins, savoring the memory of her spectacular arrival, a creature of light and flame and sweet, sweet frenzy.

"And today, you married Jeffrey," he ventured, to get the conversation moving again.

"Sort of," she said, with another sigh and another swirl and another swig.

More like a gulp.

"How do you 'sort of' get married?"

"I went through with the ceremony," she recalled. "We exchanged vows in front of that lovely gazebo, and the minister pronounced us husband and wife. We went into the lodge then, since it was time for the reception to start. Jeffrey's mother sidled up to me, all smiles, and said she was so thrilled to be going on the honeymoon with us. Turned out, Jeffrey had bought her an airline ticket, behind my back, and even reserved a room for her at our hotel."

"Uh-oh," Liam muttered, with conviction. In any other circumstances, he would have added a whistle, for emphasis.

"Jeffrey actually invited *his mother* to join us *on our honeymoon*, and I didn't see it coming. I should have, because there were plenty of warning signs, but I didn't!"

Liam was sympathetic—and fascinated. "What happened then?"

"I confronted Jeffrey, and he admitted it was true. His mommy needed a vacation, and she'd always wanted to visit Costa Rica. Can you believe it?"

Liam was stuck for an answer, so he didn't offer one.

"I told Jeffrey we were through, this time for good, and I refused to sign the license, which meant we weren't legally married. We'd been through the motions, but none of it was binding.

"Jeffrey kept arguing—he said I was being dramatic."

"Were you?" Liam asked mildly, and felt a smile tug at one corner of his mouth.

"Yes," Madison replied, after huffing out a sigh. "And I'm not sorry."

"Understandably," Liam affirmed. What kind of idiot wanted

to take *his mother* along on a *honeymoon?* "I guess this wasn't the first time Jeffrey's mother had been a problem?"

Madison drew a deep breath, causing her perfect breasts to rise beneath the silk and lace of her bodice, and exhaled loudly, in obvious frustration.

Remembering, she shook her head. "That woman—Yolanda, I mean—was always interfering. She was awful, actually. Always passive-aggressive—with *me*, that is. Clingy and possessive, too, forever fawning over Jeffrey, calling him her baby boy." She paused, shook her head. "I'm such a ninny."

"You don't strike me as a ninny," Liam observed moderately, wondering how long it had been since he'd heard that old-fashioned term. "Maybe you're being a little too hard on yourself?"

"Kind of you to say so," Madison said, softly and sadly. "But I have to take full responsibility. I wanted an ordinary man—somebody solid and dependable—not an overgrown jock like Tom. I thought Jeffrey was that man, and he said he wanted children, so I guess I was willing to overlook some of his faults—after all, I'm not exactly perfect myself."

Liam figured that was debatable, but he didn't say so. That would have been flattery, and he didn't deal in that.

"The signs were there, all along," Madison continued quietly, reflectively. "Yolanda was around way too much. She went to movies with us, for heaven's sake, and crashed more than one otherwise romantic dinner. We took a day trip to the beach once, and she followed us there."

"Wow," Liam said, because speaking his thoughts about Jeffrey's relationship with his mother would have been rude. Plus, it was none of his business.

Madison fixed her gaze on him in the next moment, eyes slightly narrowed, brows raised. "What's *your* mother like?" she asked forthrightly.

The question took Liam aback, unexpected as it was. "Different," he said, after a few long moments. "From Yolanda, that is."

"She doesn't interfere in your life? Invite herself along on your dates?"

"God, no," Liam said, trying to picture his independent mother behaving the way this Yolanda person apparently did. Cassie McKettrick loved her children, for sure, and she had been a loving, attentive parent when they were young, making sure they led active, happy lives and behaved themselves. For all that, she had always been more than a mother, more than a wife.

She was an artist, a businesswoman, a thriving entity in her own right.

Now that all three of them were grown men—he, Jesse, and Rhett, the youngest—Cassie was too busy sculpting museum-quality pieces, helping to run the family's sizeable ranch near San Diego, and serving on various charity boards to be overly concerned with what might be happening in the lives of her sons.

The faintest blush pinkened Madison's cheeks. "I'm sorry. I shouldn't have asked such personal questions."

"Don't be sorry," Liam said. He could hear car doors slamming now, female voices rising and falling, drawing nearer.

It was over, this odd encounter, and Liam wanted it to last longer. A *lot* longer.

"That will be my friends," Madison said, draining the last drops of whiskey and melted ice with an obvious swallow.

She was right, of course.

There were footsteps on the wooden sidewalk out front, and some of the chatter was discernible now.

"I'm sure she's here somewhere," a woman said.

"I saw her heading this way," said another.

"I wouldn't blame her for taking to drink," offered still another.

And then the saloon doors opened again, and four women

in voluminous gowns of pale pastels—pink, blue, green, and yellow—surged into the saloon.

"There you are, Mads!" cried the blonde in pink.

"We were worried about you," chided the brunette in blue.

"Big-time," confirmed the redhead in green.

The last of the company, dressed in yellow, wore a turban, and apparently had nothing to add to the conversation.

"Is he gone?" Madison asked, turning slightly to look back at the gaggle of bridesmaids.

She was just as beautiful in profile.

"Gone?" the blonde echoed, pink skirts swishing as she crossed the sawdust floor to touch Madison's shoulder gently. "For now, yes. He left the venue right soon after the confrontation, with Mommy tripping solicitously along behind him, tsk-tsking all the way." She laughed, and Liam decided he liked her. "I suppose they're probably at the hotel by now, recovering from the humiliation."

The brunette giggled and did a little dance. "Mads," she said, "this was absolutely *the best* wedding I've ever been to!"

"It was an s-show," Madison reminded them, somewhat dryly.

"Social media gold, as far as drama," added the redhead. "All that yelling!"

"Who's this?" purred the one in the yellow turban, giving Liam the once-over.

"This," Madison said, with an exaggerated gesture of one hand, "is Liam McKettrick, the bartender/architect/town marshal."

He inclined his head slightly, in an unspoken hello.

"Liam," Madison went on expansively, "meet my best friends—"

She reeled off their names, rapid-fire. Not one of them stuck in Liam's brain.

"I think it's time we got you home," the blonde—Alisa, Ariel, Annette?—said, turning her attention back to her friend, the flight-risk bride. "You need to get out of that dress, have something to eat—"

"And sober up," put in the redhead.

"Home?" Madison ruminated. She was definitely drunk. "And where is that, exactly?"

The blonde hooked an arm through Madison's and helped her off the bar stool.

The almost-bride hesitated, frowned. "Wait. I didn't pay for my drink!"

"On the house," Liam said.

"Thanks," said the blonde, with a brief glance his way.

With that, having surrounded her, the group maneuvered Madison toward the doors.

Liam followed, at a little distance, amused by the colorfully dressed women, all of them talking at once.

They navigated the wide sidewalk, then made their communal way around the hitching rail and water trough directly in front of the saloon.

Liam leaned against one of the poles supporting the narrow roof above the entrance, watching them move toward a white compact car waiting in the road.

Getting everyone inside was a somewhat jumbled effort, mildly comical.

And then they were driving away.

Liam watched the vehicle—most likely a rental, given its nondescript design—until it zipped beneath the archway at the end of the street and finally disappeared.

Then he went back inside the saloon.

Costumed barmaids and dance hall girls were arriving, having entered through the back way, tying apron strings and adjusting feathery headpieces as they came.

"Wait 'til you hear about that wedding over there at the Lodge, Boss," chuckled Sylvia Red Bird, the piano player and sometime torch singer. "Craziest one yet."

Liam pretended to be clueless. "You were there?"

"No," Sylvia replied, grinning. She was eccentric, to say the least, dressing herself in trousers, a pointy-collared shirt, a striped vest and a top hat for her shift at the Hard Luck. Sometimes, when she helped out in the gift shop across the street, next to the old-time photography place, she wore authentic medicine woman garb, which she created with her own hands. "Didn't need to be there. It's all over town, what happened. The ceremony went off without a hitch, according to Miranda from over at Bailey's restaurant, but when it came time for the reception, all hell broke loose. There was a lot of shouting, and then the bride tore up the wedding license and stormed out of the reception."

Liam hid a grin. "Is that so?"

"It's so," verified Molly Steel, who was paying her way through community college over in neighboring Silver Hills by dancing with, and for, saloon patrons. "I saw the videos. They're all over YouTube and Instagram and probably TikTok, too. All that show needed was footlights."

"You better show me those videos," Sylvia told Molly, "soon as we go on break."

Slowly, the saloon filled, first with staff, then with customers. A lot of these, it soon became apparent, had been guests at the thwarted wedding.

There were a lot of toasts, followed by laughter and anecdotes told from just about every perspective: old and young men alike, and their female counterparts. The caterers. Even the groomsmen, who were all in a jocular mood, despite the groom—ostensibly their buddy—being summarily dumped at his own wedding reception. They were knocking back liquor like there was no tomorrow, laughing a lot, shaking their heads at their friend Jeffrey's unnatural attachment to his mother.

Sheriff Eli Garrett stopped in around eight o'clock, as he always did whenever there was a big shindig in or around Painted

Pony Creek, accompanied by his good friend the chief of police, Melba Summers.

"Quite a day," Eli sighed, taking a place at the end of the bar.

"So I hear," Liam acknowledged. "Whiskey? Maybe a gin
and tonic?"

"I wish," Eli said. "I'm still on duty, so it's coffee for me, I'm
afraid."

Melba, truly beautiful and tough as logging chain, stood beside Eli, smiling. "Sheriff's just trying to preserve his stellar
reputation," she remarked. "Afraid I'll muscle in, one of these
election years, and push him out of office."

Liam laughed, and so did Eli.

Both officers were served coffee—like always.

"The groom's mother, Yolanda somebody, turned up at my office a few hours ago," Melba said. "She wanted her son's would-
be wife arrested for creating a public nuisance."

Eli nearly spat out his coffee. *"What?"*

"Well," Melba reminded him, "after the bride left, chaos
reigned. And somebody knocked over the wedding cake by accident. Do you have any idea how much a cake like that costs,
Sheriff?"

Eli sighed again, shoved a hand through his light brown hair.
"Actually, Chief, I do. My wife orchestrates most of these shin-
digs, and it's downright scary, the price of goods and services
these days. It's not uncommon for the bridal gown alone to
run in the thousands. And all for *one day*. I sure hope the star of
this spectacle got her money's worth, given the way the event
turned out."

Melba sipped her coffee. "The bride," she said, "is a Bettencourt. You know, *those* Bettencourts, the ones who struck silver
back in the day? The ones who built that big old house out at
the end of Sparrow Bend Road? She's not hurting for money,
I can tell you."

"I thought all the Bettencourts had died off, except for

Coralee, of course," Eli said, finishing off his coffee and shoving the cup away with a hint of reluctance. "And she's holding on by a thread, from what I've heard."

"Nope," Melba said, sounding pleased to set the sheriff straight on the matter. "She's got a granddaughter, Madison. The woman who was supposed to get married today. In my opinion, she came to her senses just in time to avoid tying herself down to a total waste of human bone and muscle."

Eli shook his head. "Small towns," he muttered. Then he thanked Liam and turned to leave.

At the Hard Luck Saloon, officers of the law got their sandwiches, sodas and coffee free. So did firefighters, paramedics and half a dozen old timers who knew how to spin a damn good yarn.

From the sound of things, Madison Bettencourt was going to be starring in more than her fair share of tall tales for a long time to come.

And Liam wanted to hear every last one of them.

2

Bliss

Twenty-Four Years Before

A butterfly with bright blue and yellow wings wafted past eight-year-old Bliss Morgan's nose, coming so close that she felt the tiniest whisper of a breeze against her skin.

She stood perfectly still, forgetting for a moment that her mother had taken off again, just a week ago, that her dad was lying drunk in the abandoned camper-trailer they'd been squatting in for a full month now, even that she was hungry. And she willed that butterfly to land on her outstretched hand, if only for a second or two, so that she could admire it up close.

The butterfly didn't cooperate—Bliss hadn't really expected it to—though she couldn't help a sigh of disappointment.

She was used to hoping for things that never seemed to happen, though, so she recovered quickly.

She found a moss-covered block of a headstone and sat down.

The small cemetery, hidden away in the woods behind the

Big House—Bettencourt Hall, it was called—was a favorite refuge, one of several secret places where her father wouldn't bother to look for her.

Not that he ever actually did that.

He just stood in the doorway of that rusted and dented metal cubicle they currently called home and bellowed her name.

Thankfully, that wouldn't be happening anytime soon; he'd come home from town late the night before, causing the camper to groan with the shifting of his weight as he bumbled toward the bench behind the tiny table and fell flat on his stupid face.

Bliss, still perched on the familiar headstone, which belonged to someone named Charles C. Bettencourt III, bent from the waist to pluck a ghostly dandelion from the tall grass.

She closed her eyes, made a wish that her mom would come back, and blew. Hard.

Moments later, she blinked, because all of the sudden her eyes stung, then watched as wispy little dandelion trees floated off into the sunlight, and she hid her wish away in her heart, along with all the others that probably wouldn't come true.

Meanwhile, birds chirped and chattered in the surrounding trees—oak, maple and birch, fir and pine, and the breeze rustled in the grass, like the footfalls of a passing fairy tribe, on its way to somewhere wonderful.

Bliss believed in fairies.

Even in Santa Claus and the Easter Bunny, though she knew she was too old, at eight, according to her recently vanished mother, for such silliness.

Ideas like that were for rich kids, Mona had said.

She never got tired of reminding Bliss that they were a poor family, mainly because her dad, Duke, was a good-for-nothing drunkard with an allergy to hard work and a penchant for rambling from one ass-end-of-nowhere town to another.

Mona preferred big cities and bright lights to poopholes like Painted Pony Creek, Montana, she'd said, and two weeks ago, just when the pinto beans and other stuff from the food bank had begun to run out, she'd taken off, Mona had.

Didn't even say goodbye.

But, then, she never did.

She'd be back one day, all smiles, with presents from the dime store and a thousand excuses for disappearing. Again.

Bliss felt sad, recalling the last time Mona had hit the road, when Bliss had come home from another favorite retreat, the hidden place where the creek, wide and rushing, bent like an elbow, splashing against big rocks, throwing up a silvery mist that struck her little-girl fancy as magical.

Liquid fairy dust.

It *was* magical, that hideaway spot, at least sometimes.

Bliss had seen and heard strange things there. Other nearby places, too.

Her dad would say she was imagining the stuff that went on where the creek bent, and maybe she was.

Bliss didn't care.

It was okay to imagine things, and it was okay to believe in them.

The way she'd decided that Jolly Old Saint Nick and the Big Rabbit were real, even if they never brought her anything.

Bliss liked to make up people and places and things.

She'd lived a hundred interesting lives, just by deciding to believe.

She believed in another family, for instance, with a father who showered and shaved and worked at a real job, and a mother who kept their nice house clean and made a lot of money selling cosmetics door-to-door and at parties.

In her imaginary family, she had sisters and brothers.

Two of each.

She had a big goofy dog named Ruffles.

She went to school, where she got smarter every single day, and she had friends, too. Lots of them. They played jump rope and hide-and-seek and tag, and Santa visited all their houses every Christmas Eve, leaving stockings bulging with toys and candy, and still more presents under the great, glittering tree in front of the picture window in the living room.

Oh, yes. Bliss was very good at believing.

And sometimes she believed so hard that her invented family seemed almost real enough to touch.

She dreamed about them at night, when she wasn't sucked into nightmares—her real dad yelling at her real mom, and sometimes hitting her. Mona screeching insults and using her fingernails on Duke's face like claws.

Bliss dreaded the bad dreams.

That was why she always practiced being with her other family in her mind, right before she went to sleep. Most of the time, the trick worked, and she ended up where she wanted to go.

A twig snapped, jolting Bliss out of her mixed-up thoughts, and she straightened her spine. Smoothed her grubby jeans shorts and too-tight T-shirt and summoned up a smile.

Her front teeth were crooked, so Bliss was self-conscious about her smile.

Mona said she'd need braces.

Her dad, Duke, said they needed lots of things, and braces were way down on the list.

Then Madison appeared, as pretty as the butterfly Bliss had glimpsed earlier, holding a big basket by its handle.

Madison was the kind of girl Bliss's mom and dad scoffed at. A rich kid, probably spoiled, with no real interest in making friends with grubby little girls who lived in sheds, tents, abandoned houses, and campers forgotten in the woods.

Except that Madison wasn't spoiled, or mean, either.

She wore good clothes, brand-new from the looks of them, and her face was always shiny-clean, like her thick brown hair.

Today, it was pulled back into a tidy ponytail that bounced when she walked.

Bliss felt a faint twinge of envy; her own hair was dirty-blond, tangled and matted in places. Her clothes were old, fished out of dumpsters or bought at garage sales.

Madison beamed at her, her big eyes bright.

"I brought food," she said, approaching. "Sandwiches and fruit and cupcakes."

Sandwiches, fruit and cupcakes.

Bliss's stomach rumbled. She'd found some blackberries growing near one of the special places earlier that day, and last night, she'd eaten a piece of cold pizza, not daring to take more than one, because her dad would get mad if she did.

Madison set the basket down, opened it, and took out a red-and-black-checked blanket, spreading it efficiently in the wide, grassy spot between Abigail Flannery Bettencourt, 1900–1918, and Franklin J. Bettencourt, 1923–1940.

Once the blanket was down, Madison bent her long, tanned legs and knelt. Like Bliss, Madison was eight years old; in the fall, she said, she'd be in the third grade.

So far, Bliss's education had been patchy, at best—during rare visits to her grandmother's house in Missoula, she'd been sent to school, and Granny H, Mona's mom, had taught her to read and count—but she knew she was smart.

She listened.

She thought about stuff.

She borrowed from the free library down by the road, which wasn't a library at all, really, but a wooden box stuck on top of a short, splintery pole. There was a door in the front, and folks exchanged books there by swapping out the ones they'd read for the ones they hadn't.

Sometimes, there was a sleeve of crackers inside, or a candy bar.

Bliss was always glad when that happened.

"Come on," Madison urged when Bliss hesitated. "Let's eat. Estelle, my grandmother's housekeeper, made chicken salad for our sandwiches, and there are sliced strawberries and green grapes, too." Another broad smile lit Madison's pretty face and danced in her eyes, which changed from green to gray to light brown, depending on what she was wearing or what mood the sky happened to be in at the time.

Today, they were green, like the worn sea glass Bliss had gathered when she and her mom and dad had lived, very briefly, in a cramped, run-down apartment someplace in California.

Mona had loved California.

Duke had hated the traffic and all the fancy people looking down their noses at him, thinking they were better.

So they'd moved on, as always.

Idaho, Washington, Oregon, Arizona, New Mexico—and now, Montana.

Though Duke was already making noises about loading their belongings into the back of his ancient black truck and heading out for wherever the road might take them.

Bliss worried her mom wouldn't be able to find them if they left before she got back.

"Bliss?" Madison prompted.

Bliss shook off the sad feeling she got whenever she thought about moving on to somewhere new and starting over. She didn't like living in the camper—it was small and there were spiders and holes in the floor, and the toilet didn't work—but the special places were here, just outside Painted Pony Creek, Montana.

She wanted to cry, just to think of leaving them.

But the prospect of real food cheered her right up.

She joined Madison on the blanket, both of them sitting cross-legged, with the basket beside them, overflowing with good things to eat.

"My grandmother thinks I made you up," Madison said, once they'd both helped themselves to a thick, delicious sandwich. The bread was soft and fresh, and there weren't any blue spots on it anywhere, nothing Bliss had to pick off with her fingers. "She says you're an imaginary friend."

Bliss chewed, slowly and carefully, then swallowed.

"I'm pretty sure I'm real," she replied. "But you never know."

She had, it was true, considered the possibility that *Madison* might be a made-up person, though. The friend she'd always wanted—clean and pretty and smart. Funny and kindhearted, too. Never judgy.

Madison often brought food along when she came to the cemetery, usually snacks in little colorful bags meant for one person, plus apples or bananas and, sometimes, candy or home-made cookies.

"You could come to my house," Madison suggested, chew-ing. "Then Coralee would *know* you're an actual, flesh-and-blood person."

Madison was the only person Bliss knew who called her own grandmother by her first name. Her mom and dad were only Duke and Mona in her mind.

Bliss shifted uncomfortably on the scratchy blanket. The fab-ric rubbed against her bare legs and made them itch.

"My dad would lose it if I went to somebody's place with-out telling him."

A mischievous twinkle sparked in Madison's eyes. Her lashes were long and thick, and her teeth were whiter than white, like the people on TV had.

Not that Bliss got to watch much TV these days.

There was no electricity in the camper.

No running water, either.

Suddenly, Bliss felt dirty. She longed for that Other Mother, the made-up one who let her take bubble baths and kept her hair squeaky-clean, brushed and braided. With pretty colored ribbons woven through.

"You don't have to tell your dad," Madison said, lowering her voice a little.

Bliss scrunched up her nose and narrowed her eyes. "He'd know," she said.

"Okay," Madison replied. Her voice was gentle. "Could I come to your house, then? Maybe if your dad met me, he'd let you come for a sleepover or supper or something."

Bliss had seen Madison's home, the back of it at least, from a hiding spot in the trees out beyond the clotheslines.

It was big and white, that house, with a lot of windows and a screened-in porch.

The porch alone was bigger than the camper Bliss lived in.

She shook her head. She might be willing to disobey her dad, under the right circumstances, but setting foot inside Madison Bettencourt's huge house was out of the question.

What if being there was so nice that her heart would split in two, since she surely wouldn't be allowed to stay long?

What if she broke something, something precious and expensive?

What if Madison's grandma took one look at Bliss, with her bare, dirty feet and her awful clothes, and ordered her outside?

That had happened to Bliss before, though the houses she'd visited had been much smaller than Madison's, and not nearly so fancy. Other kids' moms didn't trust her—they thought she might have head lice, or something else that was catching or that she'd steal something.

Sometimes, they'd given her food, half-filled bottles of shampoo, bars of soap, clothes their own kids had outgrown or simply gotten tired of, but sooner or later they always frowned at her and said something like, "Go outside and play," or, "Run along home now. We're about to have supper."

When she'd brought home the clothes and shampoo and soap—she only made that mistake once—Mona had flown into a furious fit of indignation, tearing the little T-shirt and the jeans into rags, throwing the other things into the garbage.

"We're not charity cases!" Mona had shrieked, causing Bliss

to tremble in her worn-out sneakers. "How *dare* that woman give us her castoffs, like we're beggars or something?!"

Bliss hadn't had an answer, and she'd fled the living space of the moment—it had been a cheap and very dirty motel room that time—to hide until her mom and dad had both left to do the things they did when they went to town.

"Do you think I'm a charity case?" she asked now, watching as Madison took two bottles of ice-cold soda from the basket and handed one to Bliss.

"No," Madison responded matter-of-factly. "Coralee would probably toss you in the shower, brush out your hair and outfit you in new clothes, but she's like that. If she sees a need, she wants to fill it."

"That's charity, isn't it?"

"I think it's kindness," Madison said, after a few moments of consideration. "Just because someone wants to be nice to you, and give you things, it doesn't mean they think you're a bum."

Bliss felt a pang of—something. "My dad's a bum," she said. "Granny H says so." A pause, a breath. "What's *your* dad like? And your mom? I bet she's pretty, your mom, and dresses up real nice every day, and goes places like the library and the supermarket and bingo and church."

A look of infinite sadness spread across Madison's face like a shadow. "My mom and dad are dead," she said. "They fell off a mountain when I was four. That's when I came to live with my grandmother."

"Oh," said Bliss, and that was all, because she didn't know what else to say in the face of such an enormous loss.

Madison took another bite of her sandwich. "Why do you come here, Bliss? To the cemetery, I mean?"

Because it's one of my special places, Bliss thought, but didn't say. Special places were also *secret* places, and she rarely spoke of them.

She raised one skinny little shoulder in a shrug. "It's nice here. And sometimes *you* show up, and bring sandwiches, or cookies, or apples or pears." She paused, finished off her fancy chicken salad sandwich. Helped herself to a sprig of plump green grapes, the kind that made her mouth water before she even tasted them. "Why do *you* come here? You must have your own bedroom and books and a bicycle and everything."

"I do," Madison said, but she sounded sad again. "Don't you?"

"No," Bliss replied, unwilling to share the full truth, that she lived in an old camper someone had left behind in the woods, and long since forgotten. That her dad was an ornery drunk and her mom tended to run off whenever life got too hard.

"Will you be going to school in Painted Pony Creek, or over in Silver Hills, like I do?" Madison asked.

Bliss crushed a fat grape between her tongue and the roof of her mouth, loving the explosion of tart sweetness that followed.

What would it be like to live in a house where there were grapes to eat, whenever you wanted, and lots of other wonderful things in the fridge, there for the taking?

"I'm homeschooled," she answered, after a few moments had passed.

That was what Mona told the social workers, whenever they tracked her down, though Duke and Mona's idea of homeschooling was to toss a tattered textbook her way, whenever they managed to score one from a library sale or the thrift shop, and tell her to get busy and smarten up a little.

Madison's forehead crumpled into a frown, though Bliss didn't feel looked down on, seeing her friend's expression. "Really?"

For Bliss, learning was catch-as-catch-can.

She could read as well as anybody, though, and she knew some big words. She could name all fifty states and the first sixteen presidents, clear up to Abraham Lincoln.

He was her favorite, Abraham Lincoln.

She liked his beard and his stovepipe hat and the way he enjoyed making jokes.

"What do you want to be when you grow up?" Madison asked, her tone conversational now.

"A doctor," Bliss said. "Or maybe a pole dancer."

Madison laughed, though not in a mean way. "A pole dancer?"

"They make a lot of money," Bliss replied matter-of-factly. "What about you?"

"More than anything," Madison said, looking and sounding wistful now, "I want to have a family. A *real* family, with me for the mom, and a nice husband and three or four kids."

"Four would be a handful," Bliss commented, after considering the idea for a moment or so. "Mona says that's what I am. A handful."

"Mona? Is that your mom?"

"Yes. Sometimes, she's my older sister, though. That's when Duke's off somewhere on a binge, or in jail, and she gets herself a boyfriend. Then, if I don't want a good smack, I have to say she's my sister, and I'll be going back to my regular family soon, so I won't be around long enough to get underfoot or cost any money."

Madison looked troubled. "Oh," she said.

Bliss didn't reply. She'd already said too much.

So she just took a long swig from her soda—cherry crème it was, and delicious, with real sugar instead of high-fructose syrup. Fancy stuff.

"Maybe we should go and talk to Coralee," Madison ventured cautiously. "About the boyfriends and the jail and the drinking, I mean."

Bliss stiffened, narrowed her eyes. "Don't you dare tell her anything!" she warned.

Madison leaned back a little way, startled. "She might be able to help you," she said.

Bliss got to her feet, lickety-split. Clenched her fists and fought back hot, angry tears. "I don't *want* no help from her or you or anybody else!" she shouted, regretting the outburst even as

it happened. It was as though she were two people just then—
one a tough little scrapper, the other standing slightly to one
side and watching helplessly, wanting to take everything back
and say sorry.

It didn't happen.

By then, Madison was standing up, too. Her face was calm,
her eyes full of sympathy. "Okay," she said, holding out both
palms, as if to stop Bliss from lunging at her. "Okay. I didn't
mean to make you mad."

The tears escaped then, trickling down Bliss's face zigzag-like,
probably leaving a trail because, even though she'd washed up
down by the creek a while ago, she felt as though she'd been
coated in dry dirt.

*"Don't you tell nobody about me, Madison Bettencourt! You'll be
sorry if you do!"*

Madison was still calm, still kind, and that shamed Bliss Morgan right down to the calloused soles of her bare, sunbrowned
feet.

"I won't," she said, very quietly. "I promise, I won't."

Bliss dashed away the humiliating tears with the back of one
hand, tossed the half-finished bottle of cherry crème soda to the
ground with the other, and then, without another word, turned
and ran away, as fast and as far as she could.

Mona had been right about rich kids.

Even when they were nice, it was only because they felt sorry
for you.

Pitied you.

She'd been downright stupid, thinking Madison liked her,
wanted to be her friend.

All Bliss's friends had been imaginary, before Madison, and
she meant to keep it that way.

3

Present Day

"It's a bachelorette party, in reverse!" Audra crowed as she joined Madison, Olivia, Kendall and Alexis in the main parlor of Cora-lee Bettencourt's old house.

They'd all showered and exchanged their bridal garb for shorts, T-shirts and flip-flops, and Madison, for one, felt as light as if she'd just lost one hundred eighty pounds—which she had, actually, having shed Jeffrey.

Never mind his mother.

Both of them had been blowing up Madison's cell phone in intermittent bursts of outrage since the cake incident, and she'd finally blocked them.

After stripping off her gown, veil, petticoats and high heels, then taking two aspirin and washing them down with strong coffee.

Now that she safe in the company of her very best friends, the headache was subsiding, and so were the effects of the whiskey she'd swilled at the Hard Luck Saloon. She felt semihuman—and ravenously hungry.

She'd been back at Bettencourt Hall for a full week already, but she hadn't bothered to stock the refrigerator or the pantry. She'd been too busy getting ready for a wedding that, she knew now, should never have happened in the first place.

For one thing, she wasn't sure she'd ever really loved Jeffrey, or even *liked* him, in retrospect. More likely, she'd *wanted* to love him, and made up her mind that she did. She'd been hell-bent on having the family she wanted so desperately before her biological clock ran down.

Well, she'd been a shortsighted idiot, believing marriage to the first reasonable candidate was the solution to her dilemma. This was the twenty-first century, after all, and women were no longer required to take a husband just because they wanted babies.

They could adopt or use donor sperm.

Although she still needed to process a lot of emotional stuff where her two ill-fated weddings were concerned, she *had* made a decision, one she hadn't shared with her ponytail posse, as Jeffrey had once described them.

She wanted to have the full experience of pregnancy, at least once, and now, unless a miracle happened, that would mean exploring her fertility options.

"Time to send out for pizza," Kendall chimed in, bringing Madison's full attention back to the present moment.

Kendall's shoulder-length auburn hair, just washed, hung in damp tendrils around her earnest, makeup-free face.

An actress in a popular, long-running soap opera, she lived in New York City and had mastered the art of ordering in long before DoorDash and Uber Eats came on the scene.

The others agreed to the plan, and Kendall got out her phone and started scrolling for local eateries that delivered.

Once their late lunch/early dinner had been arranged, Madison plunked down in a tattered floral chintz armchair and flung both legs over one side.

The others took seats on couches and settees and, in Audra's case, cross-legged on the floor.

Seeing her friend sitting that way sparked a memory in Madison's weary and still slightly achy head.

Bliss. The childhood friend who, by now, Madison almost believed *had* been imaginary, just as her grandmother claimed, back in the day.

The scruffy, scrappy little girl had often sat cross-legged in the grass, on the picnic blanket Madison had swiped from a cabinet in the storage room, even on top of Charles C. Bettencourt III's box-shaped headstone.

Madison had met her often in the little cemetery hidden away in a stand of trees well behind the house; they'd had picnics—Bliss was always hungry—and talked about all sorts of things.

For all their differences, they'd only argued once, and that had been pretty one-sided, since Bliss did most of the talking. Madison, always the peacemaker, had tried to reason with her friend—at that time, her *only* friend—but the other girl hadn't let her get a word in edgewise.

She'd stormed off into the woods, Bliss had, and Madison had feared she'd never see her friend again. She'd known, from things Bliss had told her, that her family was transient.

And, of course, desperately poor.

That much had been obvious, even to a sheltered eight-year-old living with her wealthy and constantly busy grandmother.

One day, when the leaves of the oaks, maples and birch trees were well into their transformation from green to yellow to orange to crimson, Madison had arrived at their meeting place with a bag of homemade cookies and a thermos full of ice-cold milk, only to find a note—a single word, actually—scribbled on the inside cover of a matchbook.

Goodbye, Bliss had written in small, tidy block letters.

That was all. Just *goodbye*.

There had been a bracelet made of braided thread tucked in behind the last remaining match—a friendship bracelet.

Where had she put that humble but profound gift, all those years ago? Madison wondered now.

Had she thrown it away?

She'd shown it to Coralee once, hoping it would serve as proof that Bliss Morgan was a living, breathing human being, not a mere figment of a lonely child's rather wild imagination. But Coralee had merely shaken her head and tut-tutted and told Madison to never mind, she'd make lots of new friends when she went back to school in Silver Hills the following week.

"Hey!" Fingers with long metallic nails snapped in front of Madison's nose. "Kendall to Mads, come in please."

Madison blinked, returned to the here and now with a jolt.

"I hope you weren't wasting perfectly good brain cells thinking about that scumbag, Jeffrey Sterne," said Kendall, tucking her phone into the hip pocket of her cotton shorts.

"Actually, I wasn't," replied Madison, sitting up straight now, with her legs in front of her, resting on one of Coralee's many wildly valuable Turkish rugs; they were all over the house, upstairs and down.

"Maybe she was thinking about that hot bartender," Alexis put in. She'd wound her dark brown hair into a knot at the top of her head, secured by two lacquered sticks. "I know *I* have been." She paused, looked from face to face. "Do you think a guy like that could handle being married to a pediatrician?" she asked.

"I think a guy like that could handle *anything*," Olivia commented dryly, and with a twinkle. She'd exchanged her gorgeous yellow bridesmaid's gown for casual clothes, like the others, and replaced the elegant turban she'd worn to the wedding with a bright paisley-print scarf.

Olivia, happily married and a very popular mommy blogger, was recovering from yet another round of chemo, having been diagnosed with breast cancer a year before. Her naturally curly near-black hair was growing back, but slowly—too slowly for Olivia's purposes.

Hence her impressive collection of scarves and turbans.

For whatever reason, she disdained wigs.

"What was it they used to say, way back when flappers were flapping?" added Audra, shaking one hand as if to cool off burning fingertips. "Hubba hubba!"

Madison looked at her friends, each one in turn, and thought, for the millionth time since she'd first met them in her freshman year of college, just how damn lucky she'd been to find them.

They were brilliant women, with good hearts and strong minds.

She cherished them.

"You're all crazy," she said, with a laugh. "I'm a two-time loser, remember? First Tom, now Jeffrey. The *last* thing I'm going to be looking for is another guy to mess up my life. And do any of you realize how much money I spent on this wedding?"

"You're a Bettencourt," Kendall said, quite unnecessarily, "and, besides that, you and Audra own a design company, with an app and everything. You could afford a hundred weddings just like that one."

"The Bettencourt fortune belongs to my grandmother," Madison reminded her friend. "Not me."

"Like you won't inherit everything," Alexis commented, spreading her arms wide to indicate their lush if somewhat shabby surroundings. The grandfather clock in the entryway ticked ponderously. "This house must be worth a couple of million, all by itself. And aren't you the only heir?"

She *was* the only heir, with Coralee's one son, Madison's father, dead all these years. But that didn't mean Madison would get the house, or a cent of the family money; her grandmother believed in making one's own way in the world. For all she knew, Coralee might leave her impressive estate to charity.

"I would never sell this house," Madison said, very quietly.

"Why not?" Olivia asked practically. "Once Coralee passes, you won't have any reason to come back here."

True enough, Madison thought. Her condo and the offices she and Audra shared were on the other side of the country, in sunny Florida. Boca Raton, in fact, one of her favorite cities.

She would definitely have to go back there, if only to make sure Jeffrey moved out of her condo, where he'd been living for the last six months, without doing any damage. *Soon.*

She'd never known him to be spiteful, but his mother was the devil's favorite sister, and Madison didn't trust that woman not to demolish the place single-handedly at the first opportunity. Jeffrey being Jeffrey, it was a pretty good bet that Yolanda had a card for the main gate and a key to the front door.

Madison made a mental note to check the security cameras.

"Coralee isn't doing well," she said, returning yet again to the moment at hand. Madison had visited her grandmother at the Silver Hills Assisted Living Center every day since her arrival in town, including that one, before donning her wedding gown, hoping Coralee might have rallied enough to attend the ceremony.

Instead, she'd gazed, befuddled, at Madison's face, clearly trying to place her, and there was no more denying the fact that Coralee, her only living blood relation, was truly fading away. It fractured her heart.

Coralee would never live to see her great-grandchildren—if there ever were any—and the dementia was definitely getting worse.

For all that, it was probably for the best that her grandmother hadn't been present when the wedding reception went sideways.

"So I'm planning to stick around for a while," Madison went on, realizing she'd dropped the conversational ball again. She and Audra had already agreed that they could conduct any necessary meetings either over the phone or via Zoom.

"How long is a while?" Alexis wanted to know, kicking off her flip-flops and wiggling her toes. "A few weeks? A month?"

Alexis wasn't nosy, really, but she was the unofficial social secretary for the group. She arranged their group chats, meet-ups and informal retreats. Since they lived in separate states, except for Audra and Madison, their get-togethers required flurries of text messages and emails, and the juggling of schedules.

Madison grinned at her very efficient friend. "I'll let you know," she promised.

After making a communal agreement not to discuss the failed wedding, Jeffrey, or his narcissistic mother, the band of sisters took turns catching the others up on recent events in their lives. Their time together was limited; the four bridesmaids were all leaving for the airport in Kalispell first thing in the morning.

The pizza arrived, and was promptly reduced to crumbs, since all of them were starving—except, that is, for Olivia, whose appetite was nearly nonexistent.

She did manage to eat half a slice, at all of their urging, but none of them pressured her. After all, she was recovering from breast cancer, and they knew she could barely tolerate food.

Olivia's health was a worry to them all, but they respected the rules she'd set early on, and kept their fears for her to themselves.

Unless, of course, she wasn't around to hear them speculate and fret, which they did, and frequently.

Olivia, for her part, swore she was on the mend, but her husband, Dave, had confided, during her most recent hospitalization, that he was afraid she was dying.

He'd found letters she'd written to him and to their children, fat envelopes sealed with colorful wax, each one marked with its recipient's name and the date it was to be opened. He suspected she'd been making farewell videos, too, when privacy allowed.

Watching her now, sitting gracefully on the settee with her hands folded in her lap, Madison felt a pang of sorrow at the prospect of a world without Olivia Denning in it.

Olivia caught her looking, smiled wanly and made a face. Mouthed the words, *Stop it. Right now.*

The evening passed, full of chatter and laughter and, inevitably, tears.

Finally, almost everyone retired to their assigned guest rooms, worn out and grumbling about how early they would have to get up the next morning.

Madison and Audra stayed behind, gathering empty pizza boxes, crumpled napkins and soda cans and carrying it all to the kitchen to be disposed of in the appropriate bins.

They were washing the breakfast dishes, left behind in the rush to get things rolling that morning, when Audra nudged Madison lightly with one elbow and asked, "How are you, Mads? Really, I mean. I know you decided not to marry Jeffrey, and I'm behind you one hundred percent, but I *also* know you must be disappointed. Talk to me."

Madison sighed, up to her elbows in hot, soapy dishwater. "I *am* disappointed," she admitted. "Mostly with myself. Audra, I think I knew all along that I shouldn't marry Jeffrey, and yet I did it anyway. I mean, I *almost* did it anyway." She drew in a weary breath, huffed it out. "What was I thinking?"

Audra, drying a plate with one of the many embroidered dish towels Coralee had collected over the years, lifted one eyebrow and grinned a little. She was a stunning blue-eyed blonde, with chin-length hair, a perfect nose and the best bone structure Madison had ever seen, bar none.

She was also a brainiac, at least in business. When it came to romance, her track record wasn't a whole lot better than Madison's. She, too, had been married and divorced, driven away by her twin stepdaughters, who had hated her on sight.

Since then, Audra had dated occasionally, though she'd kept the men she met at arm's length and fled if things started to become serious. She'd loved her husband deeply, even though he'd been almost twenty years her senior, and she'd been devastated when he'd bought into his daughters' smear campaign.

"What were you thinking," she murmured thoughtfully. "I must confess, Madison Bettencourt, that I haven't the faintest idea. From the first, we, your home girls, thought Jeffrey was a lightweight, and our impression didn't improve after we met his mother at that lovely dinner party you threw last weekend. Talk about enmeshment. Freud would have been fascinated."

Madison winced. "Well, *that* was direct," she said.

"I'm nothing if not direct," Audra replied, drying another plate. Looking thoughtful. "Truth is, I'm kind of worried about you. You're not a stupid woman, but you must have overlooked a thousand red flags on your way to today, and I'm wondering why."

"You *know* why," Madison said. "I want children, and I'm running out of time. Jeffrey agreed to start a family right away."

"Was that before or after he tried to get you to open joint bank accounts?" Audra asked. "And put his name on the deed to your condo?"

Madison flushed, a little angry, but mainly embarrassed. "I shot down both ideas right away, remember?"

"You should have shot *Jeffrey* down, figuratively speaking, of course."

Madison was cornered, and she didn't like it. She also knew she didn't have the proverbial leg to stand on.

She'd been stupid, recklessly ignored a bunch of warning signs—all because she wanted so much to be part of a family, with children of her own.

Audra was absolutely right. About everything.

"He doesn't have much of a personality," she went on. "And the mama's boy thing—"

Madison drew a deep, calming breath, and let it out slowly before answering, "I thought he'd get over that, once we were married."

Audra looked unconvinced, and the plate she'd just dried clattered a little as she placed it in the cupboard. "Woman," she said, "you need to watch about a hundred episodes of *Dr. Phil* and come to the realization that there are some real wackos in this world. Jeffrey and his crazy mama being exhibits one and two."

"You've made your point," Madison said, shoulders sloping slightly. "It's over now. Jeffrey and I are history."

Audra glanced at Madison's left hand, which was dripping soapsuds. "That must be why you're still wearing the rings," she reasoned.

Madison stiffened. With all that had been going on, she'd completely forgotten about the spectacular diamonds glittering on her ring finger, stretching almost to her knuckle.

Hastily, she pulled them off, shoved them into the pocket of her jeans shorts. She was blushing again, glad she'd never told Audra, or any of the others, that she'd bought the rings herself, with Jeffrey promising to pay her back out of his end-of-the-year bonus.

Audra smiled gently, patted Madison lightly on the shoulder. "Okay," she said, "I'll get off your back now. I just wanted to make sure you were really all right with the way things turned out, that's all."

"I know," Madison replied, choking up a little.

Yes, she *was* on the verge of tears, but it wasn't because the wedding was off.

It was because Coralee was losing ground every day.

Because Olivia was so sick.

And because she might never hold a child of her own in her arms.

"You're exhausted," Audra said. "Go to bed, Mads. I'll finish up here."

"The housekeeper will be in tomorrow," Madison said, though she was reluctant to leave a mess for Estelle to clean up.

The elderly woman had worked for Coralee for nearly forty years, and she was family.

For the past two months, with Coralee confined to the care facility in Silver Hills, Estelle had cut back to one day a week, when she dusted, vacuumed, brought in any packages or mail, and made sure things were okay in the old house.

"Estelle? I thought she was retiring," Audra said, still busy with the dish towel.

"She is," Madison answered, glad that the subject had changed, however brief the respite was likely to be. "Her daughter Connie will be taking over the job soon, such as it is."

They were both silent for a while, finishing their tasks.

Finally, Audra hung the dish towel up to dry, and Madison wiped out the sink, then washed her hands and applied lotion.

"I think it might be good for you to stay here in Painted Pony Creek," Audra said, starting toward the back stairway leading to the second floor.

Madison followed. It was early, but she was tired to the bone.

It had been a long and very crazy day.

"I have to make sure Coralee's being taken care of," Madison replied, feeling sad. If—when—her grandmother passed away, she would have no family left.

Good friends, yes. But no blood relations. No one who shared her DNA.

All the more reason to start exploring her options for conceiving a child as soon as she reasonably could.

She needed time to shift emotional gears from the Jeffrey debacle, however, and Coralee's condition would certainly be a factor, too.

Since there were no fertility clinics nearby, she'd have to do some research, find a doctor she trusted, and probably have various medical and psychological tests before she even qualified for treatment.

She'd do what she could to get the process started, then turn her attention to visiting Coralee, having any necessary repairs done to the house, and working remotely with Audra.

Fortunately, their company basically took care of itself, with some help from the technical staff, and recently a major corporation had made a breathtaking offer to buy the business. She and Audra were seriously considering accepting it.

Audra wanted to travel, and Madison, well, she'd wanted a loving partner.

So much for that.

For the time being, they parted ways, both of them yawning, Audra heading for the guest room she'd chosen, Madison slipping into her childhood quarters.

The space hadn't changed much, either in the years she was away at boarding school and college or since her last visit, eight weeks ago, when Coralee had been hospitalized for several days prior to being transferred to the place in Silver Hills.

The wallpaper, featuring tiny pink roses on a cream-colored background, was fading, but still pretty. The cushions on the window seat were fluffy and comfortable, and the beige carpet was clean, if outdated.

Estelle, bless her, had kept this room up, just as she had the rest of the house.

In a way, Bettencourt Hall—silly, pretentious name—had been Estelle's home, too. She'd spent far more time here than in her cottage in town, cooking, cleaning, keeping Coralee company.

Suddenly, Madison's eyes burned.

She crossed the large room to the wall of bookshelves, ran her hand across the spines of story after wonderful story.

For her, those books—everything from Trixie Belden and Nancy Drew to J.R.R. Tolkien's *Lord of the Rings* and Dorothy Dunnett's marvelous, multivolume *Lymond Chronicles* and monumental series, *The House of Niccolò*—had been magical portals leading from an ordinary and rather lonely world into fascinating adventures of all kinds.

Feeling nostalgic, she reached for *The Hobbit*, opened it, and flipped through the yellowed, dog-eared pages, smiling as she remembered her many visits to Middle Earth.

She replaced the beloved novel, took down another of her childhood favorites—*Through the Looking Glass*.

And there it was, serving as a bookmark.

Bliss's friendship bracelet, the one she'd left behind as a farewell gift, all those years ago.

The thing was grubby and frayed, and thinner than Madison remembered, and its colors had faded to mere shadows of the rich hues they'd been the day she'd found it, along with Bliss's abrupt goodbye note, out in the cemetery.

Madison rubbed the threads between the fingertips of her left hand, holding the book in the other, and remembered.

Bliss. Bliss Morgan, age eight.

Where was she now?

Was she even alive?

Something tightened in Madison's recently rebroken heart, remembering her lost friend.

Here was the proof. Bliss *had* been a real person, not a fantasy figure, as Coralee had claimed.

But what had happened to her? Had her parents simply skipped town with her, moved on to squat in some other empty camper in some other place?

Had she been abducted by a stranger, or run away on her own?

Madison slid the bracelet carefully onto her right wrist and made up her mind to find out what had become of Bliss Morgan, no matter what it took.

Damn it, *someone* had to care.

4

"Nobody's saying you're crazy, Liam," said Rhett, the youngest of the three McKettrick brothers, speaking, thanks to modern technology, from his place near Santa Barbara. "Everybody can benefit from therapy."

Liam pushed back in his chair, gazing at the image on his computer screen. It was Sunday, and Sundays were usually reserved for catching up with kinfolk and friends, via video calls, and for rest and recreation.

Bitter Gulch would be open for business starting at noon, but it was in good hands, and he didn't need to be there. Once the confab with Rhett had ended, he intended to gather some fishing gear, saddle his horse, and ride to the furthest corner of the ranch, where Painted Pony Creek flowed into a small lake, surrounded by trees and boulders.

"Thanks for the speech, bro," he replied gruffly, after several moments of thoughtful silence. "Where is this sage advice coming from, anyhow? Maybe your new girlfriend, Sabrina, the forensic psychologist?"

Rhett's brown-gold eyes narrowed briefly, and he thrust a hand through his sand-colored hair. Like Liam, he liked to take Sundays and Mondays off to look after his retired race horses and rescued greyhounds, leaving his second tech start-up in the hands of trusted employees.

He'd already made a fortune selling the first company, which meant he could do whatever he damn well pleased.

Today, apparently, that included pestering his older brother about things that were, to put it charitably, none of his damn business.

"Damn it, Liam, pull your head out of your butt and listen to me. You need to find out why you're letting Waverly's folks bring up *your* kids, since you so clearly want to raise them yourself."

Liam echoed his brother's earlier gesture by thrusting the splayed fingers of his right hand through his hair. "Rein it in, little brother," he said, and the words had an edge. "Living with a shrink doesn't make you an instant expert on how other people ought to manage their lives."

"Chill out," Rhett said, after expelling a soft sigh. "I'm not trying to lecture you. I just want to help."

"Did I ask for your help?" Liam knew he'd spoken tersely, and he regretted it. Rhett *was* trying to help.

He'd always been this way, even as a kid.

Rhett didn't speak. He didn't get angry, nor did he look affronted. He was his usual mellow self.

"I'm sorry," Liam said. "I shouldn't have snapped at you like that."

"No worries," Rhett answered. "You're probably under a lot of stress, what with Bitter Gulch about to be the set of a movie and all the work it takes just to run the place day to day."

"Everybody's under stress these days," Liam remarked. He

was luckier than most people, he knew that, and he refused to feel even slightly sorry for himself.

"Plus, you're lonely, rattling around in that big house—*seven bedrooms*, Liam? Who the hell needs seven bedrooms *and* a guest house? What the hell were you thinking, building a place like that?"

"I don't have a clue," Liam answered—but he *did* have a clue, of course. He'd wanted to bring Keely and Cavan, his children, home for good, and he'd hoped to find the right woman, marry her and have more kids.

Was it so wrong to want a family, and to raise several children in the same healthy, fresh-air, rough-and-tumble way he and Jesse and Rhett had grown up?

He wasn't a stupid man; he knew it wasn't wrong to want what he wanted.

But for some reason, he was stuck in Neutral.

He'd loved Waverly desperately, against his better judgment and the advice of trusted friends, and in the end, she'd nearly destroyed him. Although he'd dated a few women, after mourning the wife Waverly had never been, the one he'd tried his damnedest to conjure, he'd kept himself at a slight emotional distance, even from the best of them.

Maybe Rhett was right, and he needed to have his head examined.

And it was past time he fought for the kids he already had, bringing them home and being a real father to them, instead of a benevolent Disney dad. After all, he was the only parent they had.

"If you don't have a clue, bro," Rhett said, speaking quietly now, "you ought to go find yourself one. Maybe several. Waverly's mom and dad are getting older, and besides, they *raised Waverly* to be a self-centered witch, which might mean history will repeat itself with your kids."

"God forbid," Liam breathed. And he meant it.

At least where his nine-year-old daughter was concerned, that was one of his worst fears. Keely looked so much like her mother; he didn't want her to *act* like Waverly, too.

"*Do something*, Liam," Rhett pressed quietly. "Keely and Cavan were at the ranch last week, with Waverly's sister, Courtney, and according to Mom and Dad, they're not doing all that great. Keely's in a hurry to grow up, and I guess some of her behavior is normal, but she's more like Waverly than she ought to be, and she refers to you as a 'dumb cowboy.' As for Cavan, well, he's a little boy, Liam, and he's sadly in need of his father."

Usually, the guilt was manageable.

Today, it felt heavy enough to crush him, especially with the confirmation that Keely might be turning into her mother.

"Damn," Liam muttered. "Are you through, little brother, or do you plan on driving me off the nearest cliff?"

"If I thought you were serious about the cliff," Rhett said gravely, "I'd be landing my Cessna in Painted Pony Creek before the day's over." He paused, leaning forward a little, resting his forearms on the surface of the desk in his den, with its row of tall windows overlooking the Pacific. "Man up, big brother. I know you're reluctant to tear Keely and Cavan away from their doting grandparents, but they *need* you, Liam. You've wasted enough time kicking yourself over your poisonous marriage and Waverly's death. *Take hold*, as Dad would say, stand up to Waverly's folks, and *raise your kids*. Don't let them grow up without their father!"

"Okay, I hear what you're saying," Liam said, feeling shamed for letting the situation with his late wife's parents get out of hand.

Rhett wasn't through, despite Liam's subtle—he hoped—hint that he'd gotten the message and planned to proceed accordingly. "Frank and Marie Everton lost their daughter," he went on, "and they cherish their grandchildren. They deserve all kinds of sympathy and understanding and a reasonable amount of time with the kids, but they're also pretty damn dysfunctional, and you know it. They're not getting any younger, either." A pause. "And neither are you."

"I get the point," Liam reiterated, his voice taut.

"Do you?" Rhett persisted. When he got on his high horse, it was usually a long ride before he stepped back down to earth. "Sabrina and I spent a day on the ranch while Courtney and the kids were there, and do you know what Cavan asked me, Liam?"

Something clenched, hard, in the pit of Liam's stomach, and he identified it right away.

It was dread.

"What?" he countered.

"He looked up at me, with those big green eyes of his, and he said, 'Uncle Rhett, could you be my dad?'"

The words struck Liam like a body blow.

He was glad he was sitting down, because if he hadn't been, his knees would have given out for sure.

He breathed out a word unfit for polite company.

Not that either he or Rhett, or Jesse, for that matter, was all that polite, at least with each other.

"Yeah," Rhett confirmed, as though the word had conveyed volumes of confession.

Liam closed his eyes, hoping his brother wouldn't notice that they were wet.

They stung something fierce while he struggled to regain his composure.

"I didn't say any of that to hurt you," Rhett said, after a few awkward moments had passed.

"I know," Liam replied, his voice as rough as gravel.

"You doing okay, otherwise?"

"Yeah," Liam said, able to look his brother in the face again, but only just. "I'm just hunky-dory over here."

Rhett chuckled at that, but he sounded sad, rather than

amused. "Good," he said. "Gotta go. Horses to exercise, dogs to look after. Your turn to call me, next weekend."

"If I'm up off my figurative knees by then, brother, you'll hear from me."

"Bro?"

"What?"

"I love you," Rhett said. The man was tough, through and through, and he'd never been afraid to express his affection, when he felt it.

"Back at you," said Liam, who felt the same, but wasn't nearly as able to say so aloud.

They ended the call, and Liam cupped his hands behind his head, leaned back in his chair again, and closed his eyes.

He felt like breaking down, bawling like a baby, but, of course, he didn't.

He was Liam McKettrick, successful entrepreneur and stubborn-ass cowboy. He didn't cry—*ever*—but right now, with his brother's words echoing in his mind, and knowing what Cavan had said to his beloved uncle, he sure as hell felt like it.

After ten minutes of self-control, deep breathing and rapid blinking, in an effort to quell the burning behind his eyes, Liam reached for the phone.

He didn't call his attorney.

He didn't call either of his kids, both of whom had phones of their own.

He didn't call Frank and Marie, either.

No, he called Waverly's younger sister. He wasn't especially close to Courtney, but Liam knew she sympathized with his situation, and she helped her aging parents a lot with the kids.

"Hi, Liam," Courtney answered on the first ring. She was Waverly's polar opposite, even-tempered, friendly, compassionate. She'd been the scapegoat growing up, rather than the golden child, but instead of being bitter and resentful, Courtney was strong and independent. "What a coincidence. I was just about to call you."

Once again, something lurched painfully inside Liam, this time in the back of his throat. "The kids are all right?"

"They're just fine," Courtney said. "Mostly."

"What do you mean, 'mostly'?" he asked, sitting up straight now, anxious, all his senses on the alert.

"Well," Courtney replied, drawing out the word, "the fact is, they're getting to be too much for Mom and Dad, so I brought them here to LA. Mom's really forgetful these days, and Dad's arthritis is acting up—some days, he can barely get out of bed. Anyway, I really love having the kids here, but things are crazy at work right now. I'm pulling twelve- and fourteen-hour days, so they spend way too much time at day camp."

Liam didn't know exactly what Courtney did for a living. It had something to do with computers and the entertainment industry. He *did* know she was a devoted aunt to her sister's children; Liam didn't doubt for a moment that she loved them far more than Waverly ever had.

Waverly, he suspected, hadn't been *capable* of real love.

"I'll come and get them," he said. "Today, if necessary."

"No need for that," Courtney told him pleasantly. "My company is doing some of the special effects for the movie about to be filmed in Bitter Gulch. I'm flying in for some in-person meetings with the director midweek, which means I can bring the kids to you."

Again, Liam closed his eyes. He was glad Courtney couldn't see his reactions, the way Rhett had, during the video call. Hoped she couldn't guess them from his tone of voice.

"How are they doing? The kids, I mean?"

"Keely's a little prickly, to be honest. Cavan wants to arrive yesterday and stay forever."

Liam felt a sharp pang of love for both his children.

He missed them more than he could say.

"Keely's prickly?" he asked. "Why?"

"Mainly because she's nine going on sixteen. She'll be a bit of a challenge I'm afraid, but I think she'll come around, given some time. Cavan, on the other hand, can't wait to be with you. He wants to ride horses, go fishing, and maybe get a dog. He's even talking about being an extra in the movie." She paused. "I might be able to arrange that last part, actually. With your permission, of course."

"We'll see," Liam replied, reluctant. He mulled the possibility over for a few moments, then changed the subject. "What about your parents? How do *they* feel about all this?" The Evertons didn't have legal custody of Keely and Cavan, but they'd be able to make a good case for grandparents' rights, if things came to that, since the kids had been living with them for nearly a year now.

Just short of a full year. Separated from my kids.

WTF has been going on in my brain all this time?

"Mom and Dad are less than enthusiastic about the whole thing, as you might have guessed," Courtney admitted. "But just between you and me, they're getting to the place where they can't look after themselves properly, let alone two young children who just happen to have a perfectly good father, and they know it."

When he spoke again, Liam's voice was gruff. "Thank you, Courtney," he managed. "Thank you."

After they'd discussed arrival times, logistics, etc., knowing Keely and Cavan were with Courtney, he decided to act like a father. He wanted to speak with both his children, try to reassure them somehow that the ranch was as much their home as his, and they were welcome.

They were swimming in the pool behind Courtney's house, she told him, while two of her friends kept a close eye on them from nearby lounge chairs.

Courtney had just come inside, planning to place a call to Liam, when he had beaten her to the punch by dialing first.

"Let me go and round them up. Dry them off a little, so they won't drip pool water all over my kitchen floor. We'll call back in a few minutes, if that's all right."

The yearning to see his kids' faces, to know for himself that they were well, seized Liam by the throat and squeezed. For a moment or so, he couldn't speak.

"Liam?" Courtney prompted gently.

"Umm—I'm here. Call back when you're ready. And Courtney?"

"What?" Her tone was patient, even sympathetic.

"Make it a video call, okay? I know you're bringing the kids here in a few days, but I need to see them now."

"Ten-four," Courtney agreed, ever cheerful.

Half an hour later, the call came through.

Keely and Cavan filled the screen of Liam's computer.

"Hi, Dad," Cavan said, beaming. Like his sister, he had dark hair, but his eyes were green, like his mother's. Keely's eyes were indigo blue.

At the moment, she looked as though she'd rather be anywhere else instead of sitting in front of a computer, face-to-virtual-face with her father.

She wound a tendril of wet hair around one index finger and let Cavan do all the talking. And talk Cavan did.

He seemed so eager, so earnest, that Liam felt another rush of guilt for not being there for his son, or for his daughter. He couldn't blame the kid for being angry with him; he'd failed her, and her brother, in a thousand ways.

Combine that with garden variety tween angst, and you had the formula for a seriously broken relationship. And Cavan, as receptive as he was, probably had issues, too. He might be hiding a lot of anger and pain and, even worse, blaming himself for the way things had turned out.

The full realization of what he'd allowed to happen hit Liam like a runaway freight train. He had to clear his throat, again and again, throughout the exchange.

He'd connected with Cavan, albeit tentatively, and that was good, but Keely stayed behind that invisible force field she'd erected soon after Waverly's passing.

She'd been eight then. Far too grown-up for her age.

Once a bona fide daddy's girl, she'd begun to retreat from Liam almost immediately after Waverly's funeral service. And while they'd all had counseling, Keely had continued to back away, turning to her grieving grandparents for comfort, for affection and guidance, for everything.

He'd allowed that, unwilling to sunder the ever-deepening bond between his daughter and her mother's parents.

Frank and Marie—especially Marie—suffering through a horrendous loss themselves, had clung to the children, in their turn, and encouraged their dependence on them.

It hadn't helped that, in their view, Liam had divorced Waverly just before she got sick, and before that, in their view, kept her from achieving her lofty goals. Without him, they firmly believed, she wouldn't have ruined her otherwise perfect body by bearing two children. She'd have been a movie star, or a world-class supermodel, if only she'd never crossed paths with Liam McKettrick.

Waverly might not have died so young, and so beautiful, in the very prime of her life, if it hadn't been for her husband.

Over time, they'd sold Keely on this same viewpoint—Cavan had been too young back then to understand anything beyond the fact that his mother was gone and his Gampie and Gambie, as he called Frank and Marie, were always around, while his father was usually away somewhere, working.

When Keely finally spoke, it was at Courtney's quiet urging, from somewhere in the background.

"I'm not staying with you," she told Liam, her lower lip jutting out just a bit, and her blue, blue eyes narrowed. "This is just a visit."

Liam suppressed a sigh. "Let's talk about that in person, after you get here," he suggested. He was planning to arrange for all three of them to start family therapy right away, but he wasn't about to say so at this volatile juncture.

"*I* want to stay with you!" Cavan blurted out, with all the unbridled enthusiasm of a seven-year-old who wants a dad more than anything.

A pang of sorrow struck Liam.

This child *needed* him.

Why hadn't he registered that?

Well, actually, there was a reason, one he'd never shared with anyone besides Waverly, but that reason didn't matter much in the face of a seven-year-old's loneliness and longing to be raised by his remaining parent, instead of shunted off to his grandparents' place, with all its drama and, yes, its toxicity.

After all, Waverly hadn't turned out the way she had by accident.

Frank and Marie had favored her over her sister, encouraged her off-the-wall antics, made excuses and bailed her out of trouble time and time again, thus keeping her from learning to take responsibility for her own actions. They'd been *afraid* of her, though they wouldn't have admitted that for anything.

Waverly hadn't just gotten angry once in a while, like a regular person. No, sir. When things didn't go her way, Waverly had raged, screamed, stomped and thrown things, even physically attacked anyone who dared disagree with her.

Liam had been on the receiving end of his late wife's out-of-control tantrums more than once, and he had a few physical and emotional scars to show for it.

He'd stopped loving Waverly only a few months after Keely was born, a year after they'd gotten married, but he hadn't dared divorce her and move out, not then. He'd have had fifty-fifty custody, at best, and that meant that half the time, his daughter would be at her mother's mercy.

So he'd stayed, and things had gotten worse.

And then worse yet.

A little over a year later, Cavan had come along, unexpected, unwanted by his mother, and completely innocent. Like his sister, he would be utterly defenseless fifty percent of the time if Liam left, and that was unthinkable.

So they'd all lived in their own little corner of hell, until a few months before Waverly's diagnosis, when she'd decided she wanted her freedom, taken the kids and moved in with her parents, up in Seattle.

Obviously, the situation hadn't been ideal, but as it turned out, there wasn't much Liam could do about it, besides lease an apartment in the same city, keep building his career as an architect and spend his allotted time with his children.

At least with Frank and Marie around, the kids weren't abused, and Liam had to give them credit for that much. After being doormats for so many years, Waverly's parents had stepped up, as best they could, and protected Keely and Cavan from their mother's Category 5 tirades.

Liam had spent as much time with his children as he was permitted to, often taking them home to the McKettrick ranch to spend time with their other set of grandparents and their uncles, all the while hoping that the innate sanity of that life would influence them in positive ways.

Now he knew for sure none of that had been enough. At some point, he'd checked out. Dropped the familial ball.

Yep, Rhett had been all too right during their earlier call. Liam had had his head up his rear end for far too long, and now it was time to do things the McKettrick way.

Hands-on, toe-to-toe and for real.

"Bring jeans and boots," Liam said, realizing he'd let the

conversation lapse while he drifted through the past. "We'll be doing some riding."

Cavan cheered and bounced up and down in the chair he was wedged into, beside his still-disdainful sister.

Keely looked sour as all get-out, but she couldn't quite hide the faint flutter of interest that showed in her eyes.

Back in the day, on visits to the family ranch in California, Liam had taken her for horseback rides, with her perched in front of him in the saddle, laughing and clinging to the saddle horn with small, chubby hands.

Cutting brush, Liam had called it. Cowboy vernacular for rounding up stray cattle.

Keely would never be that little girl again, it went without saying, but maybe some of that trusting, innocent delight could be recovered.

"You have horses," she said, sounding comically doubtful.

Liam almost laughed. "You know I do," he said, when he could keep a relatively straight face. "You've been here a couple of times, kiddo, and you can't have forgotten that."

Her mouth moved, as though she were trying not to smile. "I thought those were Uncle Jesse's horses," she said. "Not yours."

"A couple of them were his," Liam allowed, "but I have several of my own."

"You still have Max the pony, right?" Cavan asked, looking worried.

"He's right here waiting for you to saddle him up, cowboy," Liam answered, having had to clear his throat again. "He belongs to you and Keely, and this is his forever home."

Yours, too, he added silently. *Like it or not.*

Keely was working hard at looking disinterested. "I'm too old for a pony," she said, with a little sniff. "If I'm going to ride, I want an *adult* horse."

"We'll see," Liam replied. Until he assessed Keely's riding

skills, he wasn't going to let her mount just any horse and head for the hills.

"I hate it when you say 'we'll see,'" she told him loftily. "Like you're the boss of me or something."

Of all the phrases he might have used, Keely's mom had hated "we'll see" as well, though not as much as "absolutely not."

"I'm your father," Liam pointed out. "For all practical intents and purposes, I *am* your boss."

She bristled at this, as he'd known she would, but what she said next surprised him plenty. "Gambie says you're just a sperm donor, *not* a father."

Damn. Another punch in the gut.

Had he been too quick to claim his parental authority, reminding her that he was in charge?

No, he decided. His daughter needed his love and understanding, of course she did. But she also needed to learn at least a modicum of respect for other people.

"Keely!" Courtney interrupted from off camera. "That was rude!"

"*And* it was *mean!*" Cavan blustered.

Keely didn't back down, nor did she apologize. She bolted.

Liam sighed for the fiftieth time that morning. "That went well," he said as Courtney dropped into the chair, shifting Cavan onto her lap in the process.

"I warned you," Courtney said, not unkindly.

Tears welled in Cavan's eyes. "Does this mean we don't get to come home, Dad?" he asked. "Because Keely's being a poop head?"

"It doesn't mean any such thing," Liam told his worried son. "I can't wait to see you again, buddy. And don't call your sister a poop head, please."

"Not even if she *is* one?" Cavan protested.

It was hard to refute the kid's logic, under the circumstances, so Liam let the question go unanswered and addressed Courtney, a softer, kinder and less glaringly beautiful version of her lost sister.

"Since you're visiting the set anyhow, I'll meet you there when the time comes and pick up the kids. Maybe we can all have lunch or dinner together, if you can spare the time."

"I'm booked for both," Courtney said, "but I'll be around for a few days. Mind if I stay in that fancy guest house of yours instead of getting a hotel room?"

"You're welcome to stay for as long as you like."

"Lunch is ready!" a female voice called from somewhere behind Courtney.

At this, Cavan chirped, "Bye, Dad!", jumped off Courtney's lap, and ran out of the room.

Convenient, Liam thought.

"At some point, we need to have a serious talk," he told Courtney. "I'm going to get Cavan, Keely and myself into family therapy ASAP, but in the meantime, I'll need some pointers on dealing with my daughter. She clearly isn't happy about coming here, *or* spending time with her—sperm donor."

"I hear you," Courtney replied, with a soft sigh of her own. "She's not an easy kid, Liam, but she's not a monster, either. She's been through a lot, for a nine-year-old, and I'm not saying that to make you feel guilty. Cavan seems oblivious to criticism where you're concerned, but Keely's older, and Waverly and Mom have laid down some pretty nasty emotional infrastructure over the years. It's going to take a real effort on your part to correct that, with or without therapy."

"Yeah," Liam agreed. "And then there's the fact that their father essentially bailed on them, thus reinforcing everything Waverly and Marie may have said and done."

"Don't be too hard on yourself, Liam," Courtney said firmly, and with sisterly affection. "Waverly was my sister, and I guess I loved her, but she was absolutely poisonous, even as a child. Almost certainly suffering from borderline personality disorder, though there was never an official diagnosis. I think Mom and Dad bought into her version of things mostly because they were afraid to rock the boat—it probably seemed a lot safer to give in and avoid the screeching."

Liam knew it was time to end the conversation—he'd be able to talk to Courtney in person soon—but he had another question, and it wasn't about his kids.

"How was that for you, Courtney?" he asked. "Growing up with your sister and your parents up to their eyeballs in alligators, just trying to deal with Waverly?"

Briefly, Courtney's pale green eyes glistened. "It was—interesting. To say the least. But I made up my mind not to feel sorry for myself a long, long time ago. I have Stan, the world's best husband, my friends, my career, and my niece and nephew. Someday, I might even have kids of my own—I certainly haven't ruled that out. I can't complain."

If anybody had a right to feel sorry for themselves, Courtney did.

She'd had to take so much abuse from Waverly.

Liam admired her tremendously, especially in that moment, for deciding not to waste time fretting over a past that couldn't be changed.

He could learn a thing or two from this woman.

"It'll be good to see you again, Court," Liam said. "Is Stan joining you on this trip?"

"No," Courtney answered. "He's busy. Big international case outside the country. He'll be away for a couple of months, unfortunately."

"Well," Liam replied, "next time you speak to him, tell him hey from me."

"Will do," Courtney promised, smiling now.

After that, they said their goodbyes and ended the call.

Liam's monitor screen faded to black.

And it was a struggle not to let his mood do the same.

5

Coralee's house, while certainly familiar, was huge, and after
her friends had gone back to their busy, varied and faraway lives,
Madison rattled around in the place like a dried pea in the bottom of a tin bucket.

On Sunday, she'd stocked up on groceries and ordered a new
router on Amazon, since the Wi-Fi service outside Painted Pony
Creek proper was on the iffy side, and the internet was vital to
her business.

Not to mention her sanity.

She'd suspected the Net wouldn't be much help in the search
for any reference to Bliss Morgan, and sadly, she was right.
Using her phone, she'd scoured the missing children websites
and come up with zip, concerning the little girl she'd first met
in the family cemetery, anyway.

Now it was Monday morning.

She'd already been for a run, showered, and dressed in jeans and a soft cotton blouse, crimson with gossamer, floral-print sleeves. She'd had a light breakfast, too, a poached egg on toast.

After backing Coralee's classic 1958 Bentley out of the detached garage, which had once been a carriage house, she set out for town, planning to stop for gas, then drive on to Silver Hills for her daily visit to her grandmother.

Given that Coralee probably hadn't used the car in years, Madison had been more than a little surprised that it had started at all.

Maybe she'd fly to Florida, pick up her small and sensible hybrid SUV, and drive it to back to Montana. If she did that, she could stop by her condo in Boca, grab some clothes and other personal items—*and* make sure Jeffrey and Yolanda weren't able to squat there, once they'd returned from their Oedipal honeymoon in Costa Rica.

In retrospect, it was glaringly obvious that Jeffrey wasn't just a mama's boy, he was quite possibly a leech, and he wasn't going to glide through life on Madison's dime.

He and Mommy would be back in the US in a few days, and Madison figured they'd either head back to Painted Pony Creek or straight to the condo she and Jeffrey had shared in Boca Raton.

Neither plan was going to fly, if Madison could help it.

She was thinking these thoughts when she reached the end of Bettencourt Hall's long and winding gravel driveway and came to a stop to look both ways, then pull out.

Five minutes later, she rolled up to a service station in the heart of town, getting plenty of curious looks in the process, shut off the engine, and got out of the car to head for the nearest pump.

She stuck her ATM card into the proper slot, pulled it out quickly as instructed by the small screen imbedded in the machine, and selected premium over regular gasoline. If she'd been driving her own vehicle, she reflected, feeling faintly embarrassed to be seen sporting a freaking *Bentley* in the heart of cattle country, she wouldn't have been so damn *noticeable.*

Given the scene at the wedding reception, though, she was probably being gossiped about—maybe even watched—at that very moment.

Madison hated the feeling that gave her.

So, in order to distract herself, she was scrolling through her phone when a gleaming red truck with an extended cab pulled in next to her, just on the other side of the pumps.

The driver's side door opened, and who should step down from the running board but her favorite bartender/lawman/architect, Liam McKettrick.

He looked better than good in his jeans, boots and white cotton shirt. Seeing Madison, he grinned, took off his sexy black cowboy hat and laid it, crown down, on the seat he'd just left.

"Hello, Madison," he said, his ink-blue eyes bright with humor and something else, something she couldn't quite identify. He gave a long, low whistle. "That's some car you've got there."

Madison, off balance momentarily because she'd initially misunderstood the whistle, composed herself but still blushed at the reference to the Bentley. It was so out of place in this small, practical, homey town.

And so was she.

"It belongs to my grandmother," she replied a beat too quickly, and that time, she couldn't stop the blush that rose to her cheeks and pulsed there. She was a thirty-two-year-old woman, not a gushing teenager, and she needed to calm the heck down.

Trouble was, being in such close proximity to this breathtakingly handsome man, it was hard to be anything but rattled.

Which was ridiculous, given that the last time she'd seen him, just a couple of days before, she'd been a classic runaway bride, complete with gown and veil. Worse, she'd proceeded to get tipsy.

Then, if that hadn't been humiliating enough, she'd had to be rescued and virtually poured into Audra's rental car by her colorfully dressed posse of bridesmaids.

Oh, yes. She'd made a spectacle of herself, in no uncertain terms. In a place like Painted Pony Creek, her wedding debacle story would surely ripen into a tale of mythological proportions and perhaps be remembered for a very long time.

Liam nodded pleasantly, but absently, and turned from her to begin gassing up his fancy truck.

She had no business wondering about this man, given that she'd been about to get married to someone else only a few days before.

But wonder about him she did.

Mentally, she kicked herself for not googling Liam McKettrick for the salient details.

Was he married? If not, did he have a girlfriend? Kids?

Annoyed with herself, Madison turned away, too, and waited impatiently for the Bentley's seemingly bottomless gas tank to finally fill up.

The smell of the high-octane fuel almost gagged her.

Or was that her injured pride, sticking in her throat and burning her eyes?

When the flow finally stopped, and she moved to put the nozzle of the heavy hose back where it belonged, Liam was still there.

He'd been looking at his phone while he waited, but he looked up right away.

"You're all right?" he asked, so quietly and with such genuine concern that Madison almost burst into tears, like an idiot.

Maybe it was the town that was stirring up all these crazy emotions.

She was used to sophisticated, bustling cities—not a place like Painted Pony Creek, even if it had, once upon a time, been her home.

She didn't fit in here, and that thought made her sad.

Still, she missed amenities like operas and symphonies, top-tier restaurants and elegant, expensive shops.

She was successful in business, and she'd been born with the fabled silver spoon in her mouth, so she didn't qualify for much sympathy, she supposed, when it came to finding and *keeping* the right man.

It hurt, feeling the way she did—lonely, humiliated, frustrated and fearful. A part of her wanted to fling herself into Liam's arms, right then and there, lay her head on his shoulder, and sob.

She imagined his strong arms around her and had to work hard to hold back the tears that would have embarrassed her beyond bearing.

Instead, she lifted her chin. "I'm fine," she said, speaking as casually as she could. "Just headed over to Silver Hills to visit my grandmother."

"How is Coralee doing these days?" Liam asked, surprising Madison.

"You know her?" she countered.

There it was again, that knee-melting grin of his. "Sure," he replied. "She's an institution around here."

Of course she was, Madison reminded herself. The Bettencourt name reached back to the settling of Painted Pony Creek, and the house, or a much smaller version of it, had been built soon after a pair of male ancestors had struck silver near the neighboring town that had been named for one of the richest veins of ore ever discovered in the American West.

"She's not doing too well, I'm afraid," Madison replied, saddened. "I keep hoping she'll make some kind of breakthrough, but she's in her late eighties, so that probably isn't realistic."

"Sometimes," Liam said, reaching into the truck for his hat and settling it on his head, "being realistic hurts too much. A little denial can be an okay thing, under the right circumstances."

It was such an odd remark that Madison was momentarily taken aback.

And was she imagining it, or was there a deep sadness lurking in those denim-blue eyes of his, hiding behind the twinkle?

"I'd better go," she said.

She was doing her best to convince herself of that, anyhow.

"I'm on my way over to Silver Hills myself, in an hour or two," Liam said. "What if we grab some lunch after I get through looking at some horses and you're finished visiting your grandmother? Noon, at the Mexican place on Pine Street? It's behind the bank."

Something fluttered in Madison's stomach, and her heart swelled.

Should she say yes? Should she refuse?

Hell, no.

She loved Mexican food, she was adrift with Audra and the others gone, and she needed something to look forward to, however small that something might be.

And the invitation *was* small, a friendly gesture to a recently traumatized newcomer.

Not that kicking Jeffrey Sterne to the curb had traumatized her.

She hadn't been hurt, not really. Once, she'd really believed she loved Jeffrey; now, she knew she'd been deluding herself.

Still, there was Coralee. She was losing her, and that knowledge bruised Madison's spirit.

"Okay," she said. "I'd like that. Meet you at the restaurant at noon."

Liam grinned again, tugged at the brim of his hat.

"See you then," he said.

"Wait," Madison said. "Do you even know my name?"

He chuckled. It was a low, richly masculine sound. "Yeah," he said. "You introduced yourself the other day, in the Hard Luck Saloon, remember?"

She *didn't* remember, actually, because at the time she'd been so riled up, she practically couldn't see straight.

"Yes," she lied. "Of course I remember."

He tilted the brim of his hat again, still grinning. "Madison Bettencourt," he said, as if to prove his earlier claim.

Madison's head felt light, and she practically dived behind the wheel of the Bentley, though she had to go around to the right side of the car to do so. The vehicle had, after all, been manufactured in the UK.

Liam remained where he was, watching her drive away.

She told herself he was just admiring the Bentley.

Fifteen minutes later, she had reached the assisted living place, a low-slung modern building with many wings and multiple windows, parked the car and signed in at the reception desk.

When she reached Coralee's spacious private room, she was heartened to find her frail, tiny grandmother sitting up, wearing a floral silk bed jacket and smiling as though she actually recognized Madison.

"Darling," she said. "How lovely to see you!"

Madison's eyes burned with happy tears as she stepped up to Coralee's bedside and leaned down to kiss her cheek. "You, too," she said.

Coralee waved a fragile blue-veined hand. "Oh, now, child, don't get all emotional. I'm not sure I can handle that."

Madison took that hand into her own, patted it gently. "It's wonderful to see you smiling, Coralee."

Coralee's brow crumpled beneath her fluffy white bangs, and her eyes, hazel in color like Madison's, twinkled. "I haven't been smiling?" she teased.

"Not recently," Madison admitted, fluffing her grandmother's pillows so she could sit up a little straighter and still be comfortable.

"How was the wedding, dear? I was *so* disappointed to miss it!"

Madison debated making up a story, and decided against it. Coralee deserved the truth.

"Things didn't quite work out," Madison said, perching sideways on the bed and still holding on to Coralee's hand, though very gently. It felt so excruciatingly delicate, like the wing of a dragonfly, far too easily crushed.

This time, Coralee's frown was real. "It didn't? Why not?"

"It's a long story," Madison replied, after planting another kiss on the old woman's crumpled forehead. Coralee's skin felt as thin as tissue paper. "It's quite a story, and it will take a while to tell, so let's discuss that another time."

"I didn't like that young man much, to tell you the truth," Coralee said, surprising Madison a little. "His vibes were off."

She smiled. "Why didn't you say so?" she asked.

"Because it was none of my business, dear. You're a grown woman, not a child. Besides, I don't think I was paying all that much attention, to be honest."

Her grandmother had never been a huge fan of marriage. She'd had a husband once, for about five minutes, as the story went, and refused to take the man's name.

She'd kept him around long enough to get her pregnant with Madison's father, and taken a long series of lovers after the divorce, though none of those relationships lasted very long, either.

A week ago, when Madison had brought Jeffrey here and introduced him, Coralee had been drifty, to say the least.

Evidently, she'd been pretending.

Now, the old woman drew in a wispy breath and went on. "Not that I think you've got much sense when it comes to choosing a partner, Madison Rose Bettencourt. Your *first* husband was a real *jerk*."

This time, Madison laughed. "Yes," she admitted, refraining from pointing out the singular irony of Coralee's remark, "and he probably still is."

That was when Coralee raised an index finger and wobbled

it under Madison's nose. "Painted Pony Creek is a wonderful town," she said with unusual firmness. "Stay right here, find yourself a good, solid cowboy and settle down."

Naturally, Liam jumped to Madison's mind then. She tried to dismiss him, but he wouldn't go.

Oh, darn it.

"It's pretty soon after the last romantic disaster to start thinking in terms of settling down with a cowboy or anybody else," she said.

"You find the right one," Coralee persisted, "and that won't matter."

Madison was still smiling, delighted to find her beloved grandmother in such a lucid frame of mind.

As soon as she'd made that observation, however, lightning struck.

Coralee began to drift. "Have you seen the little girl?" she asked, looking both confused and alarmed.

The smile wobbled. "*What* little girl?"

"I saw her in the kitchen once," Coralee said, her mind clearly wandering far from the present moment.

"Coralee?" Madison was alarmed now.

"I think she had her centuries mixed up," the elderly woman continued, bright tears shimmering in her eyes now. "She was wearing such strange clothing."

"Coralee, please—what are you talking about? *What little girl?*" Madison pressed, fidgeting with Bliss's thread bracelet as she spoke.

But Coralee began to shake her head, slowly at first, and then faster and faster.

Madison called for a nurse, and one appeared almost immediately, probably summoned by an electronic message sent from one of the machines monitoring Coralee at practically every pulse point.

A little frantic, Madison clasped Coralee's small, wrinkled

face in both hands, careful not to exert any real pressure. "Stop, *please*," she said, gently halting her grandmother's still shaking head. "Everything is all right. *You're safe.* I'm right here—"

"You need to break me out of this place," Coralee muttered after a few moments, leaning forward a little, once Madison had lowered her hands, and keeping her voice down. Conspiratorial. "I've been *kidnapped*, you know. I'm being held against my will!"

Madison tried to keep her fear from showing on her face, and she wasn't at all sure she'd succeeded. "Coralee," she said urgently. "This is a good place. Nobody here wants to hurt you!"

"It's *not* a good place," Coralee insisted, looking and sounding petulant now, like a frustrated child. "This is a *prison*! They're conducting horrible experiments here!"

The nurse, injecting something into Coralee's IV line, gave Madison a thin smile and said, "She gets like this. Don't worry."

Don't worry?

Coralee was Madison's *grandmother*, her only living blood relative. *Of course she was freaking worried!*

"Just a few minutes ago, she was fine," Madison protested, scared and defensive.

"Nature of the beast I'm afraid," replied the nurse kindly, and with the degree of patience only skilled caregivers were able to muster at times like this.

With that, the woman turned to her very agitated patient. "Miss Coralee?" the plump, middle-aged woman asked sweetly. "You were so cheerful at breakfast, and here you are, fretting again." She tsk-tsked, winking at Madison, but there was no trace of annoyance in her voice.

"She's not a nurse," Coralee confided in a raspy whisper that broke Madison's already wounded heart. "She's just pretending! She's a *jailor*!"

The nurse stood resolutely alongside the bed, across from Madison, stethoscope at the ready. "Now, Miss Coralee," she protested, still cheerful, "you know I'm not a jailor. I'm a nurse. I take care of you five days a week, remember?"

Remember?

Possibly not the best word she could have used, but Madison knew this nurse—Stella Sondheim—was unfailingly kind to Coralee, and so were all the others who attended her at different times.

Madison had made sure of that.

"Should I leave?" she asked softly.

Before the other woman could reply, Coralee gripped Madison's fingers with all the strength that remained to her.

That is, not much.

"Don't go!" Coralee cried. "Don't leave me alone in this awful place!"

"It's all right," Madison tried to reassure her grandmother. "No one is going to hurt you, I promise."

The nurse smiled. "It might be time to let Miss Coralee have a rest," she said. "Maybe come back later for afternoon or evening visiting hours."

Madison wasn't about to wrench her hand free of her grandmother's grip, so she simply nodded and waited as Coralee's frenzy began to subside, thanks to whatever sedative Ms. Sondheim had administered.

When Coralee finally fell asleep, Madison and the nurse retreated to the hallway.

"Has she ever mentioned seeing a child?" Madison asked, keeping her voice low.

She felt a scary little thrill, recalling Coralee's mention of seeing a little girl.

Could it be...?

But no, of course not. She'd been seeing things.

Her brain was collapsing.

"Most likely, she has, Ms. Bettencourt," the other woman replied. "She has dementia, and dementia patients *do* hallucinate, especially as the disease progresses."

"Please call me Madison."

"And I'm Stella," said the nurse, resting a sympathetic hand on Madison's shoulder.

Madison wrapped her arms around her torso and sighed, blinking back yet another spate of tears. "It's so difficult to see her like this," she confessed. "My grandmother was the sharpest, most sensible woman I've ever known. There was nothing, and I mean *nothing*, she couldn't do if she put her mind to it."

"I'm sorry," Stella said. "Would you like to sit down? We have a nice, quiet garden nearby, and there's a chapel, too, if you're so inclined."

Madison felt too restless to sit. She needed to be *doing* something.

Yelling. Pacing. Swinging her fists at nothing.

She checked her watch.

Still more than an hour until it would be time to meet Liam at the Mexican restaurant.

If she'd had his number, she would have texted him. Made some excuse to beg off their lunch date.

Not that it was actually a *date*.

Madison muttered a thank-you to Nurse Stella and made her way toward the nearest exit, sternly refusing to allow her tense shoulders to slump.

For Coralee's sake, for her own, she had to be strong.

Reaching the Bentley, she unlocked it, climbed in on the driver's side, and finally allowed herself to cry.

Forty-five minutes and some eye drops later, she pulled into the gravel parking lot at El Palacio Oro, the Mexican restaurant where she and Liam had agreed to meet.

His truck was parked in the lot, empty.

So he was inside.

Madison cranked the wide rearview mirror in her direction

and inspected her face. She'd applied only a little mascara and lip gloss before leaving the house, since the last thing she'd expected was to run into Liam McKettrick and get herself invited to lunch.

The mascara was waterproof, as advertised, though the lip gloss had worn off completely.

She touched up both, deciding that her eyes weren't noticeably puffy, grabbed her purse, and got out of the car.

Because she wanted to retreat, she forced herself to walk purposefully across the parking lot instead.

She pulled open one heavy, intricately carved wooden door and stepped inside. The cool blast from the AC system revived her considerably, and she was actually hungry.

Or was that plain old stress flipping in her stomach?

It took a few moments for Madison's eyes to adjust to the change from bright sunlight to a dimmer glow. She blinked, and, finally, Liam came into focus.

He was smiling at her, though there was a very slight crease of worry or concern between his eyebrows. With a nod of greeting, he hung his hat on a hook near the register, where it had other hats for company.

"This way," said the youthful waiter, menus at the ready.

"Hungry?" Liam asked, placing one hand at the small of Madison's back in a way that, oddly, made her feel cared for. Valued.

It was such a courtly gesture.

Cowboy class.

"Yes, I think I am," she answered. "What about you?"

"Starved." Liam grinned.

Soon, they were settled in a corner booth, away from the front windows and most of the other diners.

Madison was glad of that, because she wasn't *absolutely* sure that her eyes weren't puffy from crying so hard, for so long.

Fortunately, no one had asked what was wrong. She might have told them.

Both she and Liam examined their menus.

For Madison, it was a simply a habit.

She always ordered the same thing when she visited *any* Mexican restaurant: a chicken taco salad with sour cream and guacamole.

The customary starters, chips, salsa and bean dip, were delivered.

Madison placed her usual order, while Liam went for beef enchiladas, rice and beans. She asked for ice tea, and he chose beer.

"So," he began when the waiter had gone to fetch their drinks, brought them to the table, and vanished again, "how was your grandmother?"

It was a completely normal question, but Madison wished he hadn't asked it, because if she tried to explain the events of the morning, she'd start blubbering again for sure.

She might appear calm on the surface, but Coralee's outburst had left her deeply shaken. Ever since she'd left the facility, she'd been coming to terms with the fact she'd been able to deny up until then: there would be no magical turnaround; her grandmother wasn't going to get better.

"Not so great," she said, holding Liam's gaze because she wanted so desperately to avert her eyes. Coralee had taught her well; whenever she was tempted to show even the smallest weakness, she had to do the opposite. "It's dementia, so, you know—"

He reached across the table, closed one of his hands over hers, squeezed lightly. "That's tough, Madison. I'm sorry."

A brief silence fell, and Liam's hand lingered, warm and clean and slightly rough from doing manual work.

Finally, he withdrew, and Madison felt the absence of his touch.

"My turn to ask questions," she said, sitting up a little straighter.

Liam laughed quietly. "Fair enough," he replied. "Shoot."

"Are you married?" It was a brazen thing to ask, but she needed to know, though she couldn't have said exactly why.

She certainly wasn't planning on trying to get anything started between them.

"I'm sort of a widower, I guess," he answered. "My ex-wife died a year and a half ago."

Well, Madison reflected, *that* was complicated.

"I'm sorry about your ex," she said. "No girlfriend?"

This time, Liam chuckled. "No girlfriend either," he said. "Why do you ask?"

That last part came out as a drawl. A sort of good-natured challenge.

Madison blushed. "Because even though this isn't a date or anything, it might look that way to some people, and I don't want anyone to get the wrong impression."

The grin widened.

His teeth were ridiculously white, and straight, too.

"This isn't a date?" he repeated. "Damn. I thought maybe it was."

The waiter returned with their beverages just then, and Madison was glad. It gave her a few moments to recover.

"Sorry," Madison said, with a lightness she didn't feel.

"In that case," Liam persisted reasonably, "how about dinner? Tonight or tomorrow night? My kids will be coming home Wednesday morning, and between them, the movie that's about to be filmed in Bitter Gulch and all the rest, I'll be busier than usual."

Madison avoided the dinner out suggestion. "Bitter Gulch?" she asked, stirring sweetener into her ice tea with a paper straw.

"The place you visited on your wedding day," Liam said. It was there again, that twinkle in his too-blue eyes, mischief doing a little happy dance. "You must have noticed you'd stepped from the present day into the Old West—you came through those saloon doors like Calamity Jane looking for a fight."

Madison's shoulders slumped a little when she sighed. The

muscles ached from all the tension she'd been carrying there, and, weirdly, she imagined Liam's hands massaging the stress away.

"Oh, yes," she said. "I've read about Bitter Gulch, though I'd never been there until—well—the other day. It's a tourist attraction, right?"

"Yes," Liam answered. "It's also a sometime movie set. The production company will be in town for about a month, filming whatever scenes they're planning to film there. That means it will be closed to the public periodically, at least for a while—not that that will keep the curious onlookers away."

"Are you playing a part?"

He shook his head. "I might be in the background now and again," he said, "but I'm not an actor."

"What about your employees? Will they be out of work for the duration?"

"No. They'll go on about their business as usual, wearing the costumes they normally wear. Technically, they're extras, I guess. The production company is paying them for their time."

"I see," Madison said, while her brain scrambled for something to say that wouldn't make her look and sound like a smitten fangirl.

"There are some A-list actors involved," Liam went on. "*That* will definitely cause a stir around town."

Good, Madison thought uncharitably. *Maybe it will distract everybody from the runaway bride story.*

"I suppose it will," she agreed.

The food arrived, and Liam pushed the basket of chips aside to make room for their plates, which were typically huge.

Helpfully, Madison moved the bean dip and the salsa out of the way.

"So your children will be arriving soon. Have they been away for long?"

The inquiry was an innocent one, but Liam reacted to it, for a single moment, as though she'd reached over and stabbed him with her fork.

There was no anger in his expression, but there was plenty of pain.

She'd definitely touched a nerve, and she wished she could take it back.

"They've been away for way *too* long," he said. "They'd been living with their grandparents in Seattle for about six months after the divorce, and then my ex-wife died six months after that. Naturally, the kids took it hard, and they wanted to stay with Waverly's folks."

"Oh," said Madison, setting down her fork. "I'm sorry, Liam. I didn't mean to pry."

His gaze softened to good-natured sadness. "Don't be sorry," he said. "It was a reasonable thing to ask."

They both began to eat again, though slowly now, and thoughtfully.

The food was delicious.

"Is it my turn again?" Liam asked, after a silence had stretched between them for a few seconds too long.

This time, it was Madison who laughed.

She was stunned to find herself laughing after the scene with Coralee that morning, and Liam's mention of his children's grief.

"I guess that's only fair," she said presently.

"It's kind of personal," Liam qualified.

"Shoot," Madison said, echoing what he'd said earlier.

He smiled, but his eyes remained serious. "Why did you decide to marry that guy, the one you essentially ditched at the altar?"

The question was completely benevolent, though it might have been a challenge coming from someone else.

"I thought Jeffrey was somebody he wasn't," she replied, keeping her chin up, though she felt it wobbling a little now. "I loved the man I believed he was—or wanted him to be—and I finally realized I'd been deluding myself."

For a long while, Liam pondered her answer in silence. Then, just when Madison was getting uncomfortable, he surprised her by saying, "I can relate to that."

"How so?"

"In the beginning, I loved the woman my wife wanted me to *believe* she was. I don't regret that, though, because without her, I wouldn't have Keely and Cavan."

Madison didn't reply.

She didn't have to.

6

Bliss

Twenty-Four Years Before

At first, Bliss was terrified.

She'd stumbled running away from the cemetery and from Madison, fallen, and hit her head. She remembered that much.

When she woke up, there was blood dripping from a cut on her forehead, and she felt sick to her stomach. Touched her fingertips to the small cut above her right eye, winced at the sting.

Bliss was a tough kid, she'd had to be, but the sight of the blood made her dizzy. That, on top of the nausea, was too much.

She rose to her hands and knees and threw up her fancy lunch.

When she'd finished, she went to the creek, splashed water on her face, rinsed out her mouth, tried to think what to do next.

Duke was probably still sleeping off his last bender, which meant she'd probably be able to sneak past him, scrounge around in the medicine cabinet in hopes of finding some Band-Aids and iodine, and get away before he woke up and started yelling.

Her father didn't need a reason to yell; when he'd been drinking steadily for a couple of days, and without her mother around to blame for all his troubles, he'd go after Bliss, take his misery out on her.

She walked on tiptoe and kept her eyes down at times like that, and this was most likely one of them.

Her head was still spinning a little as she made her way through the trees, over the fallen log that bridged the creek, and off in the general direction of the camper, which sat, rusting and dented, in a hidden clearing, under the friendly branches of a lonely old-timer of an oak.

When Bliss reached the clearing, having watched her feet for most of the way home, since she couldn't afford to stumble again, she was mystified, then startled.

The oak tree was there, tall and welcoming, its leaves rustling softly in the cool breeze.

The camper, however, was gone.

Just gone.

So was Duke's old truck.

Had he finally gotten fed up, like he always warned would happen, and left her behind? Hitched the truck to that falling-apart camper and hauled it away somewhere?

Bliss sank to her knees, the breath knocked out of her.

She'd already barfed up her lunch, but her empty stomach cramped just the same, over and over. It was so painful that her head swam again.

This wasn't right.

Oh, Bliss had no trouble believing that her dad would desert her, just as her mother had done. That bothered her, naturally, but not as much as the flat-out weird impossibility of that old camper being loaded up onto the bed of Duke's rust bucket of a truck and taken someplace else.

Neither the camper *nor* the truck would have been able to

pull off a trick like that, since they were both good for scrap iron and not much else.

Slowly, when her stomach had finally stopped trying to hurl up a whole lot of nothing, Bliss moved toward the spot where the camper *should* have been.

Sure, Duke could have taken off in the truck. Gone drinking again, hustling money at the nearest pool hall. He did stuff like that all the time—at least, when the rig was running, which it often wasn't.

But what could he possibly have done with the camper?

There were no deep gouges in the dirt under the oak tree. No oil drips or leaked sewage, no empty cigarette packages or beer cans.

Nothing.

The grass was green and springy and thick, as though it had never been browned and bent low by the weight of an old camper. There weren't even any tracks, left by the comings and goings of Duke's truck.

Instead, buttercups, wild daisies and other wildflowers bloomed among the deep green blades in bright splashes of color.

Bliss's head began to ache.

She had to be in the wrong place. That was it.

She'd fallen and hit her head.

And she'd gotten turned around somehow, that was all. Gone the wrong way, thinking she was headed home.

Except that the oak was the same tree she'd sat under so many times. The tree she'd hugged, and felt almost as though it was hugging her right back.

Oh, yes. Bliss knew that tree well. Secretly, she called it the Grandfather; it was a friend. Until Madison, it had been her *only* friend.

She paused in her confusion to remember that she'd shouted at Madison just a little while ago. After the ruckus she'd raised,

Madison probably wouldn't want anything to do with her ever again.

Sadness nearly overwhelmed Bliss in those moments of mixed-up realization.

What should she do next?

Walk to town? Head for the Bettencourt house and ask for help?

Town was too far away—at least four miles, according to Duke. And what was she supposed to do when she got there? Go from bar to bar, with her bleeding head and her wobbly knees, looking for her father?

Her granny used to say that, if she got herself lost, she ought to find a church or a police station. Folks there would look out for her.

The problem was, Duke didn't hold with churches, *or* with cops.

The first, he said, was just a place where pompous-ass people took your money and told you lies, and the police couldn't be trusted, either. They were out to get people like them—Duke, Mona and, he swore, even little snot-nosed kids like her.

If something went wrong, and there was a poor person handy, the cops would harass, not help, them.

She could backtrack to the cemetery, hoping Madison was still there, lingering over the picnic blanket and reading a book. Or just lying on her back in the grass, smiling at the sky, like she sometimes did.

Madison was a kid, too, but she was smart, and she'd know what to do.

Wouldn't she?

Bliss squeezed her eyes shut, tight as could be, but the tears came anyway.

She wrapped both arms around the Grandfather, as far as they would reach, and hugged him. Tight.

The rough bark chafed her cheek and the cut on her head,

and it throbbed. The blood, which had slowed up a little after she splashed her face with cold water down at the creek, started flowing again.

The creek.

She'd go back to the creek, sit down in the soft, fragrant grass growing along the bank, and think things through.

So she headed for the water.

She perched nearby for a good while, knees drawn up to her chin, arms wrapped around her legs, crying and wondering and telling herself she must be crazy, to think there was any magic in an ordinary place like this one.

Lord knew, Duke had said she was loony often enough, and so had Mona.

Maybe they'd been right, though that was as hard to accept now as it had been when they said it.

The sun began to drift lower, toward the mountains to the west of where she sat, and, calmer now, Bliss wanted to sleep.

Surely, when she woke up, this bad dream, if that was what it was, would be over. She'd find the camper, fix up the cut on her head, maybe crawl onto the bunk above what passed for a kitchen, and tough things out until she felt better.

Except that Bliss knew she probably shouldn't let herself fall asleep, in case she'd done real damage to her noggin when she tripped and landed on her face.

She knew from TV that when somebody banged their head against something hard and then drifted off, well, sometimes, they croaked.

So she sat, watched a deer and two fawns make their cautious way down the hill on the opposite side of the creek, dip their velvety noses into the water and drink, ever so delicately, like ladies in a storybook sipping their afternoon tea.

The deer, after regarding Bliss with limpid brown eyes, finished drinking and wandered back the way they'd come.

Bliss felt a touch of envy. Baby deer had someone to look out for them.

Why didn't she?

She turned lightheaded again, wondering about that, and swayed a little, gripping her legs tighter so she wouldn't tip over.

There was no telling how much time had passed when she was jolted out of her stupor by the sound of someone tromping through the underbrush, whistling a catchy tune.

When the boy emerged, Bliss felt the same confusion, the same loss of balance, as she had when she'd found Duke, his truck and the camper gone from the place they should have been. And weren't.

He was about Bliss's age, maybe a year or two older.

He wore blue overalls with no shirt underneath, his feet were bare, and he was carrying a fishing pole in one hand.

It wasn't the modern kind, like Duke used when he was of a mind to land himself a clutch of rainbow trout, but a long, thin strip of wood with a string fastened to one end.

Bliss thought of Huckleberry Finn.

The boy's hair was a light golden brown, and it gleamed in the gathering dusk. To Bliss, it looked as though someone had turned a bowl upside down on his head and then trimmed off whatever was still sticking out from under the rim.

Beside him trotted a big reddish-brown dog, tongue lolling.

The dog had no collar, no jingling tags.

Spotting Bliss, the boy stopped in his tracks, and so did the dog.

The kid looked just as surprised to see her as she was to see him.

"Who are you?" he asked, frowning now. "What's your name?"

Somehow, Bliss found her voice. "I'm Bliss Morgan. Who are you?"

"Jack Bettencourt," the boy said, still all serious-faced, still hanging back, as if expecting Bliss to come rushing and holler-ing at him like somebody on the warpath. "This here is private property, and you're trespassing."

Bliss stayed silent. She didn't have the energy to argue.

Jack Bettencourt came a few steps closer, peering at her from under that fringe of shining hair. "What happened to your head?" he asked. "It's all bloody."

Bliss touched the skin near the cut, but not the cut itself. It still hurt like crazy, and it was definitely still bleeding.

"I fell down," she answered. Her voice sounded strangely normal, considering that she didn't have the faintest idea what was going on.

The boy said his last name was Bettencourt, but Madison had never mentioned him. In fact, she'd talked about being an only child, and wishing she had brothers and sisters. It was confusing.

"Do you know Madison?" she asked, silently hoping for a yes.

He shook his head, and the dog loped over to where Bliss sat, used his long, sandpapery tongue to lick her cut.

"Hobo," the boy said. "You stop that, right now."

The dog ignored him.

Bliss slipped her arms around the animal's neck and buried her face in his dusty fur, cut and all.

For the first time since this nutty dream had begun, if that was what it was, she felt comforted, though just a little.

Jack approached, after leaning the fishing pole carefully against the trunk of a fir tree, and gently pulled the dog away.

"That cut looks pretty bad," he said, squinting. Up close, Bliss could see that he had freckles, that his eyes were the same color as Madison's, hazel, and the tops of his skinny shoulders were peeling from sunburn. "Maybe we ought to head back to the house, so Ma can take a look at it."

"Ma?" Bliss echoed, puzzled. She'd never known a real per-son to say "Ma" when they talked about their mom, just the girls in the *Little House on the Prairie* stories.

Jack looked her over, his eyes widening slightly. "Where do you hail from, Bliss Morgan?" he asked, looking equally confused by her appearance as she was about his. "Ain't never seen any girl dressed like you before."

"Don't say 'ain't,'" Bliss said. "It makes you sound ignorant, and if you're really a Bettencourt, then you ought to know better."

The freckled face scrunched up a little.

She'd annoyed him.

So it surprised her when he put out a hand, pulled her to her feet.

For someone who couldn't be a day older than ten, he was sure strong.

"Come on," he said. "Ma will have my hide if I don't haul you right home, so she can tend that cut. You don't want to get an infection or anything."

Bliss ran her hands down the front of her shirt.

She'd wanted someone to help her, and here were Jack Bettencourt and his goofball dog, Hobo.

She might as well do as he said.

For the moment, after all, she didn't have a better plan.

So she followed the boy in overalls back the way he'd come, with the dog nudging her along from behind, bumping her with his wet, cold nose every time she slowed down.

7

As it turned out, Liam McKettrick had very old-fashioned manners.

Instead of saying goodbye at the door of the restaurant, he walked Madison all the way to the Bentley, doing that hand-on-the-small-of-the-back thing the whole time.

It gave her the same deliciously vulnerable feeling as the last time he'd touched her that way.

Once she had unlocked the door, Liam reached around her to open it.

She stood in the gap, looking up at him.

He adjusted his hat, grinned again. "What about that date I mentioned? Are you up for that, Ms. Bettencourt?"

Madison felt like a smitten teenager, which was stupid because, one, she was thirty-two, not sixteen, and two, she'd only called it quits with Jeffrey a couple of days before, and therefore had no excuse for being this attracted to someone else so soon.

She shouldn't be thinking the thoughts this man made her

think just by being in close proximity. Being near him made the nerve endings thrum under her skin.

She hesitated.

"What?" Liam prompted, watching her with an expression of gentle courtesy, his head tilted slightly to one side.

Madison looked away, looked back. "When it comes to dating," she confessed quietly, "I don't have the best track record."

Liam rubbed the back of his neck, pondering that statement. Sighed. "Madison," he said, finally, "I'm not asking you to move in and share my bed. I'm asking you to *dinner*." He paused, regarding her in a way that made her throat tighten and the backs of her eyes burn. "I'm going to be honest, here. I'm drawn to you—not just physically—and I have been since you came barreling into the Hard Luck Saloon in a wedding dress and a fit of fury. I think you're beautiful. I think you're smart. I think you're funny. But I *don't* have any particular agenda. I just want to spend some time with you and see if that takes us anywhere."

"No expectations? No pressure?"

"No, Madison. I just want to buy you dinner—or cook it for you, out at my place, if you trust me enough for that. I want to hear some of your story and tell you some of mine. For now, that's all."

She knew she should have said no, even as she said yes instead.

She wasn't ready for this.

She was *too* ready for this.

Talk about confusing.

"All right," she said. "I'm planning to visit Coralee again this evening, and I'll probably be pretty wrung out by the time that's over, so tomorrow would be better."

"Tomorrow it is," Liam agreed.

God, she could tumble right into the blue depths of those eyes of his and fall forever and ever, never hitting bottom.

"What shall I bring?"

"Yourself," Liam replied easily. Then he swept up the Bentley in a long, slow and admiring glance. "And this fantastic car."

"Could we ride horses?"

Madison didn't know why she'd asked such a thing of a man who was practically a stranger; it just popped out of her mouth. She had ridden a lot during high school and college, but over the last decade or so, while she was busy failing at love and marriage and succeeding in business, she hadn't made time for it.

There was something so *centering* about riding a horse, not in an arena, but in the countryside, with nature all around.

"I can definitely arrange that," Liam said. "What's your skill level?"

She laughed. "Reasonably competent and sadly out of practice," she replied.

"Got it," Liam said. "I'll choose your mount accordingly."

"What about you?" Madison countered, because for some strange and most likely silly reason, she didn't want to part with this intriguing man quite yet. "What's *your* skill level?"

"Damn good and getting better all the time," came the reply.

It was an innocuous remark, though spoken in a drawl that might have been considered sultry, and Madison's sometimes frisky mind took a leap into double-entendre territory.

She blushed.

That made Liam touch her cheek, lean in, and place a light, brief and completely world-shattering kiss on her mouth.

Damn good and getting better all the time.

Dangerous words, those, but along with that whisper of a kiss, they sent a thrill racing along Madison's nerve endings and sparked tiny fires in places she hadn't known there *were* places.

She drew back, almost as if he'd shocked her with a cattle prod, and lowered herself into the driver's seat of the Bentley, a little stunned.

A *lot* stunned.

The kiss had been a mere brush of his lips, actually, but she could still feel it on her mouth, lingering there, making her want more kisses, deeper ones, from a man she barely knew, no less. "Tomorrow night, your place," she confirmed, all business now. "What time?"

"Early, if you want to ride for a couple of hours before supper," he replied. "Say four thirty?"

"That *is* early. Don't you have to tend bar at the saloon, or keep the peace in the town of Bitter Gulch?" Madison teased, deliberately prolonging the conversation and wanting to kick herself for it.

She'd already had her emotional knees broken by two different men, and now she was flirting—yes, *flirting*—with another. What was she, anyway—a sucker for punishment?

Instinctively, Madison knew she could trust him. But could she trust *herself* to behave, alone in the wide-open spaces of Montana with a man like Liam McKettrick?

She told him she'd see him the next afternoon, closed the car door, and drove off, the kiss still resting on her mouth, thinking about the fertility treatments she planned to sign up for.

If she didn't reach a single other goal in her entire life, she wanted a baby to love, to nurture, to raise in a normal home, but if that was going to happen, it would happen in its own time. Maybe she needed to lighten up, at least for now.

She shifted her thoughts to Liam.

Keely and Cavan were, in fact, due to arrive the day after tomorrow, by Liam's own account. He'd made it pretty plain over lunch that he meant to get things right this time, make up for the months he and the kids had spent apart.

He hadn't said much about his reasons for the gaps in his relationship with his son and daughter, both of whom he clearly loved fiercely, but Madison had heard enough to make a few guesses.

His late wife—Waverly, wasn't it?—had obviously been a difficult person, and in the aftermath of her death, her parents had done all they could to keep him from taking Keely and Cavan away.

Why, Madison wondered, had such a strong man allowed his former in-laws to buffalo him that way?

Had he felt guilty for not loving his wife, even when he knew she was dying?

Had he been overwhelmed by what was absolutely a tragedy, his lack of romantic love for Waverly notwithstanding?

He'd said he'd loved the woman he believed his wife to be, rather than the woman she actually was. Perhaps he had mourned that other Waverly, the one he'd imagined.

Maybe his grief for that nonexistent partner had crushed him. Rendered him temporarily incapable of stepping up, even for his own children.

Was that even possible?

As little as she knew about Liam, Madison *had* figured out that he was strong, not only in his mind and body, but in his soul.

Madison felt a little deflated as she drove on through the town of Silver Hills and followed the highway back toward Painted Pony Creek.

She was so distracted, her lower lip caught between her teeth, that when Liam honked his horn just before turning off onto a road that probably led to his ranch, she almost jumped out of her skin.

She hadn't realized he was right behind her, though it only made sense that he would be, since they'd just left the same town and headed in the same general direction.

Not much gets by you, she told herself.

The kiss was forgotten for the moment, and Madison's emotions were in a tangle by the time she reached home—good feelings all snarled up with reluctance and no little regret.

She should have said no to the horseback ride, no to dinner, and gone about her business.

She had plenty of things to think about, after all—Coralee's deteriorating condition and the inevitable meetings with her grandmother's attorney, dealing with the aftermath of Jeffrey, if there *was* an aftermath. Maybe she'd get lucky, and the breakup would be what it *ought* to be—history. Nothing more than a bump in the road.

She'd meet with Brynne Garrett, who had planned the splashy wedding that wasn't, and clear up any financial obligations. Maybe demonstrate that she wasn't the crazy runaway bride she must have appeared to be the day she walked out on a man she'd once truly believed she loved, leaving him *and* his mother flustered and furious.

Madison liked Brynne as a person and wanted to apologize directly for what must have been the calamity of the season, if not the year, from a wedding planner's viewpoint. She'd even hoped they might become friends.

On top of all this, Madison had her business to consider. Should she sell the company, with Audra's agreement of course, and move back to Painted Pony Creek for good?

The idea had considerable appeal, though it would be a major change.

Or maybe *because* it would be a major change.

She was pulling into the driveway at home—no sense putting the Bentley into the garage, since she planned to go back to Silver Hills again after a nap, another shower, and a light supper, to spend an hour or two with Coralee—when she caught sight of the childish thread bracelet on her wrist.

Naturally, seeing it brought Bliss Morgan to mind.

Why the sudden fascination with a child she hadn't seen in nearly twenty-five years? She wasn't sure, beyond the fact that she hated loose ends.

And Bliss's sudden disappearance *was* unfinished business, to Madison anyway.

Was it possible that the little girl hadn't been real? Hadn't Coralee referred to her as an imaginary friend over and over again?

There had been no big uproar in the community when Bliss vanished, leaving only the bracelet and a goodbye, scratched into the back of a matchbook, as a farewell. But what if she hadn't been the one to leave the bracelet *or* the one-word note?

Madison had been a very lonely kid up until she went away to boarding school, and she'd had her share of imagined friendships. In elementary school, for example, she'd lived in a fantasy world for days at a time, a place populated by interesting people of the see-through variety.

Boarding school had been a turning point. There, she'd made dozens of actual, flesh-and-blood friends, and except for the odd moment of homesickness, or when she read a book that reminded her of those simple summer days in her childhood, she hadn't thought much about Bliss.

She got out of the car, shut the door behind her, and headed for the elaborate entrance to Bettencourt Hall.

She was inside, in the entryway, standing beside the beautifully carved grandfather clock, before it occurred to her that she hadn't locked the Bentley.

Alas, this was Painted Pony Creek, not some violent slum.

Most people didn't even lock their *houses*, let alone their automobiles.

She set her purse on the side table next to the Italian pottery umbrella stand and turned to lock the main door.

Madison had lived in this house until she was twelve, and never worried about thieves or home invaders, but she'd been a city dweller since then, and security was important to her.

She made a mental note to be more careful in the future.

She strolled through to the kitchen, at once anticipating tomorrow's get-together with Liam and pondering the mystery of her lost childhood friend.

What *did* she know about Bliss Morgan?

Not much.

Bliss had told her enough about her parents for Madison to

figure out that her cemetery picnic companion came from a dysfunctional home.

As for that home, Madison recalled Bliss mentioning that she lived in an old camper, "in an open place way back in the woods."

Madison had never been there, though she'd been tempted, once or twice, to follow Bliss and get a look at the place.

Bottom line, she'd been too scared. From the way Bliss described her father, she figured she would have been unwelcome. The man had sounded dangerous, and naturally Madison hadn't wanted to encounter him.

Sadly—and oddly, to her way of thinking—there hadn't been so much as a ripple of adult concern after Bliss went missing.

Madison knew that if she or any of the other kids Painted Pony Creek called its own had vanished, seemingly between one moment and the next, there would have been police from several jurisdictions and many dedicated volunteers combing the surrounding area for any sign of the lost child.

But there had *been* no police, no volunteers, no search dogs.

Surely, though, she had to be mistaken about that. Mean drunkard that he was, and as uncaring as he sounded, wouldn't Bliss's dad have raised some kind of alarm when he discovered that his daughter was gone?

He might not have known right away, Madison reasoned sadly, climbing the main stairway and making for her room. He might not have been sober enough to deal with the situation at the time. Or he simply hadn't noticed.

It was even possible, regrettably, that he just hadn't *cared*.

In fact, he might even have *caused* Bliss's disappearance, Madison thought with a shiver.

If so, he'd gotten away with a heinous crime.

Reaching her frilly, preteen girl's bedroom, she swapped out her sandals for her hiking boots and her blouse for a faded old

T-shirt with a picture of Johnny Depp on the front and added another item to her mental to-do list.

Redecorate this room to suit a grown woman.

If she decided to stay in Painted Pony Creek, anyway.

On her way down the back stairs, she grabbed a bottle of water from the fridge and went out through the kitchen door.

The floorboards of the sunporch creaked as she passed over them, and, making a rare exception, she didn't bother to lock up this time.

She wasn't going any further than the old family cemetery, and that was close by, only a few hundred yards beyond the tree line at the bottom of the overgrown vegetable patch.

If she didn't go back to Boca Raton and take up the life she'd designed to fit perfectly, like a tailor-made garment, she would restore that garden to its former glory. Raise heaps of healthy vegetables and share them with the food bank in town.

Reaching the graveyard, Madison wondered what she'd expected to find—almost certainly nothing—but that was the last place she'd seen Bliss, all those years ago.

It was, in fact, the *only* place she'd seen Bliss.

And that made it the logical place to start.

Start what?

She looked around her, noticing that the old, old gravestones and markers were almost completely hidden under deep grass and thickets of brush, thistles and all.

She waded through the bushes, thorns grabbing at her jeans and scratching at her hands and forearms, to the stone where Bliss had always chosen to sit when they met—and most likely when she was alone. She uncovered the chiseled lettering. *Charles C. Bettencourt III.*

Madison perched on that stone, listening as bees buzzed and birds chirped in the branches of nearby trees, alerting each other to the unauthorized presence of a human being.

"Bliss," she said, very softly. "Where are you? What happened?"

Of course there was no reply, but there *was* the very vaguest
sense that she wasn't alone. Perhaps there were ghosts around, she
thought fancifully, ancestors somehow tethered to their burial
places.

Not likely, she reflected.

If *she* were a ghost, she wouldn't waste her time haunting some
weedy old cemetery. She'd go where the action was, where the
living were going on with their busy, bustling lives.

She'd eavesdrop and possibly pull a few harmless pranks.

Hiding things that weren't vital to everyday living, like TV
remotes and can openers and hammers and lipsticks perhaps.

Silly thoughts.

All this visit had accomplished, really, was to add yet another
task to her schedule. Madison was the last of the Bettencourt
line, or would be once Coralee passed away, and all around
her lay her late family members, forgotten beneath their moss-
edged, tilting stones.

It was her moral responsibility, as a Bettencourt, to clean the
place up.

Pull away the weeds and the thistles and make these people's
names visible again. It would be a symbolic gesture, a reminder,
if only to her, that these remains, buried deep, had once been
living, breathing human beings. With names.

The job wouldn't be easy, though. She'd have to wear a hat to
protect herself from the sun, and she'd get blisters and scratches,
even with work gloves on.

But, as Coralee would have said, it was there to be done.

Not that Coralee had ever been one to pull weeds and tear
out thorny brush, even when she'd been physically capable of
doing so.

She'd always hired someone to perform jobs like this.

Madison stood, reasoning that she could certainly do that,

too. Estelle, the housekeeper, would know plenty of locals willing to work hard under a summer sun, and paying said laborers wouldn't be a hardship, either.

Still, for whatever reason, Madison knew this project had to be her own.

And she'd made up her mind to do it.

Resigned, she began making her way through the dense underbrush again, only realizing after she'd come out on the far side that she wasn't headed toward the house, but in the direction of the creek.

She could hear it bubbling and swirling its way between its rocky banks, smell its fresh, clean scent.

This was Painted Pony Creek proper, the stream for which the town had been named, way back in pioneer days.

Madison had rarely visited the place, alone anyway. Estelle had brought her here sometimes on hot summer afternoons to cool off. They'd sat side by side, dangling their bare feet in the shallow water, forever hurrying on to wherever, and they'd talked about things Coralee hadn't seemed interested in, like boys and school and where that creek was headed, anyway, sweeping whole legions of trout and other fish right along with it.

She smiled at that memory.

Estelle was due to return to work the next morning.

Maybe *she* would remember something about Bliss.

Estelle had always known everything about everybody for miles around, since she'd been born and raised in Painted Pony Creek.

Finally realizing where she was going, Madison walked faster, following the creek as it twisted and turned among the trees and various bushes.

She picked a handful of blackberries along the way, and nibbled at them as she made her way in the direction Bliss had pointed toward one long-ago day, indicating where the camper was but at the same time making it very clear that Madison ought to stay away from that place, because it might be bad news if her dad happened to be around when she got there.

The recollection of that warning sent an icy shiver trickling down Madison's spine, though she wasn't afraid, not in the least. She was a grown woman now, not a child, and she could protect herself if the need arose.

Probably.

It wasn't as if she knew kung fu or anything, but still. She wasn't in the habit of backing down easily.

When she reached the clearing, she spotted what remained of an ancient camper, lying on one side under a huge oak tree capped with lusciously green chattering leaves.

A crow squawked somewhere nearby.

Madison moved closer to the wreck, noting the metal peeling from the parts of it that were still visible. The thing was so rusted that it seemed a hard wind would reduce it to particles, floating like dust motes in the bright sunshine of a July afternoon.

It was well on its way to dissolution already, collapsing to the ground as though it were melting.

She looked around carefully.

For what? Tire tracks? Footprints?

She didn't know.

There was no sign that anyone had been near this relic in years.

Madison imagined the camper as Bliss must have known it, certainly nothing fancy but upright, at least, a place where people took shelter and slept and ate whatever passed for a meal.

Her heart cramped painfully at the thought of how it must have been for Bliss, only eight years old and existing—make that *surviving*—in what amounted to an oversized breadbox.

Truthfully, a garden shed probably would have been more comfortable and offered better shelter.

Madison decided she had seen enough, at least for now.

She wasn't about to climb inside that twisted mess in search of clues, like some Nancy Drew wannabe. After all this time, there wouldn't be any.

There were probably spiders, though, and mice, too. And God knew what else.

No, she'd approach this dilemma the right way.

Cautiously. Sensibly.

As soon as time allowed, she'd pay a visit to the sheriff's office in town. The municipal police department, too.

Maybe Eli Garrett or Melba Summers would be able to find something in their records. A visit to the town library was in order, too. She would look for old newspaper articles, written in the days when the internet was in its relative infancy.

Bliss, she thought, *I'm still your friend. I let you down before, but I'll find out what became of you if it takes the rest of my life.*

Why was she undertaking what was probably an impossible task? Madison asked herself that as she made her way back toward Bettencourt Hall.

It was entirely possible that Bliss was dead.

Even likely—especially if she'd been kidnapped by some pervert.

If she hadn't been taken, then there was a definite chance that her no-account father had beaten her to death in a drunken rage, buried her someplace where she'd never be found. She'd certainly shown up for a few of their casual picnics with bruises on her upper arms, and once, a black eye.

She'd refused to tell Madison how she'd gotten the shiner—or the bruises—and any attempt to press for further information was met with stubborn silence.

Madison hadn't really needed an answer, anyway.

She'd been sheltered, it was true, but not so sheltered that she didn't know fathers and mothers sometimes hit their children—or worse.

By the time the house came in sight, Madison had set all these thoughts aside to simmer, like a batch of Estelle's beef burgundy or special stew. Something would surface when the time was right.

In the meantime, she let the whole thing go.

Back inside the house, Madison showered again, washed her shoulder-length hair and blew it dry, and even applied a little lip-stick, having decided she wasn't hungry yet, and would prefer to wait and have supper after she came back from visiting Coralee.

Finally, wearing a pretty pink-and-white floral sundress and slip-on sandals, Madison locked up the house, climbed behind the wheel of the Bentley and started the engine.

She was mildly surprised, once again, that the car ran as well as it did.

Evidently, Coralee had seen that the vehicle received proper maintenance, right up until she'd had to be hospitalized. She hadn't mentioned that during their frequent telephone chats—Coralee on a landline, Madison on her cell—but there were probably a great many things the old woman had left unsaid.

Heaven knew that had always been her way, really. Especially when Madison was still a young girl, living at home.

Oh, Coralee hadn't clammed up completely, thank heaven. She'd answered Madison's questions about her dead mother and father, and shown her numerous photo albums, but she'd never actually shared anything at random, the way most people would have done.

There had been no funny anecdotes, or sad ones, either.

Coralee had never been the sentimental type.

And she'd always been far more interested in adults than children.

In those days, she'd held what she referred to as "salons" in the main parlor, hosted bridge tournaments in the home library, thrown glittering dinner parties in the elegant dining room, which looked, even now, like it belonged in a Greek palace.

It even had pillars.

Estelle had worn a uniform and served refreshments at such

events, while Madison, spellbound, spied on the proceedings from various hiding places, like the alcove behind one of the bookcases in the library.

Funny.

Funny peculiar, not funny laugh-out-loud.

She hadn't thought about that secret room in years. Back in the day, it had been the place she went to cry, scribble in her journal, or simply hide, not because she was in any danger, but because she wanted to be alone with her thoughts.

By now, she reflected, driving through the dusk out of Painted Pony Creek and onto the road to Silver Hills, her secret chamber, as she'd liked to think of it then, was probably full of dust, cobwebs and mouse droppings.

She'd take a look tomorrow, maybe do a little scrubbing and sweeping.

Had she ever told Bliss about that hideaway?

Probably, though she knew for sure she'd never been able to persuade the other girl to come anywhere near the main house. She'd seemed almost afraid of the place, as though it were somehow alive and might gobble her up.

Ridiculous, of course.

Bettencourt Hall was old, even getting crumbly in places, but it definitely wasn't scary. It was benign, through and through, and Madison had always felt safe there, secret spy space aside.

Way back when she'd first arrived at boarding school, Madison had been deeply, wretchedly homesick—not for Coralee, or even for the kindly Estelle, but for the house itself.

Every time she stepped through the front door, it was as though all those stately rooms had somehow coalesced into a living being, eager to embrace her and make her feel welcome.

It was indeed a special house.

And with every day that passed, Madison was less willing to leave it for her lovely condo in Boca Raton, or for anyplace else.

That old mansion was more than a house.

Even more than a home.

It was a sanctuary, a place to hide and to heal.

8

Bliss

The sight of the house Jack Bettencourt led Bliss to that sunny, disjointed afternoon stopped her cold, and she must have gasped aloud, because both boy and dog stopped, too, and turned to study her curiously.

"What's the matter?" Jack asked, sounding a little impatient. He probably wanted to dispense with the wandering stranger he'd found in the woods and get back to his favorite fishing hole.

Bliss was too stunned to speak, at least for the first few moments.

The house *was* the one Madison lived in, the one she herself had spied on from time to time, when she had nothing better to do.

At the same time, it *wasn't*.

It was smaller, and far less grand.

The screened-in sunporch was gone, and the back door was

high off the ground, with four steps below it, made of stones most likely hauled there from the creek, stuck together with what Jack would later describe as mortar.

There were no flowerbeds, no rosebushes.

The vegetable patch remained, and it was flourishing and abuzz with bees, but it was in a different place, over to one side of the house, not butting up to the edge of the woods, the way Bliss remembered.

All that confused her so much that the pit of her stomach quivered, and the cut on her head hurt like sin, but another surprise soon appeared.

A woman came out of the back door, carrying a basket of wet clothes, holding her burden in a way that allowed her to see where she was stepping.

Her hair was the same color as Jack's, a sort of taffy color, pinned up in a style that puffed out around her pretty face.

It was the woman's clothing, though, that made Bliss wonder if she was still lying where she'd fallen, dreaming of a place that couldn't possibly be real.

The lady wore a long black skirt, matching pinchy-looking shoes that buttoned up the front, and a blue blouse with puffy sleeves and buttons that went up her chest and stopped just beneath her chin.

Singing a song, something about glory, she walked over to the clothesline—another thing that didn't exist at the Bettencourt Hall that Bliss knew—set the basket down, took out a boy's shirt, and gave it a shake so brisk that it made a snapping sound. Then she hung the shirt from the clothesline using huge wooden pegs.

The dog—Hobo?—barked and ran toward the woman, and that was when she stopped singing, turned her head and saw Jack approaching with a stranger.

Her face crumpled for a moment, not out of disgust, Bliss thought with relief, but out of curiosity and surprise.

Forgetting the laundry, she walked over to where Bliss stood, with Jack looking on, and gave a sort of frowny-smile.

"Well, now," she said, and her voice was just as nice when she spoke as when she sang. "Who is this?" A frown shunted aside the smile as she took in Bliss's bloody forehead. "Mercy! What's happened to you, child?"

"This here is Bliss Morgan," Jack said, just when Bliss was beginning to wonder if he'd gone mute. It was clear enough that he and the woman were both as puzzled by Bliss's clothes as she was by theirs. "I found her down by the creek, just a little while ago."

He said this like she wasn't standing right there. Like she was an interesting rock or an arrowhead, discovered and brought home for show-and-tell.

"Bliss Morgan," the woman repeated. "What a lovely name." Her attention, which felt like a blessing, or a burst of sunshine on a dark day, turned to Jack. "And do not say 'this here.' It isn't proper English."

"This is my ma," Jack said, and the absence of "here" was so plain that it seemed to leave a gap in the sentence. "Mrs. Matthew Bettencourt. My pa's dead, so it's just me and Ma and Hobo hereabouts."

"Katherine Bettencourt," the woman said, introducing herself, even though her son had already done that, all the while regarding Bliss with benign perplexity. She made no mention of her dead husband. "Let's go inside and see what we can do about that cut."

Bliss hesitated.

The dream was so vivid by then that she was on the verge of tears.

And she *never* cried, in a dream or wide awake; no, not even when her dad bopped her one on the back of her head for getting underfoot or talking when he wanted quiet.

"Who are your folks, dear?" Katherine Bettencourt continued, taking Bliss firmly by the hand and leading her past the clothesline and the full laundry basket and the small blue shirt dangling from its huge pegs. "Where do you live?"

Bliss had no idea how to answer the second question, because now she was wondering if *this* place was real, and she'd only imagined the other one, where she shared a broken-down shell of a camper with her no-good father and, up until a few weeks ago, her runaround mother.

So she said nothing.

She let Mrs. Bettencourt lead her up the stone steps and into a spacious kitchen, dimly lit and deliciously cool.

The furniture was very solid, and Bliss had never seen anything like it.

There was no refrigerator, and the stove was a large, clunky black metal thing with chrome on it, though it looked nothing like a car.

Mrs. Bettencourt pulled out a chair. Weak-kneed, Bliss sank into it without being told to do so.

"Is the child unable to speak?" she asked Jack, who hovered nearby, curious himself.

"Nope," Jack answered. "I heard her talk before. I think maybe she's just scared."

His mother gathered up a dented metal basin, some bandages, a misshapen bar of yellow soap, a washcloth, and something in a brown bottle. Medicine, Bliss figured, though she was still too shook up to speak. "You run down to the Simmons place and borrow a horse," the lady went on, busy pouring water from a tea kettle into the basin. Steam rose from it. "Ride straight to Marshal Claridge's office and tell him we've got a lost little girl out here, and he needs to come see to the matter as soon as he can."

Bliss stiffened in the hard chair with its high back.

Mrs. Bettencourt was sending for a marshal?

But a marshal was a *cop*, right?

Maybe she'd be arrested, and that wouldn't be cool, even in a dream.

Bliss considered bolting, but the plain fact was, she knew her legs wouldn't hold her up. Besides, if this *was* a dream—and surely it had to be—she'd wake up soon, find herself lying under a tree or on a soft bed of moss or even in the cramped little berth in the camper, and everything would go back to normal.

The thought of that made her a little sad.

At last, she found her voice, though it was very, very small. "I'm not a crook," she said. "Please don't get the police."

Mrs. Bettencourt regarded Bliss with concern and sympathy. "Why, child," she said gently, but with emphasis, "you're not in trouble. We need the marshal to help us find your family, that's all."

Did she even have a family?

In the world where this house was big and modern, with no clothesline in the yard and the vegetable patch where it was supposed to be, down at the bottom of the big yard, she had Duke and Mona. There, her name was Bliss Morgan, and she lived in an old camper.

This world, on the other hand, was *very* different.

Which one was real?

Was she still Bliss, like before?

Too many questions flew around her head like birds, plucking at her hair with their beaks, pecking little holes in her scalp, which was already hurting plenty.

Jack had taken off right away, obeying his mother's instructions, and now Bliss was alone with this kindly woman, in her strange clothes, with her shiny caramel hair fluffed out around her face.

Bliss felt her lower lip wobble as she searched her brain for something to say.

"Never you mind, now," Mrs. Bettencourt soothed, dipping a corner of the washcloth into the basin of hot water and gently wiping at Bliss's forehead. "I reckon you'll tell me—or the marshal, once he gets here—what we need to know."

For a little while, Bliss was calmer. She even relaxed, as Mrs. Bettencourt washed her face; there was something so comforting about that.

"This is going to sting, I'm afraid," the woman said moments later, reaching for the brown bottle after she had cleaned the cut and the area around it. "I don't think you'll have a scar, though. Head wounds bleed a lot, even when they're not particularly serious."

Bliss had lapsed deeper into her haze, so that she barely heard the warning, but when Mrs. Bettencourt soaked another corner of the washcloth in smelly medicine and touched it to the cut, she sat up straight again, eyes wide-open, and scrambled to her feet.

"Ouch!" she yelled.

Mrs. Bettencourt set the cloth aside, placed her hands lightly on Bliss's now quivering shoulders, and pressed her very gently back into her chair. "The worst is over," she said matter-of-factly. She was a person who knew what she was doing—or firmly believed that she did.

"I need to go home now," Bliss said, once she'd breathed her way through the awful sting of that medicine.

A while ago, when she stayed with Gran and managed to scrape a knee or an elbow roller-skating on the sidewalk in front of the house, out would come the medicine, and it would always sting like anything.

That was because it was killing germs, Gran would say. And that was a good thing.

Well, today, those germs weren't going down easy.

They were *fighting back.*

"The marshal will take you back to your own people soon," Mrs. Bettencourt replied, deftly wrapping a long strip of white cloth around Bliss's head, like a sweatband. "And you mustn't worry. He's a very nice man, Marshal Claridge is."

"I can find my own way back," Bliss responded, though without much confidence that she could. She'd tried, after all, to go home, if that old camper could be called a home, and found it gone.

Only her favorite tree, the Grandfather, had remained of the place she remembered.

"You've been hurt," Mrs. Bettencourt said with a shake of her head. "I can't allow you to wander off all alone. In the meantime, I think you could use some food. You look very thin, young lady."

Again, the woman's eyes took in Bliss's shorts and T-shirt. Again, her forehead crumpled.

"Your clothes—" she began, but then, evidently at a loss for what else to say, she fell silent again. "I do declare, I've never seen such garments, especially on a girl."

"I might be an orphan," Bliss suggested, letting the comment on her clothes pass, and thinking of the vanished camper. There had been no sign of Duke, or of his beat-up old truck. Not even tire tracks dug into the grassy dirt. "I'm not sure."

Mrs. Bettencourt's eyes, which were hazel in color, like her son's, like Madison's, widened slightly. She laid her hand on her chest and opened her fingers wide. "An orphan?" she echoed. "My stars. Did someone *abandon* you? Is that what happened?"

Bliss considered her options.

She was no liar, but when she woke up, none of this would matter anyhow. It would be a weird story she could tell Madison, the next time they met in the cemetery for a picnic.

Besides, in a very real way, she *had* been left to take care of herself, so she was *kind of* an orphan.

And there was never any certainty that her dad would come home after the next binge, was there? And her mother was already long gone, maybe this time forever.

"Yes," Bliss said, and her lip wobbled again, and she let the tears come, simply because she was tired of trying to hold them back.

Her head hurt. She was hungry.

And the whole world—or at least, *her* world—had gone plumb crazy.

"What happened, exactly?" Mrs. Bettencourt had left off her puttering and sat herself down in a chair, looking closely at Bliss.

"My mom and dad are gone," Bliss said, telling just a *teeny-tiny* lie. "They left me down there by the creek. That's where I was when Jack came and found me."

An odd look came over Mrs. Bettencourt's face when Bliss mentioned her parents, a sort of catch in the rhythm of things, like when you were running a smooth string between your fingers and you hit a knot you didn't expect. "Your mom and dad," Katherine echoed, as though taken aback. Then, after a few moments' recovery, she went on to ask, "They *left* you?"

Bliss nodded, amazed at how true a lie could feel. "Yes," she said. "I guess they got tired of me. I can be pretty pesky."

"When did this happen?"

Bliss considered her answer for several moments.

Her stomach rumbled so loud, Mrs. Bettencourt heard it and got to her feet.

"Today," Bliss said, figuring she was on a roll now, and might as well keep on going. "We were camping," she elaborated, warming to the story and to Jack's mother's attentive sympathy. "I woke up and they were gone. They took everything and just—went."

Inwardly, Bliss smiled. The tall tale was *definitely* growing on her.

"That's *terrible*," Mrs. Bettencourt said.

She rose from her chair and walked over to a wooden box with a handle in front.

When she opened it, a soft and refreshing chill came from inside. An icebox.

Bliss had read about them in stories about the olden days.

Soon, Mrs. Bettencourt had put together a meal.

Some kind of meat, stuck between two thick slices of homemade bread, slathered with butter. *Real* butter, not margarine. A bowl of pears, taken from a jar brought from a shelf on the far wall, where there were numerous *other* jars, filled with things like beans and carrots and peeled tomatoes.

A tall glass of milk was set before her, too.

Bliss ate fiercely, trying to mind her manners, like her Gran had taught her to do, but unable to slow down.

Her stomach was like a cave dug into a mountainside, with a bear roaring inside it.

By the time Jack and Hobo returned, accompanied by a man riding a mule and wearing a funny round hat, Bliss was ready to curl up somewhere and sleep, though she didn't really want to do that and wake up back in the camper, with her belly grinding at her backbone because she'd only *dreamed* she'd had something to eat.

"The marshal was out in the countryside someplace," Jack explained as he and the man and the dog entered, one by one. "So I brought Doc Wiggins."

Doc Wiggins was a small man, wearing funny clothes—a checkered vest over a heavy cotton shirt, baggy pants and suspenders.

He nodded to Mrs. Bettencourt as he entered the kitchen, removing his hat, hanging it on a peg next to the door.

"I hear you took a bad fall," he said to Bliss, carefully removing the bandage Jack's mother had tied around her head.

He made a tsk-tsk sound as he examined the wound. Shook his gray head a couple of times.

He had a beard and a big mustache, both the same color as his hair.

"You did a good job, Katherine," he said. Then, drawing up a chair, he sat down facing Bliss, and they were almost knee to knee, which would have scared Bliss a little if she hadn't sensed that he was kind, like Mrs. Bettencourt.

He caught Bliss's chin in one hand, though lightly, and squinted as he peered into her eyes.

"Pupils look all right," he mused, as if thinking out loud. "Probably no concussion, so it'll be fine if she wants to sleep for a while. Get her strength back."

Don't talk about *me, M-mister,* Bliss thought, but didn't quite dare say, *like I'm not even here. Talk* to *me.*

That was when Jack handed Doc Wiggins a battered leather bag, black, but spotted with wear.

Bliss hoped he wasn't about to give her a shot.

She'd had all her vaccinations—Gran had seen to that—but every one of them had hurt, and she figured she'd already hurt enough for one day, bonking her head like she had.

Instead of a needle, the doctor produced a stethoscope.

Listened to her heart, nodding as he did so, and then her lungs.

"Fit as a fiddle," he said, finally.

Then, at long last, he looked at Bliss and asked, "Where are your kinfolk, little one, and where in the name of all that's holy did you get those clothes?"

Bliss didn't even have to open her mouth to answer, because Mrs. Bettencourt jumped right in and told the story Bliss had just told *her,* though she didn't explain about the clothes.

The doctor listened carefully, accepted the cup of cold lemonade Mrs. Bettencourt poured from a pitcher stored in the icebox, and spoke of other things—the doings of the "townsfolk," as he put it, the state of the nation—doomed for sure—and the new mule he was considering buying, since it was time to replace old Shadrach, the one he was riding now.

Bliss fell asleep in her chair.

And when she woke up, hours later, it was dark outside, and she was in a bed, and Jack's mother was sitting in a rocking chair close by, like if something bad tried to happen, she wanted to be there to stop it right then.

So, Bliss thought, she was still dreaming.

Or maybe she was in a coma.

She smiled and went back to sleep.

9

Madison was rudely awakened the next morning when her phone, set to ring *and* vibrate, did an annoying, clattery little dance on her nightstand.

With a groan of protest, she grabbed it, squinted at the screen, and pressed Accept.

"Audra," she muttered, her voice full of dry gravel, "do you know what time it is?"

Audra laughed softly. "Two hours earlier than it is here? So, six a.m.?"

Madison struggled to sit up, punching her pillows a few times to fluff them up before facing forward again, the phone pressed to her left ear. "That doesn't strike you as early?"

"Sounds like you didn't wake up singing about brown paper packages tied up with string," Audra observed. "Did you have a bad night or something?"

Madison huffed out a sigh. "Hold on," she said. "I need to pee."

Without waiting for an answer, she set the phone down on

the nightstand with a deliberate clunk—damn, she *was* cranky this morning—and struck out for her bathroom, which was just as girly as the bedroom it adjoined.

Another project for her growing to-do list.

When she returned, having taken longer than necessary to make the short journey, she found Audra in the same irritatingly good mood as before.

"Okay," Madison said, shoving the splayed fingers of her right hand through her hair and sitting cross-legged in the middle of her bed, like a teenager chatting with her BFF of the moment. "I'm back. Where were we?"

"I was asking if you had a bad night," Audra replied coyly.

"As a matter of fact," Madison answered, heaving out a sigh that left her usually straight shoulders slumping, "yes. I had a terrible night."

"Jeffrey?" Audra ventured quietly.

"No. My grandmother. I went to visit her last night, and as soon as I stepped into the room, she started screaming and throwing things—her water glass, her glasses, a book, her dinner tray. Audra, I've never seen Coralee quite like this—her eyes were wild and she was pale as death, and she was *terrified*."

"Of you?" Audra sounded sympathetic, but not surprised.

"Yes. Of me," Madison said. "It was awful."

"It must have been. I'm so sorry, Mads."

Madison was silent for a few moments, fighting back tears at the memory. Then she said, almost inaudibly, "Thanks." Another pause, during which she managed to pull herself together—somewhat. "I'm sure you didn't call to hear me complain about my poor grandmother, though, so tell me, is this one of those good news/bad news calls?"

Audra hesitated. "Afraid so."

"I want the bad news first," Madison said. "Let's get it out of the way."

"I stopped by your condo today, as I do every other morning, to water the plants and bring in the mail and make sure everything is okay in general, and—"

Something landed in the pit of Madison's stomach like a medicine ball, then rolled around. *"And?"*

"Jeffrey's mother was there," Audra said.

"Holy crap," Madison said.

"Yeah. She was wearing a chenille bathrobe and furry slippers, and she had curlers in her hair. Big pink ones, the spongy kind."

Madison squeezed her eyes shut, but the image of Yolanda didn't fade. "I thought she and Jeffrey were still in Costa Rica, enjoying their honeymoon."

"Nope," Audra told her. "They came back early. Some big meeting came up, I guess, and Jeffrey had to return right away."

Inwardly, Madison seethed. She'd known Jeffrey would return to the condo, if only to pack up his personal belongings—and, perhaps, annoy her a little in the process—but letting his mother stay there went way beyond personal audacity and well into brass balls territory.

"Did Yolanda happen to say what she was doing in *my* condo?"

"Yes, actually, she did." Audra sounded way too perky, either for the situation or for the time of day. "She said Jeffrey had sold his house, so they had no place to go. According to Mommy Dearest, it only made sense to live in your place for a while. Especially after you treated them so badly."

Madison made a bitter sound.

It might have been a laugh, or a dry sob. Or even a thwarted scream.

"Crap," she reiterated.

"Yeah," Audra agreed.

"That is the bad news?"

"I'd say so, Mads, wouldn't you?"

"What's the *good* news, then?"

"HammondCo made an offer on CyberDecor. It's serious

money, Mads. Enough to keep us both in designer shoes and handbags well into the twenty-second century."

"How much?" Madison asked.

Audra told her.

She gasped. Pressed her free hand to her chest.

"Yeah," Audra agreed. "It's an s-load of money, Mads. And, frankly, I'm ready to sell. Get out of here, once and for all, and leave the bad memories behind."

Madison's heart was thumping so hard, she thought she could see her hand moving.

The offer from HammondCo was huge, but Madison already *had* money. Plenty of it, it fact.

A hefty trust fund from her father's estate. Plus, the money she'd earned over the years.

She knew she wouldn't be thunderstruck by the amount, staggering as it was, for long.

Her attention made the short leap to the sad note in Audra's voice when she'd said she wanted to leave Boca—maybe even America—and forget about her ex-husband and his two spoiled, nasty daughters.

Surely there were reminders on every corner, and Madison was angry with herself for not realizing just how badly her friend was hurting, even though it had been two full years since the divorce.

There was no set schedule for getting over things like that— some people never did, really. Not completely, anyway.

If they were lucky, they found ways to cope.

"Tell you what," Madison said gently. "If you want to sell, that's what we'll do."

"Really?" Audra sounded so hopeful. So surprised.

"Maybe it truly is time for us both to move on. Start a new chapter."

"I think *you* already have," Audra said. It was amazing how fast that woman could cheer herself up. Maybe that was how she'd survived having her heart broken into fragments by a man she'd loved so wildly, truly and deeply.

Damn Brett Sinclair and his twin witches, Madison thought, knowing she'd have to lecture herself on kindness and compassion later.

Some people were so easy to hate, but the fact remained that hatred, however justified, was poisonous.

Nothing right or good could ever come of it, no matter how justified it seemed to be in the moment.

"What do you mean, you think I already have?" Madison wanted to know. It had taken her several moments to find her way back to the topic at hand. "I've moved on? How so? It hasn't even been a full week since my relationship bit the dust."

"Oh, come on, Mads," Audra teased. "You know exactly what I'm talking about—that sexy guy who was plying you with alcohol in the saloon after you ditched Jeffrey and his clingy mom. Girl, that man is *hot.*"

Madison heard herself laugh, and that surprised her a little. "Liam McKettrick," she said. Like a high school girl, she wanted to blurt out that she'd had lunch with Liam the day before, and she'd be having dinner with him tonight. Go all yippy skippy.

"That's the one," Audra said. "I googled him, you know. I figured that was slightly less intrusive than hiring a PI and running a formal background check. He's one *very* accomplished bartender, as I'm sure you know. And his family is practically legendary—the McKettricks go *way* back."

"For Pete's sake, Audra," Madison protested, but not with much conviction. "*Everybody's* family goes way back. All the way to the Fertile Crescent."

Trouble was, families didn't always go *forward.*

Hers, for example. She was literally the last of the Bettencourts, unless some long-lost relative turned up, and that didn't seem likely.

The thought was an ache, centered in her soul.

Audra went on. "I have this hunch about Liam. *And* you."

"Stop it. Less than a week ago, I was ready to marry somebody else."

"One thing does worry me, though," Audra mused, going on as if Madison hadn't spoken. "He's a widower with two children. And said his children might not take kindly to a stepmother. Believe me, it happens."

"I know," Madison said gently. "It happened to you, and that's rotten."

Audra gave a sad little laugh. "I didn't mean to make this about me. I want you to find *true* love, the real thing. What I *don't* want is to see you get hurt again. You've been through enough for one lifetime already."

"So have you," Madison reminded her friend.

"Suppose we make a pact, you and I? Next time, we'll both get it right. Deal?"

"Deal," Madison agreed, though deep down, she wondered if there would *be* a next time. With her track record, caution was advised. Audra, at least, had only struck out once.

Though that once had very nearly destroyed her.

"Have you heard anything from Olivia?" Madison asked. Her new Wi-Fi router had arrived about five minutes after she'd ordered it, but it was still in the box. Which meant she hadn't spent much time on the internet.

"Olivia isn't taking calls at the moment," Audra replied, with another sigh. "According to her blog, she's doing just fine."

"But?"

"But I don't think she *is* doing fine."

"Let's keep trying to reach her. If she ignores our messages for very long, I for one plan to fly back there and see for myself what's going on."

"That might be necessary, Mads."

"It might."

Audra drew in and released a long, audible breath. She was

very big on the curative qualities of breathing. When she spoke again, she sounded like her old self.

"So, what shall I tell the HammondCo people?"

"My vote is Yes. We'll sell."

"Mine, too," Audra said, and there was a note of relief in her voice. Successful businesswoman that she was, she didn't need the money any more than Madison did, but money wasn't the only factor in play here.

Freedom was a major part of the appeal, for both of them.

They'd worked extremely hard, starting and building their company.

It might even have been part of the reason neither of them had been able to make a marriage work.

"They'll probably want to sign off in person," Audra said. "Will you be able to fly back to Florida for the closing?"

Madison thought of Coralee, and hesitated. What if her grandmother passed while she was gone?

In some ways, given how much she seemed to be suffering, it would be a blessing when Coralee was finally allowed to rest in peace. In others, it would be heartbreaking, because even though they'd spent a lot of time apart, Madison loved her grandmother deeply.

Coralee was her only living family member, and Madison couldn't bear the thought of her dying alone.

Once the old woman had gone, Madison would be alone in a very singular way.

She'd be the very last of the Bettencourts, if that mattered.

To her, she realized, it *did* matter. If she and Jeffrey had argued about anything during their doomed relationship, besides his mother's constant interference, it was Madison's steely refusal to take his name when they were married.

And now that son of a bona fide bitch was hanging out in her condo, *with his mother.*

Still another thing she'd have to see to, and soon.

They chatted for a few more minutes, and Audra promised to follow up with HammondCo, get their take on when and where the final meeting should take place, and run it by Madison ASAP.

And then they said goodbye.

A crack of thunder alerted Madison that it was about to rain and, sure enough, the deluge began, pounding on the many levels of the roof, coating the windows in running blurs, drenching the little cemetery she'd planned to start clearing straight after breakfast.

Running was out, too.

That didn't bother her, either, though she was usually religious about it.

She returned to the bathroom, washed her face, brushed her teeth, applied moisturizer—did all the things she did every morning.

Looking at herself in the mirror, she felt a pang of impending disappointment.

This afternoon's horseback ride—an experience she actually craved—might be called off if the storm didn't pass.

Maybe the dinner Liam had offered wouldn't happen, either.

Those possibilities took some of the polish off the day ahead.

Then again, it hadn't been all that shiny in the first place.

Madison dressed, this time in sweats and her favorite pair of sneakers, pulled her hair up into a slightly messy ponytail, and headed down the back stairs, ready for coffee.

She could smell it brewing before she entered the kitchen, and for a moment, that gave her pause.

Then she remembered that Estelle was working today.

That thought cheered her up mightily.

But when she rounded the corner into the kitchen, it wasn't Estelle she saw.

It was Connie, Estelle's middle-aged daughter.

"Morning, Ms. Bettencourt," Connie said with a smile. "Mama's a little under the weather today—" thunder rolled over-head like a giant bowling ball, a brief but powerful interruption "—and it seems like we've got plenty of weather to be under, as of right now."

"Hello, Connie," Madison said, smiling. "And if you call me 'Ms. Bettencourt' again, I'll scream. You used to be my baby-sitter, remember? It's *Madison* to you."

Connie laughed outright then, and Madison was pleased to see that breakfast was about to be served. "All right, then, *Madison*," she capitulated. "Sit yourself down. I made you an omelet, and it's a dandy if I do say so myself."

Madison paused at the sink to wash and dry her hands, helped herself to a mug of coffee, and took her time-honored place at the table. "Tell me more about Estelle," she said, as Connie placed a plate of food in front of her and sat down at the opposite side of the table. "How sick is she? Is it something serious?"

"Just old age," Connie said, coffee of her own at the ready. "Her arthritis gives her fits when the weather turns like this. Barometric pressure or something. At least, that's what my grandson says."

"*You* have a grandson?" Madison asked, fork in one hand, knife in the other, eyebrows raised. Middle-aged or not, Connie seemed too young to be a grandmother.

Connie beamed. "Yes, I have a grandson. My daughter, Marion, had him young. His name is Orlando, and he's nineteen. He's starting classes at the community college over in Silver Hills this fall—wants to design video games one day—but right now, he works at Bitter Gulch. He's really a waiter in the hotel din-ing room, but he's all excited about that movie they're about to make over there. Part of one, anyway. He gets to ride shotgun on the stagecoach, and he even has a line. 'Whoa, there!' he's supposed to holler when something spooks the team of horses and they start to stampede." She paused, laughed again, shaking her graying head. It was a throaty sound, full of gentle pride. "He thinks he'll be the next John Wayne for sure."

Madison chewed, swallowed, took a sip of coffee. Like her mother before her, Connie Mendez was a *very* good cook.

The omelet was perfect. Madison said so, and thanked the other woman.

The subsequent chat with Connie lifted Madison's drooping spirits.

Rain always got her down, especially when important parts of her life were off the rails. The wet, gray gloom made her feel shut in, even a little claustrophobic, and it often ruined whatever she'd planned for the day.

Today, she decided, she would adapt.

To everything.

The commitment probably wouldn't last, life being life, but for now, it seemed the most positive course of action.

Once she'd finished her breakfast, Madison washed her plate and utensils at the sink, dried them, and put them away. Then she refilled her coffee mug and left Connie to her cleaning schedule, which began with vacuuming the entire upstairs.

Madison felt a stab of chagrin; she'd forgotten to make her bed, and now Connie would probably do it, and that wasn't right.

A grown woman should make her *own* bed, shouldn't she?

Briefly, Madison considered sneaking back upstairs and tidying up her room, but soon ruled out the idea. Connie might see her and think it was a subtle criticism of the way she did her job.

So she headed for the library and stood before the tall bookshelf facing the ornate marble fireplace on the other side of the huge room.

She ran one hand across the middle row of leather-bound classics with their vivid colors and gold-foil titles.

The hidden latch would have been imperceptible to anyone

who didn't know it was there. It was a simple metal catch, released by the pressure of one finger.

Madison pressed, then slid the entire bookshelf to one side, revealing the dark interior, a slanted ceiling and windowless walls.

There was no light switch; initially, the space had been a place to hide in an emergency, such as a raid by outlaws or renegade soldiers.

Madison pulled her phone from the pocket of her sweatpants and flipped on the flashlight feature.

She was going to need more light to clean the hiding place properly, but she could make out the shapes of several boxes pushed into a corner. She didn't remember anyone storing things here, but then again, she hadn't been inside since forever, not even during her visits home for holidays and breaks from school.

Her cell phone rang as she moved to put it back in her pocket, planning to search for a real flashlight.

Coralee had always kept one in the kitchen pantry for those times when the circuit breaker in the basement flipped a switch and turned off the lights throughout the entire first floor.

She glanced at the screen of her phone, saw Jeffrey's number glaring up at her.

Against her better judgment, she pressed Accept and said, "Hello, Jeffrey." Then, before he could answer, she added, "FYI, you're on speaker."

She was headed for the kitchen, and the pantry beyond.

Jeffrey's tone was derisive, even before he got to the point. "Mom tells me that Audra stopped by the condo this morning." *The* condo, not *your* condo. "Actually, she just unlocked the door and walked right in, and she scared my mother half to death."

"Sorry," Madison said. *Not sorry.*

"You don't *sound* sorry, Madison," Jeffrey accused her. Like Tom, the man she'd so foolishly married, the man she'd *almost* married had no intention of engaging in a rational conversation with the woman he'd once claimed to love.

He'd called to complain. Or fight.

Or both.

"Make of that what you will," Madison replied evenly, reaching the kitchen, passing over the creaky wooden floor toward the pantry.

"Aren't you even going to apologize for the humiliation you caused Mom and me at the wedding reception?" Jeffrey demanded. "You didn't even bother to explain what set you off like that."

"Okay, Jeffrey. I will repeat what I said to you before, at least half a dozen times. *Your mother* told me she'd been invited on our honeymoon. And she had the first-class ticket to Costa Rica to prove it."

"That's all?" Jeffrey sounded incredulous. This was pretense, of course. Probably a form of gaslighting, which, Madison now realized, was one of his specialties.

"Of course it isn't all," Madison said, determined to speak kindly and not be a bitch, which was going to be a major challenge, with all the anger churning around inside her. "My conversation with Yolanda was like the last piece of a puzzle falling into place. I realized that our getting married would be the worst mistake we could possibly make, bar none."

"You might have calmed down and consulted me before you made that dramatic exit, Madison. Mom and I are being *crucified* on social media. There are videos of the whole thing on YouTube, Instagram, TikTok—you name it!" Jeffrey paused, and Madison imagined him with eyes bulging out of their sockets and nostrils flared and spouting steam, like in a cartoon. "I'm *literally* a laughingstock, and Mom is devastated."

Madison spotted the flashlight in its customary place and grabbed it. "I apologize for that part—I didn't mean to cause a spectacle, I really didn't. I just wanted to get away. And I apologize for letting things go so far in the first place, because deep down, I *knew* we weren't right for each other, and I just plunged ahead, instead of putting a stop to the whole thing a long time ago, like I should have."

"But *why*? Why didn't you at least *talk to me*?"

"Jeffrey, I tried to talk to you. Many times. Think back, and if you're honest, you'll remember some of the discussions we had—especially about your mother. I was uncomfortable around her. She was always criticizing me, complaining about something I'd said or done or *hadn't* said or done, and she was *way* too involved in every decision you made."

Jeffrey was silent, and Madison couldn't begin to guess if he was finally hearing her or just waiting for her to shut up so he could leap in and defend his mother again.

Turned out, it was the latter. "Mom's a widow, Madison, and I'm an only child. She just needed some time to get used to sharing me."

"*Sharing* you? I'm not going to touch *that* remark with a ten-foot pole."

He gave an angry, bitter sigh. "Madison, you know what I meant!"

"Yes, I do," Madison agreed quietly. "I'm not sure *you* understand it, though. You're a grown man, Jeffrey, with a good career and a solid future, but for whatever reason, you let your mother run your private life—especially when it came to me. I can't live that way."

Another sigh, this one less aggrieved. "You don't understand, Madison. With Dad gone, I'm *all she has left*. I can't just turn my back on her."

"I never asked you to do that. I wouldn't. How you interact with your mother is none of my business—at least, not now that you and I aren't a couple anymore."

"What about the babies we were planning to have?"

That was a low blow, and Madison had to bite back a nasty retort. Jeffrey knew which button to push to wound her, and he's just pushed it.

"There are other ways to have children," she finally replied, with very costly self-control. *And there are other men to have them with.*

Liam McKettrick came into her mind, though she pushed him right back out.

Not that he was likely to stay gone.

"I didn't call so we could argue," Jeffrey almost purred. Was he going to try to placate her now?

Fat chance *that* would work.

Madison allowed herself another sigh. "Why *did* you call, then?"

As usual, Jeffrey didn't give a direct answer. "Look, we can give this another shot. I'll *deal* with Mom, I promise. I'll get her into therapy for her attachment issues. Let's get married for real, and start a family right away."

Tears scalded the backs of Madison's eyes, and her throat thickened, because she wanted marriage and children more than anything else—just not with Jeffrey.

"No," she said, and the word came out all scratchy-sounding and hoarse. "It's way too late for that."

Jeffrey was silent for a few moments, and Madison was just beginning to hope he would accept the facts and hang up. Instead, he turned cringey.

"I only wanted my mother to have a nice vacation," he said at long last. "What's wrong with that?"

"Nothing," Madison retorted, swinging the heavy flashlight as she walked through the house, returning to the library. Overhead, the vacuum cleaner hummed loudly, and she was glad Connie didn't have to be subjected to this end of the conversation. "Nothing is wrong with wanting your mother to enjoy a lovely getaway to a tropical climate. It's a noble sentiment, in fact. *Unless*, of course, that getaway happens to be your *honeymoon*."

He backpedaled. Sighed. "Okay, I admit it. I made an unfortunate choice."

"You can say that again," Madison responded, "but please don't. We need to let bygones be bygones, Jeffrey, and get on with our lives."

"Mom would have been such a good grandmother," Jeffrey lamented.

Amazing. The man still didn't get it.

Probably because he didn't *want* to get it. Jeffrey wasn't stupid, but he was certainly suffering from some kind of arrested development, which was sad, for sure. Maybe even tragic.

But still not her problem.

Madison closed her eyes, bit her lower lip to stem the flow of verbal fury that had welled up inside her at Jeffrey's words.

The silence stretched until he couldn't stand it anymore.

"Madison? Are you still there?"

"I don't know how to make this any plainer than I already have, but here's an attempt. I'm really sorry I didn't break this off a lot sooner, instead of at our wedding reception, but it's *over*, Jeffrey. You and I won't be getting married and starting a family. If you still want a wife and kids, then you need to find someone else, because it isn't going to happen with me."

"Would all this be happening if Mom hadn't mentioned that silly trip to Costa Rica?"

Madison nearly face-palmed. *That silly trip to Costa Rica.*

"Probably, yes," she answered evenly, "because I would have spotted her at the airport, gone home and called my attorney to have her start divorce proceedings, or file for an annulment."

"You don't think you're taking this whole silly situation a little too seriously?"

"I didn't take it seriously *enough*, Jeffrey. And certainly not soon enough."

"So much bitterness," Jeffrey murmured, playing the victim, as he had been all along, of course.

That tendency of his probably wasn't going to change short of a sky-written message from God or years of psychoanalysis.

Jeffrey would always be Jeffrey, weak, afraid of his mother, emotionally stunted.

"Stop it, Jeffrey. This is going nowhere."

"We would have had such beautiful babies," he said sorrowfully.

It was true. Jeffrey might have been a jerk—he *was* a jerk—but he had good genes. Physically, he was an ideal candidate for fatherhood.

Emotionally? Not so much.

Letting go of Jeffrey was surprisingly easy. Giving up on the family they'd planned to have wasn't. Not at all.

She thought of the fertility treatments.

Take it easy, she counseled herself. *Don't be desperate.*

Jeffrey sounded beleaguered, as though he'd been trying, with the best of intentions, to reason with a raging fool. "I suppose you want Mom and me out of the condo," he said, almost pitifully, as if they'd be homeless if she kicked them out.

Actually, Yolanda had a house of her own.

"Yes," she said. "As soon as humanly possible."

Finally, Jeffrey seemed to get the memo. "All right," he agreed. "Can you give us thirty days?"

"Sounds fair," Madison replied. "Thirty days it is."

Jeffrey agreed glumly, after mumbling something about bad investments and a tight personal budget, but Madison didn't take the bait. Thirty days was plenty, and if she decided to sell the condo, he could make an offer.

Full market value, not a dime less.

She said a civil goodbye and ended the call.

For good measure, she blocked Jeffrey's various numbers, of which there were several. Then she jammed the phone back into her pocket, flipped on the flashlight she'd fetched from the pantry—she'd had an underlying awareness of how heavy the thing was, and what a dent it could make in somebody's skull, while talking to her ex—and focused the bright light on the interior of her favorite childhood refuge.

There were, as she expected, cobwebs galore, and she caught the faint scent of mouse droppings and mildew as well.

This was no job for the fainthearted.

Good thing Madison was anything *but* fainthearted.

Two hours later, she'd swept the floor, walls and ceiling of that little hideaway.

She'd dragged the boxes out into the library to be dealt with later, borrowed the vacuum cleaner from Connie, and gone over every inch of it again.

And when *that* was done, she grabbed a mop and some rags, filled a plastic bucket with hot, soapy water—it was the first of several such buckets—and got busy yet *again*, scrubbing every surface down.

Her phone rang.

If couldn't be Jeffrey calling, since she'd blocked every possible approach, but maybe *Yolanda* had her number.

That would *really* suck.

She checked the screen.

Number unknown.

After a moment's hesitation, she answered, "Madison Bettencourt."

The voice that responded was Liam's. "Hello, there, Madison Bettencourt," he said in that low, confident drawl of his. "Guess you probably noticed the storm."

"I noticed," Madison said, about to sink into one of Coralee's chintz-covered chairs until she remembered that her clothes were filthy. "No horseback ride today, I guess?" She tried to sound cheerful, but a note of disappointment *had* crept into her voice, and Liam heard it.

"Nope, too dangerous," he said, in an upbeat tone. "We'd be human lightning rods, the both of us, riding in weather like this."

"Okay," Madison replied, still deflated by the call with Jeffrey, even though her conscience was clear.

It would be just her luck, the way things had been going, to be struck by lightning.

"Hey, cheer up," Liam said. "Dinner's still on, if you're up for driving in a torrential downpour. Or I could pick you up at your place."

An idea struck Madison then. "*Or*," she said, "you could come here. I'll make dinner."

He laughed, and it was a wraparound sound, like an invisible hug. She felt stronger, and more hopeful. "You drive a hard bargain," he said. "Got that phrase straight out of *The Cowboy's Book of Timeworn Clichés*."

Madison giggled.

"I'll have to look that up," she said.

Again, he laughed. "Good luck with that," he replied. "I think it's been out of print for a while now."

"Darn," Madison joked in return. "I was all set to read it."

"No problem. I can quote most of the content."

A burst of laughter escaped Madison at that, and she chided herself for behaving like a high school girl.

Then, determined to address the practicalities, she went on. "Seven o'clock? My specialty is lasagna. I'll make that."

"Sounds better than good," Liam replied. "Seven it is. Red wine or white?"

"No need for either. There's a fully stocked wine cellar downstairs. We'll choose something together."

She liked the sound of that, choosing something together.

Liked the soft, festive feeling it gave her, too.

"Well, ma'am," Liam said, ratcheting up his drawl by a notch or two, "I have to bring *something*. How about flowers?"

"Really, Liam, you don't have to—"

"I *want* to bring something. I'm trying to be a gentleman here."

"You're not normally a gentleman?" Madison inquired, grinning, with both eyebrows raised.

"I'm *always* a gentleman. It's ingrained."

She recalled Audra's reference, earlier, to Liam's evidently notable family and their "legendary" status. "Is that a McKettrick trait? Being a gentleman?"

Once again, he laughed, and once again, the sound moved her.

"From birth," he said. "But it's not confined to our rowdy brood, obviously."

"It's less common than you think," Madison remarked, thinking of Jeffrey and wishing she hadn't given the man space in her head. She needed to let that be over. "Sometimes it seems like good manners are going out of style."

"Sounds like you've had a hard day, and it's not even noon yet," he said.

"I'm fine," she said. *Now that I'm talking to you instead of my ex, anyway.*

"Is Coralee doing okay?" Liam asked, that being the most likely cause of upset, from his viewpoint at least.

"No," Madison answered. "She's getting worse. A *lot* worse."

"I'm sorry to hear that."

"I'm sorry to say it."

"Madison?"

"What?"

"Hold on. I'm not the cavalry, so don't expect to hear a bugle blowing, but I am a good listener. And I'll be there at seven sharp to help you choose the dinner wine."

"Thanks, Liam," Madison said, her voice a little hoarse.

"Anytime," he answered.

"One more thing," Madison ventured, almost shyly. "Let's not dress up. I'm up for a jeans-and-T-shirt kind of evening."

"Me, too," Liam agreed.

The call ended.

And Madison sat down, dirty clothes be damned, and cried in earnest.

Oddly enough, she wasn't weeping out of sadness or despair.

She was shedding tears because there was something about Liam McKettrick that fostered the belief that, no matter what happened, in the end, everything would be all right.

And that belief was new to her.

Presently, she slipped into the nearest powder room and splashed her face with cold water.

"Lunch is about ready!" Connie called from the kitchen.

"On my way!" Madison called back. During the call with Jeffrey, her stomach had declared a moratorium on food, but now, suddenly, she was hungry, and there was even a spring in her step.

Talk about *The Book of Clichés*.

When she reached the kitchen, she found a handsome young man sitting at the table.

He stood when she entered, nodded his head in polite acknowledgment of her presence, and glanced at Connie as if he were looking for affirmation.

"Madison, this is my grandson, Orlando. I hope you don't mind him stopping by for lunch. It's sort of our little routine," Connie said.

"Hello, Orlando," Madison said, putting out her hand to the boy. "I'm glad you could join us. How are things over at Bitter Gulch?"

Tentatively, he shook her hand. Then, relaxing visibly, he flashed her a bright grin. "The movie people are there, and they're all in a twist because it's raining."

"Is that why you were able to get away for lunch?" Madison asked, gesturing for Connie to take a seat at the table. There were three steaming bowls of tomato soup sitting on the counter, along with three grilled cheese sandwiches on plates, and she meant to serve them, rather than being served herself.

She wasn't royalty, after all.

Orlando nodded, watched as Madison set the plates and bowls on the table, two at a time, but he didn't sit down until she'd finished putting out all the food and pouring glasses of fresh lemonade to go with it.

"On days when Mama and I come here to clean," Connie interjected, answering for her grandson, "Orlando likes to join us, if time allows. I think he packs a lunch the rest of the time."

Orlando nodded. "Mr. McKettrick gave us all the day off, because business is really slow when the weather's bad, and the movie people would be in the way anyhow."

Madison smiled. *Mr. McKettrick.* That had a nice ring to it.

Page seventy-three, *Book of Clichés.*

It also said a lot about Orlando's respectful attitude, a not so common thing these days, especially among the youth.

"Do you like your job?" she asked, after taking a cautious first sip of her soup.

Orlando's dark eyes shone. "I *love* it, Miss Bettencourt. I get to live in the Old West, practically all the time, except we've still got all the modern conveniences, like indoor plumbing and stuff."

"Best of both worlds," Madison commented, amused. She liked this kid.

The meal was excellent, and so was the light banter that followed, and when it was time for Connie to leave, having completed her usual four hours of chores, Madison insisted on washing up the dishes.

The rain was pounding down by then, punching muddy craters into the dirt.

She watched Connie and Orlando run for an old compact car parked a few yards from the back door, and smiled again as the boy opened the passenger side door for his grandmother and then sprinted around to the driver's side.

They must have seen her at the window, water-blurred as it was, because Orlando tooted the horn in farewell.

Once the kitchen was put to rights, Madison scouted the refrigerator for the ingredients she needed to make her fabled lasagna.

They were there, since she'd overstocked the grocery supply while her friends were at Bettencourt Hall, preparing for the wedding that wasn't.

Salad greens? Tomatoes and other add-ins? Check.

This dinner would be easy to make. Even therapeutic.

Madison showered before cooking since she was so grubby from cleaning out the hiding place, washed and dried her hair, pulled on her favorite jeans—black skinny ones with rhinestones running along the seams.

For fun, she added a Bitter Gulch T-shirt, left behind by Kendall, who liked to collect souvenirs wherever she went.

She'd apply makeup closer to Liam's arrival.

Or not.

Mascara and lip gloss would be plenty, since they weren't going out on the town or anything.

Tonight, it would be just the two of them, and that was fine with Madison.

The process of cooking made up for the incessant, sky-graying rain; it was a feast for the senses, with all those bright colors, crisp, lovely textures and the singularly wonderful smell of carefully prepared, multi-cheese lasagna slow cooking in the oven.

At seven o'clock, as promised, Liam arrived.

She hurried to the front door, feeling ridiculously pleased at the prospect of spending an evening with him, and her breath caught when she saw him standing on the porch, under the portico, looking rained-on and handsome and holding a huge bouquet of yellow roses.

"These are from the supermarket," he said with a nod toward the flowers in his hand. "I was busy getting the house ready for

Courtney and the kids—they'll be here tomorrow—and the florist's shop was closed when I got to town."

Madison took the offered flowers after stepping back so he could enter the house, and buried her nose in them for a few moments. They were as beautiful as any roses she'd ever seen, and they even *smelled* good.

When she looked up, she knew her eyes were glistening a little. Maybe it was the scent, maybe it was the vibrant color of the flowers, maybe it was because Liam had chosen them just for her. She couldn't have said.

"Thank you, Liam. They're beautiful."

He shut the door behind him, tilted his head to one side as if to see her face more clearly, and crumpled his brow, just a little. "Tears?" he asked, in a tone of voice that made Madison want to set the roses aside and fling her arms around his neck.

Of course, she didn't do that.

"It's been a crazy day," she said.

"Good crazy or bad crazy?" he asked with a smile.

There had been Jeffrey, but there had been a mega-offer from HammondCo, and there had been Orlando, too.

"A little of both, I suppose."

She took his hand, and it seemed like a bold gesture to Madison, which was odd, because she wasn't a shy woman. In fact, she thought, a little reticence would have served her better than confidence at certain points in her life.

"Come on," she said. "I'll put these in a vase, and then we'll open some wine."

He glanced at her T-shirt with amused interest. "You're a Bitter Gulch fan?"

"Actually," Madison replied, feeling a little dishonest, "my friend bought this and left it behind, so I appropriated it."

He followed as she headed toward the back of the house.

Madison had expected to be nervous, being alone with Liam

in a house with no less than nine bedrooms; instead, she was at ease in a way she'd never experienced before.

The next part of the evening—dinner at the kitchen table, the wine and the sun-bright roses—was casual. Pleasant. And completely drama-free.

After dinner, they did the dishes together, side by side.

It was a curious thing, how such an ordinary task could warm a person's heart.

In all the rush and excitement and success of her life, she realized now, she'd forgotten the value of simple things. Like washing dishes with someone you liked.

Once the kitchen was in order again, Madison led the way to her favorite room—the library. She'd forgotten that her secret space was still open, since she hadn't rolled the moving bookcase back into place.

And the boxes she'd found inside were sitting in plain sight.

Liam spotted the opening to the hidden room right away, of course, and he gave a low, slow whistle of appreciation.

"Is this for real?" he asked rhetorically. "Are there secret passageways in this house, too?"

Madison smiled. She'd brought a second bottle of wine along with her, plus two glasses, and she set them down on the ornate coffee table, which had been imported from the Far East sometime in the Roaring Twenties.

"There might be," she said. "It's a big house."

"Yeah," Liam agreed, looking around at the paintings, the expensive furniture, the enormous crystal chandelier that had to be cleaned twice a year by a window-washing outfit from Silver Hills, since it was a very precarious job.

Tonight, it gleamed and sparkled.

"You haven't explored the place?" Liam asked, sounding surprised.

Madison shook her head. "Not all of it," she replied. "I was away a lot as a kid—boarding school, summer camp—" She shrugged, a slight, measured motion of one shoulder. "Then, of course, I grew up, and I've been busy elsewhere."

Liam didn't comment.

She kicked off her shoes and curled up in one of the two big armchairs facing the empty hearth, with its white marble face and heavily carved mahogany mantelpiece.

A fire would have been nice, cozy even, except that, rain or no rain, it was still summer, and the air in the room was almost muggy, as though the heat of the day had settled there to stew.

Bettencourt Hall didn't have air-conditioning.

"You forgot your hat," Madison observed, out of the blue, when Liam took a seat in the other chair.

"It's in the truck," he said with a teasing glint in his eyes. "Shall I get it?"

Madison laughed. "And get soaked in the process? I think not."

He picked up the wine bottle, looked questioningly at Madison.

"Please," she said. "Just half, though. I've got a lot to do tomorrow."

"Me, too," Liam agreed, filling a glass—halfway—for each of them. "I probably shouldn't tell you this, but I'm pretty jittery about tomorrow. I can hardly wait to see my kids, but Keely, the older one, isn't what you'd call an admirer. She might just try to scalp me in my sleep."

Madison smiled at that. "I doubt it," she said.

"You don't know Keely," Liam replied dryly, though there was light dancing in his eyes.

That was when Madison remembered that he'd mentioned another name earlier—Courtney. An adult.

She wasn't jealous—she had no right to be—but she was only human, and she wondered who the woman was, and if she and Liam had a history.

"Courtney is my sister-in-law," Liam explained. He'd been watching Madison's expression, and he'd noticed her curiosity.

She needed to develop a poker face.

"Oh," Madison said. "She'll help you with the children, right?"

"For a while," Liam answered, looking solemn for a moment. "A week, maybe." A pause while he took a sip of his wine. He set the glass down in a way that indicated he didn't plan to pick it up again. "I'm grateful, don't get me wrong, but getting these kids used to being with me, in a new place, is going to be a lot like jumping onto a moving freight train—the way they did in all those old movies—and I can't see Keely adjusting in just a week. Cavan, okay, but not Keely."

Madison wanted to reach over and squeeze his arm or his hand, reassure him, but something held her back. "I take it Keely and Cavan are close to Courtney?"

"Very. In a lot of ways, she's been more of a mother to them than Waverly ever was. But she's got a life—a job, a husband, a social circle, all of it. Besides, the kids are *my* responsibility, not hers."

"What about Waverly's parents—and yours? Wouldn't they help?"

"Waverly's folks have done enough," Liam replied, and Madison couldn't tell whether that statement had been a compliment or a criticism. "And my parents love Keely and Cavan to distraction, but they've raised their children. I can't—and won't—expect them to raise mine, too." He rested his lower arms on his knees and let his hands dangle between, fingers interlaced. "Furthermore, they're both busy, doing all the things they didn't have time for while they were raising my brothers and me."

Madison knew she was on sensitive ground, but she also guessed there was more Liam wanted—or needed—to say. "Yesterday, at lunch, you said the children have been with their grandparents for a little over a year. That's a long time."

"I tried," Liam replied, apparently fine with the question, personal as it was. "Every time I brought them home with me, though, even for a weekend, Keely panicked. She cried and begged to go back to her Gambie—that's what she calls Waverly's mother. And it wasn't just a matter of a little kid throwing tantrums—Keely and I had counseling, trying to resolve the situation, but that didn't work. The therapist advised me to let Keely stay with her grandmother for a while, since she was grieving hard for Waverly, and of course that meant Cavan would stay, too, because he really clung to his sister."

This time, Madison did reach out. She laid a hand on Liam's, closed her fingers around it. "You're going to get through this, Liam."

His eyes shone for a moment, and he looked away, though he'd turned his hand in hers so that their palms were touching.

"I know," he said. "But I'm scared."

It amazed Madison that Liam was strong enough to admit being afraid. Most of the men she'd known would have been incapable of telling *anyone* that.

"I'm just a friend," Madison said, very softly. She was scared, too, scared of the big feelings unfolding within her; she *wanted* this man, and not just sexually. Scared of being too hasty, as she had been with Jeffrey and with Tom, and making another mistake. "But I'll help you if I can, Liam."

He looked at her, his eyes gently taking her measure. "Come here," he said in a husky voice.

He pulled her onto his lap, and Madison didn't resist in the slightest.

10

Within five minutes of her arrival in Painted Pony Creek, hauling her small frame laboriously out of Courtney's rental car, Keely made it absolutely clear that she would have preferred to be anywhere else on the planet besides some backwater town in Montana.

And *with* anybody else but her father.

Cavan, on the other hand, unbuckled himself from his booster seat and bolted out of the back of the subcompact to rush Liam like a football player going for a touchdown.

"Dad!" the little boy cried, beaming.

Nearly knocked off his feet, Liam laughed and swept him up into his arms, spun him around. "Hey, cowboy," he said hoarsely, looking away for a moment because he knew his eyes were wet. "Welcome home."

"Aunt Courtney says we get to *stay* this time! *Forever!*" Cavan crowed.

"That's right," Liam said, nearly choking on the words. "For-ever."

Keely meandered toward him, frowning.

Even as a still gawky nine-year-old, Keely was a strikingly beautiful child.

And, as evidenced by her expression, a very unhappy one at the moment.

She reached Liam's side, eventually, and allowed him to shoulder-hug her, though just briefly.

Bending to set Cavan back on his feet, Liam kissed the top of his daughter's head.

"What if I *don't want* to stay here forever?" she asked, and al-though she was doing her best to be snarky, Liam glimpsed a flicker of uncertainty in her wide eyes.

"You probably won't," Liam replied, after clearing his throat. "You'll grow up and go to college and have a career all your own."

"Gambie said I could have been in TV commercials, but you said no," Keely reminded him. "She said I could have won a lot of beauty pageants, too, but you wouldn't even let me *try*."

Liam didn't attempt to make a case for his decisions. He had nothing against children getting into show business or entering beauty contests—as long as they weren't *his* children.

He simply wanted his kids to have a chance to *be* kids, that was all.

He sighed and exchanged glances with Courtney, standing nearby.

Courtney, too, was beautiful, but not in the same dazzling way Waverly had been, and Keely almost certainly *would be*.

Her personality was nothing like Waverly's, and Liam saw that as a good thing, though of course he wouldn't have said so. In spite of everything, Courtney had loved her sister.

And that, Liam knew from experience, wasn't easy.

Keely was still looking up at him, waiting stubbornly for a response to her complaint.

He took off his hat and plopped it onto her head, so it covered half her face.

"No commercials and no pageants, Keel. Not before you're eighteen, anyway," he said, gently but firmly. "Take your time and be a kid while you can, because you're going to be a grownup before you know it. And for the rest of your life."

Keely tilted her head back, regarding him solemnly.

She wasn't going to give Liam an inch, if she could help it, and that was fine.

He was a McKettrick, too, and he liked a challenge.

In the meantime, Cavan caught the hat before it fell into the dirt of Bitter Gulch's main—and only—street. Put it on his own head. "Look Dad," he grinned. "I really am a cowboy now. Can I be in the movie?"

"We'll talk about that another time," Liam said, smiling at Courtney and mouthing the word, *Thanks.*

"Hello, Liam," she greeted him, rising onto her toes to plant a sisterly kiss on his cheek.

They were good friends, he and Courtney, but nothing more.

And, though it was another thing he'd never say, the mere prospect of marrying back into that family made him think of sticking his right arm into a wood chipper.

In any case, he didn't want to lay his family problems on his ex-sister-in-law.

He shook off the thought, but for a moment, he was back in that amazing house, the night before, with Madison on his lap, *this far* from carrying her to the nearest bed and making love to her until they were both exhausted.

He hadn't, of course, because it was way too soon for sex.

Madison was still broken, in terms of romance. She'd said so herself.

And he wasn't exactly whole himself.

He needed to get his act together, and that had to begin with his children.

He loved them both fiercely, but they were going to need some convincing—especially Keely.

"If you let Cavan be in the movie," Keely said, breaking the train of his thoughts and bringing him back to the here and now with a bone-jarring crash, "I'm gonna be real mad!"

Liam suppressed a grin. He was heartened by the fact that, attitude aside, his daughter was still leaning into his side, and she hadn't shaken off the arm resting lightly around her shoulders.

"Why?" he asked, baiting her a little, just to hear her voice. Even if it was a little on the snippy side.

"It wouldn't be fair," Keely pointed out, her cheeks flushing pink. "If I can't have a career until I'm eighteen, neither can my brother!"

"Fair enough," Liam replied.

"Could we get hamburgers?" Cavan interjected, still rocking the hat. "And milkshakes and curly fries?"

"Or something healthy?" Courtney offered. "Like salad, maybe?"

"Noooooo!" both children chorused.

"Hamburgers," insisted Cavan.

"Curly fries," Keely cried.

Courtney laughed and rolled her eyes.

Under ordinary circumstances, Liam would have taken all three of them to the hotel dining room right there in Bitter Gulch, except that the place was swarming with various film crews busily setting up for the first scene, which would involve a shootout in front of the Hard Luck Saloon.

"We'll eat at Bailey's," he decided. "It's a great place. Everybody in Painted Pony Creek goes there—or to Sully's Bar and Grill, but that's on the other end of town."

"Can we walk there?" Courtney asked. "To Bailey's, I mean?

My legs are stiff from sitting on a crowded plane for almost two hours, then spending another hour and change in the car."

"There wasn't even a first-class section on the plane," Keely kvetched, determined, apparently, that nothing about this day would be classified as fun if she had anything to say about the matter. "It was *really* little and *really* crowded."

"Terrible," Liam teased.

"And we didn't get any pretzels, either," Cavan said when Liam reclaimed his hat and patted the boy's head. He couldn't quite summon up a complaint, it seemed, probably because he was a glass-half-full kind of a kid. Always had been.

"Bailey's is just a few blocks away," Liam replied to Courtney's request, over the children's heads. "Let's get there before the noon rush." The kids were walking beside him as he started in the appointed direction, one on his left, one on his right, and he rested his hands on their shoulders, verifying their presence to himself. "It's only ten thirty, so they're probably still serving breakfast, if that sounds good to anybody."

"Hamburgers," Cavan repeated, with less emphasis than before, but plenty of certainty just the same.

"Curly fries," Keely confirmed.

Courtney, keeping pace, shook her head and smiled. "Do they get that hardheaded attitude from our side of the family?" she asked. "Or from yours?"

"A little of both, I'd say," Liam said. When it came to stubbornness, which usually manifested as grit, the McKettricks were world-class. In light of what he knew about the family history, that was nothing new.

Courtney laughed. "Very gracious of you," she said. She was probably thinking about Waverly, and how difficult she'd been at times.

Bailey's Restaurant and Bar practically functioned as a community center, it was so popular with locals.

There, among the Formica-topped tables and booths, people

met to talk about books they'd read, or to play canasta and pinochle, or simply to enjoy comfort food and company.

At Bailey's, men and women planned to get married, or to get divorced. They laughed and cried and cheered each other on when times got tough.

It was, in fact, one of the reasons Liam loved the town.

The place was genuine, and so were the people.

Alice Bailey, a tall blonde, still beautiful into her late sixties, greeted them with a bright smile. "Liam!" she called, as though his arrival might just be the high point of her day so far. She swept the kids and Courtney up in her welcome. "I'm Alice," she added. "Who do we have here?"

"This is my sister-in-law, Courtney," Liam answered, proud of his little crew. "My daughter, Keely, and my son, Cavan."

"Glad to meet you all," Alice replied, and the great thing was, she wasn't just being polite. She meant it. She indicated an empty table—the last one in the place, as a matter of fact—and they all sat down.

Liam and Courtney were on one side of the table, Keely and Cavan on the other.

While the adults looked the lunch menu over, the kids waited impatiently to order as planned. Breakfast was still being served, but Alice made an exception because the kids were so eager.

Courtney chose a Cobb salad and ice tea, while Liam asked for the special of the day, chicken-fried steak with mashed potatoes and green beans.

He'd skipped breakfast that morning, too wired to eat, and now he was half-starved.

He wanted something with gravy on it.

Cavan did most of the talking, at least at first, between bites of food.

He pronounced the hamburger at Bailey's to be the best one he'd ever eaten, while Keely argued for the curly fries.

Liam's bruised heart swelled inside him as he watched them,

his children. How had he even *survived* living apart from them for a day, let alone a year?

In those moments, his regret was so ferocious that it nearly tore him in two.

The problem with regret was, it didn't change anything, and if you dwelled on it too long, it could do serious harm. Its only real value was in the lessons it taught, like making up your mind to do better, *be* better, and not to make the same mistakes ever again.

It wasn't an easy pit to avoid, since there were so many things he wished he'd done differently, from the first time he met Waverly Everton right up to this very moment.

Still, whatever her faults—and his—Waverly had given him these kids.

That made everything else worthwhile.

Liam's throat tightened, and he lowered his eyes for a second or two.

The eyes really *were* the windows of the soul, and just then, he didn't want anyone to see inside him.

Especially not his kids.

It would be too easy for them to misunderstand the things he was feeling.

"Can I have a horse?" Cavan blurted out, stopping his father from drifting and reeling him right back into the present moment. The seven-year-old had been chattering along, though Liam had missed some of it, lost in his own thoughts.

"You already *have* one," Keely told her brother, elbowing him in the arm for good measure. "You have Max the pony here. And Papa and Mimi just gave you that little pinto, Domino."

Papa and Mimi were the names they called Liam's parents.

"Domino," Cavan said pointedly, "*is in California.* And Max is *just* a pony. He's for little kids. And *I'm not a little kid anymore.* I'm *seven.*"

"We'll see about the horse," Liam said, but neither Keely nor Cavan seemed to be listening.

"*And,*" Cavan went on, "you said you didn't *want* a horse, so Papa and Mimi didn't give you one!"

"Hey," Liam interjected, more firmly this time. "I said we'd talk about that later."

"When grown-ups say they'll talk about something later," Keely protested, pushing away what was left of her lunch, "they mean *never!*"

"Keely," Courtney said mildly. "Stop. That isn't true, and you know it."

Keely hunkered down, puckered up her entire face, and kicked at the legs of her chair with the heels of her sneakers.

"They're tired," Courtney added, glancing Liam's way. "Both of them."

"It's a big change for them," Liam agreed. Then he turned his attention back to the kids. "Stop kicking the chair, Keely," he said evenly. Firmly. "You're too old to act like that."

Keely stopped kicking, but apparently that was all the concession she was willing to make, because her arms were still clenched tight across her chest, and she wouldn't look at Liam.

"You're not the boss of me," she said, in a tone that told Liam she was testing the parental waters. Looking for the border between what would and would not be tolerated.

"On the contrary, Miss Keely McKettrick," Liam replied, ignoring another glance from Courtney, who clearly wanted to smooth things over, "for all practical intents and purposes, I *am* the boss of you, at least until you grow up, and you'd do well to keep that in mind."

"Or what?" Keely whispered, with less confidence than before.

"Or you'll be doing a lot of extra chores instead of, say, watching videos on your tablet or your phone. You've been to Papa and Mimi's place plenty of times, so you know just how many chores there are to do on a ranch."

"That isn't fair."

"Isn't it?" Liam's voice was quiet, even respectful, and there was no anger in it. If there was anything he could do to stop his daughter from taking after her mother, as far as her behavior went, he was going to do it.

"Can we leave now?" Keely persisted.

"No," Liam replied. "We're not going anywhere until everybody's finished eating."

"I wish I'd stayed in the car!"

"I'd stop talking right about now, if I were you," Liam advised calmly. He knew the kid was still baiting him, trying to get a rise out of him, maybe just for the fun of it, and *maybe* because she resented him in so many ways.

And that resentment wasn't entirely unfounded, of course.

"I'm not hungry anymore," Cavan said, a little sadly.

Keely had clearly popped the kid's bubble with her mini melodrama, but he'd eaten plenty, for a kid his age, so Liam wasn't troubled by that.

He hadn't expected any of this to be easy.

And he knew it was just the beginning.

Mentally, he pushed up his sleeves and prepared himself for an uphill battle.

It was a skirmish he fully intended to win, because the well-being of his children was at stake, and that meant giving up wasn't an option.

Not that any McKettrick he'd ever known—Keely, included, for better or for worse—*ever* gave up.

Not even when they should have.

When the meal was over, and Liam had paid the bill, they left Bailey's for the sunbaked sidewalk.

Madison was just getting out of the Bentley, having parked

on the other side of the street, and Liam's flagging spirits rose a little, just at the sight of her.

She wore a simple cotton top, jeans and running shoes, and she nearly took his breath away.

She smiled, waved, looked both ways, and then hurried across the street.

"Is that your car?" Cavan asked, clearly impressed by the Bentley. The kid had never met a stranger, which was *mostly* a good thing.

Madison smiled and braced her hands on her knees, bending down to look Cavan directly in the face. "No," she said. "It belongs to my grandmother, but I'm borrowing it these days."

Liam remembered his manners.

Remembered that he was standing on a sidewalk in Painted Pony Creek, Montana, and not on a fluffy cloud somewhere over the rainbow.

He made the introductions.

Courtney and Madison shook hands.

Keely, thankfully, was reserved, but not out-and-out rude.

Cavan looked delighted, and a little bewitched.

Liam could identify with that.

He heard himself speaking, but he felt disassociated, too.

As if he were still suspended in midair.

Cue the cartoon birds, twittering a happy tune.

He invited Madison out to the ranch that coming Saturday for the horseback ride they'd had to postpone just yesterday, when it rained, and a barbecue afterward.

"I want to go riding, too," Keely said.

"No you don't," Cavan protested. "You don't even *like* riding horses."

"Enough," Liam said, resettling his hat, a thing he'd always done when there was any kind of conflict, benign or otherwise.

Get used to it, cowboy, advised the voice in his head. *The chute's open and the bronco is bucking fit to kick holes in the sky.*

Madison's smile didn't waver, and her eyes told him she understood, though he couldn't help wondering if she actually did.

"A horseback ride and a barbecue sound like a lot of fun," she said. "What time, and what can I bring?"

"Bring your car," Cavan put in. "I'd really like to ride in it!"

"I think that can be arranged," Madison replied, and her focus shifted to Keely, who was probably just as impressed by the light in this woman's eyes and in her voice as her brother was, though she'd most likely die before admitting it. "How about you, Keely? Would you like a ride in the Bentley too?"

Keely shrugged. "Maybe," she muttered. "And I *do too* like riding horses," she added, side-eying her brother. "No matter *what* Cavan says."

Madison lifted one wrist, glanced at her watch.

It was the old-fashioned sort, not particularly expensive, the kind that had to be wound and did not play music, predict the weather, signal for help or send and receive texts.

As small an observation as that was, it struck Liam as one more thing he liked about this woman.

And those things were mounting up, fast.

"See you Saturday," Liam said. "Around noon?"

"I'll be there," Madison promised. She turned back to Courtney, put out her hand again. "It's nice to meet you, Courtney," she said.

Just then, Melba Summers pulled up and parked right behind Madison's grandmother's car.

"We're meeting for lunch," Madison explained.

Liam couldn't help feeling concerned. After all, she lived alone in that happy monstrosity of a house. Maybe something had happened, or she felt threatened for some reason?

"Is everything all right?" he asked, remembering how good it had felt to hold her the night before, on the couch in her library. They'd done quite a bit of kissing, and he'd sensed that she wanted more as much as he did.

And they'd tacitly agreed that it was too soon to go to bed together.

"Yes," Madison assured him, though she seemed pleased that he'd cared enough to ask. "This is about something else, something that happened a long time ago. I'll tell you about it another time."

Melba had crossed the street to join them by then.

She was a beautiful woman, innately feminine.

She was also the local chief of police, and she was in uniform, all smiles and warmth and good-natured authority.

More introductions were made.

This time, Keely didn't try to hide the fact that she was impressed. She'd taken note, it was obvious, of the shining silver badge, the service belt and revolver, the shoulder radio.

Her blue-violet eyes were wide, and they shone with admiration.

Inwardly, Liam celebrated.

After a few moments, Melba and Madison said their farewells and went into Bailey's. Liam's curiosity had been aroused—*what* "something" had happened "a long time ago"?

He'd just have to wait to find out.

He and Courtney and the kids returned to Bitter Gulch, or at least to the fringes of it. The filming had begun, and two actors, one of them very well-known, were squaring off in the street, with the saloon in the background.

They looked like the Earp gang, with their long, fitted coats, round-brimmed hats and Colt .45s.

There, Courtney parted ways with Liam and her niece and nephew, as it was time for a meeting she'd scheduled with one of the producers and a few of the techs. She would drive out to the ranch later, she'd said, in the rental car.

Liam collected Cavan's booster seat, carried it to his truck, which was parked nearby.

"Now *this*," Cavan pronounced exuberantly, "is a *truck!*"

Keely rolled her eyes, but said nothing.

Liam grinned. Helped his son scramble up into the back seat and onto the booster.

Cavan fastened his seat belt on his own.

"Can I ride in front, with you?" Keely asked.

Damn. The first remotely friendly thing the kid had said to him and he had to refuse her request. "Sorry, Squirt," he said, with genuine regret. "You're not quite tall enough for that to be legal."

"I don't need a booster seat, like Cavan," the girl reasoned. She was small for her age, delicate, and so, at the moment, was her voice. "So why is it against the law for me to sit in front?"

"Something to do with the airbags," Liam responded. "If there was a crash, and those bags deployed, you could be badly hurt. Even killed."

The thought of *that*, of course, was downright intolerable.

No way he was giving any ground on *this* one.

"That sucks," Keely said, but she didn't argue any further. She just climbed into the back seat with her brother, wrenched her seat belt into place, and snapped the buckle shut.

"So much of life does," Liam replied mildly. "That's why you have to choose what's important enough to get bent out of shape over, and what doesn't matter enough to justify a hassle."

Keely just looked at him.

Not even a tween-ager yet, and she'd already mastered silent contempt.

Liam sighed. Shut the passenger side door and walked around to the driver's side. Climbed in.

There was no sense in arguing, especially with this particular kid.

Instead, he decided to follow his own advice and save himself for more important battles.

God knew there would be plenty of those.

11

Although Madison tried to be prepared for everything, at all times, running into Liam, the children and Courtney outside Bailey's had thrown her a little.

Her mind had been focused on the lunch meeting with Melba, and with the morning visit she'd made to Coralee, over in Silver Hills.

Her grandmother was still having scary episodes, and that morning, she hadn't even known Madison was there—unless, and this was a horrible thought—Coralee was trapped inside herself, well-aware of her situation and unable to communicate.

Considering that possibility again—it had been haunting her all morning—made Madison squeeze her eyes shut for a moment, as if that would make it all go away.

"Madison?" Melba's rich, smoky voice was gentle, the voice of a friend.

They were seated at a table next to the front window of the restaurant, coffee before them, salads on the way.

Madison opened her eyes, sighed, tried to smile and faltered. "I'm sorry," she said. "It's been a challenging morning."

"How's that?" Melba asked, stirring sweetener into her coffee, her expression pensive. "Anything to do with our little get-together here at Bailey's?" A speculative smile twitched at one corner of Melba's full mouth. "Or maybe it was the way that red-hot hunk of a cowboy, Liam McKettrick, was eating you up just now with those ridiculously blue eyes of his?"

Madison laughed. Blushed.

Both at the same time.

"He was doing no such thing," she said.

"Whatever you say," Melba replied.

The salads arrived, and with them came the memory of the way Coralee had looked that morning at breakfast time, when Madison had first stepped into her room at the care facility.

Nearly catatonic, her white hair sticking out in every direction, with patches of pink scalp showing through, Coralee had looked at once frantic and bewildered. Her rounded eyes seemed to be searching beyond her immediate surroundings for the approach of something extremely frightening.

Madison's appetite receded like an outgoing tide.

"What is it?" Melba pressed, serious now. The woman was astute—*too* astute.

"It's my grandmother," Madison said, her voice small. Defeated. "She has dementia, and it's killing her."

And it's killing me, too.

"I'm really sorry," Melba said sincerely, her voice quiet now, and warm.

She reached across the table and took Madison's free hand, squeezed briefly before letting it go.

"Thanks," Madison said, equally sincere. Nothing had changed, of course—Coralee's fate was sealed—but Melba's strength and concern were powerfully soothing. "That isn't what I wanted to ask you about, though."

"Let's hear it," Melba urged. She took up her fork and stabbed it into her salad, so Madison did the same.

She knew that, even though she didn't want food at the moment, her body needed it. She'd been running on coffee and a single slice of toast all morning.

Between bites, Madison told Melba what she knew about Bliss Morgan. How they'd first met, when they were both eight years old, in the overgrown family cemetery hidden away in the woods behind Bettencourt Hall. How they'd picnicked there, on subsequent days, and how hungry Bliss had always been.

She told Melba about the old camper Bliss had claimed to live in with her father, a drunkard whose name she'd never mentioned, at least as far as Madison recalled, and her mother, who apparently came and went.

She showed Melba the tattered friendship bracelet Bliss had left for her just before she vanished, along with the one-word note. *Goodbye.*

And when she'd said it all, she sighed, all too aware of how little she'd given the chief of police to go on.

"Morgan is a fairly common last name," Melba said, looking out the window as she mused.

"I know," Madison said. "She's probably fine. Her folks weren't the kind to settle down anywhere for long, I'm guessing. It's entirely possible that they simply moved on, taking Bliss with them." She paused, bit her lower lip, went on. "But a big part of my brain doesn't believe that."

Melba met Madison's gaze, raised an eyebrow. Her question, though unspoken, was entirely clear.

What do you think happened?

Madison pushed her plate aside. Answered. "I don't know for sure." Her voice was tentative. "But I believe there was something terribly wrong. That Bliss might have been kidnapped, or even murdered."

She'd half expected Melba to declare that this was all speculation, that too much time had gone by, that the police were busy enough with *current* cases and didn't have the time or resources to investigate crimes that might not have happened at all.

"I presume you've done some research on the web," Melba said.

Madison nodded. "Yes, and I came up with nothing, so I'm going to the library this afternoon to check old newspapers and the like. I was just hoping that you—well, that there might be something in police records. Anyone named Morgan who might have been in Painted Pony Creek back then and gotten into some kind of trouble—"

"I'll do what I can," Melba told her. "But that might not be much. Lots of records are expunged after a certain length of time. Others are simply lost, even with all the modern technology that's available now. You know, glitches, system failures and the like. And then, of course, there are always the hackers. Some of them really get a kick out of sabotaging entire databases for no other reason than that they can do it."

"But surely most records survive?"

"I'll check it out," Melba reiterated, and Madison knew the chief of police wasn't just brushing her off. If this woman said she would do something, do it she would, no matter what.

"Thank you," Madison said.

A seasoned waitress—her name tag read Miranda—approached the table and asked if there was anything else they wanted.

Both Madison and Melba said there wasn't.

Madison picked up the check.

"You planning to stick around town awhile?" Melba asked conversationally.

With the failed wedding growing smaller and smaller in the rearview mirror now, Madison was more relaxed about staying in Painted Pony Creek.

She liked the community, liked being back in Bettencourt Hall.

Liked being with Liam McKettrick, accidentally or on purpose.

And, of course, there was Coralee.

Madison had already reached out to Audra via email and asked her to handle the sale to HammondCo, since she didn't want to travel.

With her grandmother so obviously failing, there was no way she could leave the area. Besides, contracts could be signed digitally these days, and if a meeting turned out to be vital, well, that too could probably be done remotely.

Her mind had wandered again, back to that morning's interlude with Coralee, and Melba's next words presented such a contrast that she almost asked her to repeat them.

"We have a book club—well, several of them—but the one I belong to is the most flexible, time-wise, and it's made up of half a dozen women around our age. I guess what I'm trying to get at is, we'd sure like it if you'd join us."

Madison's first reaction was a surprised and silent, *Really?*

She loved books, and she needed some local friends, since her posse was so far-flung.

But she was still a relative stranger in Painted Pony Creek, so the invitation surprised her.

In her experience, people wanted to get to know another person pretty well before they included them in social events, however informal. Especially in tight-knit communities like this one.

"I'd like that," she managed after a few moments.

"Good," Melba replied. "We're meeting tonight at seven thirty out at Brynne Garrett's place. You know Brynne, right?"

"We're acquainted," Madison said. She'd worked with Brynne putting last-minute touches on the wedding. "She probably thinks I'm crazy, though."

Melba laughed. They were outside by then, walking across the sunny street toward their cars. "Not for a moment. I reckon she'd have thought you were crazy if you went through with that marriage, though."

Madison blushed a little, hoped Melba hadn't noticed.

Melba was a cop, though, and obviously a good one. Which

meant she missed very little. "Like I said, we'd be happy to have you," she said quietly.

"But what if I haven't read the book you're discussing?"

Melba laughed. "Well, then we'll have to drag you over to Bitter Gulch and hang you," she joked. "We just finished Kristin Hannah's latest, and we'll be picking something new tonight. By consensus, though I'm voting for a Debbie Macomber story. We don't have a president or anything like that, and we rotate our meetings so everybody gets to host when their turn comes up."

"I'd love to come, but—"

"But?"

"But there's a lot going on right now. When's the next meeting?"

"Two weeks out," Melba replied.

"Maybe we could hold it at Bettencourt Hall? It would be a lot of fun to entertain again—I've been so rushed lately, and I'm seriously trying to shift gears. Get some kind of emotional traction."

"I hear you," Melba sympathized good-naturedly, and then smiled her approval. "I'll suggest that to the group tonight," she said. "I think the ladies would jump at the chance to get a look at the inside of that house. It's famous around here, you know—even fancier than the old Worth place."

Madison did know. "Back in the day, there were parties there all the time," she recalled somewhat wistfully. "It's almost as if the house itself is lonesome for the hustle and bustle of people coming and going."

If Melba caught the whimsical nuance of that statement, she didn't comment on it. Or maybe it didn't seem out of character for someone who'd flee the scene of her wedding, after creating an uproar, for the surprising solace of the Hard Luck Saloon.

In other words, for a slightly crazy person.

The two women said their goodbyes then, and Melba drove away in her cruiser, tooting the horn as she passed the Bentley.

Madison, already behind the wheel, tooted back.

And something swelled inside her.

A sense of belonging, and of discovery, very similar to what she felt whenever she was with Liam.

The library was only a few blocks away—she could have walked—but since she was in the car anyway, Madison drove there, humming under her breath.

The town's only source of books was housed in a low-slung brick building two blocks from the courthouse.

Madison parked in a shady spot—there were only two other vehicles in the lot—grabbed her purse, and headed inside.

The interior of the building was wonderfully cool, and the satisfying, dusty and unique scent of books permeated the quiet atmosphere.

The first order of business, Madison decided, was to sign up for a library card.

Maybe, she thought fancifully, her name was still in the system, since she'd been a loyal patron until she was twelve.

She approached the main desk and was greeted by an elderly lady in a floral dress. Her white hair was neatly arranged into a French twist, and she wore a string of pearls and matching earrings.

Her smile was welcoming—and vaguely familiar. Very vaguely.

"Good afternoon," she said. "How can I help you?"

"I'd like a library card, to start, please," Madison replied, feeling strangely shy, as though she were a child again, barely able to see over the desk. "And to check some newspapers, if you have them on file. They go back quite a way, actually—almost twenty-five years."

"Don't you recognize me?" the woman asked, not unkindly, but with mischievous interest, letting Madison's request slide for the moment.

Madison studied the powdered, still pretty face, the bright blue-green eyes.

Something niggled at the back of her brain, then disappeared. She shook her head.

"Why, Madison Bettencourt, I'm surprised at you! I'm your grandmother's best friend, Althea James, and I've spent almost as much time at your house as my own." A pause, a little tut-tut sound, crisp but entirely benign.

Her eyes grew misty, and before Madison could respond, she went on. "Poor Coralee. Such a bright, beautiful woman—why, to see her end up like this—"

Madison suddenly realized that she *did* remember Mrs. James.

She and Coralee had been bosom buddies back in the day, forever having lunch together, attending various meetings around town, participating in bridge and mahjong groups, exchanging favorite books, sometimes giggling like a pair of schoolgirls. They'd gone on art retreats and shopping expeditions and traveled to Vegas twice a year to see a few shows and play slot machines and blackjack.

Madison's eyes burned, because it hurt to know that Coralee would never again be that lively woman, always up to something.

In the moment, she couldn't speak.

"I try to visit her every Sunday, right after church," Althea James confided sadly, "but it breaks my heart. The poor darling hasn't a clue who I am." She paused, sniffed, thrust her shoulders back a little, lifted her chin. Her smile was determinedly bright, if a little shaky. "Nevertheless, I'm there every single week, because she's still my best friend in the world, and I'm lost without her, even though she isn't gone yet!"

"I know it's hard," Madison said, and she did. She was already grieving the loss of Coralee, and of course there was her friend Olivia's illness. Unlike Althea James, she couldn't go and sit with her friend on a regular basis, because of physical distance.

Olivia wouldn't have allowed it, anyway, but not being there still bothered Madison a lot. And she knew Audra, Kendall and Alexis felt the same way.

That kind of helplessness was painful.

Mrs. James fretted on, paying no apparent heed to Madison's brief comment, shaking her head as she spoke. "Coralee and I were little girls when we met—we both attended the old one-room schoolhouse—it's long gone now, of course—and we formed an alliance straightaway." The librarian looked dreamily off into the invisible, smiling. "I don't know why this should come to mind, but once there was a garden party at Bettencourt Hall—so lovely—but you wouldn't remember that, of course. You came along much later." She paused, looked away, and then looked back. "Coralee and I were playing hide-and-seek, out by the old cemetery, and she got lost. We searched for what seemed like hours, and when she finally came wandering along the road from town, she was pale, and wouldn't talk at all. Not for *days*." Althea stopped, huffed out a breath. "Forgive me, Madison. I'm rambling. I seem to do that more and more lately."

"That's all right," Madison said, all her senses on red alert now.

Again, Althea didn't seem to register her response. She busied herself preparing the library card, handed it over. She hadn't asked for identifying details, and why would she?

Althea James was an old friend of the family.

She knew all about Madison; Coralee, before her dementia took hold, would have filled her in.

And she'd always been kindly, and a marvelous storyteller to boot.

Now that she'd been reminded, Madison recalled coming to the library as a very small child, and sitting among a circle of other children at Mrs. James's feet, absorbed in story hour.

Much younger then, obviously, Mrs. James had been an attractive woman, full of laughter and high spirits.

But Madison's mind was awhirl as she went back over the

story of Coralee getting lost during the long-ago garden party at Bettencourt Hall. There had been a careful search that ended only when she came "wandering back," as Mrs. James had put it.

"That day—the day of the garden party, I mean—did Coralee ever tell you where she'd been during the time she was missing?"

Oddly, Althea laughed, waved a cheerfully dismissive hand. "Yes, but it was nonsense. Everyone thought she'd made it up—including me. She was a very imaginative child, you know. Used to come up with the *most* complicated games of pretend you've ever heard of."

Madison was vaguely angry on her grandmother's behalf.

Why did people always assume that children made everything up?

Yes, they had active imaginations, most of them. They played make-believe, drifted off into daydreams sometimes, lost themselves in books and games and movies.

But to have made *everything* up?

To Madison, that seemed like a stretch.

"What did she tell you?" she asked very carefully, all but holding her breath.

Mrs. James sighed, shook her head again. "She said she'd stumbled into another place, where everything was different."

"Different how?"

"Different as in, Coralee truly believed she'd found her own personal wrinkle in time. We'd just read a similar book the previous week, so I guess that much made sense—"

"But…?"

"But Coralee swore she'd seen the *old* Painted Pony Creek, complete with wagons and buggies and strange buildings. Her description was quite detailed, actually, but then again, she *was* a fanciful child, just as I said before."

Coralee had never mentioned that experience to Madison, though she'd loved regaling her grandchild with tales of the good old days.

So why hadn't she told that one?

Madison felt strangely lightheaded and at the same time breathless with excitement. She was also more than a little annoyed with her grandmother, since she'd brushed off every mention of Bliss Morgan and her strange and sudden disappearance.

You're making it up, Madison, Coralee had accused her, each and every time. *You spend too much time alone, and now you're inventing imaginary friends for yourself. I guess I don't blame you for that, but it's not safe, wandering the countryside the way you do.*

After a while, Madison had given up asking, out loud, anyway.

She'd pondered the situation plenty in each of her five-year diaries, small plastic-covered books with a little lock and key to protect her secrets.

Such as they were, in those days.

She recalled now that she'd received a brand-new one every Christmas—a familiar square bulge in her stocking.

Where were those diaries now?

Had she tossed them?

Maybe. Maybe not.

All thought of spending the afternoon scouring old newspapers on a computer screen, relics of a time nearly a quarter of a century in the past, fled her mind.

If anything official had happened concerning Bliss or her family, Melba would find it.

Madison's job was to go home and turn Bettencourt Hall inside out, if she had to, to locate her own humble journals as well as Coralee's.

For she had been a journal keeper, too, once upon a time.

Another option would be to sit with Coralee until a lucid moment presented itself—and how unlikely was *that?*—so she could pounce and ask about her grandmother's alleged visit to the Painted Pony Creek of yesteryear.

She'd definitely ask, if and when she got the chance, but for now, in the state Coralee was in, it would be a waste of time and energy.

No, Madison would go straight home to Bettencourt Hall and search high and low, from the attic to the basement of that old house, a place full of stories of its own, and she would ferret out those journals.

If there was an account of Coralee's experience the day of her disappearance recorded anywhere, she would locate it.

"Thank you, Mrs. James," she said, and hurried out of the library, clutching her library card in one hand and her car keys in the other.

Fifteen minutes later, she was back home.

She parked the Bentley in the detached garage and hurried around to the back of the house, letting herself in by way of the sunporch and the unlocked door leading into the kitchen.

The house offered a silent, familiar welcome, very much like a hug, though, naturally, there was no pressure of strong arms, no firm solace of a warm, muscular chest.

Liam.

In that moment, Madison truly craved his presence. She wanted, even needed, to tell him what had happened to Coralee when she was a child, and what *might* have happened to Bliss as well.

It sounded impossible, even ludicrous.

But what if...?

Madison brought herself up short.

Probably, being a rational man, Liam would say what Coralee had always said.

That Madison was imagining things.

Even in that case, though, she would have been comforted just by the act of confiding in him. He'd told her before that he was a good listener, and it was true.

She'd told him so much the previous night, before the kissing had started, sweeping them both up into a sweet storm of passion that never came to fruition.

In some ways, Madison regretted their mutual restraint.

Lovemaking would probably have been downright therapeutic, if ill-advised.

She shook that off, along with the idea of texting Liam, just to maintain some kind of contact, however limited.

Liam been separated from his children for too long, and she wasn't about to get in the way of any bonding that might be happening, now or later.

She set aside her purse, hung the Bentley's keys from their appointed hook beside the pantry door, and shifted her focus to the mission of the day: searching for her childhood diaries, and for Coralee's journals.

She began the search upstairs, in Coralee's massive bedroom, with its deep carpeting, its beautifully papered walls, its bay windows and balcony.

Standing in the middle of the room, hands on her hips, Madison fought down a rush of guilt—she *was*, after all, invading someone's private space—but she was committed to her purpose.

There were bookshelves along one wall, and Madison inspected them carefully, tome by dusty, well-thumbed tome, without finding anything that resembled a journal. She even felt for a hidden catch, in case the shelves could be moved aside like the ones downstairs.

Perhaps there was another hidden room here, like the one in the library.

But no. There wasn't.

A search of the dresser and bureau drawers was fruitless, as was her careful examination of the contents of Coralee's vanity, desk, nightstands, blanket chest and closet.

The bed itself was gigantic, as though built for an Amazon queen rather than a tiny, elegant and very mortal woman living alone for most of her long life.

There was nothing hidden under the mattress, or stuffed behind the headboard, or gathering dust under the bed itself.

Madison ran a hand through her hair and sighed.

Then she remembered the boxes she'd dragged out of the secret room downstairs just the day before, pronounced herself at least marginally an idiot, and set out for the library via the broad, curving stairs at the front of the house.

The thought struck her, apropos of nothing, that even though her grandmother's will would not allow her to sell Bettencourt Hall, she ought to do something constructive with it at some point.

Turn it into a bed-and-breakfast, perhaps, or a retreat center.

Or a home for wayward armadillos.

Get a grip, Madison, she thought. *You're getting carried away.*

The tattered but otherwise sturdy cardboard boxes were right where she'd left them after cleaning out the hidden space the day before.

After Liam had gone home, she'd been too tired, and too caught up in steamy fantasies, ones that made her ache in private places, to bother with whatever was inside them.

She had to fetch a box cutter to open the first and largest of the containers; all of them had been duct-taped shut, *wrapped* in the stuff, as though they contained top secret documents or maps leading to a buried treasure, like in a pirate story.

She smiled, because when she thought of pirates, she thought of Johnny Depp, and when she thought of Johnny Depp, well, she smiled.

The box contained old clothing—*very old* clothing—women's shirtwaists fronted with about a million tiny buttons, heavy woolen skirts and bombazine dresses, long and all in drab grays and browns. All ridiculously tiny.

The combined smells of mildew, mothballs and generations of mice indicated that the duct tape—added years after the boxes were filled—hadn't kept out vermin.

Madison coughed and wished she could open a window.

She couldn't, unfortunately, because this was the library, and the floor-to-ceiling windows were sealed in their frames.

Madison went through the box, however unpleasant that was, garment by garment.

There were no journals.

She wondered who the contents had belonged to—certainly not Coralee; these items of clothing had been fashionable in the late nineteenth and very early twentieth centuries, well before her time. And why had they been hidden away in the secret room at some later date? They definitely hadn't been there when Madison was a child, spying on cocktail parties.

Where was Trixie Belden when she needed her? Where was Nancy Drew?

Madison laughed to—and at—herself. Maybe she really *was* losing her marbles, trying to solve a dusty old mystery that really had no bearing on her present-day life.

Still, something compelled her to learn what had happened to Bliss, something powerful.

Wasn't it worth searching for lost people even when they'd been gone for more than two decades, and no one else seemed to care?

To Madison, it was.

Bliss had been a living, breathing human being, not a fantasy, whatever Coralee might have believed. And she'd been Madison's friend, if only for part of one childhood summer.

Bliss was important, if *only* to her.

She tackled the next box, and then the next.

More clothing, a few books, a packet of very old letters, bound by the time-honored ribbon, fading and frayed at the edges.

Finding the letters, Madison felt a little thrill, examined them briefly, then set them aside. They had been special to someone, written long, long ago, and clearly cherished through the years, but they'd been written well before Coralee's birth, never mind Bliss's.

They'd been postmarked between 1870 and 1885, and addressed to one Katherine Bettencourt in a strong, clearly masculine hand.

That name was familiar to Madison, of course. Katherine had been her great-great-grandmother. She'd lived in this house, borne several children here and died here.

The letters were family history, and Madison intended to preserve them carefully, and certainly to read them, but for the time being they would have to wait.

The last and smallest box, bound tightly with twine instead of duct tape, finally, finally yielded journals, bound in scuffed leather, embossed with flowers, each one tied shut with a tasseled black cord.

A quick—and breathless—examination of the first volume revealed that these, like the letters, had belonged to Katherine, not to Coralee.

Madison scanned a few pages, penned in splendid copperplate handwriting, the ink a faded, almost ghostly blue.

Katherine had begun the journal at the age of nine, with an account of her cousin Lucy's wedding. She'd been the flower girl, and delighted by her assignment.

Madison smiled at the essence of childhood joy, which came through so clearly, even after more than a century had passed.

Because Katherine's journals almost certainly contained a lot of interesting information about the Bettencourts of days gone by, they were naturally important to Madison. She decided to have them scanned, as soon as she could arrange for that to be done, so that their contents would never be lost. Perhaps she would have them transcribed, as well.

As fascinating as the handwritten books were sure to be, they, like the letters, were filled years before Coralee was born, including the latest one, dated 1906.

She lifted each of the leather-bound volumes gently, almost reverently, from the darkness that had housed them these many years, and stacked them on the end table, alongside the love letters.

Presently, Madison cleared away the ancient clothing, placing the garments on the sunporch bench to air out, then carried the fusty, falling-apart boxes out to the burn barrel, to be set alight at another time. Maybe the clothing could be donated to the local historical society, or a museum.

She poured herself a tall glass of ice tea, with a slice of lemon added for pizazz, and sat down at the kitchen table to rest for a few minutes and figure out what to do with her discoveries, such as they were.

She'd tackle the attic next, she decided, daunting though the prospect was. The space extended across the entire width and breadth of the house, and it was doubtless draped in spider webs and gauzy fabrics that would shift and flutter like ghosts when disturbed.

A sweet thrill went through her at the prospect of opening the attic door and stepping into the realm of memories.

There were mysteries tucked away in this grand old house, just waiting to be brought to light.

And Madison was ready to get busy doing just that.

12

Bliss

1897

Bliss kept expecting to wake up, but the dream went on.

And on.

By the third day, she had begun to hope she would never wake up.

She considered the possibility that she might be dead, and caught in some kind of afterlife—not like heaven or anything, because there were no angels flying around playing harps, and no pearly gates or streets of gold, like Gran always said there would be.

Plus, when she pinched herself, it hurt.

It was all so weird, but not in a scary way.

In most ways, this place was like the one she remembered from before—the sky was blue, there were trees everywhere, the ground had substance under the soles of her feet, and so did the floorboards in the house.

The bed she slept in was solid, and the food she ate—that was almost the best part, that there was always plenty to eat—filled her stomach and made her feel stronger.

She wasn't homesick for the camper or Duke, that was for sure, and she'd pretty much gotten over missing Mona, but she *did* wish she could go back—wake up?—just long enough to tell Madison she was okay.

If, that is, she *was* okay.

There was no telling whether she was or not; already, this dream world seemed far more real than the other one, where she'd been so lonesome so much of the time, so hungry, so tired of living in that filthy old wreck of a camper, of wishing Mona would come back and be a real mother, and that Duke would change.

Here, she had a whole room all to herself, and around that stood an entire *house*, with windows and ceilings, floors and a sturdy roof. There was a *really* cool hiding place in the book room, which the family referred to as the library—Jack had shown her the secret space and made her swear never to tell anyone about it, *ever*.

His pa had built that room special, Jack told her, before he died in a mining accident, when Jack himself was still a baby. And there were others like it in other parts of the house, too, though he refused to reveal them just yet. A cubbyhole like that might just save all their lives sometime, he'd added in a raspy whisper, in case of a raid by outlaws or Indians.

"Native Americans," Bliss had corrected him at the time, but he'd just rounded his eyes at her and shaken his head.

"Never mind that," he'd said. "You've got to keep this a secret, like Ma and me do. If everybody and his Aunt Bessie knows about this place, it won't make any sense to hide here, now, will it?"

Bliss had had to admit that it wouldn't.

That had happened the day after she wound up in this place, and two *more* days had passed since then.

Now, it was Sunday morning, and Mrs. Bettencourt made Jack put on pants, a shirt, suspenders *and* a jacket, though it was hotter than blue blazes out, even before breakfast.

Jack's mom had cut down one of her own dresses to fit Bliss, calling it a "calico," which made Bliss wonder if it had something to do with California. Mrs. Bettencourt had been busy sewing up more girl clothes for her, too, whenever she got the time.

Her shorts and shirt had disappeared as soon as the cut-down dress was ready to wear, and Bliss suspected that they'd probably been burned in the kitchen stove.

She'd had a bath, too, and Mrs. Bettencourt had scrubbed her down good, from head to toe. Her hair was shiny clean now, brushed and braided, and her fingernails—and toenails—no longer looked as though she'd been digging holes in the ground with her hands and feet.

Only her sneakers remained, and she figured those wouldn't be around long, either, since every time Mrs. Bettencourt looked at Bliss's feet, she sighed and shook her head and said, "Lord have mercy."

The woman had a list going, and a lot of what was on it was about Bliss.

She was never still, it seemed, except when she read her Bible in the early morning and late at night, always sweeping, cooking, mending, weeding the vegetable patch, making butter in a big wooden thing she called a "churn," carrying laundry to and from the clothesline, after washing everything in a machine that didn't plug into the wall. After all that, when the shirts and blouses had been dried by the sun and the wind, she started pressing out the wrinkles with a big metal iron—not the kind that plugged in, though, because there weren't any wall sockets, anywhere. This thing had a big wooden handle and had to be heated up on the stove, along with the tea kettle and, most times, a pot of soup, simmering away at the back.

Yesterday, Mrs. Bettencourt had baked bread, first mixing flour and salt and other stuff in the biggest bowl Bliss had ever seen—she'd had to stand on tiptoe to peer inside—and then pushing up her sleeves and washing her hands to knead and knead and knead the dough.

After that, she set the goop in bread-shaped pans to "rise."

Bliss hadn't really understood the idea behind that, but she'd been fascinated by the whole process, just the same.

And when that stuff went into a hot oven to bake, the smell was so delicious that Bliss couldn't bring herself to leave the kitchen, even though it was sweltering hot and Jack had invited her to go down to the creek, where it was cool and shady, and fish with him.

The only thing better than the scent of that hot, fresh bread was smearing it with butter and eating as much of it as she could hold. Mrs. Bettencourt kept chickens, but she bought milk and cream from the neighbors just down the road. She'd had a cow once, but the critter kept getting loose and making straight for the garden, where she'd eaten her fill of vegetables and trampled the rest, so she'd sold it.

Back in the Other Place, which was all Bliss could think to call the different-and-yet-the-same world she'd come from, bread came from a rack at the dollar store, if there *was* bread, and nobody *ever* cooked anything that smelled that good, either.

She was making notes in her mind all the time, because if she got lost from *this* place, she wanted to remember everything about it.

So she paid attention.

Jack and his mom lived alone in that wonderful house, since *Mr.* Bettencourt was gone, and as far as Bliss had been able to see, there were no men coming around the house to flirt with Katherine.

That seemed strange to her, since Katherine was so beautiful, but it was a relief, too, since Duke was pretty much the only grown-up man she knew, and she sure didn't miss him, not one bit. He was too unpredictable, quiet one moment, loud and angry the next.

Nope. Men couldn't be trusted, and it was safer to stay out of their way.

"Are you two ready for Sunday meeting?" Mrs. Bettencourt asked, there in the kitchen, next to the stove, which was so hot it gave off little mirages, shifting and shimmering in the thick air.

She was adjusting Jack's collar, which was white and stiff and had already chafed his neck, leaving red marks that looked itchy.

"Yes, ma'am," Bliss said eagerly. She wanted this strange adventure to keep right on unfolding, uncovering new and interesting parts of itself.

Today, for instance, they were going to town, where the church was.

They'd be traveling in an actual *buggy*, drawn by a huge gray horse named Solomon.

Sure enough, when the three of them, Jack, Mrs. Bettencourt and Bliss, were squeezed together on the single narrow seat, and Mrs. Bettencourt had taken up the reins and then slapped them down very gently onto the horse's back, at the same time making a *click-click* sound with her tongue, they were off to Painted Pony Creek. Or the edge of it, anyhow.

Bliss took it all in—the smell of leather and horse sweat and dust, of laundry soap and clean cloth, the deep and cloudless blue of the sky, the twisty road, with its deep ruts and patches of grass growing in the middle.

In places, there were trees lining their way, so tall that they blocked out the bright sun for a few moments and cooled the damp skin at the nape of Bliss's neck and under her chin.

When the trees gave way to open fields, the buggy, with its spindly wheels, cast a skinny, spidery shadow that rippled and flowed alongside them, fast and fluid, reminding Bliss of the heat mirages in the kitchen.

She was enchanted.

And a little confused.

There was no figuring out what was happening to her, or if it was real or not.

The hard seat of that buggy sure seemed real enough, since, with all the bouncing the rig did, as the wheels bumped over rocks and ridges of packed dirt, it was already making her bottom sore.

The church was small and white, with a wooden cross on top, and it sat in a big field, right at the edge of the town.

There were more buggies there, and wagons, too.

There were horses and donkeys, tied up under shade trees.

And there were people—too many to fit into that little church, it seemed to Bliss—all of them dressed like actors in a Western movie, except their clothes, though clean, were scruffy, and the colors were plainer.

The men looked like cowboys, mostly, and their hats weren't fancy. The women, like Mrs. Bettencourt, wore long skirts, blouses and high-button shoes that probably hurt their feet.

There were kids, running and shouting in the grass in front of the church, dodging between wagons and grazing horses, now and then tipping over a water bucket that had to be refilled so the animals could drink.

Jack leaped out of the buggy before it came to a full stop and raced off to join the others.

"That boy," Mrs. Bettencourt muttered, not sounding mad. "I swear, it will be the death of me, teaching him simple manners."

Bliss barely heard. She sat spellbound, staring hard, memorizing the sights and sounds.

Katherine—Bliss thought of her as Katherine, or "Jack's mom," though she had soon figured out that calling her by her first name wouldn't be a good idea—found a shady spot so

Solomon could wait out what promised to be a *very* long sermon, which Jack had warned Bliss about earlier, without getting too hot.

Jack's mom pulled an empty bucket from beneath the seat and was headed toward a stone well with a little roof over it when a man stepped up, tipped his hat, and took the bucket from her.

Bliss tried to stay close without getting underfoot.

She wasn't scared, exactly, but there were a lot of people around, and they were dressed all weird, and she didn't want to answer a bunch of questions.

And there *were* questions.

Bliss could see them in the eyes of girls with long finger curls and big bows in their hair. These were the kids who stayed close to their parents, instead of chasing around with the others.

She wasn't fooling them; they knew she was different somehow.

They just didn't know *how* different.

The man who'd taken Katherine's bucket had filled it by then, and carried it back to Solomon so he could drink from it.

Bliss wondered if Katherine knew the guy wanted to be her boyfriend, or even her husband. She'd smiled and thanked him for his help, but had she really *noticed* him?

Bliss didn't think so.

After a few minutes, when everybody seemed to be talking at once, and *nobody* seemed to be listening, a bell began to ring, slow and deep.

Bong—bong—bong—

Katherine took Bliss's hand in her gloved one and started toward the church door, the two of them jammed into the funnel flow of people.

Someone—an older boy or a man, Bliss thought—gave a long whistle, so shrill that it hurt her ears, and the kids who'd been running wild were suddenly quiet.

The inside of the building was simple, but it amazed Bliss, just the same.

It looked nothing like the church Gran sometimes attended.

No stained-glass windows, no big wooden cross, no altar, no choir in matching robes, hymnals open, mouths ready to sing.

There were rows of long benches instead of folding chairs or polished pews, some with backs and some not.

The walls and floors were rough, unpainted, and splintery-looking.

People seemed to know where they belonged, though, and they found their places.

A lot of shuffling and whispering happened while they did so.

Katherine led Bliss to a seat on one of the benches with no back, and they both sat down.

Jack came out of the crowd, dragging his feet a little and looking like he had an attitude, but he made his way toward them and sat down next to Bliss without saying anything.

The hard heel of his right boot made a thumping noise as he bounced it off one of the legs of the bench.

"Jack," his mom hiss-whispered.

Jack stopped kicking the bench leg.

Bliss, though she'd noticed this, was too busy looking around to care much what Jack Bettencourt did. He was nice enough, but he was still a boy.

She straightened hard when a thunderous note of music filled the crowded space, echoing off the ceiling and the walls.

A thin, happy-looking woman was playing an organ, up near where Bliss expected the preacher would stand.

Looking back, Bliss decided she'd liked going to church, but that was before Gran and Duke had a falling-out over him not working a job, like a good husband and father ought to, and he stopped letting Bliss visit so often.

Gran had ranted like crazy the day they got into that fight.

She'd said she hadn't raised him to be a no-good, waste-of-skin bum.

Duke had been angry, too, accusing Gran of nagging him half to death, every moment of his life.

After that one fight, which certainly wasn't the first, trips to Gran's place had gradually tapered off to nothing.

The organ made a wheezy sound between storms of pounding notes, and brought Bliss back from Gran and Duke and their yelling. She sat up even straighter, trying to get a better look at the tiny woman up there thumping away at the keys.

The preacher appeared, coming in through a side door, and the gathering of people settled down a little.

The last notes of the organ tune banged their way into silence.

Bliss took in the man standing up front, dressed in an old-fashioned movie suit that looked too tight for him. Like Jack, he had on a high, starched collar that came up to his chin. Unlike Jack, he had sideburns and a big ole mustache that looked as though he'd sprayed it with WD-40.

He tugged at his collar with one finger, like it was choking him, and cleared his throat.

Here we go, Bliss thought, bracing herself. *The man is getting ready to holler.*

Gran had always favored preachers that hollered. Said it was because they meant what they said, and they wanted to get their point across.

Beside Bliss, Jack gave her a nudge and whispered, "If you see me fall asleep, don't you go wakin' me up for anything."

Bliss made a face at him.

If Jack Bettencourt wanted to sleep, he could do it at home, in his own bed, because if she had to listen to a long and probably boring speech, so did he.

It was only fair.

Five minutes into the longest prayer Bliss had ever heard anybody offer up—not that she'd been around much praying—Jack's head fell forward.

Bliss elbowed him.

He straightened up quick, and glared at her.

There was some singing, and more organ playing along with it.

Bliss knew the songs were called hymns, but she didn't know the words to any of them.

They were all about God, she'd figured out that much.

He sounded nice in some of the songs, and real mean in others. Nobody she'd want to cross, that was for sure.

Bliss didn't believe or not believe, actually, but Katherine seemed to take in every word, every note, every silence, her expression earnest and happy, in a soft way.

The speech was, as Jack had warned, very, *very* long. Somewhere in the middle, Bliss left off jabbing Jack in the ribs to wake him up and struggled hard not to fall asleep herself.

She was glad—*real* glad—when the whole thing ended, at least two hours after it started, and she and Jack and Mrs. Bettencourt made their way back to the buggy and patient Solomon, who was twitching his tail when Jack stepped up to collect the water bucket and pat the sweaty horse on the neck.

People lingered everywhere, chatting, discussing the sermon, making plans for the afternoon and the week ahead, but Katherine didn't pause to join in. She greeted the others in passing, and took up her place on the buggy seat.

This time, Jack didn't ride with Bliss and his mother.

He straddled Solomon, harness and all.

Bliss's mind was full of wonder as they made their way back to the house; on the inside, she was sorting out the experience and trying to make sense of it.

Nothing made sense, however.

And that figured, she decided later, because that night, when everyone else was sound asleep and the big house was quiet, except for the ticking of the grandfather clock near the front door, Bliss went back to the Other Place.

13

"I hate you!" Keely screamed, from somewhere out of Liam's sight.

Liam, seated at the table in his big, sunny kitchen, with its state-of-the-art, top-of-the-line appliances and long wooden table, rolled his eyes and rose from his chair.

Courtney, seated to his left, hands encircling a cup of hot coffee, gave him a sympathetic look. "Be careful, Liam," she advised gently. "This is all new to the kids, and as I'm sure you've noticed, Keely isn't adjusting as well as Cavan is."

No shit, Sherlock, Liam thought, though he kept the remark to himself.

None of this was Courtney's fault, nor was it her responsibility.

That fell squarely on *him,* one hundred percent.

As he strode through the house, he wondered why the hell he'd made the place so big.

What had he been trying to prove? That he was successful?

Well, yeah, he *was* successful. Sort of.

He had a flare for making and managing money.

Whoop-de-freaking-do.

None of that mattered, since he had nothing to prove.

What *did* matter? He *sucked* as a father, that was what, and maybe as a human being.

He found the kids in the media room—an effing *media room*—what had he been thinking?

Keely, clad in turquoise shorts and a matching tank top, stood on the leather couch, gripping the controller for the Xbox, hopping from one bare foot to the other and shooting poison out of both eyes.

Cavan stood his ground, glaring back at her. "I hate you, too!" he said, just before both of them spotted Liam.

"Keely," he said, in the most even and reasonable tone he could manage, "get down from there. Now."

She hesitated, defiance in miniature, then leaped off the couch.

"Give me the controller," Liam said.

Keely held the plastic device close against her middle for a long moment, then extended it, grudgingly.

He took it from her, set it on a high shelf, well out of the kids' reach.

Unless, of course, one or both of them climbed the bookcase to retrieve it.

Liam made a mental note to make sure the thing was bolted to the wall.

"It was *my turn*," Cavan complained. "I said so, and Keely said I was stupid and I said she was mean, and then she said she hates me, so I said it back."

Liam sighed, closed his eyes for a moment, opened them again. "'Hate' isn't a word you can throw around just because you're angry," he said. "It's ugly and it's poisonous."

Cavan's dark eyes widened, and Liam felt a stab of sorrow

over the one thing he never wanted to say to this child, but had to, someday soon.

"How can a word be poison?" the boy asked.

Keely folded her arms and looked upward, as though praying for peace.

Yeah, right.

"Words have power," Liam tried to explain, already knowing he was probably missing the mark. "They can hurt people, do real damage that lasts a long time—maybe forever—or they can make things better."

"Can I have my turn now?" Cavan asked, rather meekly.

Clearly, he didn't understand the morality speech Liam had just offered, and there was no surprise in that, was there?

The kid was only seven.

"No," Liam answered. "For today, it's game over. For both of you."

He picked up the remote from the coffee table and shut off the massive TV he'd thought was such a good idea when he'd bought it at Costco, while the house was still under construction. Back then, he'd naively pictured himself watching wholesome movies with his kids on that enormous screen, and thrown in the Xbox and a few game cartridges because he'd imagined that, too. Playing happy video games, all of them together.

So far, family time bore no resemblance to his preconceived scenario.

Keely and Cavan had been there, on the ranch, for four days.

When she wasn't making trouble, Keely stayed mostly in her bedroom.

Like the TV, and the size of the house in general, the kids' bedrooms were a study in conspicuous consumption—for Keely, there was a canopy bed with matching nightstands and chests of drawers, a desk, built-in bookshelves, and a closet almost as big as the bedroom itself.

The space had track lighting, nooks for shoes and girly stuff.

And, of course, there was an adjoining bathroom, just for her.

Liam had figured it would cut down on drama once she hit her teens—thank God it would be a while before *that* happened—and started spending every free moment messing with her hair and putting on makeup.

Cavan's room was the same size as his sister's, masculine in design, with a much smaller closet and a much less elaborate bathroom, but it was still over-the-top fancy, a rich kid's room, with a race car bed as its focal point.

Silently, Liam chided himself for a being a sap.

Spoiling these kids was one of the worst things he could do. He didn't want to screw up their values, make them think the world owed them a living, turn them into self-centered, vapid nobodies with unrealistic expectations of everybody and everything.

His *own* parents were wealthy, but they hadn't raised their sons in luxury, hadn't spoiled them.

They'd had horses, he and his brothers, admittedly a luxury for a lot of kids, but the animals weren't playthings, they were living, sentient beings, to be properly trained and treated with respect and kindness. Like their riders, those horses worked, running fence lines, rounding up strays, hauling cows out of mud holes and from between the slats of cattle guards.

Liam, Jesse and Rhett had had their own rooms, good clothes, not necessarily expensive and definitely not designer. They'd attended public school, done chores every day, played sports, and when they were old enough, the chores got more intense, so they were paid for bucking bales, chopping wood, shoeing horses and driving cattle from one grazing area to another.

With their modest wages, they'd bought used cars, paid for gas and maintenance and insurance out of their own pockets.

Yes, they'd had hefty trust funds, all three of them, but they hadn't been able to access them until they had (1) graduated from college and (2) reached the hopefully sensible age of thirty.

Liam still hadn't touched his, and he doubted his brothers had, either.

In other words, it was okay to be rich, but it didn't give you added value as a person, or entitle you to any kind of special treatment.

How, then, had he gotten so far off track with his own kids?

Liam sighed again, shoved one hand through his hair, and sent the kids to their rooms to think about all the bad things hatred could make a person do.

When he returned to the kitchen, where he and Courtney had been discussing the logistics of filming a movie in Bitter Gulch, she'd gathered up her purse and gone to the back door, which led out onto a large, sheltered patio.

Just beyond its edge, there was a swimming pool, empty as yet, because Liam had been too busy of late to think about filling it.

"I've got some emails to answer," she said quietly. Then, a pause. "You okay, Liam?"

Courtney had been staying in the guest cottage, and she was headed there now.

She'd been a big help with the kids, but she'd wrapped up her meetings, and now she was ready to head back to LA.

Liam gripped the back of a kitchen chair and lowered his head for a moment, breathing deeply and slowly.

"No," he answered finally. "I've totally screwed up this father thing, and we're only a few days in."

Courtney smiled gently. "You haven't screwed up, Liam. And you're being *way* too hard on yourself. You're a good man, and that means you'll be a good father. Maybe even a great one, if you take after your dad."

Liam shook his head. "I don't know," he said.

His father was a hard act to follow.

"Yes, you do," Courtney countered. "Stop tying yourself up in knots. Easy does it, remember?"

"I'm worried about Keely," he confessed, keeping his voice low, even though her room was a half-day's hike from the kitchen. "She reminds me a little too much of her mother sometimes."

Courtney made a scoffing sound, though kindly. "Trust me, Liam, Keely is *not* like Waverly, not in the way you mean. I was *there*, remember? I grew up with Waverly, and I took the brunt of my sister's temper enough times to know there is no comparison between her and Keely."

"What was the matter with Waverly?" Liam asked, of himself as much as Courtney. "She was so beautiful and yet—"

"She was damaged, Liam. I don't know what broke her, but something did, and it must have happened pretty early on, because I don't remember a time when she wasn't a sworn narcissist, and damn proud of it."

"Didn't your parents ever talk about Waverly's—problems?"

"Sometimes, in hushed whispers. But if they know what turned her into what she was, they haven't confided in me. Waverly was the golden child, remember, and they never held her accountable for anything she did. They seemed to believe that she needed to be protected from the big, bad grouchy world, even if that meant throwing their younger daughter—me—under the bus."

Liam forgot his own concerns for the moment, and it was a relief. "It must have been so hard for you. I can't imagine what that would be like, living that way."

Courtney's smile was sad, and she adjusted the shoulder strap of her bag, maybe out of reflex or simple habit, her free hand still resting on the door latch. "Don't feel sorry for me, Liam," she said softly. "I couldn't bear that."

"I don't," he said gruffly.

"Good," she said. She worked the latch, pulled the door open. A cool breeze seeped into the room. "Keely will be fine, if you stand your ground and let her know your love is stable, that you're in this for the long haul. She never had that with Waverly, or with my parents. My theory is, she's testing the boundaries, trying to see what you'll let her get away with, or if you'll just throw up your hands, call it quits and send her back to Seattle."

"I would *never* do that."

"I know, Liam. But Keely doesn't. Sure, you're the man who visited, the man who took her and her brother places, taught her to tie her shoes and say her alphabet and count to a hundred. But you're also the man who wasn't around all that often when Waverly was being—well—*Waverly*. If you prove to Keely that you won't leave her, that you'll be there when she needs you, she'll come around. She wants to love you, Liam, but she needs to know it's safe to do so."

"Court?" Liam straightened his back, released his white-knuckle grip on the chair back.

"What?"

"Thanks."

She grinned, waggled her fingers in farewell. "See you later, cowboy. Gotta get those emails out of the way, and then I might just haul off and take a nap."

"Madison's coming tomorrow," he reminded her in parting. He'd been looking forward to seeing Madison again, taking her horseback riding, grilling burgers for her out on the patio.

Maybe he'd stick a hose in the pool.

"I know," Courtney said. "I like her a lot."

"You'll be here, right?"

Courtney was outside now, standing on the doormat, watching Liam with amusement in her eyes. "No, Liam," she informed him, "I will not. I'd be a third wheel, and you know it."

Liam opened his mouth, but Courtney cut him off before he could say anything.

"It will be you and Madison and the kids. They need to get to know her, and she needs to get to know them. Don't complicate matters by adding to the guest list, okay? Not at this point, anyway."

With that, Courtney closed the door and left.

Liam rubbed the back of his neck.

He went to the other side of the house, stood between his children's closed bedroom doors—they were directly across from each other—and just listened.

He didn't know what he'd expected to hear—crying maybe. Or one of them talking on their cell phone, begging Gambie to come and rescue them from a fate worse than death. As in, living with their father.

But there was nothing.

He rapped lightly on Cavan's door and, getting no answer, quietly opened it.

The kid was sprawled on his stomach, arms out wide, in the middle of his race car bed, sound asleep.

It looked as though he'd been circling the room like an airplane and come in for a crash landing.

Liam smiled, closed the door again and crossed to Keely's side. Knocked softly.

"Come in," Keely said. She sounded almost meek, not testy like before.

Liam opened the door and stood on the threshold, wishing for wisdom, knowing he lacked it sorely. "You're doing okay?" he asked.

Her eyes searched his face, and he felt a crack zigzag its way down the center of his heart.

If he couldn't reach this child, it would be the biggest failure of his life.

"I guess," she said, and bit her lower lip.

"Know what?"

"What?"

"I love you, Keely. And no matter what you do or say, I'm never, *ever* going to give up on you."

She studied him for several long, silent moments, her head tilted a little to one side, her expression thoughtful. Wary.

When she spoke at last, it was as though she'd hurled a live grenade at his middle. "Mom said you *don't* love us. She said you didn't want her, and you didn't want Cavan and me, either, so you divorced *everybody.*"

Liam nearly doubled over at that, but he managed to keep his spine straight and then to sit down on the edge of his daughter's bed.

He wanted to stroke her hair, or cup her chin, or simply take her hand, but he didn't dare do any of those things, because this was a very shaky bridge they were standing upon. One wrong move, one wrong *word*, could send them both hurtling into heartbreak—the kind that lasted a lifetime.

"Listen, sweetheart," Liam began carefully. "Your mother and I had a lot of problems. Some of them were my fault, and some of them were hers. The rest could be blamed on both of us. When your mom told you I didn't love you and Cavan, she was probably angry with me. She knew it wasn't true, but maybe, for some reason we don't understand, she just had to say it."

Hope flashed in Keely's eyes, just for the briefest moment, and then receded.

"You're going to have to prove you love us," she said, sounding, as she often did, like a grown woman only pretending to be a kid. "Cavan will believe it. It's easy to make him believe things. But *I'm* not a little kid. And I'm not stupid. I'm going to know if you mean what you say, or if you're just trying to smooth things over."

Liam was, in that moment, at a complete loss for words.

Keely raised both eyebrows. She didn't speak, either, but the look in her eyes said, *Cat got your tongue?*

But, wait. That was *Waverly* talking, whispering from the back forty of his brain, not Keely.

"Give me a chance, Keely," he said quietly, glad they had a

family therapy session, their first, scheduled for Monday afternoon. "Will you do that?"

Automatically, he braced for a smirk, and had to remind himself all over again that he wasn't dealing with Waverly, but with his daughter, an innocent nine-year-old with reason to question his commitment as a father.

Yes, he'd done his level best to spend as much time as he could with his children over the past few years, as much time as he'd been allowed to, but that hadn't been enough.

To them, he was essentially a Disney dad.

It was discouraging.

He should have fought harder. A *lot* harder.

He came from a long line of honorable, if somewhat rowdy, men and women who didn't turn and run at the first sign of trouble.

Nope. The tougher things got, the deeper they dug their heels into the ground.

So why had he let himself be hornswoggled—by Waverly, by her parents, by Keely herself?

While Liam was thinking all these thoughts, Keely had been watching him. Maybe even considering what he'd said before.

It was probably a stretch to believe she'd actually *listened*.

"I don't want to stay here," she said, striking a second, harder blow, though Liam didn't allow himself a visible reaction. "I want to go back to Seattle. My friends are there. Gambie was going to sign me up with a talent agency."

"Your grandmother is too sick to look after you, Keely. You can stay in touch with your friends easily enough, too—" he paused, indicated her phone, which she was holding like a tiny shield "—via the miracle of technology. And you'll make lots of new friends here."

"I don't care about any of that."

"Well, darlin'," Liam said, "that's too bad. Because you're staying here, with Cavan and me. This is your home, from now on."

"I hate it here," Keely replied.

Liam gave a raspy sigh, searched the ceiling for a long moment, then met the challenge in his daughter's eyes, and just like that, he was back in full McKettrick mode.

Finally.

"I guess that's another thing that's too bad," he said, standing now, ready to leave. "You may have run the show in Seattle, kiddo, but that's not going to be the case here. You're a kid. I'm an adult. You're my daughter, but I'm your father, and that means I call the shots."

Keely's lower lip jutted out. "I can make a lot of trouble if I need to," she threatened.

"Not as much as I can," Liam replied, and he wasn't bluffing.

She reddened.

"I know stuff," she said.

Liam didn't fold, which seemed to surprise her a little. Throw her off her game just a bit.

"So do I," he countered.

"Like what?"

Like that I'm not going to let you behave the way your mother did.

"Like, you're playing in a whole new ball game, kid, and you seem determined to learn the rules the hard way."

"*What* rules?"

"For one, you're going to stop swinging the word 'hate' around like a light saber."

"If I don't?"

One. Two. Three...

"You'll be sorry," Liam responded, after he'd counted all the way to ten in his mind. Before she could ask how, in that snippy tone she so favored, he went on. "You'll be sorry," he repeated, "because you'll be mucking out stalls with a pitchfork, and your phone, iPad and access to my computer will be cut off—for a full week every time I hear that word come out of your mouth. Of course, the TV will be off-limits, too. And the Xbox."

Keely rolled her eyes, but she shrank back a little, too, no longer so confident that she could bulldoze her way through to victory.

"Why are you so against one stupid *word*?" she asked.

"I told you before, it's poisonous. Hate isn't just a word, Keely, it's an *energy*, one that can do a lot of damage. *Irreparable* damage, sometimes."

"You hated Mom. She said so."

"I loved her." *Once. When I thought she was another person entirely.*

"I don't believe you."

"Then you're not as smart as you think you are. I never hated your mother or anybody else. I didn't necessarily *like* her much, a lot of the time. That much is true."

"How can you say you didn't hate her, if you didn't like her?"

All in all, it was a reasonable question, coming from a troubled child facing big changes in her life.

He drew a deep breath, exhaled it slowly. "It's possible to love someone, Keely, and really dislike the things they do and say."

"Is that the way you love me?"

"No," Liam answered, and he meant it. "You're my daughter and I'll love you forever, whether you like it or not. When it comes to your behavior, on the other hand, I haven't been crazy about that. And furthermore, I'm not going to tolerate it, so you might want to rethink your action plan."

Tears welled in Keely's eyes, and Liam wanted to gather her into his arms and hold her close, but he didn't.

He'd drawn an important line in the sand, and he didn't want to minimize that.

"Just go away," she said, rolling onto her stomach and burying her face in her pillows, her small shoulder blades jutting out like a fledgling's wings as she cried.

Liam's throat constricted, and the backs of his eyes burned.

He took his battered heart and quietly left the room.

Outside, on the patio, he hooked up a hose, hung it over the side of the large, empty swimming pool, and then went back to turn on the water.

It would probably take a full twenty-four hours to fill the thing, but maybe by tomorrow afternoon, when the horseback rides were over, they could swim.

Heartened by the prospect of seeing Madison Bettencourt in swimwear, he swung a leg over one of the benches lining the picnic table and took out his phone to text her.

Bring a swimsuit tomorrow, he wrote, using the sides of his thumbs.

Her response didn't take long. Okay. What else?

Just yourself.

Seriously, Liam. How about a green salad? Or some kind of dessert?

Sounds good. *McKettrick*, he thought, *you are a wiz with words.*

What do the kids like?

Cavan likes anything. Keely doesn't.

Madison's answer was a laugh emoji. Sounds ominous. I take it the parenting is as tough as you expected it to be?

Tougher, Liam confirmed. He needed to change the subject, since he hadn't reached out to Madison to whine about his problems. What have you been up to? It's been a few days since we've spoken.

I've been playing Nancy Drew. And visiting Coralee, of course. Before you ask, she's no better.

I'm sorry to hear that. What's this about playing Nancy Drew?

Just something I'm curious about, really. I'll tell you about it in person, when the time is right.

Fair enough. He wasn't ready to let her go. Their contact, tenuous as it was, was a lifeline. It was keeping him afloat. What else have you been doing?

Tackling the weeds in the family cemetery. Haven't gotten past doing the outside edges, though. And I've hired someone to scan some old journals I found in the secret room.

The secret room. I haven't told anybody about it, by the way. Liam added a smile emoji of his own, one wearing a cowboy hat.

Thank you. Telling would defeat the purpose, obviously.

If you need help cleaning up the cemetery, I'll be glad to pitch in. Anything to be near her, to look into her eyes, to hear her laugh.

Seems to me you have enough on your plate without hacking away at weeds and thistle bushes in the hot sun.

There's a method to my madness. I've been threatening my daughter with chores, and given her reaction, I might have to prove I'm serious. And prove I love her, despite what her mother and grandparents have told her about me.

We'll see. I don't want Keely to associate me with punishment, even indirectly.

It's okay, Madison. I'm the one she's going to be mad at. Make that, I'm the one she IS mad at.

She'll come around, Liam. Not that I have any business commenting.

Behind Liam, the patio door slid open.

"Dad?" It was Cavan. Keely hadn't called him that since she was about four years old, and back then, it had been Daddy, not Dad.

He grieved that time, when his daughter had loved and trusted him.

Better go, Liam thumbed. Duty calls.

See you tomorrow. And I am bringing a salad. Maybe a pie, too. Shall I raid the wine cellar as well?

I've got that covered. The wine I mean.

Later, then.

Inwardly, Liam marveled at how much better he felt, even though the text exchange had been pretty low-key.

There was a whole lot more he wanted to say, but he was bound and determined to do things right with Madison. No sense in getting all riled up and blowing his chances with her.

Later, he confirmed, and set his phone aside.

"What's up, buckaroo?" he asked, watching Cavan.

"Can we go riding again?" The boy sounded shy, braced for a no. "Just you and me?"

Liam patted the bench beside him, indicating that Cavan take a seat. "Suppose we just talk for a while?"

"Okay," Cavan replied, but he didn't sound all that enthusiastic.

Liam grinned, ruffled the kid's hair. He looked more like his mother than ever, but he was his own person, even at seven.

Most likely, Keely was her own person, too. He needed to be careful not to think of her as a clone of Waverly; that was unfair.

Sure, the kid was snarky, but she was undergoing some major transitions, and being snarky went with the territory.

She'd been through a lot, and so had Cavan.

If he had to remind himself of that every five minutes, he would.

"Keely said you don't want us," Cavan confided, looking as though he might cry.

Liam sure wanted to right about then.

He wrapped an arm around his son's shoulders and held him close against his side for a few moments. "Keely's upset. She misses her friends. But she's dead wrong about me not wanting you, son. I love you both, with all my heart, and that's not going to change."

Cavan cheered up a little. Even managed a crooked grin. "I guess I miss my friends, too," he confided. "But I missed you a lot more, Dad."

Liam had to look away for a few moments. Blink his eyes.

"No more than I missed you, buddy." The words came out sounding like they'd been coated in gravel, with a few rusty nails in the mix.

Cavan's small, freckled forehead crinkled. "I'm sorry, Dad."

Liam cleared his throat. Tried to brighten up a little. "For what?"

"All those times you wanted us to come live with you, and I said no. It was because Gambie and Keely said I'd be sorry if I left them, because you were always working and I'd be alone all the time."

"Your mom was gone," Liam said gently, "and you were used to living with your grandparents. It would have been hard to be away from your sister, too." Again, he ruffled the boy's hair. "Everything's going to be all right, buddy. So stop worrying, okay?"

"Okay," Cavan replied agreeably.

The kid was so positive. The world's one and only seven-year-old motivational speaker.

"Know what?" Liam asked.

Cavan grinned. It was a silly game, but it was theirs. "What?"

"Chicken butt," Liam answered.

And the sound of the kid's laughter was like a medicine, soothing Liam's troubled heart.

14

At ten the next morning, having been out for an early run and then showered and dressed herself carefully in too-new jeans and a long-sleeved T-shirt, Madison searched the back of her closet for boots, hoping to find leftovers from her riding days at boarding school or in college.

There were none, because, unlike Coralee and her predecessors, Madison didn't save things unless they had sentimental value or might actually continue to be useful in some way.

Therefore, she had to settle for an old pair of Converse, black with grungy white laces.

She was going to look like a rube, out there riding the open range with Liam and the two little McKettricks, who would all be correctly outfitted, she knew, with sturdy gear, as in proper boots. Most likely, the kids would have helmets too.

Sneakers, on the other hand, were a greenhorn's choice; the danger of getting a foot caught in a stirrup and then being dragged over hill, dale, thorn bush and gopher hole was much greater, since the soles were slick and flat.

That was why Western boots had heels, she thought, in self-lecturing mode, even though she didn't usually beat herself up. In Madison's experience, there were plenty of people in the outside world ready to rise to that particular challenge.

After settling a beat-up blue baseball cap on her head and pulling her still-damp-from-the-shower ponytail through the gap in back, she huffed out a sigh, descended the back stairs and collected her purse and the keys to the Bentley from the hooks on the pantry door.

She'd applied sunscreen upstairs, along with a swipe of mascara to her upper lashes, but that was the extent of her makeup.

She wanted to have fun today—she'd be with Liam, and she hadn't ridden a horse in way too long—so she wasn't going for glamor.

Not that she hadn't been tempted, but practicality won out.

This would be an active day, and she would probably sweat.

Perspiration and haute couture cosmetics didn't make for a good mix, so she skipped the Dior and Chanel lipsticks, foundations, blushers and eye shadows she'd bought for her almost-marriage and nonexistent honeymoon.

For now.

Besides, she didn't want Liam to think she wanted him to like what he saw when he looked at her, even though that was true.

Shaking her head at her own nonsense, Madison let herself out the back door, locked it behind her, and crossed the sun-porch to the screen door.

Just for a moment, standing there on the back step, poised to head for the garage, she felt an odd, fluttering sensation in the pit of her stomach, which stopped her where she was.

Madison would have sworn someone was watching her, and she scanned the edge of the woods, eyes narrowed in alert concentration.

She saw nothing, heard nothing.

But the experience yielded one benefit: she had a few moments to remember the salad she'd made earlier, and the coconut cake she'd baked the night before.

She went back inside to collect them, both already packed in their specially designed plastic containers, carried them as far as the battered jute doormat, and set them down on a bench long enough to relock the back door.

The sense of another person lurking just out of sight had passed by then, and Madison put it out of her mind.

Today promised to be a very good day, and she meant to enjoy every minute of it. She made sure the sealed salad bowl and the cake carrier were stationary in the back seat of the Bentley, buzzed open the garage door, got into the car and backed out.

And nearly ran right over a small gray dog, sitting with forlorn resignation in the middle of her driveway.

Madison muttered, jammed the Bentley into Park, shut off the engine and got out to approached the little dog, slowing her steps so she wouldn't scare him—or her—any more than she already had.

"Hey, fella," she crooned, crouching. "Where did *you* come from?"

The dog's eyes were mournful, and Madison felt a sharp pinch in her heart.

He—or she—looked considerably the worse for wear, fur matted, nails overgrown, tongue lolling.

There was no collar, so no tags.

"Looks like you've been on your own for a while," Madison said gently, tentatively stretching out a hand to pat the dog's head. "Wait here while I get you some water and something to eat, okay?"

The dog gave a tiny whimper, but didn't move.

For the second time that morning, Madison went back into the house.

There, she grabbed some sliced lunch meat from the refrigerator and filled a bowl with water, then hurried outside again.

She'd feared the little critter would be gone, but there it was.

She crouched again, set down the water bowl, tore the lunch meat into bite-size pieces with her fingers.

The dog drank lustily, obviously parched, and ate the offered lunch meat from the palm of Madison's hand.

Now that the poor thing was standing on all fours, she saw that it was male.

What to do now?

She glanced at her watch. She was due at Liam's place in twenty minutes, but she couldn't just leave the pup out here alone, and she wasn't comfortable confining him to the house, either. He'd be lonesome, and heaven only knew what damage he might do.

Madison made a quick decision.

She picked the dog up in her arms and set him in the front passenger seat, since the cake and salad were in back.

Then she took her phone from her purse and texted Liam.

I'm going to be a little late. I found this dog in my driveway a few minutes ago, and I'm taking him to the vet.

Liam's response was gratifyingly prompt. See you when you get here. In the meantime, do what you need to do.

Thanks, she tapped out. Hopefully, this won't take long.

With that, the "text-versation," as Audra had dubbed such exchanges, ended, and Madison and the dog were headed for town.

Along the way, Madison considered stopping at the town's one animal shelter and dropping off the dog. It was a good shelter, one Coralee had supported for as long as Madison could remember, and one she'd contributed to as well, but something made her choose the local veterinarian's clinic instead.

Fifteen minutes later, Madison and the dog were in an examining room.

A vet's assistant ran a hand scanner over the back of the little guy's neck, shook her ponytailed head. "Nope," she said, looking resigned. "No chip."

Madison sagged at the news. She'd been hoping to witness, or at least *set in motion*, an ecstatic reunion between pet and owner.

She rallied within a few seconds. This was reality, not a Disney movie.

"I've got to be somewhere else for a few hours. Can you ask the doc to check him over?"

"Sure." The girl smiled. "We have a groomer on staff now. What do you say we clean this bad boy up a little, too?"

Madison smiled back, relieved. "That would be great." A pause. "Does he need to be neutered?"

Again, the assistant shook her head. She was petite, and probably in her twenties, though to Madison, she looked only slightly older than Keely McKettrick.

A sure sign that she, Madison, was getting old.

That brought her upcoming fertility consultation to mind.

Her first appointment was a month away, the earliest opening available.

Maybe she should just adopt this dog, if he wasn't claimed soon.

It wouldn't be the same as having a real, *human* baby, but it would almost certainly be a heck of a lot easier.

Inwardly, Madison shot down *that* idea.

A biological child, just one child, was what she wanted most in all the world, all the *universe*. After that, she could foster children, or adopt, or whatever. She would love them all the same, of course, but she wanted the *experience* of carrying and delivering a baby.

"What do you call him?" the assistant asked, jolting Madison back to the here and now with a bang.

For a second, she thought the girl had read her mind, that she was asking about the baby Madison intended to have.

Then she realized that wasn't possible.

And the dog certainly deserved a name, especially when you considered all he'd probably been through before he'd found his way to the middle of Bettencourt Hall's gravel driveway.

"Charlie," Madison decided aloud, having plucked the moniker out of the ether. "His name is Charlie."

The assistant was still grinning. She gathered the dog up into her arms, held him securely and said, "Let's get you all spiffed up, Charlie."

Charlie whined softly as the girl carried him out of the exam room, yearning for Madison with his eyes.

Madison just stood there for the length of several heartbeats—she could almost feel the steady *thud* of them against her breast bone—wondering what she'd just gotten herself into, taking a dog into her home. Into her life.

What if it turned out to be a mistake?

She bit her lower lip as she returned to the front office, swiped her credit card for any and all charges that might arise, and, after washing her hands in the rest room, set out for her original destination.

Fifteen minutes later, she pulled up in front of one of the most amazing houses she'd ever seen, and that was saying something, considering the places she'd been and the people she'd known.

Liam's place, magnificently simple, sat surrounded by greenery—young maple and oak trees, and beyond that, grasslands and more trees, and in the near distance, the rolling foothills trailing off from their brethren, the Rockies.

The little boy—Cavan, she recalled—came bounding out of the house, and Madison stopped the Bentley a little farther from the grand, pillared portico than she would have otherwise, for safety's sake.

Cavan McKettrick was all smiles, and he'd grow up to be a

heartbreaker, Madison thought, even though he didn't really resemble his handsome father.

"Did you bring the dog?" he cried, almost breathless with excitement.

Liam came out of the house, grinning, looking five kinds of delicious in his worn jeans, T-shirt and scuffed boots. His longish dark hair gleamed in the sun like a raven's wing.

Keely stood behind him, on the threshold, watching intently. She didn't approach, or speak.

"I had to leave Charlie at the veterinarian's office for today," Madison explained to the boy, smiling as she opened the back door of the Bentley, on the driver's side, and reached in for the large plastic container of green salad.

It was a dandy, laced with every fresh vegetable she'd had in the fridge, and the dressing was her own super-secret special recipe.

"Carry this for me?" she asked, noting the polite disappointment in the child's face. He'd really wanted to meet Charlie.

"Sure," Cavan said gamely, holding out both hands.

Madison handed him the salad.

"Is he sick?" the boy asked earnestly. "Your dog, I mean?"

"I don't think so," Madison answered, with a gentle shake of her head. A strange new tenderness welled up inside her as she looked into Cavan's fretful little face, and she realized she could love this child, given half a chance. "He's been lost a while, it seems, so he needs some extra help."

By then, Liam was there.

The sight of him, and his soap-and-sunshine scent, made Madison a little dizzy.

She tugged the brim of her baseball cap down a little further over her eyes, hoping he hadn't noticed her reaction to him.

It was physical, yes. But it was so much more.

She was glad she'd given the salad to Cavan to carry, because she might have dropped it right there in the driveway if she hadn't.

Liam let his gaze slide from her face to her sneakers.

The glance was not invasive, just appreciative.

"Bad choice of shoes," he commented dryly.

"I didn't bring riding boots," she replied, feeling foolish, bending to grab the cake carrier while she scrambled to regain her wavering dignity. "When I came back to Painted Pony Creek, I mean. They wouldn't have matched my wedding gown."

Liam chuckled, and the sound affected Madison like an intimate caress.

She shivered, and it was a pleasurable sensation, one she'd never experienced before. Damn, but this man, it seemed, could make love to her using his eyes and his voice. No hands required.

He took the cake carrier. "Come on," he urged, reaching out to close the rear door of the Bentley, almost as if he expected her to jump back in the car, scramble over the seat, to get behind the wheel, and speed out of there. "Let's put this food away and see what we can come up with in the way of boots. I'm thinking Courtney's might fit you—she has a couple of pairs, I think."

For a reason she couldn't have explained, Madison blushed.

It wasn't as if Liam had offered to loan her some of Courtney's underwear, for pity's sake.

And that was when she remembered.

"I forgot my swimming suit," she blurted.

Liam actually laughed then. "Chill, as my kids would say. If necessary, we can drive back to your place later on and fetch it."

Madison relaxed just a little. Looked around.

The property was gorgeous, and the house resembled something out of *Town & Country* or *Architectural Digest*. For all she knew, it might have been, or soon would be, featured in one or both publications.

It was that beautiful and that unique.

Like the man who'd designed and built it.

"Is Courtney around?" Madison asked lightly. She didn't want to give him the impression that she felt competitive or anything like that.

Liam shook his head.

They were approaching the front doorway by that time, and Keely receded into the shadows, like a very colorful little ghost.

"I invited Court to join us on the ride, but she's leaving for LA pretty soon, so she wanted time to pack and all that. I'll send Keely to ask her about a swimming suit and the boots, though."

Madison felt embarrassed. Unprepared.

It wasn't a thing like her.

She followed him into the house, and as they passed through the spacious, light-filled rooms, Madison couldn't help comparing the place to Bettencourt Hall, not in a better-or-worse way, but simply because the contrast was so plain.

Coralee's house was gigantic, of course, and elegant to the nth degree, but the rooms there didn't have the airy, wide-open feel of those here.

Cavan ran ahead of them, clutching the salad container to his middle with both hands and yelling, "Keely! Dad wants you to ask Aunt Courtney for a swimsuit and some boots!"

Liam laughed, a low, affectionate sound that warmed something in Madison she hadn't realized was cold, and shook his head.

When they reached the kitchen, Keely was there, standing by the long, rustic wooden table, with benches on both sides and chairs at either end.

She was wearing blue jeans and a pink tank top, and her arms were folded across her little-girl chest.

Madison knew the girl was nine years old, but she was petite, and her size gave her the look of an even younger child.

Her face, however, wore a grown-up expression, one of wariness and suspicion.

"Hello, Madison," she said, without the slightest hint of welcome. Her attitude was faintly hostile, in fact. "Cavan said you need to borrow boots and something to swim in."

Inwardly, Madison sighed, and her smile wobbled a little on her mouth, though she managed to hold on to it, not let it slip away.

Cavan was clearly an easygoing child.

His sister, on the other hand...

"That's right," Madison managed to say.

Out of the corner of her eye, she saw Liam's jaw harden, just for the briefest of moments. "Keely," he said, and there was a warning in his tone, moderate but still definite.

Keely still looked obstinate, but something flickered in her incredibly beautiful, almost purple eyes. She sighed, and her little shoulders sagged briefly.

Madison felt sorry for the girl, and made up her mind not to let that show.

Liam's daughter was hurting, however hard she might try to disguise the fact, and Madison would have hugged her, under any other circumstances but these. Putting her arms around this child, as a virtual stranger and quite possibly a threat, would have been like embracing a porcupine.

It was too soon for any of that, naturally. Too soon to say, *I know how you feel, little one, because I've been there myself. I never really knew my mom and dad, and my grandmother loved me from a proper distance.*

Watching Keely, Madison remembered when she'd been sent away to boarding school when she was only a few years older than this defiant child.

Even now, years later, that "proper distance" still separated her from her grandmother, as much as she loved that compli-cated, rapidly diminishing old woman.

Keely looked at her father, sighed loudly. "Boots and a swim-suit," she affirmed, her tone as glum as her manner as she turned toward the back door. "But Aunt Courtney is smaller than you are, so her stuff probably won't fit you."

"Keely, that's mean," Cavan objected.

"True that," Liam said, plainly annoyed.

Keely stiffened momentarily, then opened the door and bolted for the guest house, just visible from where Madison stood, feeling as though she'd blown it somehow.

As the child ran past the pool, she came so close to the edge that Madison flinched, thinking she might fall in.

"I'm sorry," Liam said. He sounded tired. Incredibly so.

"Don't be," Madison answered, having pulled herself together enough to put on a happy face. "I'm not that easy to offend."

Cavan drew close to Madison's side, leaned in a little. Looked up at her with wide, questioning eyes. "Are you anybody's mom?" he asked.

The question pierced Madison's heart, and she felt as though she were hanging from her own smile by the tips of her fingers. In other words, just barely.

"No," she said, and though the smile held, she knew there was sadness in her voice. "I haven't been that lucky."

Liam looked at her with curious concern, though he shook that off quickly and assumed that devastatingly mischievous grin of his.

As it turned out, Courtney's borrowed boots *were* a little tight, but the bathing suit, a blue-and-white-striped one-piece, looked as though it would work well enough.

"Thank you, Keely," Madison had said, when the girl shoved the items into her hands, after dragging her feet all the way back from the guest house.

"You're welcome," Keely muttered begrudgingly.

Liam opened his mouth to protest, but Madison stopped him by holding up one palm and giving him a look.

"Let's ride," he said, after a brief silence. "The horses are saddled and ready to go."

"I helped Dad put the saddles on," Cavan announced, beaming.

"Get your helmets," Liam said, and both kids left the kitchen, one eager to obey, the other reluctance personified.

Madison sat down on the nearest bench, facing away from the table, kicked off her Converse and tugged on Courtney's boots.

"This table," she commented, mostly to make conversation about anything other than Keely's attitude. "It's different from the rest of your furniture. Not so modern."

Liam grinned, grabbing two bottles of water from the huge, gleaming refrigerator and setting one down next to Madison's elbow. "That's because it's an antique. Belonged to my grandfather, Angus McKettrick, several greats back. He was a *genuine* cowboy, the real deal, and so were his four sons—my branch of the family is descended from one of them."

"Which one?" Madison asked, even though she hadn't a clue who Angus McKettrick might have been, much less his sons, and no matter what answer Liam gave, it wouldn't enlighten her. She just liked hearing his voice, and little tidbits about his background, such as this.

"Jeb," Liam answered. "He was the youngest."

Madison stood, shifted her weight from foot to foot, making sure she could wear Courtney's boots without setting herself up for long-term podiatry.

"How much do you know about them?" she asked. Her tone was light, but she really wanted to hear the reply.

Liam shrugged. "A lot, actually. But we're about to mount up and ride, and my mind's on that. If you still want to hear the tall tales, I'll tell you everything you want to know, but for right now, I'd rather concentrate on the fact that you're here, and we're going to ride together."

Madison grinned. "I'm going to need a whole bag of Epsom salts in my bath tonight," she told him. "I haven't ridden in several years."

Liam smiled. Placed his hand lightly on the small of her back, gently steering her toward the front of the house.

"You'll be fine," he said with quiet confidence.

And she *was* fine.

The horse Liam had chosen for her was a spirited little bay mare named Coco.

His own mount, whom he introduced as Xerxes, was a large black gelding, who presented himself, it seemed to horse-loving Madison, as a stallion. He was proud, this animal, and his coat shone like Liam's hair in the sunshine.

Cavan rode a small pinto named Scooby, and Keely's horse was a pretty palomino she called Lady. Both kids mounted up without assistance, and Madison, who had surprised herself a bit by swinging effortlessly into the saddle, without help from Liam, was impressed with both of them.

Keely sat straight-backed, and though her saddle was Western, she was clearly used to dressage, like Madison herself.

Liam gave his children instructions to stay in sight and not to run their horses, and they trotted off, through the pasture gate and onto the open range.

Way off in the distance, there were cattle grazing, a mixture of Herefords and Black Angus.

Madison beamed, standing in the stirrups, filling her lungs with a greedy plentitude of fresh air.

Liam, still on foot, shut the big gate behind them, latched it, and then mounted Xerxes with the ease of someone who'd literally learned to ride before he could walk. And maybe he had, growing up on a ranch.

"This place is beyond beautiful," Madison said, taking in the staggering view.

"I think so," Liam agreed quietly. Then, with a sidelong glance, his eyes dancing, he asked, "Just how out of practice are you, Madison Bettencourt?"

"A lot," she replied honestly, "but not so much that I wouldn't challenge you to a race."

He laughed. "A race, is it? It's only fair to warn you, Xerxes and I are a pretty good team." He pointed to a lone pine tree standing way off in the distance. "Let's see if you can keep up, City Girl."

Such joy welled up inside Madison that she threw back her head and laughed into the blue, blue sky. Then she loosened the reins, leaned forward in the saddle, and nudged Coco's gleaming, muscular sides with the heels of Courtney's boots.

The mare blasted off like a rocket, reaching a full-out run in three strides, and the race was on.

Liam and Xerxes kept pace easily—his was clearly the more powerful horse—and Madison knew they were both holding back, Liam willingly, Xerxes under protest.

Tears of pure happiness blurred Madison's vision as she and Coco dashed through the deep grass, bounding headlong toward that single, solitary tree, which was still far away.

She looked sideways, watching Liam traveling alongside her.

He was as magnificent as his horse, so at home in that saddle that he almost seemed to be *part* of Xerxes.

Cavan and Keely, meanwhile, had both stopped to watch.

Cavan was cheering, while Keely smiled, most likely in spite of herself.

Just as they reached the tree, Liam reined in his horse, and Madison and Coco shot ahead to victory, circling the tree, coming back around to face Liam, who grinned and resettled his hat while Xerxes pranced beneath him, probably disgruntled.

"You let us win!" Madison accused, exhilarated. Standing in the stirrups once more as she and Coco rode in circles so the mare could cool down.

Liam adjusted his hat again. It was a simple gesture, but one that Madison knew she would always associate with him, whether their time together was short or long.

"You said it yourself. You're out of practice," he reminded her.

Dear heaven, his eyes were so *impossibly* blue.

Cavan and Keely trotted over to join them, and Madison thought she caught a look of respect as the girl took her in.

"You can really ride," Keely said, watching Madison as she finally brought Coco to a stop and leaned forward to pat the animal's sweaty neck.

"Thanks," Madison replied lightly, because she didn't want to make this into a big deal. "I was around your age when I started."

Cavan looked at his father. "Dad won't let us race," he said.

Liam rode close to the boy and plopped his hat onto his son's head, covering both his helmet and his eyes.

When Liam took it back, Cavan's mood had shifted back to its usual mode of innocent goodwill. *"Dad,"* he crowed. "Why do you always *do* that?"

Liam rested a hand on his chest, seemed to recede a little in the saddle. "Do what?" he asked guilelessly.

"Put your hat on my head like that!"

"Couldn't say," Liam replied, in the same *who, me?* tone of voice. "Guess it's a mystery."

Cavan looked happily exasperated.

Even Keely was smiling, though there was something cautious about her expression, too. As though simple happiness wasn't to be trusted.

Madison felt another pang of sympathy, wondering what this girl had been through before she and Cavan had come to live with their father.

Keely caught her looking, and the smile slowly faded.

After that, they rode, the four of them, never exceeding a trot.

Perhaps an hour had passed when Liam suggested they head back and get the barbecue started. While the coals were heating up, he said, they could cool off in the pool.

Of course the horses had to be attended to first, and Madison enjoyed that process almost as much as the ride. When it came to taking off the saddle and bridle and wiping the animal down with a sponge dipped in lukewarm water, muscle memory kicked in. She could literally have taken care of Coco in her sleep, and that made her feel strong again, in charge of her own destiny even.

At what point, she wondered, had she begun to feel weak?

She never had, actually. But she'd lost the particular sense of confidence riding gave her, and rubbing down the horse was like balm to her spirit.

The ride had been more than an hour or so of fun.

It had been therapeutic.

It had brought her back to herself, which was a revelation, since she hadn't realized until then that she'd wandered away in the first place.

The sense of homecoming, of belonging right there in her own skin, was transformative.

Once the horses had been turned out into the pasture for the rest of the day, Liam, Madison, Keely and Cavan returned to the house.

Madison was shy about putting on the borrowed bathing suit, thinking her legs were white and she should have gone over them with a razor that morning in the shower, but soon she was in the pool with the others, splashing in the still-icy water.

Liam admitted he'd filled the pool just the day before, which meant it really hadn't had time to warm up much.

He'd added the proper chemicals, though, so the water was clean, and a pretty turquoise color, drawing blue from the famous Big Sky arching over them like the dome of some celestial cathedral.

Madison was practically bursting with the simple joy of it all.

And that scared her a little, deep down, because in her experience, every peak led to a valley.

15

Bliss

It was very dark.

There was a strange, silent hum in the air around Bliss, out-side of her at first, but then it seeped into her somehow, caught in her middle with a hard yank and a roar she felt rather than heard. It was if she'd swallowed Duke's greasy old chainsaw whole, and it was about to cut her in two.

Panic didn't pay. She'd learned *that* lesson long ago, though knowing she shouldn't freak out didn't always help her stay calm. Sometimes, it just took the edge off so she could think.

Tonight, standing beside her narrow bed in Katherine Betten-court's spare room, just down a back hallway from the kitchen, she shivered, even though she was wearing a flannel night-gown, cut down and stitched back together to fit her, like the dress she'd worn to church the previous morning, and it was a steamy hot night.

She didn't hear voices or anything like that, but she felt a strong pull toward the yard, the woods, the little cemetery she knew lay hidden among the trees.

It felt like somebody had tied a rope around her middle, ready to lead her to somewhere she might or might not want to go, and they were pulling hard, leaning-back-on-their-heels hard.

Bliss knew she wouldn't be able to resist, and she was both scared and intrigued.

She'd hidden her worn-out tennis shoes under the bed so Katherine wouldn't burn them, like she had the shorts and top she'd been wearing when she found herself in this new place, sitting by the creek with her knees drawn up, and with Jack Bettencourt and his dog coming toward her, looking none too welcoming.

Bliss pulled on her sneakers—they were falling apart, for sure, but they were better than the shoes she'd been given to go with the church dress. Katherine had dug those out of a trunk in the attic, and they were at least a size too small.

If she needed to run, either to something or away from it, she'd be a lot better off in her own shoes.

She tied the frayed laces carefully, tightly, in case they came undone and sent her sprawling to the floor. *That* would surely wake up both Jack and his mother, and then she'd be stuck in the house, expected to explain what she was doing out of bed in the middle of the night.

The invisible rope would still pull on her, but she wouldn't be able to follow where it wanted to take her, because Katherine would definitely object to that.

The moon was just a sliver of silver, transparent and offering very little light; Bliss had seen it when she'd looked out the window just before she'd climbed into bed.

She bit down on her lower lip, thinking hard.

Wishing for a flashlight.

Here in *Little-House-on-the-Prairie*-ville, there was no such thing.

She considered swiping a candle, or even the kerosene lantern in the middle of the kitchen table, but decided against both, because the candle would just blow out when the first hint of a breeze came up, and the lantern scared her.

If it tipped over, she might set the woods—or herself—on fire.

So, she decided, she'd wing it.

Find her way as best she could.

When she stepped out onto the back steps, careful to close the door quietly behind her, she realized she literally couldn't see her hand in front of her face.

She waited. Blinked. Waited some more.

And her eyes began to adjust. Even here, she thought, in what seemed like absolute darkness, there was light. It must have come from the stars, scattered across the sky like diamonds.

A shuffling beside the steps, followed by a huge dog-yawn, told her that Hobo was there, probably keeping watch. Sneaking out of the house was one thing, Bliss realized, but sneaking back in would be another, with him on the job.

"Hobo," she whispered, her tone urgent, "it's me. Bliss."

Hobo made a low, uncertain sound, way down in his throat. It was probably intended as a growl, but it came out more like a rumbly whimper. A canine question.

Bliss prayed the dog wouldn't bark, though barking would have been pretty logical right about then, she reminded herself. It was Hobo's *job* to make noise when somebody or something was moving around in the night—or at any other time—wasn't it?

"Shhhh," she said, sitting down on the high threshold and patting his head. "Everything's okay. I'm just going for a little walk, that's all."

A little walk. In the middle of an almost moonless night.

Sure, Bliss.

Heck, even a *dog* wouldn't believe that.

Especially not a dog.

"Come with me," Bliss whispered. "Something's pulling on

me, and I've gotta go." She paused, bit her lower lip again, scanned the shadowy edge of the woods.

At the moment, following this strange inner leading didn't make a whole lot of sense, but then, neither did falling down and hitting your head in one version of the world and coming to in another, and that had happened.

Unless she was dreaming.

Or in a coma.

Or dead.

Bliss leaned over and pressed her face into Hobo's furry neck.

In some ways, the new place was harder to live in.

There were no light switches, no cars, not even blue jeans, which Bliss missed more than her shorts and too-small top from Goodwill. Water had to be lugged up out of the well in a bucket and carried inside. Wood had to be chopped and carried in for the cook stove, and those things were just the *beginning* of the constant work it took just to live out an ordinary day.

In spite of all that, though, Bliss loved the new place.

If she was dreaming, or in a coma, she didn't want to wake up.

If she was dead, well, this must be heaven.

The air was so fresh, the sky so blue, the grass so green.

And here, with the Bettencourts, she always had enough to eat. *More* than enough, in fact.

She slept in a real bed, not on a bare mattress like back there, in a room half again as big as Duke's whole stupid camper, and, best of all, Mrs. Bettencourt—Katherine—seemed to genuinely care what happened to Bliss, referring to her as "the little visitor," smiling at her, gently combing the tangles out of her hair, tucking her in at night and kissing her forehead.

Thinking of all that, Bliss felt her eyes start to burn, and her vision blurred.

Hobo, loosely tied, panted in her face.

His breath wasn't the best.

The pull of that unseen rope hadn't eased off, and even though

Bliss could make a much better case for staying than for going, dog or no dog at her side, she sensed there was a *reason* for the strong tug at her middle.

At least the chainsaw had shut down, though she was still nervous. No getting around that.

"Come on," she repeated in a loud whisper, and started toward the woods.

Toward the cemetery.

She had no idea why anyone, especially her, should be drawn to a graveyard in the dark, but that was where she needed to go.

Hobo walked along beside her, but slightly ahead, acting as a Seeing Eye dog for someone who wasn't even blind.

She might as well have been, though.

Thistles snagged her nightgown as she made her way through the dense underbrush, and Bliss was glad she'd brought Hobo along for company. He'd probably run off and leave her if a bear or a cougar showed up, but his presence was soothing, all the same.

When they reached the little cemetery, the very one where she and Madison had met for the first time, Bliss still didn't know why she'd come there, though she had a strange sense of satisfaction, even accomplishment, as though she'd cleared the way for something new and important to happen.

It was still dark out, and Hobo was still beside her, which probably meant she was still in the new place. The place where she belonged, where she was wanted, looked after, maybe even loved.

She sat where she had so often sat before, in the other time and place, on top of that low, blocky headstone.

Hobo let out a little whine and plunked himself down at her feet.

The pull on Bliss's middle had stopped, but the buzzing sound was back.

She felt herself slipping. Dissolving.

When she opened her eyes, she had a terrible headache.

It was daylight instead of night.

And Hobo was gone.

Another mystery.

There was no sign of Madison, which was kind of a letdown, even though Bliss hadn't really been expecting to see her friend again.

Hard to say what she *had* been expecting.

She sat there for a long time, waiting for the buzzing to stop, and for her stomach to stop doing backflips against her spine.

When she'd recovered enough, she stood, teetered a little as she waited for her legs to stop shaking, and then sort of stumbled off into the surrounding trees.

She found the creek, knelt and splashed water on her face.

That was when she noticed that the leafy trees had turned from soft greens to blazing yellows, oranges and crimsons.

Fall. It was *fall*.

Somehow, she'd stepped right out of summer, into autumn.

There was a crisp nip in the air, too, she noticed.

Bliss shook her head, more confused than she'd ever been before.

What was happening to her?

She just plain didn't know, and wondering made her headache worse, so she tried to stop the thoughts racing around and around in her brain, making her dizzy all over again.

Bliss made her way through the woods, staying close to the creek, comforted by its busy, rustling whisper. It hurried along, over rocks and tree roots, as if it were trying to keep up with her.

When she reached the clearing, the camper was there again.

Duke's truck was parked next to it, and he was inside, leaning forward, passed out on the steering wheel. His dark red hair fanned out around the bald spot on top of his head like a clown wig.

Bliss wanted to cry.

The man was her father, but she would have given anything to be far away from him, back in the other, better place, with Katherine and Jack and poor Hobo, wherever he'd disappeared to. Maybe Hobo *hadn't* vanished, though. Maybe he'd just gone off and left her, chasing a rabbit or a squirrel.

Bliss crept past the truck, grateful not to come face-to-face with Duke. He was bound to be in a bad mood; he always was when he'd been on one of his benders.

As she moved, she let herself think about how it was daylight here, when it had been dark in the woods with Hobo.

How could that be?

Maybe she *wasn't* dreaming, or in a coma, or dead.

Maybe she was crazy.

She groped for another possibility. Had she fallen asleep in the cemetery, of all places? Slept the night away?

That didn't explain her clothes.

And it sure didn't change the fact that she'd been smack in the middle of a summer night one minute and in a cool autumn day the next.

The dizziness returned, worse than ever, and once again, Bliss almost threw up, but she stopped herself, because she didn't dare make any noise.

Puking was usually a loud business, and Duke, dead to the world as he was, might hear.

Resolved to hold steady, she crept into the camper, looked around.

It was the same as ever: cramped, messy, smelling of stale beer, cigarette smoke, and sweat.

Crap, she thought.

What was she even doing here? Why hadn't she stayed in the cemetery, waited for Hobo to come back, or for Madison to turn up?

The thought of Madison reminded Bliss of why she'd come here, to this stinky camper.

She definitely wanted to go back to wherever she'd been be-fore, with Katherine and Jack and his dog. But she'd *also* wanted, all along, to say goodbye to Madison, the only friend she'd ever had, besides her Gran.

Sure, there was Jack, but he could be ornery, and it was pos-sible he wasn't even real.

Heck, maybe Madison wasn't real, either.

Maybe *she*, her own self, wasn't real.

Quickly, because Duke might come to at any moment and stumble-bum it into the camper, looking for a fight.

He was always furious after a binge, acting as though some-one had forced him to drink himself stupid, and he'd been help-less to stop them.

Duke had never been one to admit he might be in the wrong.

Bliss shook off the memories of her father's crazy rage and scrabbled through empty pizza boxes and other garbage until she found two things, a pen and a used matchbook.

She opened the matchbook, wrote *goodbye* on the inside of the flap, pressing hard so there would be no mistaking what she'd written. Then she'd tucked the matchbook into the pocket of her shorts.

She found her shoebox, where she kept her treasures—a few pretty pebbles, some colorful postage stamps Gran had given her to keep, a birthday card Mona had given her once when she'd come down with a brief case of motherly love, and the best thing of all, a friendship bracelet, made of colored thread.

She'd woven it herself, one lonely afternoon, hoping she'd have a real friend to give it to someday.

Bliss took that from the shoebox, stuffed the box in the back of the only cabinet in the camper, and sneaked out into the sun-shine and fresh air.

Duke was still passed out on the steering wheel.

She tiptoed past the truck again, and her unconscious father, and once she'd cleared both man and vehicle by a dozen feet or so, she broke into a run.

She *tore* between the trees, through the bushes that scratched her legs and snagged her clothes.

Once again, she was grateful to be wearing her sneakers, instead of those funny black shoes Katherine had scrounged up for her from some trunk in her attic.

She wouldn't have gotten far in those.

But *was* there a house at all, with or without an attic?

Was there a Katherine?

Bliss wondered as she ran.

Her head still pounded, and her stomach was rolling around inside her like it had come loose from whatever muscles usually held it in place, but she didn't slow down.

Duke was a big man, with a beer belly, but when he was mad, he could run *real* fast, and Bliss knew he could have woken up, seen her speeding for the woods, and decided to catch up with her, grab her by the hair, and drag her back to the camper.

He'd done it plenty of times before.

But this time was different, in more ways than one.

It was daytime, and it wasn't summer, like it had been when Katherine had kissed her good-night just a few hours ago, but full-on fall.

Either the whole universe had gone crazy, Bliss thought, or she had.

Back in the cemetery, she took the matchbook and the thread bracelet from her pocket, secured the bracelet by tucking it behind the few remaining matches, and set the works on top of the gravestone she had been sitting on earlier.

Afraid both things might blow away since they were so light, Bliss found a mossy rock and used that to hold them in place.

Then she sat down, on the ground this time, with her back to the gravestone, and waited for whatever was going to happen next.

By then, the headache was so bad, she could barely stand it. Her stomach quivered violently.

She closed her eyes.

And she must have slept for a long time, because when she opened them again, the headache was gone, it was dark out, and Hobo was licking her face.

16

Sweet exhaustion flooded Madison, body and soul, as she leaned against the counter in Liam's kitchen, back in her regular clothes, her hair still damp from the pool, her stomach threatening to burst with all the food she'd eaten—barbecued chicken, salad, corn on the cob, baked beans and, unbelievably, dessert.

The kids were in another part of the house, taking showers, changing clothes—in general, getting ready for an early bedtime, since they'd expended a lot of energy that day. The swim, especially, had left both Cavan and Keely yawning.

For the first time since she'd arrived, Madison was alone with Liam.

It was a delicious interlude, with him standing close to her, so close that with another half step, his hard, strong body would be pressing against her softer one.

At some point, Madison knew, sex with this man would be inevitable, but for the moment, they were both dealing in restraint.

The kids were in the house, after all.

And it was still early in the game.

Madison was no virgin—she'd been married, and had several serious relationships between her first husband and Jeffrey, her discarded groom—and it seemed that her whole self was straining to be with Liam, to join with him, not just physically, but on a much deeper level.

Sex almost seemed superfluous, compared with all that might be possible between them, much of it a mystery still, and yet so enticing as to be patently irresistible.

This was a journey she had to take, wherever it might lead.

Liam kissed her, very lightly.

"We have to wait," she told him in a whisper, licking her lips with the tip of her tongue in an effort to take that kiss inside her, taste it, swallow it, hide it away in her heart.

Liam groaned, his voice low and thick. "I know," he agreed, with the utmost reluctance. "But I don't have to like it."

She laughed, then moved her arm between them, consulted her watch.

It was after six, and the vet's office, where she'd left Charlie for a badly needed physical update, would close at six thirty.

"I have to go and pick up my dog," she said. "Wouldn't want him to think I've ditched him."

Liam smiled, tucked a lock of her moist hair behind her ear. "For a runaway bride," he teased, "you place a high value on loyalty."

She arched an eyebrow, grinned a little, soaking in the warmth of him, the nearness of him, the sweet safety she found in his presence.

"Was that a jibe?"

Liam shook his head. "Just an observation," he replied.

Madison drew a deep breath, exhaled. "Maybe I'm too loyal for my own good," she informed him. "And I don't think of myself as a runaway bride. I think of myself as a woman who came to her senses just in time to avoid certain disaster."

His smile widened, tilting up on one side, somehow accentuating the chiseled lines of his handsome face. Before he could say anything, though, they heard footsteps pounding in their direction, approaching fast.

They drew apart just as Cavan came sliding into the kitchen like a runner making a mad dash for home plate. He was wearing Spiderman pajamas.

"Good!" he almost shouted, beaming at Madison. "You aren't gone yet!"

"I'm still here," she confirmed, and some of her baby fever, always with her, the pulsing subtext to almost everything she did, melted away. Yes, she could definitely love this child; perhaps she already did, just a little.

"I wanted to say good-night," Cavan told her, rapid-fire, almost breathless with relief. "And say thank you for the salad and the cake and could you please let me meet your dog Charlie real soon?"

Madison laughed. "Good night to you, too, Cavan McKettrick," she said, "and thank *you* for your hospitality, you're very, very welcome and yes, you can definitely meet Charlie, and soon." She glanced at Liam for confirmation, thinking she might have overstepped by offering an introduction to the dog she barely knew herself, and he gave her the slightest nod of approval.

Cavan gave an ear-splitting shout of pure joy.

Liam winced, made a big deal of covering his ears with his hands. *"Buddy,"* he said. "Dial it down just a little, okay? That yell went through my head like a spear!"

"Okay," Cavan agreed charitably. "When can I see Charlie?"

"When Madison and I have talked about it and decided on the best option," Liam responded. Then he reached out, mussed his son's dark hair with one hand, and sent him off to finish getting ready for bed, promising they'd read a story together later.

After Cavan had retreated to do as he'd been asked, Liam walked Madison outside and across the front yard to the Bentley.

That was when she realized she hadn't taken Cavan for the ride she'd promised the day they all met up on the sidewalk in front of Bailey's.

She'd left the cake and salad containers behind since there were leftovers inside, but she wasn't going to worry about that.

Loose ends usually bothered Madison, even the smallest ones, but in this case, she was glad to have any reason to see Liam again, no matter how mundane.

"Next time you talk to Courtney, thank her for me," she said, referring to the loan of the swimsuit and the boots. Liam's sister-in-law had already left for the airport, after hugging and kissing both children, evidently not caring that they had just climbed out of the pool, soaking wet of course.

Madison had fretted quietly, after Courtney had gone, because she was wearing the swimming suit at the time and could hardly have returned it sopping wet and unwashed.

Liam had assured her that Courtney had planned to leave some of her things at the ranch anyway, since she'd be returning for more meet-ups with the movie people.

"How's that going?" Madison asked now, standing beside Coralee's classic car, which was dusty after traversing country roads. "The movie project, I mean?"

Liam laughed, standing near her again, holding open the car door. "Thanks for clarifying," he said. "That question could cover a lot of hot topics."

"Sometimes I don't do segues," Madison explained, smiling, ready to fetch her dog from the vet's, go home, soak in a hot bubble bath and crawl into bed, where sweet dreams surely awaited. "I was thinking about Courtney, which led to the movie, which led to my asking how it was going."

"It's going. I stay away as much as possible—and I've been pretty busy with the kids. Frankly, I'll be glad when they wrap the thing up and move on, but the people of Painted Pony Creek are getting a big kick out of the whole process, and that's good. They like running into movie stars in the grocery store, I guess."

"Don't you?" Madison asked, actually curious.

Liam sighed. Could be that, like her, he was pleasantly worn out. "I don't much care, to be honest," he said. "When I'm starstruck, it's by *real stars*, Madison. The kind that spill across a midnight sky like billions of tiny pinpoints of silver. *That* impresses me."

You impress me.

That was the message she saw in his eyes, but of course, she could have been imagining that.

"You're quite the poet, Liam McKettrick," she said.

He grinned. "If you say so, Madison Bettencourt," he replied.

They were silent for a minute or so, just looking at each other, taking each other in. For Madison, the interval was so profound that she had to fight back tears.

"If you'd like to watch some of the filming, I'm sure I can arrange something," Liam offered presently, breaking the spell, and as lightly as he'd spoken, she could see that her answer mattered to him.

"I'd like that," she replied.

"Are you free tomorrow?"

Madison shook her head. "I have Zoom meetings all morning—Audra and I are in the process of selling our company—and then I plan on visiting Coralee." She paused, sighed. "Somewhere in between, I need to get acquainted with Charlie, buy some dog gear, like a leash and food and toys, take him out for a walk or two, that kind of thing."

"I'll text you after I speak with the director," Liam said. "There's no hurry. They have a lot of street scenes to film, evidently, plus a few in the hotel lobby, the church and the saloon."

"That sounds good," Madison said, reluctant to part from this man, and all the intangible pleasures of being near him. It was powerful, this feeling, almost mystical, and for the time being, she wasn't interested in defining it, or putting it into a category.

Even the word *love* didn't cover it.

He kissed her again, not so lightly this time, but not with any pressure or tongue, either.

"Good night, Madison," he said huskily.

Madison responded in kind, nearly floated onto the car seat.

She was strangely disassociated as she drove toward town, but fully alert, too.

Did it mean anything that never, ever, in her whole life, had she felt what she was feeling now?

The residual joy of riding again, at full throttle and with Liam beside her, lingered, and so did the time the four of them had spent in the pool, laughing and splashing each other.

Madison could admit it now—she already adored little Cavan.

As for Keely, well, the kid might well be seeing her as a potential wicked stepmother, even though marriage wasn't a factor.

Not yet, that is.

Maybe never.

Quite possibly what she had with Liam was nothing more than infatuation, a sort of rebound thing, since she'd only recently parted with a man she'd believed she loved.

Surely it wasn't smart to shift gears so quickly.

Was it?

When it came to romance, Madison wasn't ready to trust herself.

She'd already made two huge mistakes, marrying Tom and *almost* marrying Jeffrey. A third screwup of that magnitude might be more than she could bounce back from. She was a strong woman, but she wasn't superhuman, for Pete's sake.

To make matters more complicated, her grandmother, her only living blood relative, was dying, and her dear friend, Olivia, might be, as well.

Plus, she was selling the company she and Audra had built

together, and that was a major shift in its own right. They'd worked tirelessly, endlessly, for *years* to build their design service, to create and maintain the app. They'd each put a big chunk of themselves into the enterprise, traveling all over the world, consulting top-flight designers, working crazy hours, succeeding and failing and succeeding again.

Madison wondered who she'd be, exactly, without the business, and she knew Audra well enough to be sure her friend had to have similar concerns.

There would be a huge payout if the deal didn't fall through, and even after taxes, she and Audra would be even richer than they already were.

Managing all that money would be an even bigger challenge than earning it in the first place, quite possibly a full-time job in and of itself, even with the help of accountants and financial advisors.

Madison was sure of only one thing where the money was concerned: she could have gotten by without it.

She had enough fancy jewelry, designer outfits, bags and shoes.

Too many, in fact.

She lived in a house she loved, and she was driving Coralee's Bentley.

She had excellent friends who truly had her back, as she had theirs.

And she had *something* with Liam McKettrick, though she couldn't have said what it was.

Her desires in life were simple.

She wanted to love and be loved.

She wanted a family.

And, yes, she wanted to make a difference in the world.

A big difference, like paying to have freshwater wells dug in developing countries, contributing to the cost of medical care and education for those who needed it most, helping with the most pressing causes of the times.

Madison Bettencourt wanted to be more than an heiress who'd sold her half of a business for a fortune.

She'd been receiving all her life.

Now it was time to give.

Madison was thinking all these thoughts when she drove into the parking lot behind the vet's office, got out of the car, and made her way around to the front.

The receptionist, clearly ready to close the place, met her with a grin and a spiffy little dog with pointy gray ears, wearing a bandana over the collar he'd been given.

Madison's heart swelled as her new companion hurried toward her.

"Charlie," she greeted him, choking up a bit. "You look like a different dog!"

"A bath and a good meal did wonders," the receptionist said cheerfully. She was called Kathy, according to her name tag, and she was dressed in pink scrubs with tiny white cats printed all over them. "Dr. Valerie says he's healthy, just a little undernourished. He's had his shots, and he has a chip now, too." She paused and handed Madison the leash, then a bag that had been waiting on the counter in front of the desk. "Here are some samples to tide you over until you can go shopping—packets of wet and dry food, eye wipes, a tennis ball. Stuff like that."

"Thank you," Madison said as Charlie rose onto his hind feet and scrabbled at her legs with the front pair. She couldn't resist picking him up, and she was surprised, once again, by how little he was, how light. "Everything covered moneywise?"

"We ran your card when Dr. Valerie was finished," she said, with a big nod and an even bigger smile. "Added the cost of the grooming in, of course."

"Of course," Madison said agreeably, pleased that all the dots had been connected.

Charlie licked her cheek. Maybe he smelled the barbecued chicken she'd eaten at Liam's a little while before.

Or maybe he was just glad to see her.

Her eyes burned with a new kind of happiness as she headed for the door, which would soon be locked behind her.

"Come on, Charlie," she said, nuzzling his neck as she walked toward the Bentley. "Let's go home."

Soon, Charlie was sitting obediently in the front seat, his ears up.

It occurred to Madison, not for the first time, that Charlie might not have been abandoned, as she'd thought. He might have run away from home, or gotten lost.

Maybe someone was searching for him even now, heartbroken.

However short their acquaintance, Madison knew she would be devastated if someone showed up and claimed him. And that could happen.

Turning onto the road that led to Bettencourt Hall, she decided not to worry.

What was the point, really?

If Charlie belonged to someone who loved him, someone who was searching for him at this moment, she would surrender him, even though it would hurt. Her heart had wrapped itself around this little fellow the moment they met up in the driveway, and letting go wouldn't be easy.

But suppose he'd been purposely neglected instead of loved, tossed away, even abused?

Well, in that case, she'd fight to keep him.

With everything she had.

Thus resolved, she reached over and patted Charlie's furry head. His coat was soft and shiny now that he'd been bathed and brushed, and she would have sworn he was smiling as he looked over at her.

There was still plenty of light when they got to the house, and

Madison was glad of that, because, despite the benign spirit of the place, it was isolated, and there were plenty of places to hide.

She'd feel safer with Charlie around, not because he'd be of any real use as a guard dog, featherweight that he was, but because he could serve as an early warning system.

He was a mixture of small breeds, mostly terriers of one kind or another, Madison thought, and that meant he would bark if he heard, smelled or merely sensed danger.

Madison parked the Bentley in the garage, and then she and Charlie made their way around to the back of the house.

Charlie paused at the foot of the sunporch steps to lift a hind leg.

At least, Madison thought charitably, he hadn't waited until they were inside to do his business.

Once she'd flipped on the kitchen lights, she set the goody bag from the vet's office on the counter, along with her purse, and crouched in front of Charlie to cup his funny little face in her hands.

His eyelashes were long enough to envy.

"You'll be happy here, buddy. And safe, too. I promise."

Charlie whined softly, then laved her face with his quick little tongue.

Madison laughed and leaned back slightly to avoid more of the same. "You're a kamikaze kisser," she said. She'd have to watch out for incoming volleys of canine affection in the future. "Let's get you settled in for the night," she concluded, getting back to her feet.

She opened the goody bag, took out a packet of dry food, and emptied it into a bowl, then filled a second bowl with water and set them both down in a far corner of the kitchen.

Charlie ignored the food, but he lapped up some water.

He'd been fed at the vet's office, and evidently his last meal was sticking to his ribs.

She shut off the kitchen lights and started up the back stairs,

Charlie following in little bounding leaps. He'd need license tags, a real dog bed—maybe two—and, of course, a proper leash and collar for walks in the countryside. The people at the vet's office had provided temporary ones, but they wouldn't hold up as well as the ones Madison intended to buy.

As she'd told Liam, she didn't expect to have very much free time tomorrow, between back-to-back meetings with HammondCo and their lawyers, accountants and various other advisors, and her daily visit to her grandmother over in Silver Hills.

She felt a flash of guilt as she took a wool blanket from the linen closet, folded it into a thick square, and laid it down on her bedroom floor for Charlie to sleep on.

She was going to have to leave the dog home alone for a couple of hours while she was with Coralee; no way around it.

He ignored the improvised dog bed and immediately hopped up onto its counterpart, designed for humans, curling up near the footboard, yawning, and closing his expressive brown eyes.

Madison sighed and shook her head.

She didn't have the heart to remove him, so she found a nightgown and went into her bathroom.

There, she filled the big claw-foot tub, adding in a generous squeeze of liquid bubble bath, and stripped off her clothes while steam filled the room and clouded up the mirrors.

Finally, with a big sigh, she sank into the tub, sliding down until her chin touched the water and the bubbles tickled her nose.

Now that she felt the sheer relief of soaking in a hot bath, she realized that her thighs, bottom and lower back were aching from the horseback ride with Liam and his children.

Both Keely and Cavan were naturals on horseback, like their father, though Keely hadn't seemed to enjoy the experience nearly as much as her little brother did.

Madison couldn't help wondering if it had been her presence that had caused Keely to tamp down the delight she obviously felt, astride her dainty palomino mare, Lady. Without a word, the child had made it clear that Madison was—extra.

An outsider.

With a sigh and then a huge yawn, she decided she was reading too much into a very small thing. She was a stranger to Keely, and therefore, somewhat suspect; that was entirely natural.

If what Madison had begun with Liam turned into something lasting, and Keely was still withdrawn, she'd find a way to deal with that.

In the meantime, she had plenty of other things to keep her occupied.

For example, Coralee's longtime attorney, Ezra Clark, had emailed her twice already, wanting to set up a meeting, each time stressing that it would be wiser to go over the details of her grandmother's estate in advance of her death.

And each time, Madison had put him off, not only because she'd been busy settling in at Bettencourt Hall and spending as much time as possible with Coralee, but because she preferred to ignore the depressing fact that Coralee was dying.

It was true that Madison and her grandmother had been apart for long stretches of time, but that didn't mean they didn't love each other.

Yes, Coralee had held herself a step removed from her, emotionally, for as long as Madison could remember, but along with Bettencourt Hall itself, the old woman had been a touchstone, anchoring Madison to her identity, her heritage, her family history.

Furthermore, the kindly distance Coralee had kept between them had strengthened Madison rather than scarred her.

She'd been a lonely kid, sure.

But she'd known all along that Coralee was doing the best she could, all things considered.

It couldn't have been easy to lose her son and daughter-in-law so tragically and then find herself responsible for the four-year-old daughter they'd left behind.

Coralee had *adapted*, and sometimes, that had to be good enough.

Soon, the bath began to cool off, and instead of turning the hot water spigot to add more, Madison lathered herself up, scrubbed, rinsed and climbed out of the tub, which was long, wide and deep enough to serve as a horse trough.

She wrapped herself in an oversized towel before bending to pull the plug, and after brushing her teeth and applying moisturizer to her face and lotion to the rest of her body, she returned to the bedroom and tossed back the covers on her bed.

Charlie, still ensconced at the foot of it, opened his bright button eyes and then closed them again.

Madison smiled to herself.

She was tired, so tired.

Normally, it took her a while to fall asleep; she needed time to settle her busy mind, to slow down on the inside, not just the outside.

Sitting up with her pillows propped behind her, Madison considered the packet of letters and the stack of leather-bound journals waiting downstairs in the library, on a side table.

She'd intended to sit down and read through every word, ever since she'd found them in that box from the secret room, but for some reason she couldn't explain, she was reluctant—not in a negative way, though.

No, she wanted to be ready, that was all.

Whatever being ready meant.

Madison sighed, plugged her phone in to charge, switched off her lamp, adjusted her pillows, and slid down beneath the lightweight summer covers.

Charlie began to snore, and although Madison knew she should have made him get down off the bed, she couldn't bring herself to do it.

Anyway, it was nice to feel his weight near her feet.

She shifted this way and that, trying to get comfortable, having to maneuver her feet around the warm lump that was Charlie each time she moved, but eventually, sleep overtook Madison and sucked her down into the realm of disjointed dreams.

They moved and changed like colorful glass shards in a kaleidoscope, her dreams, mental fragments of a busy day.

Meeting Charlie in the driveway.

Riding hard over open rangeland, with Liam riding beside her.

His children, splashing and laughing in the swimming pool.

That soft, special kiss in Liam's kitchen.

And then, from somewhere in the depths of her unconscious mind, stranger images arose, displacing the happier bits.

A little girl, a familiar one, running breathlessly, frantically through darkened woods.

Bliss?

Yes. Yes, of course, it was Bliss.

Who—or what—was pursuing her, and why?

Vaguely aware that she was asleep, indeed that she was dreaming, and none of this was real, Madison was nonetheless struck by the child's desperation and fear.

As her dream-self, she called out to Bliss, tried to run toward her, but she was stuck fast, as though her feet were mired in rapidly drying cement.

Bliss didn't slow down. She crashed blindly through the underbrush, looking back over her shoulder every few strides, stumbling, righting herself again.

Running. Running.

The light of a waning moon illuminated the small figure, then the shadows swallowed her again.

Madison called out. "Bliss, wait! *Wait!*"

And then Bliss was in the cemetery, their meeting place.

Madison could see the girl's bright eyes, her halo of brownish-blond hair, tangled and unkempt, rioting around her small, freckled face.

A face filled with fear. And something else.

Determination?

Again, Madison tried to move, to get to Bliss, to save her somehow.

But she was still stuck, as though caught in waist-high quicksand.

Bliss hopped onto the gravestone where she'd liked to sit, spine straight, legs crossed, like those of a miniature and very skinny Buddha.

Next, to Madison's bafflement, a shimmer rose around the girl, not fog or smoke, but the energy, the *essence* of those things.

Through the haze, Madison saw her lost friend press both hands to her ears and squeeze her eyes shut, as though she were in the worst kind of pain. She cried out, swaying atop that rectangular marker—and then—

And then, she simply *disappeared*, as if absorbed by the strange mist.

The shock was so great that Madison was jolted from the depths of sleep to full wakefulness in the space of a single heartbeat.

Her skin was moist and very cold.

Her heart was pounding, and so was her head.

And Charlie stood at her side, on the mattress, his ears perked, watching her.

Clearly, she'd startled him, waking up with such a violent jerk that she could still feel it in her muscles and joints.

What the hell was that *about?*

Like everyone else on the planet, she'd had bad dreams before. She'd had full-on nightmares. But this had been something more—much more.

More like a memory than a dream.

Yet she'd never seen Bliss in such a state, running as if for her very life, perching on the grave marker and pressing her little hands hard into the sides of her head.

Giving a hoarse shout of indescribable pain.

And then vanishing.

Just vanishing.

Madison sat up, careful not to send Charlie flying off the bed in the process, and swung her legs over the edge. Planted her feet firmly on the floor, the way she'd done once or twice in college, when she'd gotten carried away at some party, drinking more than she should have.

Now, as she had then, Madison felt a need to anchor herself.

To stop the room from spinning around her like a carnival ride gone out of control.

Her breath came hard and fast, and she rested a hand on her chest, felt the thud of her heart right through flesh and bone and the fabric of her nightshirt.

Charlie whimpered and crawled into her lap.

She hugged him gently, whispered reassurances she needed to hear herself.

"It's all right," she said, after a long time spent rocking back and forth and trying to slow her breathing down enough that she wouldn't hyperventilate. "It's all right."

It wasn't, though.

The dream haunted her, prodded at her. It lurked, as if it might pounce on her, even now that she was awake.

Bliss. Poor, terrified, lost *Bliss.*

What, Madison asked herself for the hundredth time, had happened to her friend?

In the dream, Bliss had been fleeing from something or someone, flying along as if her life depended on it.

And maybe it had.

"Shake it off," Madison told herself aloud, easing Charlie off her lap so she could stand up. "It was a dream, that's all. Only a dream."

Alas, it wasn't that easy.

Dream or no dream, it had *felt* real.

As real as the room she stood in.

And it had left her shaken, even a little traumatized.

Could a simple dream do that?

If so, Madison had no reference point for such an experience, because she'd never had one quite like it before.

She'd *been there*, in the woods, under a nearly full moon, watching, straining to get to Bliss, to rescue her somehow.

And she'd been unable to move.

That had been the worst part.

Madison stumbled into her bathroom without bothering to switch on the lights, turned on the cold water faucet in the sink, and splashed her burning face over and over again.

Slowly, very slowly, she began to calm down.

When she felt strong enough to stay upright without leaning against the pedestal sink, Madison left the bathroom, grabbed her phone from the nightstand, and crossed to her door. She entered the hallway and started down the rear stairway.

Charlie followed, his recently clipped nails tap-tap-tapping on the wooden steps.

In the kitchen, she turned on the lights, flipped the switch on the electric teapot, found a package of chamomile tea bags in the cupboard, and dropped two into a mug.

Chamomile wasn't going to cut, it was the best she could do at the moment. She didn't have any meds for anxiety, and just then, the thought of alcohol of any type turned her stomach.

She glanced at the phone, checking the time.

It was late. After one a.m.

Too late to call Audra, or any of her other friends.

Certainly too late to call the person whose voice she most wanted to hear—Liam.

While she waited for the kettle to boil, she practiced taking slow, deep breaths.

Charlie nuzzled her bare calf with his very cold nose, and she took a moment to bend down and give him a pat on the head.

She was being silly, she lectured herself.

She'd had a dream, that was all.

Just a dream.

The kettle reached a rolling boil, and she lifted the pot from its base and poured scalding hot water into her mug, causing the tea bags to float to the top.

Just as she was about to sit down at the table and wait patiently, *sanely* for her jitters to stop, or at least abate a little, her phone rang, startling her so much that she jumped, and poor Charlie skittered backwards in alarm.

Madison frowned, pressed the button to accept the call, and said hoarsely, "This is Madison Bettencourt. What is it?"

"I'm Jenny Baker, and I work at Silver Hills Assisted Living Center," replied a female voice. "I'm calling about your grandmother, Coralee Bettencourt."

17

Coralee was awake, sitting up in bed, and she was lucid.

Her eyes were calm, her wrinkled hands didn't tremble, and she greeted Madison with a smile of recognition, weak though it was.

Bone-weary, Madison hovered in the doorway of her grandmother's private room at the assisted living place. She'd literally thrown on her clothes in her hurry to get to Coralee, and there was a real possibility that her T-shirt was on inside out and that her shoes didn't match. Her jeans were the same ones she'd ridden in earlier, with Liam and the kids.

"You asked for me?" she said, almost in a murmur, approaching Coralee's cranked-up hospital bed.

That had been the subject of the call from Jenny Baker. Coralee was cognizant and wanted to speak to her granddaughter immediately.

Coralee put a hand to her ear. "Speak up, Madison," she ordered. "I'm an old woman, and my hearing isn't what it once was."

Madison moved closer.

She'd glanced at her watch on the way into the building: 1:27 a.m.

It seemed lucidity was no respecter of time.

Not that it mattered, of course.

For whatever reason, Coralee Bettencourt was truly in her right mind for the first time in weeks, if not months. And there could be no doubting that the internal weather change would be temporary.

Madison's heart skipped a beat or two; she wanted to grab on to this moment with both hands and cling, lest it escape too quickly.

Because escape it would.

She went to Coralee's bedside, touched the old woman's hand.

Coralee was wearing *lipstick*, at this hour of the night, and even a touch of blusher on her papery cheeks. Her favorite ring, an oversized sapphire that had probably cost more than the Bentley, graced her right-hand ring finger, and—Madison squinted in the dim light—yes, those were Coralee's Jackie O. pearls, as she'd long since dubbed them, hanging around her neck.

Instead of making her feel better, the old woman's efforts at looking her best were mildly disturbing.

Madison found her voice. "You look—beautiful," she said.

Coralee waved a dismissive hand, the one Madison wasn't holding. "No time for flattery, young lady," she replied. "I'm going to die soon, and there are things I need to tell you. Pull up a chair and sit down."

Ignoring the instruction to take a chair, Madison perched on the edge of Coralee's bed instead. She didn't want to let go of that fragile bird's wing of a hand.

"I'm listening," Madison said, and her vision blurred slightly as she watched her grandmother's face, with all the lines time and life had carved into it.

"Most of what you'll need to know is already on record, with my attorney. You've probably heard from Ezra by now."

Madison nodded.

"There's a considerable estate, as you probably know," Coralee went on briskly, "and most of it, including the house, will come to you. I want you to do something constructive with Bettencourt Hall, Madison. It's a very special place. A refuge of sorts. There's plenty of money, so you won't need to sell the place or any of the property."

"Okay," Madison murmured, clinging to her grandmother's hand, though not hard enough to hurt, but not so loosely that it could slip from her grasp.

"I've made bequests to Estelle—maybe she'll finally retire—and of course to my favorite charities. There's a particular bracelet, rose-gold, set with emeralds, that my good friend Althea admires very much. I would like that to go to her—you'll find it in the safe hidden away in my bedroom closet. Ezra has the combination."

"All right," Madison said. A part of her wanted to change the direction of the conversation, because she didn't care about the money, and she'd never have let Bettencourt Hall go if she could help it. Nor did she begrudge the chatty librarian, Mrs. James, Coralee's emerald bracelet.

"I hear your wedding to that Jeffrey person was a flop," Coralee said brightly. There it was, Madison thought with a faint smile. The change of subject she'd hoped for—well, sort of, anyway. Jeffrey and the foiled wedding were not the direction she'd hoped her grandmother would take.

Still, she was there to listen. She owed Coralee that much and a lot more.

It surprised her, though, that the older woman had retained that much information, given her many cognitive lapses.

Probably, the nurses gossiped, too, and in a clear-minded moment, Coralee had probably overheard the account.

"Yes," Madison agreed belatedly, when she realized her grand-mother was waiting for a reply. "It's all for the best, though, so don't worry."

Again, that dismissive wave of the hand. "You'll find the right man eventually," Coralee said with conviction. "He'll most likely show up when you stop looking."

Madison nodded. There wasn't time to explain her attraction to Liam; this kind of mental clarity was rare for Coralee, obviously, and Madison didn't plan to waste it.

"Tell me about that summer," she ventured as the pause lengthened, "when you got lost in the woods. Althea told me something happened to you, and I'm curious about what it was."

Evidently, Coralee knew what incident her granddaughter was referring to, because she blew out a breath of frustration and said, "Althea never believed a word I said—nobody did—and I can't imagine why she's yammering on about it at *this* late date. When your best friend in the world confides in you, you ought to believe them!"

"I agree," Madison said. "But what happened, Coralee?"

Coralee seemed to deflate a little; her energy was already ebbing away. "My journals are somewhere in the house," she replied. "I forget where. You can read about what happened when you find them."

Madison hid her own frustration, which matched Coralee's. "Why did you call me here?" she asked gently. "I know all about the will, and you know I'll make sure your wishes are followed. Why now, in the middle of the night?"

"I told you, I'm going to die soon. And I need to warn you. I should have done it a long time ago, but—"

"Warn me about what?" Madison interrupted softly.

"The woods. There are places out there, along the creek, around the cemetery, that are—dangerous." Coralee closed her eyes, sagged against her pillows. She was drifting, and once she floated out of reach, there might be no bringing her back.

"Dangerous how?" Madison asked, with a quiet urgency she couldn't hide. "In what way are those places dangerous, Coralee?"

The old woman opened her eyes, looked directly into Madison's, and said, "It's all in the journals. Find them."

With that, she faded back into her usual state of bewilderment and something that vaguely resembled fear.

"Coralee, please," Madison whispered, clasping her grandmother's hand with both of her own. "Don't go—not like this—"

Coralee shook her head, very slowly, very slightly.

"I'm sorry," she said in a croaky whisper. "I'm so sorry."

In the next instant, Coralee drew a breath, expelled it shakily, and retreated into a sleep that was more than sleep.

It was oblivion.

Despite the monitors that conveyed Coralee's vitals to the nurses' station, Madison reached for the buzzer and pushed the button, still unwilling to let go of her grandmother's childishly small hand, now limp in her own.

Two nurses, one male and one female, entered the room.

The man checked the monitors while the woman gently eased Madison away from Coralee's bedside and used her stethoscope.

Madison didn't need to be told that her grandmother was gone.

Her knees melted, and she dropped into the nearest chair, lowered her head, and struggled to breathe.

Beyond that first shock and the weariness that followed, she felt nothing.

One of the nurses removed Coralee's ring and strand of pearls and placed them in a zippered bag for safekeeping. They were now part of an estate, and they would be handled accordingly.

Madison didn't care one way or the other.

She signed forms but refused to leave the room, though she

was urged, however gently, to go home and rest, because there was nothing more she could do there at the facility.

She sat with Coralee until the people from the funeral home came, shifted the tiny, used-up body onto a gurney, covered her up and rolled her out into the hallway.

Still unable to feel anything, Madison stared at her phone.

Should she call someone?

Audra, or one of her other close friends? It was too early to disturb them.

Liam?

Well, he would be kind.

But he had young children at home.

He couldn't be expected to leave them alone.

Still, it would have meant so much just to hear his voice.

Madison stood, finally, and the muscles in her legs and back throbbed in protest. First the horseback ride, and now an hour or two sitting stiffly upright in a chair in her grandmother's room.

The female nurse came back, her beautiful mahogany face a study in sympathy. "Is there someone we can call?" she asked gently.

Madison was dazed, but her composure remained in place.

She'd known Coralee's time was short—the woman had been in her late eighties, after all, and her health had been going downhill for quite a while now—and yet the loss of her would, at some point, be a powerful blow.

For now, though, she seemed to be coping.

Holding the inevitable grief at bay.

She shook her head, tried to smile. "No," she whispered, her voice raspy, "I'll be fine."

"You're sure you're all right to drive?" the nurse persisted.

The name Julie was stitched into the upper right hand corner of her scrub shirt. Aqua blue, with pants to match.

Funny the things you noticed when you were stunned to numbness.

"Yes," Madison said. "I can drive home. Nothing to worry about."

Looking unconvinced, Julie walked Madison out of the room without further protest, down the long corridor, past the doors of sleeping patients, through the quiet, softly lit reception area and out to the parking lot.

She waited while Madison unlocked the Bentley, opened the door, sank into the driver's seat. The keys jingled in her shaking hand as she tried to line one up with the ignition.

Julie opened her mouth, closed it again.

Madison acknowledged her concern with a stiff nod, said nothing, and started the car.

She drove home, hardly aware of doing so, parked the Bentley in the garage, and went inside, as usual, by the back door.

Charlie met her immediately, jumping up, making a soft whining sound in his throat, his paws brushing her blue-jeaned legs repeatedly.

And it was then that the loss finally hit her with the force of a tsunami.

Or a Category 5 hurricane making landfall.

The tears came, floods, *rivers* of them.

She knew this was more than a reaction to her grandmother's death; it was the result of being hurt, many, many times, and not allowing herself to let down her defenses long enough to process her pain.

Now, Madison slid down the counter nearest the door, landed on her backside on the floor with a thump that raced up her spine and immediately blossomed into a headache. Charlie scrambled into her lap, licking her face almost frantically, as though desperate to stop her from crying.

Madison clung to that sweet little stranger, holding him as close as she could without hurting him, weeping into the soft warmth of his coat.

She wasn't sure how long she sat there, though the sun was

coming up when she finally collected herself, moved a sleeping Charlie off her lap, and stood.

She ran cold water in the sink, splashed her face with it.

Her skin felt raw, chafed by all that salt water, by the constant rubbing, by Charlie's rough tongue, but the headache was fading fast.

After cooling herself down a little, she brewed coffee.

And finally, when the hour seemed decent, she called Audra.

Her friend didn't answer with a hello, a yawn, or a recrimination for phoning her so early in the day. Except that in Florida, it *wasn't* that early.

"What?" Audra asked, her voice anxious.

Madison had to swallow the lump in her throat before she could reply. "It's Coralee," she said. "She's gone." She paused, gave a humorless chuckle, painful to utter, painful to hear. "Dead, I mean."

"I'm sorry, Mads," Audra said. "I'll be there as soon as I can."

Madison remembered the Zoom meetings scheduled for that morning. They were important, and no matter how stricken she was by Coralee's death, she meant to get through them.

More than get through them.

She was a professional. She would do this right.

"We have the meetings—"

"We can reschedule them, Mads. Right now, you need to handle arrangements. You need to grieve."

"Oh, trust me," Madison sniffled, crying again, but not sobbing like before. That was something. "I'll do all that, especially the grieving. But business—"

"*Please* don't say 'business is business.'"

"Okay," Madison agreed, dashing at her eyes with the back of her free hand. "But it is."

Audra sighed heavily, and Madison could picture her as clearly as if they'd been using FaceTime: chin-length blond hair, always slightly—and attractively—mussed, large china-blue eyes, emphasized by thick lashes, pretty mouth lipsticked and wobbling just a bit because this woman was one of the most empathetic people Madison had ever known.

"All right, Mads, you win. We'll get through the meetings together. But the minute they're over, I'm going home to pack a bag, book a flight, and arrange to rent a car. I'll be at your place by tomorrow night at the latest."

The trip would almost certainly disrupt Audra's otherwise well-ordered life, but talking her out of it would have been a waste of breath, time and energy.

"I could pick you up at the airport," Madison suggested.

"No need," Audra responded. "I'll rent a car."

"You're sure?"

"Yes," Audra replied, unfazed. "It's only an hour or so, a drive I can manage quite easily, thank you very much. And anyhow, I'm going to need wheels once I get there, aren't I?"

It wasn't the kind of question that required an answer, so Madison offered a question instead. "You're sure you want to do this?"

"Of course I'm sure. And the drive is beautiful. I'll enjoy it."

Madison smiled slightly, in spite of the great sorrow churning within her. "You could enjoy the scenery from the Bentley," she said reasonably. "If I picked you up at the airport, I mean."

Audra made a *pffft* sound. "Bentley Schmently," she said. "Have I mentioned that I think that car is highly impractical? You live in rural Montana now, and I'll bet the winters are one long blizzard. Hence, you need a pickup truck instead. Or at least an SUV." A pause. "Or a team of huskies and a sled."

"That's it," Madison replied. "This conversation is officially off the rails. Let's concentrate on selling our company for an s-load of money, for today, anyhow." A pause. "And Audra?"

"What?"

"Thanks for being exactly who you are."

Now it was Audra who sniffled, though she had her brave

voice up and running in the next second or two. "Shall I call the others? Let them know about Coralee?"

"The others," of course, were Kendall, Olivia and Alexis.

"No," Madison said, perhaps a mite too quickly. "They're all dealing with their own stuff. Especially Olivia. And besides, the four of you were just here. Which is—"

"They'll want to know, Mads," Audra interrupted.

"I'll send emails. I really don't want to burden them, Audra, and while I'm super-glad you've decided to come back, I feel a little guilty about it, too. You shouldn't have to drop everything and hop on a plane."

"I *want* to be there," Audra replied, sounding more upbeat now, and less sniffly. "And I promise I won't get underfoot, okay? I get the subtext, kiddo. You love the girls, and you really don't want to inconvenience them, but you *also* don't want a houseful of people just now. Am I right?"

"You're right," Madison sighed. "Sometimes I think you're a mind reader."

There was a smile in Audra's response, a kind one. "I'm like the algorithm on Amazon, sweetie. I see all, I hear all, I know all." She was quiet for a moment, probably taking a sip from her ever-present water bottle. "We've been friends for a long time, remember, and I'm *very* observant. I probably know almost as much about you as you know about yourself."

"And you still like me. Amazing."

"Hush," Audra scolded her good-naturedly. "See you on Zoom."

"See you then," Madison answered, touched by her friend's determination to help out in whatever way she could—including flying across country for the second time in under two weeks because "Mads" needed her.

"Wait," Audra said just as Madison was about to thumb the End button.

Charlie was scratching at her legs, this time because he

needed to go outside. He'd already eaten and lapped up his water. "What?"

"Does the cowboy bartender know about Coralee—that she's passed?" Audra asked, sounding slightly breathless, as though she'd set her phone down, crossed a large room, and then run back to ask the question.

"His name is Liam McKettrick," Madison said, mildly amused in spite of the cavernous loss she was feeling at the moment. "And, no, I don't think so. At least, I haven't told him. Given that this is a very small town, however, I imagine he'll hear about it before he's had his second cup of coffee." A moment of biting down on her lower lip, then, "Why do you ask?"

"You know darn well why I ask," Audra replied crisply. "He's a man. You're a woman. He'll want to offer comfort."

The kind of comfort Madison wanted from Liam McKettrick had little or nothing to do with Coralee, God rest her soul.

"He'll know soon enough," she said very quietly. "And it's up to him how he reacts. I'm not going to call or text him, Audra, and beg him to drop everything and rush over here to hold my hand."

"Touchy much?"

"*Tired* much. Lost my *grandmother* much."

"Sooooorreee," Audra said. As in, *Sorry. Not sorry.*

Madison couldn't help laughing, though it was a broken sound that scraped painfully at her throat. "*Later*, Audra. I've got a dog to walk, a company to sell, a guest room to prepare, and, finally, a chat to have with Coralee's lawyer. I expect him to call at any time."

"What dog?" Audra said, having apparently skipped over the rest of Madison's to-do list for the day.

"Another story for another time," Madison said. "Thanks for listening—I really mean that—and *goodbye*, for now, anyway."

With that, the call ended.

Madison skipped most of her usual morning run, not sure how much stamina Charlie had, or if he could keep up.

He more than kept up, as it happened.

When they got back to Bettencourt Hall, circumventing the woodland paths weaving through the trees and along the creek behind the house because she'd remembered Coralee's strange warning about the dangers of the area, Madison felt better, if only marginally.

The mystery of Coralee's warning was something she didn't have the bandwidth to mull over presently, and it would have to wait. Still, she couldn't shake the strange sense of urgency, or the fear underlying it.

Don't wait too long, chimed a familiar voice in her head.

Coralee's voice.

A little shiver traveled the length of Madison's spine as she and Charlie reached the backyard.

She used the steps to brace herself as she stretched her aching legs, thighs and calves. Never mind all that had happened since; she was still suffering the effects of yesterday's horseback ride.

Had it really only been *yesterday*?

It seemed as though a month had passed since she'd last been with Liam, not mere hours.

Pride, she reflected, would be her downfall.

Audra had been right; Liam *would* have found a way to help her. He was that kind of man.

Still, like her other friends, Liam had problems of his own.

Not the least of which was winning the trust of his daughter.

And that, clearly, was not going to be easy.

It might take years, in fact. Or never happen at all.

Although it hurt her heart, Madison concluded that she ought to back off in more ways than not expecting him to comfort her. She had a lousy track record with men, she reminded herself, and she probably wouldn't be doing Liam any favors by holding on.

Romantically speaking, she was a hot mess, and the best thing

she could do for him, most likely, was to walk away, before both
of them were in too deep.

She needed to straighten out her life.

Give Liam a fighting chance to mend his broken family.

What, after all, was more important?

Nothing, that was what.

Friendship came a close second, but blood was blood.

And now, with Coralee gone, Madison had absolutely no one.

These depressing thoughts lingered while Madison showered,
blew her hair dry, dressed in clothes left over from college—a
boatneck shirt in bright blue and her only clean pair of jeans.
They wouldn't show during the meeting, unless she stood up,
and she didn't intend to do that unless something dire happened
and she and Charlie had to flee for their lives.

Dramatic. Both Tom, her first husband, and Jeffrey, her almost husband, had accused her of being dramatic.

Strange, when neither one of them had ever managed to
make her cry.

Determined to keep her thoughts on an even keel, Madison
applied makeup, using more than she would have on an ordinary day, perused the notes on her laptop, mostly compiled by
the always diligent Audra, and drank more coffee.

Charlie, meanwhile, curled up at her feet beneath the desk
in the library. He was tuckered out from the run, but happily
so, judging by the way he'd grinned up at her from beginning
to end.

Coralee's attorney called just as she was finishing up her prep-
arations online. Getting ready for the Zoom meeting had raised
her spirits, reminded her of just how much she and Audra had
accomplished, working together. *Small-town girl makes good*, she
thought, grateful for the distraction the morning's activities had
provided.

The lawyer's call brought reality thundering home, though.

"Ms. Bettencourt?" he began as soon as Madison had said

hello. When she confirmed that she was indeed Ms. Betten-court, he went on. "This is Ezra Clark. I am—or was—your grandmother's legal advisor. Allow me, first and foremost, to offer my sincere condolences. Coralee and I were old friends, as well as associates, and I will miss her very much."

"Thank you," Madison said, glad she was sitting down, be-cause she suddenly felt weak all over.

Maybe she shouldn't have gone out for that run, short-circuited as it was.

"I trust you received my emails?"

"Yes," Madison replied. "I'm—I'm sorry for not replying yet. There has been so much going on."

"So I've heard," Clark said kindly, and with a touch of amuse-ment.

Madison bristled, wondering if he was referring to her de-bacle of a wedding, decided it wasn't important one way or the other, and said, "You want to discuss the will."

"Yes," Clark agreed. His voice was melodious and deep. "I was hoping we could meet today, in fact. There are stipula-tions, you see, about how Coralee wished to be buried, among other things."

"I was under the impression she wanted to be cremated." Was she really discussing this? *Cremation?* It was hard to think about, not just for the obvious reasons, but because this was *Coralee* they were talking about. The woman who had been so vital, so full of life and energy, until very recently.

Mr. Clark cleared his throat. "Well, yes, but there's more. She requested that her ashes be buried in the Bettencourts' family cemetery in two weeks' time, give or take a day or two. You see, your grandmother wanted a proper 'send-off,' as she called it, not a standard memorial service, when we last spoke. It's to be held in the rose garden there at the family home, and she arranged for caterers, musicians, decorations and, of course, a preacher, far in advance of her death. She asked for one—" the lawyer paused, apparently consulting his notes "—Daniel Summers to officiate at the service. Interestingly enough, the man is a former navy SEAL."

Madison knew about Daniel Summers, who happened to be Melba Summers's husband, though she'd never met him. Coralee had taken a liking to the man when he became a minister a while back, though she hadn't been a churchgoing woman. Not as far as Madison knew, anyway.

There had been a lot she hadn't known about her grandmother, after all. Coralee had been loving, but she'd been reticent, too. And sometimes mysterious.

"I wonder if I might drive over and meet with you this afternoon, Ms. Bettencourt. I've given you an overview, but there is a letter, as well as a very detailed list of instructions. These things would be much more effectively discussed in person."

Madison thought about the business meetings, the first of which was scheduled to begin in less than half an hour. It would be followed by two others, each an hour long.

The idea made her head spin, but as she'd told Audra, business was business.

As much as she would have liked it to, the world wasn't going to stop turning just so she could catch her breath.

They agreed that Mr. Clark would arrive at Bettencourt Hall at approximately three p.m. He lived in a town on the other side of Silver Hills, some fifty miles from Painted Pony Creek, and there was roadwork in between that could cause delays.

Once the call was over, Madison reached for her bottle of water and the two over-the-counter painkillers she'd shaken into her palm before she sat down at the computer.

If she didn't have a second headache now, she told herself, she surely would by the time the morning was over.

She knew she would need all her strength to get through this day.

18

Bliss

He'd seen her.

This time, Duke had seen her.

She'd braved the terrible headache and the violent empty-ing of her stomach to get back to the world she'd nearly for-gotten about, all so she could steal the bottle of aspirin her dad kept in the glove compartment of his truck. He always took a dose when he thought he had a hangover coming on, and he wanted it handy.

It made Duke mad when he had to rummage for something he figured he needed right now, like a bottle opener or a Bic lighter or the dried, stinky ground-up stuff he kept in a baggie.

Bliss wasn't thinking about hangovers.

She wanted the aspirin because Doc Wiggins said Jack's fever was going to kill him if it didn't break soon. And she'd remem-bered, in a flash of desperate inspiration, that Gran had given her baby aspirin when she was little. Whenever she'd hurt herself, or gotten sick and had a temperature, that had been part of making her feel better.

Duke's aspirin was for grown-ups, not babies or little kids, but it would have to do.

Too bad he didn't keep penicillin around.

Having decided on a plan of action, dangerous as it was, Bliss had gone back on her promise to herself, after her last visit to the other place, that she would never risk another attempt. It had hurt too much, and besides, she was scared of getting stuck in the twenty-first century and having to be Duke and Mona's kid again, instead of Katherine Bettencourt's ward.

Tonight, after three or four days of sweating and tossing and turning and calling out to people who weren't there, it looked like Jack was as close to dying as he could get without his heart stopping.

Katherine had been sitting with her young son day and night, trying to cool him off with a cloth she soaked in cold well-water, wrung out, and soaked again, hardly taking her eyes off Jack for an instant.

On this new journey, Bliss had expected to land in the cemetery, like she had before, but that night was different.

It was like being shot straight up into space without an astronaut's suit; she was surrounded by jagged shards of ice-cold emptiness, and she couldn't draw a breath for the life of her. The pain was searing, and she was aware of every part of her body, it seemed, all of the different pieces crashing into each other.

No wonder, then, that she'd fainted on impact, and when she woke up, dizzy and disoriented, it took her a while to recover, and still longer to realize that she was *inside*, not leaning on that old marker in the cemetery or sitting by the creek.

Wherever she was, it was darker than dark, but there were a few narrow cracks of light coming through one of the walls.

Was she in a barn?

No. There was no animal smell, no scent of dusty hides and hay and manure.

This was a house.

She was sitting on a box or a chest, she realized, and when she realized that, her confusion cleared up in a moment.

She was in the secret room in Bettencourt Hall, a place she'd explored often enough with Jack before he took sick.

But the streaks of light were too bright to come from lanterns or oil lamps.

Had she found another way to go back and forth from then to now?

She stood, waited until her knees felt strong enough to support her weight again, and crept to the wall to peer through the cracks.

The library was there, so this *was* Bettencourt Hall, but it had changed *a lot*.

There were fancy couches and chairs with flowers printed all over them, and the lamps were the modern kind, electric. A fire snapped and crackled in the huge fireplace across the room—and that, too, was different. In the house she'd just left, determined to get that bottle of aspirin from Duke's truck and bring it right back to Katherine, there had been a smaller fireplace, made of simple river rocks and mortar, like the steps off the kitchen.

It seemed there were no people around, but that was a crap shoot, as far as Bliss was concerned. Bettencourt Hall was a *big* house with lots of rooms, even in the new-old days, where Katherine and Jack lived.

At least, Bliss *hoped* Jack was still living, that she could get the medicine and hightail it back to him and Katherine in time to be of help.

She waited for what seemed like a long time, then slowly and carefully pressed on the lever Jack had shown her. That done, she waited again, breathing as quietly as she could, and gave the wall a push at one end.

Sure enough, the bookshelf that hid the secret room slid slowly to one side.

Bliss stopped it with one hand when there was just enough space for her to slip through. After drawing a deep breath and offering a little prayer to the God Gran believed in, she made her move.

She was in the rear hallway, almost to the back door, when she saw the woman.

And the woman saw her.

All Bliss really registered was that this wasn't Madison, the only person she had hoped to run into, and that this might not be the part of time Madison lived in, either.

The woman was small and slender, and young, too.

It looked like she was dressed up for a party, or planning to go out someplace fancy, because her dress was short and bright red, slim-fitting but ruffled from the neck to the hem. She wore a sparkly band around her head, and there was a black feather sticking up at the back.

While Bliss was looking at the woman, of course, the woman was looking back, taking in the homemade calico dress Katherine had made for her, the high-button shoes, everything.

"Hi," Bliss said nervously, edging toward the outside door. She knew there was probably a bottle of aspirin here in the house, but trying to find it would take too long, especially if the woman decided to stop her.

The woman stared, her pretty, heart-shaped mouth in a perfect crimson O, and the glass of bubbly stuff she held in one hand dropped to the floor and shattered with a series of sounds that were almost like music, or tiny chimes.

"Gotta go," Bliss added.

The woman's knees buckled, and she folded gracefully to the floor in a faint.

Bliss bolted.

The moment she was outside, a powerful wind struck her,

and for a few moments, the headache and the need to puke were back, full force.

Don't send me back, she pleaded silently. *Please don't send me back before I get Jack's medicine!*

In an effort to compose herself, Bliss paused, looked over her shoulder at the house where magic happened.

Tonight, under a waning moon, the place was different. *Very different.*

Did that mean Duke's camper and, worse, his truck wouldn't be in the clearing, sheltered by the Grandfather tree?

She couldn't take the time to mull the question over for another minute, she concluded, because Jack was so sick—his illness had started with a tumble into the creek and a bad cold to follow, and gotten steadily worse after that. The aspirin she intended to swipe might be the only chance he had.

Of course, there were no guarantees. Even if she got back in time, would the pills work?

If she knew Duke Morgan, they were probably past their expiration date.

She ran, ignoring the pain her stupid shoes caused, swiping at low-hanging branches as she tore through the woods, stumbled alongside the whispering creek, her eyes burning with tears the whole time.

The camper was there.

And so was the truck.

Bliss stayed out of sight, breathing hard, while she assessed the situation.

Until then, it hadn't occurred to her that Duke might have been in town at one of his watering holes, which meant the truck would have been gone, too.

That idea struck her like a punch in the stomach.

There were so many things that could have gone wrong, and still might.

She waited a little longer, trying to see inside the truck, but it was dark in the shade of the Grandfather tree, and she was too far away.

Duke might be behind the wheel, like last time, either passed out cold or just waiting until his head stopped spinning.

She was going to have to chance it and get closer to find out.

He wasn't in the truck.

Bliss let out the breath she'd been holding almost long enough to make herself faint dead away again and went around to the passenger side. Tried the door.

It wasn't locked.

Duke was probably too fuddle-headed to remember to take simple precautions like that one.

With luck, he was in a snoring stupor, set to stay that way for a good long time.

Very, very slowly, Bliss worked the door handle.

It made a clanking, metallic sound, and she winced. Waited.

Unfortunately, the passenger side of the truck was facing the camper, not away from it, which would have been a little bit safer.

She waited for a sound from the camper, but nothing happened.

Still, there was a tightness in the air, like a rubber band pulled to the snapping point, fit to sting when it clapped back.

Terrified that she'd be discovered if she dallied too long, forced to stay, forced to explain where she'd been, only to be called a liar, Bliss yanked open the truck door with all her strength, climbed onto the running board, and fumbled wildly through the junk in the glove compartment, searching with her hand because she was using her eyes to watch the camper door.

Her ears felt like they'd come to a point, she was listening so hard.

Finally, just when she thought she might collapse out of pure fear and maybe wet herself, her hand closed around a small plastic bottle.

Aspirin.

It had to be aspirin, or all this would be for nothing.

And Jack would probably die.

Just as she jumped down from the running board of that rusty old truck, lantern light flared and then swayed inside the camper, splashing across the cracked, grimy glass of the little window by the door.

"Hey!" Duke yelled.

He was just a bulky shadow behind the lantern he carried, but there was no mistaking who he was, or what he'd do if he caught her.

Bliss ran, stumbling and groping her way into the dark woods, following the moon-dappled course of the creek, her heart swollen big enough to fill her windpipe and burn the back of her throat like she'd taken a big old swig of kerosene.

Behind her, keeping pace despite his size and the state he was in, but not quite catching up, Duke cursed and roared and threatened.

"Come back here, you little thief!" he shouted, nearly upon her by then.

Did he recognize her, in her strange other-world clothes?

Had he missed her at all, or even wondered where she'd gotten off to?

She didn't know, and she didn't want to find out.

One thing was clear: the house was too far away, and the woman was there, probably recovered from her fainting spell, and there was another of those sickening headaches somewhere in between, like an invisible wall.

A wall that would probably shatter Bliss if she tried to go through it.

Reaching the secret room again was clearly impossible, so she headed for the cemetery, for the old gravestone, the place where she'd come through the time wrinkle—if that was what it was—before.

The brush was high and thorny, and it tore at her skirt as she passed, with Duke storming along behind her, still shouting and breathing so fast and loud that she knew he must be almost close enough to grab her.

She got to the stone, clutching the bottle of aspirin, and climbed onto the cool, mossy surface of it.

At the edge of her vision, Bliss saw Duke, just a few yards away, scowl in fury and lunge toward her.

Then the humming sound came, drowning out his voice, and her head pounded like it might split wide-open. She shoved the aspirin bottle into the pocket of her dress, covered her ears with both hands as if to keep her skull from bursting, and held her breath.

She felt Duke's hand brush against her side, then fall away, solid at first, then nothing more than a faint breeze.

After that, the world was quiet again, except for the usual night sounds, the scratchy chirp of bugs, the flow of the creek, the random hoot of an owl.

Bliss took several minutes to settle back into herself, and when she had, she shoved one hand into her dress pocket, terrified that the bottle of aspirin wouldn't be there.

But it was.

She took it out of her pocket, squinted at the contents, visible through the clear plastic container.

It was about half-full.

She would see that Jack took the recommended dose—two tablets every four hours until his temperature went down. If Katherine objected, and she might, since there were no plastic bottles of aspirin in the world she knew, Bliss wasn't going to let that stop her.

If she had to sneak those pills into Jack's mouth and push them straight down his throat, that's what she would do.

19

Holding his breath, Liam watched from a comfortable distance as Landon Reece, stunt double for A-list actor Bram Finley, took an imaginary bullet to his middle and toppled headfirst off the roof of the Hard Luck Saloon, a distance of more than thirty feet, and did a somersault in midair.

The camera followed Reece until he hit the trampoline waiting below to catch him, rolled triumphantly onto his feet and held both arms in the air to acknowledge the applause of the sound and camera crews and the exuberant cheers of the local lookers-on, who were farther away.

"Wow!" Cavan said, looking up at Liam, who was wearing his marshal's getup because he'd been in the background of a few shots that morning. "That's what I want to do when I grow up! I want to jump off of buildings!"

Liam resettled his hat. Offered no comment, although he was thinking, *Over my dead body, buckaroo.*

"If that's what you want to do," Keely told her brother, "you're stupid."

"Enough," Liam muttered. The bickering between his kids was constant, and most of the time, he felt more like a referee than a father.

Good thing the three of them would be heading off to Silver Hills for their first meeting with Angela Winston, family therapist, right after lunch. That woman had her work cut out for her, dealing with a trio of mixed-up McKettricks all at once.

He kept his gaze on the scene that was being filmed, pretending an interest he didn't feel. The fact was, Liam was tired of the whole showbiz thing and more than ready for the Hollywood gang to wrap up their time in Bitter Gulch and move on to wherever they were headed next.

It wasn't that he didn't like the people; they were okay. It was the *process* he didn't care for. The disruption, not only in the Gulch, but in Painted Pony Creek proper.

The movie was about all anybody talked about, and he supposed that was normal, given that the project was a definite novelty in a town where the biggest events of the year were the annual rodeo and the lighting of the community Christmas tree.

He was glad he'd be hanging out with three good friends that night; almost since the day of his arrival, he'd been part of the bimonthly poker game in the back room of Sully's Bar and Grill, commonly referred to simply as Sully's.

The founding members included Eli Garrett, the county sheriff, Cord Hollister, a horse trainer of renown, and J.P. McCall, rancher and financial wizard, but the group had expanded over the past year or so. Now, besides Liam, it included Dan Summers and several others.

Liam enjoyed the game, the beer and the occasional cigars, but he valued the friendships most of all.

There was a game that night, and he meant to attend, hoping it would distract him, help him shake off some of the things he was dealing with, if only for a little while. Miranda, a wait-ress at Bailey's, had agreed to look after Keely and Cavan for a few hours, and they both seemed to be okay with that, which surprised Liam a little, not on Cavan's account, but on Keely's.

The girl seemed determined to balk like a spooked pony at every suggestion, especially if it came from her dad.

Liam smiled to himself. She was a tough kid, but there were a few chinks in that unnecessary armor she wore so often.

He turned his thoughts back to the organized pandemonium going on in front of him, wondered why the hell anybody would want to be in the movie business anyhow.

It sounded glamorous, sure, but the reality was anything but.

Liam knew he couldn't have stood it, the mind-numbing rep-etition of filming the same scenes over and over again, ad nau-seam, the waiting between calls to the set, the long hours, the constant changes of plan.

As an extra, he was in just enough background scenes that he had to hang around, when he would have preferred to be elsewhere.

With Madison, for instance.

Doing just about anything that didn't involve the movie.

Sure, he respected the director and the rest of the creative staff, and he actually liked Landon Reece. Although Reece earned his living by being shot off roofs, beat up by outlaws and dragged by horses and behind runaway wagons and stagecoaches, he was a down-to-earth kind of guy, reserved but not moody, confi-dent but not arrogant.

The same couldn't be said of Bram Finley, who strutted around between scenes, charming the women and girls watch-ing from the far end of Main Street, ordering Liam's people around like they owed him their allegiance, stretching every scene he was in until the very air shuddered, like it did when a sudden storm was about to strike.

Now, while Reece crossed to stand next to Liam, much to

the delight of the kids, the trampoline was pulled out of camera range by a couple of gofers, and Bram swaggered into the scene as if he were Laurence Olivier about to spout Shakespeare.

Inwardly, Liam sighed, and he just barely kept himself from rolling his eyes.

Reece must have sensed Liam's reaction, because he chuckled.

He was the same height as Finley, about six feet, lean and well-built. Like the man he replaced in every action scene, he had brownish-blond hair, on the long side and usually tucked behind his ears.

Beyond those things, there was no real resemblance.

"Seems like you might be getting tired of us hanging around your town, Marshal McKettrick," Reece remarked in a leisurely drawl, when Keely and Cavan had ventured far enough away to peer through the souvenir shop's display window.

Across the street, Finley rolled headfirst onto the ground and came up with pistols drawn, one in each hand. They were high-quality fakes, those guns, but they made plenty of noise and spewed smoke when fired.

"I might be getting tired of some of you, Reece, but not all."

"Call me Landon," Reece said. "You like it around here, in Painted Pony Creek, I mean?"

Liam gave a semi-shrug, ignoring the scene across the street and looking straight at Landon Reece. "I'm Liam," he replied, and they shook hands. They'd met before, but never exchanged first names. "And, yes, I do like the Creek. It's a special place."

"How's that?" Landon asked, looking as though he really cared about the answer.

And maybe he did.

"It's the people," Liam said, after a few moments' thought. *Madison Bettencourt in particular.* "Definitely the people. Most of them are decent to the core. They're always ready to lend a hand when somebody's in trouble, for one thing."

Landon looked pensive. "I've wondered sometimes if there

were any places like that left. There's so much turmoil and strife out there—enough to make a man think the good folks have all died off, or just decided it wasn't worth it to try anymore."

"Guess that's another thing that makes the people here different," Liam ventured. "They don't give up. Doesn't seem to be in their nature."

"Makes me want to stay here when the filming is done," Landon said, his expression serious, almost solemn. "Buy myself a piece of land, raise crops and maybe a few cattle."

Liam grinned, hoping to lighten the moment. "And leave Hollywood?"

"That would be the best part," Landon said, and he grinned back. "I know there are a lot of fine people there, like there are anywhere, but the overall mindset of that place gets to me, if I let it."

"You'd be starting from scratch as a farmer, right?" Liam asked.

The kids were back, arguing again under their breath.

Like Liam wouldn't notice.

Landon shook his head. His blue-green eyes were at once thoughtful and alight with whatever vision he had for the next part of his life. "I grew up on a farm, back in Iowa. It's gone now—my dad lost the place when the last recession hit—but I really miss the life."

"I hear you," Liam said, feeling a stab of sympathy for Landon and his family. A loss like that could destroy a person if they weren't made of strong stuff.

Which, he suspected, Landon Reece was.

Just then, the director, a balding man in chinos, a T-shirt and a windbreaker, without a trace of cowboy to him, turned around, scanning faces, finding Landon's.

"Reece!" he called out. "We need you over here again!"

"Lucky me," Landon murmured, but he stepped off the high board sidewalk and headed back across the street.

Watching him go, Liam decided he'd like to have a friend like Landon Reece, and he hoped the man *would* decide to stay on in Painted Pony Creek and start living the life he'd lost. He'd make a point of inviting the man to that night's poker game, for a start.

"Can we get lunch now?" Cavan asked, tugging at Liam's coat sleeve.

It was too damn hot to be wearing a wool coat, and Liam pulled it off, slung it over the nearest hitching rail.

"It's a little early," he said to the boy. "Are you really hungry, or just bored?"

"*I'm* certainly bored," Keely said, with such gravity that Liam almost laughed aloud. He felt a surge of pure love for the girl, despite all the drama she'd brought into his life. "Do you have any more walk-ons today?"

"One," Liam said. "If they get that far."

"Why don't you ask the director?" Keely pressed. "It looks to me like they're about to make Mr. Reece make another dive off the roof." She gave her brother a sidelong glance. "He needs a new job. One where he won't break his neck."

"He's not going to break his neck!" Cavan protested, alarmed.

Liam ruffled his son's hair. "Don't worry, buddy. The man knows what he's doing."

"Accidents can happen to anyone," Keely insisted, with a little sniff and a toss of her head. Then, without preamble, she caught Liam's eyes and asked, "Are you going to see Madison, or send her flowers or something? Because her grandmother died?"

The question brought Liam up short, inwardly at least, because Madison and her recent loss had been in the back of his mind ever since he'd heard about it that morning, at Bailey's, when he'd stopped in for coffee.

He'd texted Madison immediately, offered his sympathies, and asked if there was anything he could do to help.

She'd texted back right away, saying she appreciated his concern but she needed some time to herself.

The response, reasonable as it was, had stung Liam.

Time to herself?

She was pushing him away, obviously. Maybe she thought things between them had been moving too fast, or she was having second thoughts.

He came with baggage, after all, and it might well be that Madison had decided to keep her distance. Find someone who didn't have two kids to raise.

"You look sad," Cavan said, his lower lip quivering a little.

"I *am* sad," Liam confirmed. "I didn't know Madison's grandmother, but she'll be missed, I'm sure."

"We could visit Madison," Cavan persisted. "Meet Charlie the dog."

Liam gave the boy a thin smile. "Another time," he said. "Madison's got a lot to do right now, and she'll probably get more company than she needs. We'll hang back a while, until she's ready to hear from us."

"Can't we even send *flowers*?" Cavan wanted to know.

"Yeah. We can do that," Liam replied gruffly. Looking down into the boy's upturned face made something catch inside him, something both painful and sweet.

Just then, a girl with a ponytail and a clipboard bustled across the street, smiling up at Liam. "Mr. McKettrick? We're ready for you now."

"*Yes!*" Cavan said. His sadness had passed quickly, as it usually did.

Keely said nothing at all, but Liam saw a flash of excitement in her eyes. Her dad was going to appear in a major motion picture, however briefly, and that probably gave her bragging rights with her friends back in Seattle.

Liam grabbed his coat, put it on, and crossed the street, resigned to another great moment in cinematic history.

Last time, he'd ridden up to the saloon on a horse, dismounted, and strode inside, like he was mad enough to fight bears with a stick of kindling.

On this occasion, he was instructed to stand in the middle of the street and fire two shots into the air, using the rifle provided. He was supposed to look angry, without a clue why.

This wasn't *High Noon*, and he wasn't Gary Cooper.

He did as he was told, and the director was satisfied with the first take.

Liam was excused for the day, like a schoolboy who'd finished his homework in study hall, and the implications of that chapped his hide a little, but at the same time, he was glad to leave Bitter Gulch and go on about his personal business.

He and the kids chose a bouquet of flowers at the florist's shop to be delivered to Madison at Bettencourt Hall, and all three of them signed the card.

Next they had lunch at a burger place on the far end of town.

And after that, they set out for Silver Hills and their appointment with the shrink.

Angela Winston greeted them herself.

She was a tall woman, with full lips, striking gray hair and dark eyes, impeccably dressed in a charcoal pantsuit that fit her so well it was probably custom-made. She was in her fifties, Liam estimated, and she looked more like a runway model than a therapist.

The beginning of the session was awkward.

Liam had no idea where to start, and Keely's mood had darkened again, which gave him the feeling he was about to step onto an emotional minefield.

Which he most likely was.

Cavan was intrigued. Interested. Almost eager.

Keely, of course, glared daggers. Liam didn't know where else the kid wanted to be, but it wasn't there.

"Let's get to know each other," Ms. Winston said with a

broad, bright flash of a smile. Her teeth were almost too white: veneers, probably. "Who wants to start?"

"My name is Keely McKettrick," announced the most unlikely volunteer, "and I don't like it here. On my dad's ranch, that is. Your office is okay, I guess."

Liam closed his eyes, realized that was a tell, and opened them again. His jawline felt tight.

"And you?" Ms. Winston asked without missing a beat, turning to Cavan.

"I'm Cavan McKettrick," he said, with a note of pride that touched Liam's heart like a warm fingertip and left a sweet, throbbing bruise behind. "I'm seven and I have two horses—three if you count the one at Papa and Mimi's place in California—and my dad is in a movie."

"Excellent," the therapist chimed, nearly singing the word.

She turned her deep brown gaze on Liam, raised her eyebrows, and waited.

"Liam McKettrick." He gave up the name reluctantly, and his voice came out sounding hoarse.

"And you're here because?"

Liam looked from Cavan to Keely, and for no reason he could define, the tension inside him began to ease.

"Because I love my kids," he said.

Cavan beamed.

Keely sighed, long-suffering. Waverly in miniature.

Angela Winston said, "Good, good! We're off to a great start then, aren't we?"

You tell me, lady, Liam thought. He'd half expected her to clap her hands, she sounded so enthusiastic.

After ten minutes of what seemed to Liam to be casual chatting, the therapist asked to see each of them separately.

Cavan was up first, while Keely and Liam sat in the otherwise empty waiting room, side by side, not speaking, staring straight ahead.

When Keely broke the silence, it was with a thunderbolt. "Are you going to tell Ms. Winston about Cavan? That he's a mistake, I mean?"

Liam was struck dumb for the next few moments, staring down at his daughter in shock. *"What?"* he finally gasped. Then he paused, recovered a little, though it involved a struggle. "Cavan *isn't* a mistake, Keely." Another brief interval while he tried to make sense of what she'd said. "And neither are you."

"Mom said he was. So did Gambie. They said you left because of him."

The bottom dropped out of Liam's stomach and swung like a trap door on faulty hinges, dangling over an abyss. *Surely,* he thought desperately, *even Waverly and her mother wouldn't stoop so low as to tell a kid a lie like that.*

It was the equivalent of emotional napalm.

Keely looked defiant, then stubborn, and then, for just a fraction of a heartbeat, regretful. "You need to tell Cavan that you're not really his dad," she said.

Liam closed his eyes again. His world rocked on its axis.

Then, straightening his spine, he looked into Keely's face, now slightly pale, and told her, "I *am* Cavan's dad, Keely. As much as I am yours."

She leaned toward him a little, whispered accusingly, "He's not even a McKettrick."

Liam worked hard to control his temper, usually an easy thing to do, but not this time. This time, it cost him. Cost him plenty.

"Cavan *is* a McKettrick," he said. The assertion was completely true, as far as he was concerned, because the boy was part of his heart, part of his soul. "That isn't going to change."

The receptionist returned from wherever she'd been, a slight woman with a lively smile and a streak of bright green in her hair.

Keely bit down on her lower lip and fell silent, but there was a look of triumph in her eyes that took the starch out of Liam's knees. *What is* wrong *with this kid? Why is she so eager to reveal something devastating, something she should never have known about in the first place?*

No answer came to him.

Soon enough, Ms. Winston opened the door, and Cavan came bounding out of her office, looking ebulliently happy, as he did most of the time.

Liam's heart cracked down the middle; he wanted to sweep the kid up into his arms and carry him out of this place. Away from his sister.

And that felt worse than wrong.

Ms. Winston looked at Liam. "Can we speak now?" she asked. She nodded toward the receptionist, who was settled at her desk by then, tapping away on a computer keyboard.

Liam stood. Looked at Keely, then at Cavan.

He wasn't about to leave Keely alone with her brother, not after the things she'd just said. *He* wanted to be the one to tell his son—*his son*—the truth, fouled up as it was, but not *now*, damn it. Not until Cavan was older, better able to understand.

As things stood, he couldn't trust Keely not to drop the bomb on Cavan first chance she got.

"Maybe next time," Liam answered at length, feeling weary to the marrow of his bones. "I'd rather you spoke with Keely instead."

Keely looked up at him with a combination of confusion and fury. "I don't think I have anything more to say today," she said.

Liam seethed, but his love for his daughter ran every bit as deep as the weariness he felt. How was it possible to care so deeply for a child and, at one and the same time, want to throw up his hands in frustration and send her straight back to Seattle, to return only when she'd developed an entirely new attitude?

He sighed, thrust a hand through his hair.

And he stood his ground. Glad Cavan wasn't in the room.

"Why don't you tell Ms. Winston what you just told me,

Keely?" he asked, and there was no mistaking the anger in his words.

Keely flushed pink, lowered her eyes. "I don't want to," she said in a very small voice.

"Well," Liam replied evenly, "right about now, I don't really *care* what you want."

Ms. Winston's incisive gaze traveled quickly between father and daughter. Clearly, she wanted to ask what was going on, but she was too experienced and well-trained to jump in over her head that way.

Keely stood up, shoulders stooped, head down, and walked past the therapist into the office.

"I think we need separate sessions in the future," said Angela Winston before she closed the door. "Starting with you, Mr. McKettrick."

Liam merely nodded.

He couldn't sit still, so he paced, while Cavan perched on the edge of a chair, feet swinging, and watched him.

The receptionist left again.

"How come you're mad at Keely?" Cavan asked the moment she was gone.

"I'm not mad at her, son," Liam said, and before he could accuse himself of lying, he realized he was telling the truth. Keely was a kid. She'd been hurt by the divorce, and then by the loss of her mother.

Now she was living in a new place, in a different house, under a whole new set of rules. If she was a little spiteful, well, he could understand that.

The real problem here *wasn't* Keely herself. It was figuring out how to resolve this situation before it blew up in all their faces.

He stopped pacing and went to stand at a floor-to-ceiling window, taking solace from the view of Silver Hills and, in the distance, the mountains. He felt small, until things shifted, and he became part of all that scenery.

Usually, that only happened when he was on horseback, alone on the range.

His phone pinged in his pocket, and he took it out, consulted the screen.

J.P. McCall, one of his poker buddies.

"Hey," Liam said.

"Back at you," J.P. replied. "Just checking to see if you're coming to the game tonight."

"I was planning to," Liam answered, surprised by how calm he sounded. How ordinary. "How about you?"

"I'll be there," J.P. assured him with a laugh. "I need to win back what I lost to Cord last time."

"Don't we all," Liam responded lightly, wondering how he was going to manage all this, since he felt like he'd have to stand between his son and daughter from now on, like a bodyguard, to avert certain disaster. On the other hand—

"Do you think anybody'd care if I invited a new guy?"

"Nope," J.P. said with confidence. "Who do you have in mind?" he asked.

"His name's Landon Reece. He's a movie stuntman."

"If you think he's all right, it's cool with me." J.P. paused, cleared his throat. "Bram Finley, on the other hand—"

"He's on his own," Liam said.

J.P. laughed. "Good. He's already had at least one run-in with Eli—drunk and disorderly—so it's probably best to keep them apart."

"Drunk and disorderly?" Liam echoed, not the least surprised. "He won't get an invitation from me. For one thing, he might try to hog all the beer."

Again, J.P. laughed. "I'd like to see him try," he said lightly. "See you later, Liam."

"Later," Liam confirmed, still wondering how he was going to swing this, given Keely's attitude and Cavan's innocent vulnerability.

The answer was obvious, of course.

He would have to sit down with Cavan, explain as best he could that Waverly had made a mistake, and help the boy understand somehow that his biological paternity didn't matter to Liam or anyone else, besides Keely and Marie Everton, her she-dragon of a grandmother.

How was he going to say all this to a seven-year-old who wore his heart on his sleeve? What could he say—*without* saying that Waverly had slept with another man while she was still married to his dad? That she'd done it out of meanness and spite, because she'd wanted to hurt Liam as badly as possible?

For all that, what mattered was this: he, Liam McKettrick, was Cavan's dad, and that was the reality. Period.

After twenty minutes or so, Keely emerged from the therapist's inner sanctum, looking chagrined rather than smug, like before.

What had gone on in there?

Angela Winston crooked a finger at him.

He hesitated, looked at his kids again, each in turn.

"I really need to speak to you privately, Mr. McKettrick," the therapist said.

Liam gave Keely a look full of warning, and once again, she ducked her head.

"Sherilyn will look after the children," Ms. Winston assured him, nodding to indicate the receptionist, who looked up from her monitor and smiled. Then, with more import, she added, "They'll be fine."

Liam stepped into the office, and Ms. Winston closed the door.

"Sit down," she said.

"I'd rather stand, thanks," Liam replied.

Ms. Winston sighed patiently, nodded, and stepped behind her desk. Took a seat in her swivel chair. "Keely is very troubled," she said.

Now there's an insight worth two hundred dollars an hour, Liam thought, impatient. "Yes," he said, keeping his voice moderate, though he knew he probably wasn't fooling the elegant shrink behind the immaculate desk. "I know."

"She's furious with you."

"I know that too. What I *don't* know is how to get through to her. She's had a lot of upheaval in her short life, and that kills me. I'd do anything to help her." *And anything to see that she doesn't hurt her brother.*

Or turn out like Waverly.

"Keely is a very intelligent, resilient child," Winston went on. "And, believe it or not, she doesn't hate you. She's simply testing you—that's my theory at least, and I've seen this a lot in my years of practice. She wants to see if you're cut out to be the kind of father she needs."

"Did she tell you what she said to me, about Cavan?"

"She did," Winston confirmed. "I must admit, I fail to understand why any responsible person would say such a thing to a child. It's a terrible burden for Keely to bear."

"If you'd known her mother, you would understand completely."

Winston merely nodded.

Liam shoved a hand through his hair. Hoped he wasn't coming off as intimidating, though in all fairness, this woman didn't seem open to intimidation of any kind, even if it was accidental. "I guess I shouldn't have said that," he admitted.

"Was it true?"

"Yes."

Ms. Winston spread her smooth, manicured hands. "All right, then. We can explore that another time. But we *do* need to explore it, Mr. McKettrick. The children aren't the only ones who've been wounded, and if you really want to raise them in a happy, healthy home, as I'm convinced you do, you're going to have to work through some things. So, can I expect your cooperation?"

"Yes," Liam said for the second time.

"You're still worried?"

He nodded, tired of the verbal version. "Cavan isn't ready to hear the truth, but Keely seems bound and determined to tell him."

"I'm afraid there's a real danger of that," Winston agreed. "Keely is very angry right now, with just about everyone, not just you. The obvious answer to the most pressing problem, of course, is the wisest one as well—you need to tell Cavan the truth, in a way he'll understand, and you need to do it soon." She paused, considering. "I can say for certain that Keely loves her brother, and she realizes how much an outburst could hurt him. She and I have an agreement, for the time being, that she'll stand back and let you handle the problem. That said, she's nine, which means she may have a lot of trouble controlling her impulses."

"I haven't seen her try," Liam admitted, with a slight grin.

"I will need to meet with her again, of course. And you. Cavan, as I've said, is in remarkably good shape for a seven-year-old who's lost his mother."

"Thank you," Liam said, and he meant it, although he couldn't wait to get out of that office and back to the ranch, where he could breathe.

First, though, he had to stop in at Bitter Gulch, find Landon Reece, and invite him to that night's poker game.

He might have to back out himself, of course, because Keely might strike out at Cavan, tell him what she knew.

His daughter was subdued when he returned to the waiting room, where he made appointments for her and for himself for the following week.

Cavan got a pass.

Somehow, in spite of everything, the kid wasn't messed up.

He would be, though, if Keely felt the need to strike out at somebody.

They took the elevator downstairs, left the building, got into the truck.

Cavan sat in his booster seat, Keely quiet and introspective beside him.

Liam hesitated, then climbed behind the wheel.

It was time to head back to Painted Pony Creek. He'd speak to Reece about the poker game, then make a quick stop at the grocery store for things they were running low on, like milk, bread and eggs.

After that, Liam decided, he'd have a word with Keely.

Remind her that she was a McKettrick, and he expected her to act like one.

Especially with Cavan.

Keely was silent on the way back from Silver Hills; periodic glances in the rearview assured Liam that she was pondering something deeply.

Cavan, on the other hand, chattered constantly, exuberantly, as if he'd just been baptized in the Jordan River and was out to spread the gospel, far and wide.

Presently, they reached home.

Liam changed into work clothes and went out to the barn to tend to the end-of-day chores, and Cavan stuck to his side like a burr to Velcro.

When they returned to the house, Keely was sitting in the kitchen, scrolling through images on her iPad. She looked up as they entered, her eyes solemn, and when Cavan had raced off to clean up and change clothes, she said quietly, "You think you need to save him from me."

Liam paused, crossed the room, and crouched in front of Keely's chair, took her hands in his. "Do I?" he asked gruffly.

Tears filled her luminous violet-blue eyes, and she bit her lower lip, shook her head. "No," she said. *"No."*

"I got a different impression from what you said today, in Angela Winston's waiting room."

One tear escaped the barrier of Keely's thick lashes and raced, zigzag, along her cheek, and Liam brushed it away with the side of one thumb.

"I'm sorry," Keely whispered. "It's just—"

"It's just what, Keely? That you think I love your brother more than I love you, maybe because he's a boy, and you feel the need to punish him for that?"

Keely just stared at him for a long time. Then she asked a question so poignant that it nearly knocked Liam off his feet. "*Do* you love me, Dad?"

Dad. It was the first time she'd ever called him that; she'd skipped from "Daddy," when she was little, to what amounted to a disdainful "hey you" during and after the divorce.

He cupped her small, wet, earnest face in both hands. "Keely McKettrick," he said, "I love you more than I love my next breath. I always have. And if you'll give me a chance, I promise I'll prove it."

She threw her arms around his neck then, and sobbed into his shoulder while he held her.

He cried, too, but silently. Carefully, so she wouldn't see.

He wasn't naive enough to think the gulf between him and his daughter had been bridged, once and for all, but they'd made progress, and the relief he felt nearly undid him.

20

The Zoom meetings had gone as well as could be expected, and despite her still-fresh sorrow over losing Coralee, Madison was encouraged.

Her actual participation had been minimal, since Audra had done most of the talking, bless her, but Madison had been present and very much in the loop.

The deal was done.

Technically, the company was sold, though documents had to be signed, funds transferred, all the usual things involved in a major financial deal.

For the time being, Madison was glad she didn't have to think about business.

She *did* have to think about Audra's imminent arrival, however, and about the upcoming meeting with Ezra Clark, her grandmother's attorney. Although he'd given her a comprehensive overview of the issues at hand earlier, over the phone,

Mr. Clark was a lawyer and therefore a detail man. He wanted to go over the terms of Coralee's estate one by one, in person.

Since it was only noon, and Mr. Clark wasn't due until three o'clock, Madison decided to run a few errands in the interim.

She loaded Charlie into the Bentley and headed for town, stopping first at the print and copy place, where she'd left Katherine Bettencourt's journals to be scanned and transcribed. The young woman who brought the dusty volumes—the actual transcription would be sent to Madison by email—was very quiet, almost frightened, it seemed.

She met Madison's gaze only long enough to say, "I'm so sorry for your loss, Ms. Bettencourt."

Madison thought her reticence was odd, but soon dismissed it on the grounds that most people find it awkward when they encounter someone recently bereaved.

Taking the journals and the receipt for services rendered, she returned to the car, where she was welcomed by Charlie as joyously as if she'd been gone for a month instead of ten minutes.

The next stop was the pet store, and Charlie was delighted anew when he realized that this time, he got to accompany Madison and actually go inside. She fastened the leash the vet's assistant had given her to his collar, also meant for temporary use, and headed inside.

Charlie pranced like a proud little horse as they entered, sniffer working overtime, head turning constantly to take in all the wonders surrounding him.

Madison couldn't help smiling, and for a few minutes, her grief subsided.

Together, she and Charlie chose a harness, a strong leash, food and water bowls, half a dozen squeaky toys, a fluffy dog bed, and a big bag of kibble.

The experience raised Madison's spirits all over again.

Charlie still needed a license tag, but she could register for that online.

Their final destination was the grocery store; there, Charlie had to wait in the Bentley again, with one window rolled partway down. Madison's grocery list was short, so woman and dog weren't separated for long, though, as before, the little guy greeted her with eager face licks, squirms and a low, happy whine.

Back home, Madison carried in all the loot, Charlie keeping pace as she went back and forth between the car and the kitchen, and when that task was finished, she fitted him out in the new harness, clipped on the matching leash, and took him for a walk.

Last time, they'd followed Sparrow Bend Drive toward town, but on that day, they went in the opposite direction, going as far as the rusted mailbox in front of the neighboring farmhouse, which was technically next door to Bettencourt Hall.

Since both properties encompassed many acres of land, it was a good trek.

In adulthood, now and on previous visits home, Madison had tended to avoid the derelict, long-abandoned place, but when she chanced to see it, all run-down and forgotten, she felt sad.

There had been a For Sale sign out front since forever.

Back when she was very young, before Coralee sent her away to boarding school, a family had been living there, a thriving, rambunctious bunch including two parents, three young sons, and one daughter.

The Hallidays, Madison recalled. That was their name.

They'd been such happy people, obviously poor, but maintaining the property, diligently keeping the grass mowed, the house and picket fence painted, and the barn shored up, which couldn't have been an easy task, given that the structure dated back to the nineteenth century.

The Hallidays had grown most of their own food, cultivating and tending a huge garden, keeping chickens and pigs and a milk cow they called Ida. Mr. Halliday had earned a hardscrabble living raising corn, alfalfa and hay, and Mrs. Halliday sold eggs, cream and milk year-round and vegetables in season. The boys were rowdy, and their clothes were shabby, but they were good kids. The youngest, named Martha, was painfully shy and breathtakingly beautiful, even as a little girl.

Where were they all now?

Madison had no idea. All she knew for sure was that hard times had struck that family at some point, and evidently, they'd lost everything.

She recalled Coralee remarking dismissively that the Hallidays were land-poor.

They owned nearly a hundred acres, and barely made enough money to keep the proverbial wolf from the door.

Today, though, there was a newish car parked in the driveway, and a woman Madison didn't recognize had just hung a Sold sign over the forlorn original.

Seeing Madison and Charlie standing by the mailbox, the woman waved and smiled. "Hello," she called cheerfully. "Isn't it wonderful? The old Halliday house is going to be a home again!"

Madison smiled. "Yes," she answered, while Charlie sniffed around the pole supporting the mailbox and then lifted his leg to pee on it. Back in the day, Coralee had considered buying the place herself, just to keep another downtrodden family from moving in. She'd planned to have the house, barn and other outbuildings bulldozed to the ground and burned, but for whatever reason, she'd never sealed the deal.

The real estate agent approached, put out a hand to her. "I'm Alice Redding," she said. "And, unless I miss my guess, you're Madison Bettencourt. I was very sorry to hear about Coralee's passing."

"Thank you," Madison said. She searched her memory for any recollection of meeting Alice before, and came up dry. "You know me?"

Alice was still smiling. She was about Madison's age, slender to the point of being skinny, with short, spiky dark hair and wide brown eyes. "You're sort of famous around here. Because of the wedding."

Madison blushed. Was that what she would be known for from now on? Running away from Jeffrey at the last moment?

"Oh," she said. "Well, *that's* a little embarrassing."

Alice patted her arm. "Never mind all that," she said warmly. "Stuff happens. As for your initial question, the Halliday farm will soon belong to one of the movie people—his name is Landon Reece, and he seems to be a very nice man."

"A movie star is buying this house?" Madison asked, surprised.

Alice chuckled. "Not exactly. Mr. Reece is a stuntman. He's working as a double for Bram Finley." She paused, patted her chest with one hand, fingers splayed. "Be still my beating heart."

Madison *had* heard of Finley, and even seen a few of his movies, but she'd met enough celebrities in the course of her career to know how ordinary most of them were. The best ones were invariably modest, and somewhat amazed by their own success, but a few were insufferable egotists.

She had no idea which category Bram Finley fell into, and she didn't care.

"Well," she said, at a loss for anything relevant to add besides a platitude, "it's nice to think of the old place being cleaned up and lived in again."

Alice nodded, looking back at the house and the landscape in general, her expression wistful. "I think the Hallidays would be glad," she said very quietly.

"Do you know what happened to them?" Madison asked, picking up on the other woman's sadness and matching it with her own. "The family, I mean?"

Alice turned back to her. Sighed. "Mrs. Halliday—Geneva— got sick. Pancreatic cancer, I think. After she died, Mr. Halliday just gave up on the place, let it go back to the bank. He took the kids and moved away, but I don't know where they went. None of them ever came back, as far as I know. Another man bought it when it had sat empty for a few years, but he put it up for sale after six months or so. It's been on the market ever since."

Madison nodded, her question answered. She'd run out of small talk.

"I'd better get back home," she said. "Lots to do."

"If you ever want to sell Bettencourt Hall," Alice said, producing a business card, "give me a call."

Madison accepted the card, tucked it into her jeans pocket, shook her head. "I won't be selling it," she said, undoubtedly dashing Alice's hopes for another commission. "But if I ever need the services of a real estate agent, I'll be sure to contact you."

Alice didn't seem disappointed. She probably didn't expect the house to be offered for sale, but nothing ventured, nothing gained.

Like Madison, she was a businesswoman.

"It was great to meet you," Alice said, looking and sounding sincere. "Maybe we'll run into each other again."

"Maybe," Madison agreed, liking Alice.

They parted ways then.

Alice went toward her car, and Madison and Charlie headed for home.

When Alice passed them on the road, she gave the horn a merry toot in farewell.

Back at Bettencourt Hall, Madison unhooked Charlie's leash, removed his harness, and ruffled his ears, telling him he was a good, good boy.

Apparently exhausted, Charlie lapped up some water and curled up on his new bed in a corner of the kitchen.

Madison hurried upstairs, feeling a little rushed now, where she showered and put on black slacks and a white blouse. She added a touch of mascara and some lip gloss, then went back downstairs.

Since it was almost time for Mr. Clark to arrive, she put the matter out of her mind, to be dealt with later.

She was tidying up the library when the doorbell rang.

Evidently, the roadwork hadn't slowed Mr. Clark down; he was a little early.

But when Madison opened the heavy front door, she found a thin young man standing under the portico, holding an enormous vase of white lilies.

A pang of fresh sorrow tore at her heart.

She took the bouquet, asked the boy to wait, and carried the flowers into the library, setting them down on the coffee table. They smelled heavenly; they also brought tears to her eyes.

She recalled once, as a child, she'd stuck her face into a bouquet of lilies, greedy for more of that marvelous scent. And after that, she'd walked around, unaware, with a yellow, powdery smudge of pollen on her nose—much to Coralee and Estelle's amusement.

The memory was especially poignant now that her grandmother was gone.

After raiding her purse, she went back to the door, handed the boy a tip and thanked him. Given how many friends Coralee had had in Painted Pony Creek and the surrounding area, this might be the first of a number of such deliveries, though most well-wishers would probably wait for the memorial service.

Once the boy had taken the tip, thanked her and gone, Madison went back to the library and read the florist's card.

Both Keely and Cavan had signed with their first names, and their father had added, in his strong, slightly slanted scrawl, "We're here if you need us. Liam."

It was fortunate that Madison was standing in front of an armchair, because her knees were suddenly weak, and she sank onto the cushion, bouncing a little.

Her eyes burned with appreciation and something else.

The feeling wasn't hard to identify, nor did it take very long.

A singular loneliness—for one person alone.

She wanted to call or text Liam, *right now*, and ask him to come over, to listen, to hold her close while she cried.

But she couldn't do it.

Her need for Liam was a wild, elemental thing, and that was the very reason she had to step back, at least for the time being.

She had just come out of a relationship.

She had lost her grandmother and sold her company, almost simultaneously, and though she didn't regret selling, it would be a while—maybe a *long* while—before she'd sorted through all that.

Much as she wanted to turn to Liam, she could not allow herself to do it.

It would be unfair to him, for one thing. And to her.

Liam had been badly hurt by the breakup with Waverly, and he deserved a healthy, uncomplicated love, not one that might be nothing more than a knee-jerk reaction to loneliness and loss.

Plus, he had two children to care for, and they obviously needed a lot of attention, especially Keely.

Anyway, Madison still wanted a baby, and her first fertility appointment was a month away.

How could Liam possibly fit into that plan?

He probably didn't want any more kids, especially one that wasn't biologically his.

Of course there was a chance he felt differently, but Madison's baby clock was ticking, and she couldn't afford to wait around much longer. With every passing year, the risks of pregnancy were greater.

As for the undeniable attraction between herself and Liam, well, it would take time for a relationship to develop. Suppose she and Liam decided to take a chance, see where fate would take them, with her hopes rising higher and higher as time passed, and then Liam chose not to have a baby with her?

No. Having a child of her own was too important to Madison.

She needed to move forward with her own plans.

Mr. Clark's arrival was a welcome distraction, and Madison was composed and businesslike as the two of them sat down to go over Coralee's rather complicated last wishes.

Charlie, curious about the visitor, moseyed in from the kitchen, sniffing the aging lawyer's pants cuffs.

Ezra smiled and petted the eager dog's head.

Madison decided she liked this man. He was probably close to Coralee's age, but he soon proved himself competent and sharp.

He politely refused Madison's offer of refreshments—cookies and coffee or tea—saying he was cutting back on sugar, and he never took caffeine after lunch, and they settled down to business.

Besides the emerald bracelet set aside for Althea James, Coralee's librarian friend, there were other miscellaneous bequests, ranging from exquisite pieces of antique china and jewelry to cuttings from certain plants in the garden.

She'd left sizable amounts of money to Estelle and Connie, and even provided a college fund for Orlando.

Madison was impressed. She'd known Coralee was a generous woman, but she'd definitely outdone herself with the wide range of gifts she'd bequeathed to different individuals and to literally dozens of charities.

Madison was to receive the house and most of its contents, with the exception, as already stated by Mr. Clark, of the items she'd earmarked for various friends and acquaintances. In addition to Bettencourt Hall, there was a significant sum of money.

Between what Coralee had left her, what she'd earned over the course of her career, and her share of the sale of the company she and Audra had built together, she would never need to work another day in her life if she chose not to.

That, however, was a choice Madison had never intended to make.

She loved working, feeling useful, making a difference.

Although the idea was still in the early stages of its development, she planned on starting a charitable foundation, and running it would be a full-time job in and of itself.

She would hire employees and run the operation out of Bettencourt Hall.

God knew there was more than enough room.

Once Mr. Clark had outlined the contents of the will, plus Coralee's comprehensive plans for her own memorial service, he pulled a sealed envelope from a pocket in his briefcase and held it out to Madison.

She took it slowly, thoughtfully, recognizing her grandmother's custom stationery with its distinctive embossed seal.

Ezra Clark smiled gently at her apparent reluctance to open the missive.

She wondered if the lawyer knew the contents, then decided he probably didn't. It was sealed, and chances were, that had been Coralee's doing. She'd always had a flare for the dramatic.

"I'd best be going," Mr. Clark said, rising carefully, because Charlie had been sleeping at his feet with his muzzle resting on the man's shoe, and he clearly didn't want to startle the dog. "If you need anything, anything at all, please don't hesitate to get in touch," he added. "I'll let you know when the will has been properly registered and executed, and my wife and I do plan to attend the memorial service."

Madison, subdued now, walked Ezra Clark to the front door, Charlie trotting after them as if to provide an escort.

When the lawyer was gone, she returned to the library, sat down in the same chair she'd occupied throughout the visit, and, her hands trembling slightly, inspected the envelope.

Again, she thought of Liam, wished he were there with her to provide moral support—even though she wasn't entirely sure why she *needed* moral support.

As sad as she was over Coralee's passing, she understood her duties as her granddaughter perfectly well.

She was to plan the memorial service, invite the whole town, and make sure the event lived up to her grandmother's high expectations. After the service, she was to distribute the china, jewelry and other gifts.

Mr. Clark, thankfully, would disperse the allotted funds.

It was all cut and dried. So why did she feel such a grinding need to be in Liam's presence?

She wouldn't call him, wouldn't text him.

She'd already decided to steer clear of Liam McKettrick from now on, or at least until she had her own life under control.

Besides, Audra would be arriving soon.

She could confide in her friend, her business partner, the person she trusted completely. She'd feel better then, surely. Forget all about Liam and the powerful attraction between them.

Madison sighed, admired the lilies, allowing the envelope to rest unopened in her lap until she heard the grandfather clock chime ponderously.

Five o'clock.

She checked her phone for messages.

Audra had left a voice mail. She'd been held up in Boca Raton and would be arriving tomorrow instead of tonight.

Madison was disappointed, but she rallied quickly enough. As the real estate agent had said earlier, stuff happens.

The text from Liam was not so easily dismissed.

Thinking about you. Say the word, and I'm there.

Answer him! The voice in Madison's head, surprisingly, was not her own, but Audra's. Sometimes the empathy between them bordered on spooky.

Madison fumbled, nearly dropping the phone.

She bit her lower lip. Debated with herself.

And her sensible side lost. Resoundingly.

She texted back.

Tell me what "the word" is, and I'll say it.

She waited.

Less than thirty seconds passed before his response bounced down from the satellite and landed hard, not only in her phone, but in her heart.

On my way.

Liam must have been in town instead of on his ranch, because he was at the front door in less than fifteen minutes.

He was alone, freshly showered and dressed in jeans, a neatly pressed cotton shirt, and polished boots.

Madison didn't say anything.

She just threw her arms around his neck and held on.

Liam pushed the door shut with one foot, holding her.

"Hey," he said. It was a low, raspy rumble of a word.

"I'm sorry!" she all but wailed.

He kissed the top of her head, rocked her gently in his arms.

Charlie danced eagerly around them, excited to welcome another visitor.

Liam held her away from him, but not very far, because she was still within the warm radius of him. "What do you have to be sorry for?" he asked, still sounding hoarse.

"Disturbing you," Madison said, calm enough to be mildly embarrassed by her neediness. She did *not* want to come off as needy, even though, at that moment, she was. "Where are Keely and Cavan?"

He touched her nose. "With Miranda, over at Bailey's. She volunteered to babysit for the evening."

"So you had plans, and now I've messed them up."

"Shhh," Liam said. "No matter what else is going on, Madison, I always have time for you. Always."

She took his hand, led him through the house, to the kitchen.

In places like Painted Pony Creek, she reflected, the kitchen was always the heart of the house, the place where people tended to gather, in good times and in bad. Even in a house like Bettencourt Hall.

"Sit down," Liam said, putting his hands on Madison's shoulders and pressing her lightly into a chair at the table. "I'll make coffee, or tea, or whatever you want."

"I just want to be in the same room with you," Madison confessed. "I don't need anything else."

Liam pulled back a chair of his own, sat down. "I'm here, and I'll stay as long as you want," he told her very quietly.

"You were going out?" Madison framed the words as a question, but she wasn't really asking one.

"It's poker night at Sully's," he said. "But that's later."

"I don't want to keep you."

"I'm pretty adaptable, actually," Liam responded with a slight grin. "And there will be other poker games. But you can only lose Coralee once."

Madison felt foolish, tearful, and very grateful that Liam was there.

"I wasn't going to text you. Or anything. I thought—*think*—we might be rushing things a little."

He looked sad. He also looked as though he understood completely. "Why do you think that?" he asked reasonably.

"Well—it was only a few weeks ago that I broke things off with Jeffrey, and—"

"And?"

"I might be on the rebound. I *am* on the rebound."

"If you say so, I won't argue. Which doesn't mean I agree."

Madison laughed, actually *laughed*, then clapped both hands over her mouth, embarrassed again.

Still.

"Go ahead," she ventured, after long moments of drinking

Liam McKettrick in with her eyes. It seemed then that her very *soul* was thirsty for him. "Argue."

He chuckled, took her hands in his and squeezed. "Okay," he said, drawing a breath and then releasing it slowly, as though summoning up his courage. "I've never wanted a woman the way I want you, Madison Bettencourt. From the moment you came barreling into the Hard Luck Saloon looking as though you could pull up railroad spikes with your teeth, I haven't been able to think straight."

She stared at him. Hopeful. Confounded. And unable to utter a single word in response.

Liam's strong rancher's hands released hers, then rose to cup her face so tenderly that her breath caught and her heart skipped a beat.

"Madison," he began, "I understand that you're not ready for a full-on relationship. I get that you need time to sort things out in your head, and that's okay."

"What about sex?" Madison blurted, and then blushed so hard that her cheeks burned.

He leaned forward in his chair, nibbled briefly, lightly at her lips, causing her mouth to tingle and things to open and expand inside her.

"Sex," he repeated with a sigh. "I think about it a lot. I'd love to take you to bed. I don't deny that, not for a moment. But I care about *all* of you, Madison, and what I feel runs a lot deeper than sex. With you, it's going to be *lovemaking*, being part of each other, something sacred. And when it happens, I want everything about it to be right." He paused. "No groping. No fumbling. The time has to be—well—*the time*—because I'm not going to bungle this. It's too important."

Madison was so stunned that she swayed a little in her chair.

"You're honestly willing to wait?" she asked, amazed. Liam McKettrick was the first man she'd ever gotten close to who didn't want to jump her bones, the sooner, the better.

"Didn't I just say that in so many words?" he asked, with a teasing note in his voice and a mischievous sparkle in his eyes. "Don't get me wrong. I'm as horny as the next guy. But this is different. *You* are different."

Madison felt a lump rise in her throat, aching there, and her eyes burned. "There's one thing I have to tell you."

Liam made a show of bracing himself. "Let's hear it."

"I have an appointment next month. I'm starting fertility treatments."

He dropped his hands from her face, sat back in his chair.

She tried to read his expression and couldn't.

"Why?" he asked, after a brief silence that pulsed between them, so intense that it was nearly palpable.

"I'm thirty-two years old, Liam," Madison heard herself say. "I want a child. Before it's too late."

"I see," he said, after another long lapse.

"You don't want more children?" she dared to ask, almost in a whisper.

"I don't know," he replied. He was so purposefully honest.

"So we have a problem. I can't wait around to see if things work out between us, Liam. Because if they don't, I might *never* get what I want most in the world."

Liam nodded. Clearly he understood her point.

And just as clearly, he wasn't ready to make any promises.

"Go," she said, after what seemed like an eternity. "Go to your poker game. I'll be fine."

He leaned forward, kissed her, and it was a *real* kiss, not a mere brush of his lips against hers.

Then he stood. "You're sure you'll be all right?" he asked.

"Yes," Madison replied readily enough.

But, of course, she wasn't sure at all.

21

Coralee's Letter

My darling Madison,
If you're reading this, as the old chestnut goes, I'm either dead or incapacitated.

Not that there's much difference between the two. Given the choice, I'd definitely prefer the dignity of death.

By now, Ezra Clark, or one of his successors, should I outlive him by any length of time, will have filled you in on the details of my will and outlined my personal wishes in regard to my memorial celebration and the various belongings I have earmarked for certain friends and acquaintances.

And, obviously, he will have given you this letter.

My journals tell my story in exhaustive detail, so I will speak here only of the most urgent matters. If for some unfathomable reason you are curious about the way I've chosen to live my one precious life, you'll find everything you could possibly want to know in the diaries I've kept, on and off, for most of my life.

Here, I must restrict myself to the unbelievable.

It's conceivable, I suppose, that an intelligent young woman such as yourself will see that what I'm about to tell you is the truth, but sadly, I'm almost entirely convinced that you won't.

You'll think I'm demented. Senile. Or simply a very imaginative storyteller.

Nonetheless, given the fact that I am now dead, or permanently comatose, I must say what has to be said while that is still possible. Believing or not believing is your choice, of course, but I warn you—*not* believing is dangerous. Possibly deadly.

You do understand, I think, that Bettencourt Hall is no ordinary house. The place has a magic all its own.

The danger lies outside the walls of this grand old place, along twisting paths through the woods, beside the creek and, perhaps most especially, in and around the family cemetery.

There are strange, invisible passageways out there, Madison. They open and close, like shimmering veils of nothing. They appear and disappear—and they can swallow the unwary.

This happened to me a very long time ago, and I have seen evidence of it happening to others. Most likely they will never admit to it, for obvious reasons.

Do you remember your little friend, Bliss? The one who vanished? The one I insisted was imaginary, a product of your lonely childhood?

I cannot forgive myself for not reporting that child's disappearance, Madison.

You see, I knew she was real.

And I knew exactly what had become of her.

Why didn't I tell the police? I was a coward, that's why. I had tried to tell my own story—as a small child, I wan-

dered into another version of Painted Pony Creek, in another time. I returned so stunned and disoriented that I
could not speak at all for a while, let alone share what I had
experienced with anyone.

When, after many days, I found the courage to tell Papa
what had happened, he didn't believe me. He said I was
telling tales in order to garner attention, and that that was
a wicked thing to do. I was punished.

I never confided in another adult after that, though I did
tell my closest friend, Althea. I told her everything I could
remember—the people in strange, old-fashioned clothing,
the horses drawing wagons or buggies, the rutted roads,
the odd, rustic buildings that shouldn't have been there,
but were.

Alas, Althea didn't believe me, either. I'm fairly certain
that you've already guessed that much. I was shattered by
that, though I disguised it well, I think. We've remained
the dearest of friends, Althea and I.

Why, you ask, should I attempt to tell you, especially
at this late date?

Because I was fortunate to return from that place, Madison.

It wasn't some awful black-and-gray version of hell; the
trees were green, like the grass, and the sky was blue.

But I didn't belong there.

And because I had—and have—no understanding of
how or why such a thing could happen, I was terrified of
stumbling back through some invisible portal, unable to
get home again, to Mama and Papa and Bettencourt Hall,
as I knew it. I avoided the cemetery, even though I had
helped Mama pull weeds and plant flowers there for as long
as I could remember.

You see, I was hiding there, behind a tombstone—Althea
and I and a half-dozen other children were engaged in a

lively game of hide-and-seek, while the grown-ups laughed and chatted and indulged in champagne cocktails—and I was determined not to be found—when suddenly my head began to spin, and then ache, in the most horrendous way. I honestly believed I was dying in those terrible moments.

The headache intensified, and I felt as though I were hurtling through the most complete darkness I could imagine—not a *pinprick* of light anywhere—and the pain! Oh, Madison, the crushing pain in my head was so terrible, I could not bear it. I lost consciousness, and when I came around again, I wasn't in the cemetery, but on my feet, and well along the familiar road into town.

Or a version of that road, at any rate; there was no gravel, and it bent in different directions in different places. There were no mailboxes along its sides, and no houses, either.

If I'd had the clarity of mind to make such an observation, I would have thought that, like Dorothy and Toto, I had been swept away to the land of Oz.

Except this *wasn't* Oz. It was Painted Pony Creek, Montana.

And it *wasn't*.

I believed I was asleep, having a dream.

Maybe I was.

All I can say on that score is, the whole experience seemed thoroughly, irrevocably real.

I got as far as town—it looked like something out of an old Western movie or TV show, Madison—and the people, men, women and children, were dressed accordingly, except that their skirts and trousers and short pants weren't like costumes. The garments were clean, in most cases, but shabby.

All the men and most of the boys wore hats, and the women and girls were in long skirts and dresses.

There were horses tied to hitching rails along the street.

It must have been Sunday, because most everyone seemed to be headed toward the edge of town, where a white clapboard church stood proudly on a grassy knoll. A bell rang in the belfry.

Being only seven years old, I was overwhelmed.

I had no desire to explore, or to ask questions.

I just wanted to go home.

I remember running back the way I'd come, desperate. Frantic.

At some point, I stumbled and fell, striking my head against the hard-packed dirt along the road.

This time, when I woke up, I was lying alongside the creek, face down in the rocky soil that lined the banks. I remember having another terrible headache, one so intense that I lost the contents of my stomach.

I don't know how I knew, but I was aware that I was back where I belonged.

The most tremendous joy and gratitude surged through me, in spite of the pain, which was already beginning to subside; I didn't even fret that Mama would be sorely vexed because my beautiful organza party dress was torn, and further spoiled by mud and dirt. She'd had it made especially for the garden party taking place at Bettencourt Hall, and now I'd ruined it.

I didn't care one whit.

I knew *I was home.*

I raced back to the house, where there was much consternation, because I had been missing for several hours, as it turned out.

Mama and Papa were so relieved that they didn't scold me for vanishing, or for the wholesale destruction of my once lovely party dress. Not then, anyway.

Later, as I've said, Papa could not accept my explanation.

Years passed, and when I was all grown up, and not only

a mother, but a *grandmother*, and you told me about your missing friend, I did you the same disservice my father and best friend had done me.

I couldn't admit that I believed you, and I am sorry.

I wanted to tell you a hundred times that I suspect other Bettencourts may have had a similar experience to mine, and chosen not to tell, for reasons I've already stated.

Papa, for instance, grew up in Bettencourt Hall, and he never mentioned his childhood. It was as though he'd never had one, he was so reticent.

I have no way of knowing, though I can't help suspecting.

Much later, before I was married to your grandfather— as you know, the Bettencourt women never change their names when they take a husband—I was dressed up for a party, waiting for my date to arrive.

Mama and Papa were away at the time.

Anyway, I thought I glimpsed a little girl in the kitchen at Bettencourt Hall, not a ghost or a hallucination, but a *genuine, flesh and blood child*, and she frightened me so badly that I dropped one of Mama's best glasses, let it crash to the floor and shatter at my feet. I didn't recognize her, and of course it didn't occur to me until years later that she might have been your lost friend.

I had not been able to convince myself that she was simply a child who'd sneaked into the house without my knowing. She had been wearing a calico dress and high-button shoes, for one thing, and for another, Bettencourt Hall was four miles from town, and thus quite isolated.

Back then, we didn't have any close neighbors, and strange children did not barge into other people's homes, at least not in my—at the time—limited experience.

She did not belong there, as surely as I had not belonged in that earlier incarnation of Painted Pony Creek.

Who can comprehend the tricks of time, or of illusion? Certainly not I. To this day, I remain mystified.

It's possible, I suppose, that I did indeed imagine my experience, and the presence of that little girl in the kitchen, too. Still, the image of her is vivid in my mind all these years later, as I compose this letter.

I can't quite accept the fantasy theory, sensible as it sounds, because what mere *dream* has the power to weave itself into a person's life to such an extent that it becomes a lasting part of them, as surely as arms and legs, or the color of one's hair and eyes?

Thus, Madison dear, I am bound by my love for you, and the dictates of my own conscience, to warn you. You will surely have children one day, and I know they will spend time at Bettencourt Hall, even if you wind up living somewhere else.

I ask you, with all the fierce sincerity of a grandmother who cherishes you, to be careful. I remain convinced that the house itself is a safe haven, truly benign, though strange things have happened there from the very beginning.

I pray you will believe me, not for my sake, but for your own.

If you don't, however, you don't.

You can decide this letter is nothing more than the ravings of an old woman whose mind is gradually fading away into confusion.

But please know, my dearest, that while I have not been the most demonstrative of grandmothers, I have loved you with my whole heart, from the day you were born.

Perhaps you wonder, then, why I sent you away to boarding school when you were so young, and you'd lost both your parents, and wanted so very much to stay here at Bettencourt Hall.

I did it to protect you, Madison, for no other reason

than because I loved you too much to lose you. I had already lost too much.

Still, it broke my heart—the heart I was forced to harden.

Maybe I was wrong, and should have begged your forgiveness.

I don't know.

Of one thing, I am certain. I am...

Truly yours,

Coralee

22

Audra sat on the sofa in Bettencourt Hall's library, her long, slender legs curled beneath her, Coralee's letter in her hand. "This is wild," she said, fluttering the pages gently beneath her chin, fanning herself. A long, long pause followed, while she studied Madison's face, her cornflower-blue eyes squinting a little, for any sign of what she was thinking. "Do you believe it, Mads? Do you believe Coralee actually traveled back in time?"

Madison, seated in the nearest armchair, clad like Audra in shorts and a tank top, shrugged one shoulder. "I'm not sure," she confessed. "I know it sounds ridiculous—*impossible*, given that her mind has probably been disintegrating for longer than I realize, and yet—"

"And yet?"

"My grandmother was always a practical, down-to-earth person, not given to fanciful ideas. In fact, I'd go so far as to say she was the skeptical type."

Audra looked concerned, as well as weary. She'd had a long

day, leaving Florida early that morning, enduring several flight delays on her way to Montana. *"Time travel,* Mads?" she asked.

Mercifully, there was no scorn in her voice or in her manner. Just worry.

Maybe she thought Madison, who was obviously considering the possibility that Coralee had been telling the truth when she penned that strange letter, albeit with great misgiving, might be afflicted with dementia, as her grandmother had been, though of the early-onset variety.

"I know it's crazy," Madison fretted. She was thinking of Bliss now, not Coralee.

Briefly, she suspended all disbelief.

Had Bliss, like Coralee, slipped through some fold in the fabric of time?

The universe was an undeniably strange place, full of chaos and mystery, tumult and contradiction. Modern science could explain some phenomena in fairly concrete terms, but most conclusions were merely theoretical, weren't they?

Who could say that time was only linear, that it could not turn back on itself, like a snake changing direction?

"I'm getting a headache," she said.

"Not surprising," Audra replied, setting the letter carefully aside on the nearest end table. "The journals you mentioned, the ones you had transcribed...?"

"They were Katherine Bettencourt's. She was Coralee's grandmother."

"Have you read them?"

"Not yet," Madison replied, rubbing her temples with the fingers of both hands.

Charlie, lying at her feet, a warm, furry little stumbling block, gave a low whine that might have been sympathy.

"Little wonder," Audra conceded. "You've had so much going on. I was just wondering if they might shed some light on— well—Coralee's background. What she was like as a child."

"Katherine was dead by the time Coralee was born. Coralee's parents were Jack and Caroline Bettencourt—she was much younger than her siblings—and as far as I know, neither of them left any letters or diaries. All I know is that they didn't believe Coralee when she told them what happened during that afternoon garden party—or at least, her father didn't. She didn't mention discussing the experience with her mother, did she?"

Audra frowned, picked up the letter, scanned it quickly. "No," she said. "But that doesn't mean—Caroline, was it?—didn't know."

"True," Madison agreed, using one bare foot to idly stroke Charlie's silky back, in an unconscious effort to ground herself in a solid, predictable and—above all—realistic world. Finally, she sighed. "I'm sure you're right, Audra. Things like that just don't happen."

Now Audra yawned, straightened her legs and planted her feet on the floor. "I'm not so sure about that. That I'm right, I mean. Bottom line, we're probably never going to know what did or did not happen to Coralee. Or to your little friend, Bliss."

Madison had told Audra what she knew of Bliss's story, which was precious little. And it was Bliss's fate that niggled at the back of Madison's mind now; Coralee's was already settled.

It didn't really matter whether her story was real or made up, did it?

Moreover, if by some incredible fluke of nature, things had happened just as Coralee claimed they had, Madison wasn't sure she *wanted* to know.

Reminded of Coralee's sober warning, that not believing could be not just risky, but actually dangerous, she shook her head.

If this thing really *had* happened to Coralee and Bliss, then it might happen to anyone. Including her.

And that was scary as hell.

As Madison considered what it would mean to be separated from the world she knew, from Liam, uncertain as things were between them, now that she'd told him about her plans to have fertility treatments, from Audra and her other friends, even from little Charlie, her stomach lurched and her knees went spongy.

And suppose her own child, the baby she intended to conceive in a Seattle fertility clinic, or those she planned to foster or adopt later, were somehow spirited into another niche in time?

A shiver trickled down her spine and then back up, and she shook it off as she rose from the easy chair, careful not to step on or trip over Charlie, and stretched, raising both hands high into the air.

Like a certain heroine, in a certain well-loved novel, Madison decided she would think about the family mystery tomorrow.

Or the day after.

Since they were both tired, she and Audra made it an early night, retreating to their rooms after a light supper and a few cups of chamomile tea.

Madison slept soundly that night, without dreaming, and she awakened rested, grateful for Audra's presence, and mildly amused at herself for thinking, even for a moment, that Bettencourt Hall and the surrounding properties could ever be part of a *Twilight Zone* scenario like the one Coralee had outlined in her letter.

Coralee had clearly believed the experience had been real, and for that reason, it had been—for her. Madison felt no disrespect for her grandmother, and no pity.

She simply missed her.

She and Charlie went for a run, as usual, and when they returned, Audra was up and dressed in jeans, an apricot-colored blouse and white high-top sneakers.

"Let's have breakfast in town," she said, smiling over the rim of her coffee as Madison and Charlie entered the kitchen via the back door. "And then let's sneak over to the movie set and watch for a while. Your friend Liam won't let them chase us off, will he?"

Madison grinned, shook her head in mock amazement. This

morning, her grief was lighter, more manageable, and she appreciated small graces. "You think I have sway with Liam McKettrick?" she asked.

"I *know* you do," Audra replied. "Hurry up and get ready. As my old granddaddy used to say, we're burnin' daylight."

Madison widened her eyes in a look of pseudo-alarm and climbed the back stairs, while Charlie, the little traitor, stayed behind to charm Audra out of a treat or two.

By the time she got back to the kitchen twenty minutes later, Madison had worked up an appetite.

Her last conversation with Liam, the night before last, had left her feeling a little off-balance. He'd said wonderful things to her, things no other man had *ever* said, and she'd believed him. He hadn't exactly reacted with enthusiasm, however, when she'd told him about her plans to start treatments soon.

A small, cowardly part of her wanted to avoid him, but she knew Audra had made up her mind about visiting Bitter Gulch, probably hoping for a good look at Bram Finley, though she never would have admitted that.

Leaving Charlie behind to snooze on his bed in the kitchen, the two women hopped into Audra's rented compact, since the Bentley seemed bulky by comparison, and headed for town.

They enjoyed a quick breakfast at Bailey's, where they ran into Melba Summers, who had stopped by to pick up a takeout order for the crew over at the police station.

She came to Madison and Audra's table and rested one hand gently on Madison's shoulder. "I'm so sorry about your grandmother," she said.

Madison thanked her, tearing up a little in the process, and introduced Melba and Audra to each other.

They exchanged greetings, and Madison brought up the book club meeting, which was to have been held at Bettencourt Hall in just over a week, but would need to be postponed until after Coralee's memorial service.

Melba agreed, and then she said, "I checked on your missing friend, like we agreed. I'm afraid I didn't find any reference to a Bliss Morgan. There was a man who squatted in that old camper you told me about, though. He was only here for a few months before he moved on. Name was recorded as Duke Morgan, and he came to a bad end, according to my rusty-dusty outdated sources. Wound up in prison on drug charges, and he died there of unknown causes."

Madison felt a sinking sensation as she listened.

"There was no mention of a daughter?" she asked when Melba fell silent, looking sad and more than a little frustrated by the whole situation.

"None at all," she replied. "I'm tempted to team up with Eli and his people and conduct a ground search, but it's been so long, I doubt the dogs could catch a scent, even if that poor little girl is buried out there somewhere."

Madison felt a strong, sudden urge to warn Melba that the area behind Bettencourt Hall was perilous, but she managed to override it.

What was she supposed to say, exactly?

Had it all been a dream?

She didn't know. And right then, she didn't want to think about it.

That the searchers might accidentally vanish, tromping around out there, only to find themselves in another Painted Pony Creek, in another century?

"Let me know what you and Sheriff Garrett decide," she said instead, while Audra looked on in silence, frowning pensively.

After a delicious—and only partially eaten—breakfast of stuffed French toast, bacon and fruit, accompanied by plenty of coffee, Madison texted Liam, asking permission to stop by Bitter Gulch with Audra. She wasn't going to just show up; sometimes the set was closed to observers, and besides, she didn't want to come off as presumptuous.

Liam's response, however, was both quick and friendly.

I'll meet you on Main Street whenever you're ready. The crew is filming in front of the church.

Madison texted back that they were on their way.

After settling up the breakfast bill, she and Audra walked to Bitter Gulch, since it was only a few blocks from Bailey's, and Madison's heart quickened when Liam, clad in jeans, boots and a T-shirt instead of his usual Old West marshal's getup, leaned in to greet her with a kiss on the cheek.

He turned to Audra next, with a smile, and put out a hand. "Welcome back to the Creek," he said. "You're Audra, right?"

"You have a good memory," Audra replied.

"I work at it," Liam said.

Audra smiled, shading her eyes from the bright morning sunlight. Like Madison, she'd forgotten her sunglasses that morning. "Thanks for letting us come over," she said. "I've never been on a movie set before, so this should be fun." Then, probably remembering why she'd returned to town so soon after the last visit, she lost some of her natural sparkle. Patted Madison's shoulder gently. "Maybe *fun* isn't the right word—"

Wanting to spare her friend unnecessary discomfort, but also to tease her a little, Madison said, "Audra wants to ogle Bram Finley. That's why she's *really* here. She's a super-fan."

Audra didn't pat Madison this time. She gave her a light jab in the upper arm with one finger. "I *do not* want to 'ogle' anybody, Madison Bettencourt," she protested. "And I am *not* a super-fan, either."

"Sorry," Madison said, wiggling her eyebrows once. "I would have sworn you were."

Liam laughed. "If you want to meet him, I can arrange it."

Audra shook her head vigorously, folded her arms. "I *don't*," she insisted.

Down at the end of the street, in front of the picturesque little white church, a cluster of crew members was busy setting
cameras and sound equipment in place.

Liam, Madison and Audra kept to the wooden sidewalk, and
while the women focused their attention on the hubbub outside the
church, Liam was looking in another direction, grinning a little.

When Madison followed his gaze, she saw a man on a
powerful-looking black horse. The creature's raven-dark hide
rippled over muscle and bone and sinew, and it tossed its head
in impatience. For all that, the man controlled the animal easily, and at first, Madison thought he was the famous Bram Finley, live and in person.

At a shout from the director, or one of his minions, a scene
began, and the cameras rolled.

A bride and groom rushed out through the church's open
doors, clad in period wedding clothes, ducking while celebrants
showered them with rice.

The bride looked around, as though searching for someone,
and then, in the next moment, the big horse was thundering
down the dirt street, his rider looking masterful in the saddle. He
rode close to the steps of the church, leaned down and hooked
an arm around the bride's slender waist, hauling her deftly up
in front of him.

They raced off then, while male members of the congregation
leaped forward and fired pistol shots in their direction.

"Cut!" the director called.

The rider turned the horse around, eased the bride carefully
down to the ground.

Her movie-rescuer remained in the saddle, the beautiful horse
dancing beneath him, probably still reacting to the gunshots.
Or simply wanting to run.

"That isn't Bram Finley," Audra said, squinting at the rider.

"No," Liam agreed with another grin. "Finley would fall off

a rocking horse if he was glued to the saddle. That's Landon Reece. He's the stunt double."

"Hmm," Audra said.

Liam might not be picking up on the vibes, but Madison certainly was. Audra was drawn to the man on horseback, though she probably thought she was being subtle.

Right on cue, Reece rode over to the high sidewalk. He nodded to both Madison and Audra, and then grinned at Liam. "So far," he said, his distinctive blue-green eyes alight, "this day has been easy."

By the time he'd finished the sentence, he was looking only at Audra.

"Landon Reece," he said, leaning down with a creak of saddle leather to put out a hand to Audra.

She leaped back a step, then blushed.

Reece laughed. "You're safe," he said. "I was only going to shake your hand, not yank you off the ground and carry you off into the sunset."

Audra's blush deepened, and she looked more flustered than Madison had ever seen her, which was saying something, since they'd been through so much together over the years that they had few if any secrets, but she stepped forward and, very tentatively, accepted the man's leather-gloved hand.

"Audra Lassiter," Madison said when Audra didn't introduce herself. "And I'm Madison Bettencourt. It's good to meet you, Mr. Reece. That was quite an impressive ride."

"Thanks. And call me Landon," he replied, tugging lightly at the brim of his hat. "It's a pleasure to make your acquaintance, Ms. Bettencourt." His gaze slipped, mischievous, to Liam's face, then back to Madison's. "I've heard all about you," he said.

Liam looked away, resettled his hat.

Madison naturally wondered what Landon Reece had been told.

Audra was still watching Landon, as though he were a puzzle with a few key pieces missing. "You do this for a living?" she asked.

Although she was kind and well-meaning, Audra wasn't the most diplomatic person in the world. She was naturally direct.

"This and other stuff," Landon said. Watching Audra, his eyes softened, and Madison figured her friend hadn't noticed that, either.

"Like what?" Audra asked.

"Like rolling headfirst off buildings," Liam put in.

Audra stiffened. *"Really?"*

"Really," Landon confirmed. His voice was strangely husky now.

"Reece!" a man's voice bellowed from somewhere in the crowd gathered in front of the church. "Let's try that again!"

Landon rolled his eyes, but his grin didn't falter.

"Ladies," he said, once again tugging at the brim of his dusty hat—cowboy chivalry at its most breathtaking.

And then he rode away.

"What an idiot," Audra muttered. "Risking his life like that. And for what?"

Madison and Liam exchanged glances, smiled, and said nothing.

Audra paced back and forth on the sidewalk, keeping her eyes on the crowd assembled near the church.

Or was she watching Landon, who was at once containing the fitful horse and bending in the saddle, listening carefully to instructions from someone on the crew?

While she was distracted, Liam took Madison's elbows gently into his hands and turned her to face him.

"You look amazing," he said.

"Flatterer," Madison replied, though she was pleased, and she didn't really try to hide it.

"We need to talk, Madison," Liam went on, and his eyes were serious now. "About the fertility thing."

Madison stiffened slightly. She was sensitive about "the fertility thing," and as much as she enjoyed Liam's company, she didn't see her reproduction plans as any of his business. "What is there to talk about?" she asked quite crisply.

The change in her mood seemed to affect the surrounding atmosphere.

"Us," Liam said.

Audra interrupted just then, calling from the door of the souvenir shop a few yards away, her voice back to its usual perky good cheer. "I'll just be a minute, Mads. I need to pick up a few T-shirts for my nephews."

Madison didn't look her way, and neither did Liam, although they both gave an abrupt nod.

"Is there an 'us'?" Madison asked, feeling cornered and defensive, though she knew she was overreacting. This happened to her sometimes; she turned contrary without understanding why. At least, not fully.

"That's one of the things we need to talk about," Liam said, not giving an inch of ground.

"Liam, my grandmother just died. I'm planning her memorial service, and it's a major production. She left a lot of miscellaneous stuff to a lot of people, too, and I'm supposed to pass it on to them. I have a house guest, and there was this crazy letter, and I just sold my half of the company Audra and I built from nothing, and I'm—" Her throat tightened, and her eyes burned. "And I'm pretty overwhelmed at the moment!"

"I know," Liam said with a sigh. He squeezed her shoulders and went on. "I'm sorry—I get that this isn't the ideal time or place." He paused, and his blue eyes darkened a little as he regarded her. "What crazy letter?"

"I can't begin to explain," Madison answered, and that was true. If she told Liam what Coralee had written on those featherlight sheets of stationery, he would think *she* was crazy, not the letter. "Maybe one day, but not now."

Liam withdrew his hands then, and his jawline hardened, just for a moment. "Okay," he said. "Right. You need time."

"Is that a problem for you?" Madison asked, not as a challenge, but because she really wanted to know.

"It might be," he conceded, after a silent but visible struggle with some emotion—anger? Frustration? Impatience?

She couldn't tell.

"What does that mean, Liam?"

Liam said nothing. He pretended an interest in the goings-on at the far end of the street, where Landon was wheeling the movie horse around, heading their way, ready to gallop up to the church steps and scoop up the bride again.

Madison felt stubborn. "Liam?" she prodded. "I asked you a question."

He turned back to her, and this time, he looked sad. "Later," he said. "I'm busy right now."

And with that, he turned and walked away, crossing the street without looking back at Madison, who stood, strangely stricken, on the wooden sidewalk, watching him go.

She was startled when Audra materialized at her side, a bulging shopping bag in one hand. "I leave you alone for five minutes," she scolded in a good-natured whisper, "and you manage to butt heads with Mr. Right. What *is* it with you, Mads?"

Madison had to blink hard to keep back angry, injured tears. "Who says he's Mr. Right?" she retorted with a snap in her tone, but she was watching Liam, not Audra, as she spoke.

"I do," Audra said softly, touching Madison's arm. "Maybe the timing isn't great, sweetie, but this might be the chance of a lifetime. Have you thought about that?"

Madison loved her friend, so she didn't answer just then, knowing anything she said would be confrontational. Defensive.

And probably stupid.

"Mads? What happened just now? What's upset you so much?" Audra was successful for a reason; she never gave up. She'd been raised by a struggling single mother, and she'd learned the value of bullheaded persistence early on.

What she *hadn't* learned, apparently, was when to cut her losses and run.

She'd probably still be trying to make her doomed marriage to Brett Sinclair work if he hadn't filed for divorce and moved, with his two teenage daughters, to the south of France, where he reconciled with an ex-girlfriend.

"It's the fertility treatments, isn't it?" Audra asked.

Even though she'd experienced it a thousand times before, Audra's insight surprised Madison, and it angered her a little, too.

"Maybe," she said stiffly.

Without making a verbal agreement to do so, they left Bitter Gulch and made their way back to Audra's car, which was parked in front of Bailey's.

"Madison," Audra insisted once they were in the car, with the motor running and the air-conditioning on full blast, "*talk to me. I'm your best friend, not your enemy.*"

Madison gazed straight ahead, her backbone still stiff. "He wants to have a serious talk," she said.

Audra checked the mirrors and the camera and backed into the street. *"No,"* she said. "A serious talk? *That's awful.*"

Madison pushed her bangs back, lifted both hands to tighten her ponytail. Then she huffed out a breath, though she still wouldn't—or couldn't—look at Audra. "You're not being funny, if that's what you think," she said.

Audra laughed. "Maybe not," she retorted, "but *you* are. What's the matter with you, Mads? Why would you hold back when that man—that *good* man—so clearly adores you? Do you think guys like him are commonplace? That there's one around every corner, just waiting to love you like you've never been loved before?"

Madison bit her lower lip. Breathed through her nose for a few seconds. "Of course not," she bit out when she trusted herself to speak. "But may I remind you, my nosy friend, that just a couple of weeks ago, I was all set to marry somebody else?"

They were headed out of town by then, traveling in the direction of Bettencourt Hall, and while Audra kept her eyes on the road, she was committed to the conversation and not about to back off.

"'All set'? Is that what you were, Mads? Or were you just trying to go with the flow because everything had already been set in motion and you didn't want to throw a wrench in the works?"

Madison sighed loudly. Clamped her back teeth together. Forced herself to relax. At least a little.

"You noticed, I presume, that I *did* throw a wrench in the works? Or were you looking the other way when the whole situation went south?"

Again, Audra laughed. "Now *that* was quite a show," she said. After a pause, her tone was more serious. "Don't blow things with Liam, Mads. You might never get another chance like this. You realize that, don't you?"

Inexplicably, and to her great annoyance, Madison began to cry. "He wants to talk me out of having fertility treatments, I just know it. If you'd seen his face when I told him I was planning to conceive a child, you'd understand."

Now Audra spoke with such gentleness and affection that Madison couldn't help crying harder. "Mads," she almost whispered, feigning impatience. "If Liam objects to you using donor sperm, maybe it's because, if you're so set on having a baby, he wants the child to be his."

"I *wish*," Madison said. "Liam already has two children, and he has his hands full raising them."

"What if you're wrong, Mads?" Audra pressed quietly. "What if he *does* want more kids? More importantly, what if he wants to have them with *you*?"

"That would be wonderful," Madison admitted with a sniffle. "But it's also pure speculation."

"Exactly. And you won't know *what* he wants—what you *both* want—if you don't talk it through with him."

"There's too much going on right now," Madison insisted.

"There will *always* be a lot going on, Mads. It's called life."

"My judgment is bad when it comes to men. You *know* that, Audra. You've had a front row seat. I chose Tom. Then I chose Jeffrey. And both of them seemed like the right man at the time I fell for them."

"Like you've fallen for Liam McKettrick?"

Madison concentrated on the scenery, the trees and the mountains and that big, wonderful sky. "Yes," she said after another extended silence. "Like I've fallen for Liam McKettrick."

"So you admit it? You're in love with him?"

"Yes, oh grand inquisitor. I admit it."

They'd reached Bettencourt Hall, and Audra signaled the turn onto the driveway. "So here's the plan: I spend an evening out—go shopping, take in a movie, whatever—and you invite Mr. Gorgeous over, and the two of you discuss the situation like sensible adults."

Madison thought about mentioning Keely, just to make a point. The girl was obviously having trouble accepting her new circumstances, and she probably wouldn't like it if her father had a girlfriend, let alone a potential stepmother. Stepchildren were a touchy subject with Audra, with good reason, since her own had torpedoed her marriage to a man she'd loved deeply, and if Madison brought up her reservations about Liam's daughter, it might be construed as a retaliatory dig.

So she kept her mouth shut.

And she and Audra spent the afternoon making plans for Coralee's splashy memorial service, well aware that the time between now and then would go by fast.

23

Caroline, Age Thirty-Two

Most of the time, Caroline didn't think about the other place, the other life, the other, very different childhood, lived under a different name.

And what a strange name it had been.

Bliss.

She believed she'd imagined that, along with all the other things she allowed herself to recall now and then, when her mind wandered.

And it was wandering that day. Meandering.

It was a hot Saturday morning in midsummer, and she was kneading bread dough at the kitchen sideboard, while Katherine, elderly now, sat nearby in her rocking chair, in front of the big window Jack had put in when they'd added on to the house, and awash in the sunlight streaming through the glass.

Katherine's hair had long since gone silvery-gray, but it was still lush and shiny and thick. Her back remained straight, her shoulders strong, and Caroline loved her as dearly as if she'd been born of her sturdy body, not that of some forgotten woman.

The old woman was knitting as she rocked, her fingers working nimbly, though unlike the rest of her, they were twisted and gnarled. She'd turned her thoughts inward, a common thing these days, and she hummed under her breath and smiled at whatever she'd found tucked away inside herself.

Caroline smiled fondly in her mother-in-law's direction. "What are you thinking about?" she asked.

Katherine didn't pause in her knitting, though she gave Caroline a sweet glance. "Well, my dear," she replied, "I was thinking about you. When you came to us that day, seemingly out of nowhere."

It seemed more than coincidence to Caroline that she'd been thinking of that, too. "Tell me what you remember," she said gently, rolling the mound of yeasty dough in the big wooden bowl and then pressing it down with floury fists.

"I was washing clothes," Katherine responded, her tone musing, her gaze fixed on the long-ago. "Jack had gone fishing with his dog—you remember Hobo, I'm sure—and he came back long before I expected him, and instead of bringing back trout for supper, there you were, dressed in the strangest clothes—I still can't imagine where you would have come by such a costume, I swear." She paused here, shook her head, mildly marveling at the memory. Then she made a tsk-tsk sound and went on. "You were *so* disheveled, dear. Your hair was so matted it took me hours to comb out the tangles, and as careful as I was, it must have been an ordeal for you. But did you complain? No. And when I fetched something for you to eat, why, you gobbled that food as if you'd been starved for weeks!"

Footsteps sounded outside on the little porch—Jack's handiwork, like the kitchen window—and he stepped inside, tall and so handsome that Caroline's heart tripped at the sight of him, even after twelve years of marriage.

He approached Caroline, kissed her cheek, patted her rounded stomach with one work-roughened hand.

"Good day to you, Mrs. Bettencourt," he said.

Caroline beamed at him. And the child moved in her belly, as though to welcome him back from the fields. "And to you, *Mr.* Bettencourt," she replied.

This baby—*their* baby—was a miracle, due in only a few weeks.

And every time she felt a kick or a shift, she rejoiced, because she and Jack had lost three other babies within a month or two of conception.

This little one, likely to be their only offspring, given Caroline's previous difficulties, seemed determined not only to hold on, but to launch itself into the world with tiny fists flying and feet kicking.

Having greeted his wife, Jack crossed the room to bend down and kiss his mother's forehead. "Another baby blanket?" he teased, with a little nod toward the small panel of blue yarn now resting in her lap.

"One can't have too many," Katherine replied, smiling.

Jack squeezed her shoulder, smiled back.

He turned to the big porcelain sink this time, and pumped water to wash his hands and splash his face. "Don't stop chatting on my account," he said. "I'm just here to rest my feet and gulp down about a gallon of water before I go back to tilling the cornfield."

"We were just remembering the day you found Caroline down by the creek and brought her home to me," Katherine said brightly. Sometimes she was forgetful, but today, her mind seemed sharp. "Do you recall those odd clothes she was wearing, Jack?"

Jack filled a tall drinking glass with water from the sink pump, crossed to the table, turned a chair backwards, and sat astraddle of it. "Yes," he replied. "I've never seen anything like them, before or since. And those shoes." He paused, shook his head. Looked up at his wife. "You called yourself Bliss back then, remember?"

Caroline covered the bread dough with a clean dish towel and went to the sink to wash the flour and butter from her hands, as Jack had washed away field dirt and sweat. Then she stepped up behind him, leaned down, and kissed the sun-reddened nape of his neck.

"I suppose that must have been my name at the time," she said, lowering her bulky self carefully into a chair beside her husband's. "But it doesn't suit me now," she added. She'd chosen the name Caroline herself, out of a book. That mysterious child of long ago, the one called Bliss, was a vague curiosity to her now rather than a person.

Although she must have been abandoned sometime before Jack discovered her, dazed and sitting on the bank of Painted Pony Creek, she didn't remember much about the time before that.

She'd had wicked parents, and one friend, a pretty young woman named Madison.

All part of a fantasy, she supposed.

The dream—the *dreams*—had all been so vivid, seemed so real.

But how could they be true?

She'd gone back, in a later dream, she recalled now, to steal medicine for Jack, as he'd been so sick with a fever that even Doc Wiggins had expected him to die.

Recalling that made her tense.

Jack *had* taken ill when he was just ten years old, almost consumed by a high fever. And he'd recovered.

"Do you remember the medicine?" she asked, and then wished she hadn't spoken aloud. The memories crept closer when she did that, and there was always the danger that they'd catch up with her.

Katherine was rocking again.

Jack was leaning back in his chair, his eyes closed.

"What a peculiar thing *that* was," Katherine said with a

thoughtful nod. "You brought me a handful of little white tablets, and begged me to give some to Jack. I was desperate enough to try anything by then. And to God be the glory, he got better after that. Where on earth could you have gotten such a thing, Caroline?"

Caroline bit her lower lip. Was it possible to cross over between dreams and everyday reality? Surely not, but there *had* been that medicine. She'd stolen it from a box in a strange metal carriage standing outside a strange metal *house*.

And a man had chased her into the cemetery, snatching at her arm, shouting profanities. He'd intended to hurt her, she'd been sure of it.

Then, suddenly, the nightmare had ended with a terrible, aching burst of energy, and Hobo the dog was there again, licking her face.

He'd led her home through the dark woods, and—

And she'd opened the little bottle, in the yard behind Bettencourt Hall, poured the pills into the palm of her hand. Lost a few in the grass when they overflowed.

If she'd been dreaming, where had the bottle come from? It, too, had been odd, made of something hard, something she could see through, though it definitely wasn't glass.

She'd hidden the thing under a bush near the back door, she remembered now, and a few days later, she'd retrieved it, secretly buried it down by the creek.

Caroline began to feel dizzy, and she clutched at the table's edge with both hands, afraid she might swoon.

Jack reacted instantly, wrapping a strong arm around her shoulders, holding her steady so she wouldn't topple from her chair. His gentle face was etched with worry as he studied her face with those changeable hazel eyes of his, eyes that reminded Caroline of someone else.

Briefly, an image flickered in Caroline's mind. A girl, with Jack's light brown hair and chameleon eyes.

Before she could even attempt to put a name to the face, it faded away.

"Shall I fetch the doctor?" Jack asked in a raspy whisper.

No doubt he was thinking of those other babies, poor little things, lost before they'd had a chance to come into the world.

"It isn't that," Caroline said, breathless. When she tried to focus her eyes, the room pitched and dipped and swirled, like the deck of a boat sailing a stormy sea. "It isn't the baby."

She clutched at Jack's arm. Held on.

"You need to lie down," he fretted. "You've overdone it again."

"The bread—I have to finish—"

"The bread must rise for an hour before it can go into the oven," Katherine put in. "Let Jack help you, Caroline. Please."

It wasn't a matter of "letting" Jack do anything, Caroline thought, even more disoriented now. She didn't have a choice, because the room hadn't stopped moving, and she knew she wouldn't be able to stand on her own two feet.

Jack carried her easily up the rear stairway and along the hall to their bedroom.

There, he laid her gently on the bed.

She clutched at him, squeezed her eyes shut to stop the incessant spinning sensation.

"I'm getting the doctor," Jack told her in a voice that brooked no argument. "Something is really wrong."

"No," Caroline protested. "Please. Please don't leave me, Jack."

He bent over her, kissed her forehead, and she breathed in the earthly scent of him. "Mother will keep you company, if that's what you want, but I'm heading for town. You need help."

This wasn't about the baby being born too soon, but she didn't know how to convince Jack of that.

No, this was about memories she'd called dreams, recollections she didn't want to entertain.

For whatever reason, things were flooding back, filling her with images she couldn't explain, not even to Jack, who was the husband of her very soul, as well as her heart and her body.

She'd loved him since she was eight years old.

Don't make me remember, she pleaded silently, listening as Jack strode out of the room. His boot heels made a steady thumping sound on the back stairs, like the firing of a Gatling gun. *Please don't make me remember.*

But it was all coming back, and there was nothing she could do to stem the flow of vivid pictures, visceral impressions. They twisted and turned before her mind's eye, like colorful glass shards moving inside a kaleidoscope.

It was a good thing Jack had carried her to the bed, she thought miserably, because she was coming unraveled, physically *and* mentally.

Fearing she might not be able to put herself back together, Caroline clutched her distended belly in both hands and tried to lie still, to breathe slowly, to calm herself down.

She heard Katherine climbing the stairs, walking along the hallway, entering the room she and Jack's long-dead father had once shared.

Katherine's hand rested, cool and comforting, on Caroline's forehead.

"Don't fuss, now. It isn't good for the child."

Caroline didn't protest that the baby was all right; Katherine's concern was justified, if wholly misguided. She longed to confide in this woman who had been a mother to her long before she was a mother-in-law.

But how would those confidences be received? As the ravings of a mad woman?

My name was Bliss Morgan, and I was eight years old.

I lived outside Painted Pony Creek, but it was the last part of the twentieth century, not the first, like now.

My father was called Duke, and my mother was Mona.

Duke was a mean drunk and Mona left us, because she needed free-dom and fun.

I never really blamed her, because I wanted those things, too. I just didn't know how—or where—to find them.

Duke and I lived in an old camping trailer because we were poor and there was nowhere else to go.

Those odd clothes and shoes you remember me wearing? Those were—will be—worn by kids everywhere. Shorts. A T-shirt. Sneakers.

And that medicine? It was aspirin.

Caroline pressed her hands to the sides of her head, trying to push the memories—could visions of the distant future be called "memories"?—back down into the deepest, darkest part of her brain.

"I shouldn't even be born yet!" she wailed, because in that moment, just as the images wouldn't stay down, neither would the words hammering the back of her throat in an effort to escape into the world and be recognized at long last.

"Hush, child. You're not making sense," Katherine murmured, sitting on the bed beside Caroline now and patting her hand.

"I'm not losing my mind!" Caroline cried. "I'm not!"

"Shhhh," purred Katherine. "Of course you're not losing your mind, dear. Something bad happened to you before you came to us, and now it's made its way to the surface. Try to breathe very slowly and deeply."

Caroline began to sob. Emotionally, she was a human volcano, erupting, and there was nothing she could do about it. Nothing at all.

She remembered everything.

24

Liam had made up his mind to give Madison space; whatever his own needs might be, he knew it would be wrong to crowd her. Worse than wrong.

If he tried to crowd her, she'd run, and who could blame her?

So it was that, during the next two weeks, Liam McKettrick functioned as best he could without seeing Madison, hearing her voice, touching her.

He stuck around home most of the time, since Bitter Gulch was still occupied territory and hanging around a movie set had proven to be boring as hell. It was a mystery to him how anybody could work in that weird, hurry-up-and-wait business without going out of their ever-loving skull.

Ordinary duties sustained him; there were plenty of chores to be done on the ranch, like always, and he went riding with the kids most days.

He and Keely attended weekly therapy sessions, separately and together, and progress seemed painfully slow.

Courtney came back from LA twice for short visits, and when she was around the home place, Keely was usually tagging after her.

That worried Liam, although he knew it was reasonable for a young girl to want a feminine influence in her life. When Courtney was present, she seemed happier, more hopeful, but when it was just Liam and Cavan keeping her company, she often withdrew, hiding out in her room, reading books or texting back and forth with her friends in Seattle.

Liam coped as best he knew how—by loving his children and making sure they knew it. At least, *Cavan* knew it. Keely was still wary, as though she expected her father to sprout horns and a tail and run her through with a pitchfork at any moment.

It was on a Thursday, two days before Coralee Bettencourt's big deal of a memorial was to be held, when fate finally intervened and nudged him out of Neutral, into Drive.

Liam was in Murphy's Hardware Store, across the street from Bailey's, buying bolts to fix bookshelves to the walls of his house so that said shelves wouldn't tip over and crush one of his children, when Madison appeared.

Half a dozen plastic wasp traps lay in the bottom of her shopping cart, and she was examining strings of fairy lights when she glanced Liam's way and caught him staring at her.

He rustled up a smile, though on the inside, he felt as nervous as a pimply fourteen-year-old about to ask out the prettiest girl in school.

"Hello, Liam," she said, and there was a wistful note in her voice. "How are you?"

"I'm fine," Liam replied, though that wasn't strictly true. Being near this woman was like flinging himself into a pool of cool, clean water after crossing a blazing desert naked. It literally took all the restraint he could muster not to enfold her in his arms and hold her as close as he decently could, in a hardware store, in broad daylight. "How about you? All ready for the memorial?"

"Mostly," Madison answered with a small sigh. "Audra and I have been running ourselves ragged, ordering food and flowers, renting tables and chairs—" She paused, glanced down at the contents of her cart. "Orlando is stopping by later to hang these lights around the backyard. We're expecting the party to run well into the evening."

Liam knew Orlando and liked him. He was a good kid and a responsible worker.

He merely nodded in response to Madison's remarks, not quite trusting himself to say anything more.

I love you, Madison. I love your courage, your independence, your determination to get things right. I love that you made room in your life for a little dog, lost and alone. And for so many other reasons.

The words thrummed in his brain, at the back of his tongue, clamoring to be spoken.

Madison tilted her head slightly to one side, squinted a little as she studied his face. "Are you all right?"

No. No, I'm not all right. And I won't be until you're mine.

"Uh—yeah," he said, word virtuoso that he was.

Madison seemed to be waiting for him to say more. The expression in her eyes was sad and curious, but it also seemed to caress him, to ripple against his heart like dangling ribbons fluttering in a soft breeze.

"Do you need any help?" he heard himself ask.

A soft and very faint smile lit her beautiful eyes, and he thought he saw her lips tremble ever so slightly.

"Actually," she said, very tentatively and very quietly, "I *could* use some help, Liam. Audra had to leave town briefly to check up on her mother, and Orlando's been busy doing background scenes in the movie, so I'm pretty much on my own, and the cemetery is still a mass of scrub brush and weeds. I have to get it cleared before Coralee's—" she stopped, swallowed, went on "—Coralee's ashes—can be buried."

Liam smiled, spoke gently. "I'd be glad to help."

Madison beamed. "Wonderful," she said. "Could you bring the kids along? Cavan still hasn't met my dog, you know, and I promised. He and Keely could play with Charlie while we clear the cemetery." Another pause, a slight blush. Liam imagined peeling away this woman's clothes, slowly, garment by garment, nibbling at everything he uncovered in the process. More than anything else in the world, he wanted to taste her, caress her, love on her until she was frantic with pleasure. Until she clawed at his bare back with her fingernails and cried out his name. "It isn't very big, the cemetery, so it shouldn't take long with both of us working."

The simple practicality of these last words blasted Liam out of his fantasy.

He reached for a box on the shelf and held it in front of him, casually he hoped, in order to hide the evidence.

"How does this afternoon sound?" he asked. His neck felt warm.

"Perfect," Madison said.

I want to put my arms around her, offer her comfort. Tell her I love her.

But what he said aloud was, "Meet you at your place in an hour?"

Madison nodded. Her eyes were shining, and her countenance was strangely soft, sweetly pliable. "I'll be ready," she said.

Inwardly, Liam groaned, though he knew she meant she'd be ready to start pulling weeds in the cemetery.

"Good," he replied.

She waggled her fingers at him in a funny little wave that made his heart swell, then turned and headed to the cash register.

Liam waited until he was decent again, put the box he'd used as a shield back in its place on the shelf, and made his way forward to pay up.

WHERE THE CREEK BENDS 337

He had never felt more alive, more fully present in the current moment, but he was also dazed, almost to the point of stumbling.

The kids were with Courtney over at the public library, and Liam considered leaving them in his sister-in-law's care for the rest of the day, even though Madison had specifically asked him to bring them along to Bettencourt Hall.

If he did as she'd asked, there wouldn't be a feather's chance in a high wind of getting Madison into bed, obviously.

Don't press your luck, cowboy, advised a voice in his head as he left the hardware store, headed for his truck, which was parked at the curb, and climbed in. *Take your time, and don't rush the lady. This isn't the time for a stampede.*

Because he had to get through a full hour before he could reasonably knock on Madison's door, Liam made a quick trip back to the ranch.

There, he raided the tool shed for pruning shears, a shovel, a rake and a hoe.

He carried work gloves in the glove compartment of his truck, so that was covered.

After grabbing a tube of sunscreen, he drove back to town, trying not to speed.

There was still plenty of time.

Too much time.

He stopped by the library, parked and went inside.

The air-conditioning came at him in a refreshing rush.

Courtney, Cavan and Keely were standing at the checkout desk, each of them holding a stack of books.

"Guess you're planning on sticking around for a while," Liam observed with a glance at the books Courtney had selected.

"More meetings," she said with a sigh.

"You're all coming to the memorial, I hope," said the librarian, an elderly but spry woman wearing a jersey dress and a name tag that read Althea James. "Coralee loved a party, and this one will go down in history."

Courtney looked confused. "A *party?*" she echoed.

"It's a Bettencourt tradition," Ms. James explained cheerfully. A particularly beautiful emerald and diamond bracelet flashed on her left wrist as she scanned the books into the system. "They like to go out in style."

"Oh," said Courtney, still bewildered.

Liam rested a hand on each of his children's shoulders.

Keely flinched away, a move that was just barely perceptible, but Liam took note of it just the same, and he sighed.

Determined to keep things from deteriorating into another crap-storm, he focused on Cavan for the moment, being in need of a receptive audience as he was. "We've been invited over to Madison's place, to help get ready for the—party. Here's your chance to make the acquaintance of the legendary Charlie the Dog."

A visible jolt of joy went through Cavan, and his smile was wide. *"Yes!"* he shouted.

Ms. James put a finger to her lips. "Shhh," she said. "This is a *library.*"

"Sorry," Cavan said very quietly, but he was still grinning.

Keely nudged him with one sharp little elbow. "Doofus brain."

Liam decided to choose a different battle and let this one slide. So far, knocking heads with his daughter had gotten him nowhere.

She was, after all, as much a McKettrick as he was.

And that gave her a real knack for being stubborn.

"Do you want to go with Cavan and me or not, Keely?" Liam asked in what he hoped was a reasonable tone of voice.

"We could sit by the pool and read, if you'd rather go back to the ranch," Courtney offered, addressing Keely, as they all made their way toward the doors.

Liam cleared his throat. Gave his sister-in-law a look.

"On the other hand, I need to get ready for those meetings I've been yakking about lately," Courtney said, too quickly. "I don't think I can take the time to sit around reading right now, much as I'd love to do just that."

Keely made the decision to go to Madison's place when they reached the parking lot. She handed the books she'd chosen to her aunt and said, with dramatic reluctance, "I guess I'll go with Dad and Cavan."

At least she was calling him Dad now. That had to be a good sign, right?

Courtney placed all the borrowed books in the back seat of her rental car and leaned down to kiss both kids on top of the head, first Cavan, then Keely.

"See you later, Al E. Gator," she teased.

It was a lame joke, but the kids loved it.

"After 'while, Crock E. Dial," they responded in unison.

It was discouraging that, after getting off to a fairly good start, the kids were practically at each other's throats during the ride to Madison's house.

In his head, Liam heard his own father's voice, coming from long ago and far away, in response to his three young sons, arguing in the back seat of some dusty rig.

Don't make me stop this car.

He chuckled at the memory.

"What's funny?" Keely asked, her tone a little terse.

"Everything," Liam replied lightly. "*Life* is funny."

"Whatever," Keely muttered, worldly wise.

Glancing in the rearview mirror, Liam saw his daughter turn her head to look out the side window. He wished he knew how to reach her, in the moment, but he didn't.

"You're a Grinch, Keely McKettrick," Cavan accused. "And it isn't even Christmas!"

"And you're a butthead," Keely retorted idly, still staring out the window.

"One more word from either of you," Liam interrupted

firmly, "and you're both grounded until three weeks after the Second Coming."

He didn't know if they'd caught the reference or not, but they both fell silent, so he counted it as a win.

Cavan had cheered up considerably by the time they pulled into Madison's driveway, and he began to bounce up and down in his booster seat when he spotted her watering flowers in the front yard with her dog jumping at her feet, trying to catch hold of the hose she was wielding.

"There's Charlie!" Cavan whooped. The wait to meet Madison's dog had probably seemed interminable to him, and now the moment had arrived, and he could barely contain his excitement.

You're mighty slow on the uptake, McKettrick, Liam chided himself, parking the truck and shutting off the engine. *Your kids need a dog. Get one. Better yet, get two.*

Both Keely and Cavan were unbuckled and out of the truck before Liam realized that he was gawking at Madison in her trim jeans and long-sleeved shirt, stricken by the sight of her.

So much for holding back, playing the waiting game, being afraid of jumping the gun.

The hell with all that. He was ready for serious action.

He wouldn't rush Madison; he hadn't changed his mind about that, but he wanted her, needed her, not just physically, but with the whole of his being, body, mind and soul.

And he was done hiding what he felt.

Waving a welcome, Madison turned off the water and wound the hose, hanging it from a hook on the side of the house.

Her smile unfurled things inside Liam that he couldn't identify, since they ran far deeper than ordinary feelings.

As a distraction, he unloaded the tools he'd brought from the ranch.

Madison stepped forward to take a set of pruning shears, and Keely, to her father's hidden surprise, took the hoe. With Charlie at his heels, Cavan stepped up to claim the rake.

"This is going to be hard work," Madison warned good-naturedly, probably offering the kids an out, but neither of them took it.

After touching Liam's face with her gaze, she turned and led the way around the side of the house.

There were canopies everywhere, with long tables beneath them, where food and beverages would be served, no doubt, and flowers displayed. Chairs were scattered around in pairs, trios and quartets, placed carefully in the shade of oaks and maples and cottonwoods with their shimmering leaves.

There was nothing funereal about the setting; this was, as the librarian had said earlier, the scene of a celebration, a feast, bright and colorful and welcoming—the figurative embrace of a small town, making space for old memories and new ones, too.

Looking around made Liam's throat tighten.

Not noticing his reaction, Madison continued the trek toward the cemetery, hidden in the woods behind the great and venerable house, a structure of such moment that it had a name.

Keely walked directly behind her, with Charlie and Cavan following, and Liam brought up the rear.

He was thinking that Madison Bettencourt was a woman of infinite mystery, and he was ready to devote a lifetime to learning all about her.

The very private graveyard was overgrown, except for a small patch at one side, where Madison had probably been pulling weeds for days.

Without speaking, she began whacking away at a cluster of blackberry vines, taking them down to the roots.

Liam pulled on his work gloves and started yanking brambles out of the ground.

Keely and Cavan, who started out with good intentions, soon drifted into the shade.

Because he was concentrating on the task at hand, a lot of the work was done before Liam lifted his head and realized that the kids had wandered off.

He wouldn't have worried if Madison hadn't gone still and lost some of the color in her sun-kissed face.

"The kids—" she murmured, clearly alarmed. "Did they go back to the house?"

Liam set the shears he'd been using aside, his gaze held fast by Madison's expression. Even though he'd worn heavy-duty gloves, his hands felt blistered, and suddenly, he was scared. Inexplicably so.

"I don't know," he replied grimly. "Why do you...?"

Before he could finish the question, he heard a shriek, followed by the shrill barking of the dog.

It was Cavan who had cried out, and he sounded terrified.

Liam bolted through the surrounding brush. "Cavan!" he yelled. "Keely!"

Madison was right behind him.

When they reached the creek bank, where the water widened to form a quiet pool, Cavan and the dog were there, a huddled ball of fur and flesh, but there was no sign of Keely.

Cavan's face was streaked with tears. "Keely said you're not my dad!" he wailed, inconsolable. "She said I'm not even a McKettrick!"

Liam closed his eyes for a moment, but his daughter was gone, and he knew this was more than a fight between two kids. He had to find Keely *now*, because something terrible was going to happen if he didn't.

That certainty meant leaving Cavan, who needed him, to Madison, who dropped to her knees in front of the boy and pulled him into her arms, holding him tightly, murmuring that everything would be all right.

The boy sobbed in her embrace, his head buried in her shoulder.

"Keely!" Liam yelled again, not in anger, but in desperation.

"Liam, wait!" Madison cried, getting to her feet. "Wait!"

He *couldn't* wait. He was already plunging into the thick brush, looking for his daughter. The fear that enshrouded him was dark and thick, full of images that brought bile surging into the back of his throat

"Stay right here, with Charlie," he heard Madison telling Cavan. *"Do not move."*

She caught up to Liam, grabbed his arm. "Let me do this, Liam. Let me find her. *Please.*"

Liam felt as though he'd stumbled into a bog, part of the smothering darkness, pulling him down and down, to flail uselessly in oblivion. "No," he said. "No!"

But suddenly, for reasons he could not begin to understand, he was unable to move.

Madison squeezed his arm and ran past him.

25

As Madison ran on, leaving Liam behind, it was as though a great unseen vise was tightening, tightening around her head.

Sickness boiled, bitter and vile, into her throat.

She'd gone only a hundred yards or so before she was forced to her knees by the sheer force of the pain.

She clutched her stomach, leaned forward and vomited.

The pain was excruciating, intolerable, intractable.

Her vision blurred, then was blanked out by a dazzling eruption of light.

"Keely," she choked out. "Keely! Where are you?"

The strange light brightened, blazing around Madison like a consuming fire.

She swayed. Then, with all the strength that remained to her, she fought her way to her feet, unable to see into the glare that surrounded her. Teetering, nearly falling again.

"Madison." It was a female voice, not Keely's, but that of an adult. "It's you!"

Madison blinked, desperate to clear her vision, and made out the shining shape of a woman, rimmed in light. Her clothes were of another era: skirts long, blouse fitted, with puffy sleeves. And she was clearly pregnant.

"Keely—" Madison whispered. This was her fault; she should never have allowed Liam to bring his children to the woods behind Bettencourt Hall, knowing what could happen.

"She's here," said the woman, stepping forward into a patch of leaf-dappled shadow. It was easier to see her there, where the light was muted.

Keely must have been standing behind the stranger, at least partly, for her appearance startled Madison, made her heart leap and flail in her chest.

Madison held out a hand to the child.

Keely hesitated, looking deathly pale, but then she stepped forward, took Madison's hand. Madison wrenched her close, held her even more tightly than she'd held Cavan just minutes before.

Keely huddled against Madison's side, whimpering.

Madison lifted her eyes to the woman's pretty, and faintly familiar, face.

She had caramel-colored hair, done up in a bun at the back of her head, and her eyes were pale amber. Her protruding stomach indicated that she might give birth at any moment.

"Bliss?" Madison said, stunned by the insight, knowing this couldn't *possibly* be her old friend, all grown up.

"It's Caroline now," came the soft response. "Caroline Bettencourt. But I was Bliss Morgan once—a long, long time ago." A wistful smile touched her full mouth. "Or somewhere in the future. I couldn't say which."

Madison felt as though she'd been gut-punched.

This cannot be happening.

But it *was* happening.

"How did—how could…?" Madison was unable to frame the question.

"Go quickly," urged Bliss-now-Caroline. "There's no time to talk. I haven't come this way in years, but it feels different. I think—I think the passage is closing, probably for good."

Madison stumbled backwards, pulling Keely with her, never taking her eyes from Caroline's gentle but worried face. "Were—*are*—you happy?"

"Yes," said Caroline. "I've left messages for you in the margins of Katherine's journals. But you *must* go now, and hurry!"

Madison turned then, suddenly convinced that if she and Keely lingered too long, they might never get back to their own time. To Liam and Cavan and Charlie. And that was unthinkable, so she bolted, dragging a stumbling, still-whimpering Keely along with her.

Almost immediately there was another blast of pain and light, so intermingled that she could not separate them. Beside her, Keely screamed.

They fell, the two of them, face-first into the stubbly grass.

Madison couldn't look back—she didn't have the energy. Or the courage.

Keely was the first to get back on her feet, though her hand still clasped Madison's in a fierce grip. Her clothes—shorts, sneakers, a little sun top—were smudged with dirt, and she'd skinned her knees badly enough to bring tiny speckles of blood to the surface of her flesh.

Madison was scrambling to stand upright when she heard Liam's voice and the sound of brush and tree limbs being shoved aside.

"Keely!" he shouted. "Madison!"

Keely let out a huge, wailing sob and then cried, "Daddy!"

Liam appeared. With a confounded glance at Madison, he gathered his little girl up in a single motion of his entire body, held her.

Long moments passed, and then Cavan and Charlie were on the scene.

Cavan's grubby little face was raw and red from crying.

Charlie bounded over to Madison and leaned his full weight against her calf.

"I'm sorry, Daddy," Keely sobbed, "I'm so sorry—"

Liam murmured something in the child's ear, but he didn't set her down.

His gaze moved to Madison, questioning. Bewildered.

"What just happened here?" he asked.

Madison had no answer—at least, not one that would be believed. She wasn't sure she believed it herself.

"I'm not sure," she said, and that was the blunt, unvarnished truth.

I left messages for you in the margins of Katherine's journals. She heard the words of the woman she'd known only as Bliss in the back of her mind.

Keely pulled back in Liam's arms, peered earnestly into his face. "I felt sick—*really sick*—and there was this lady—"

Liam kissed his daughter's grubby little forehead. "Shhh," he said.

His gaze was still fixed on Madison, and it was searing into her flesh like a branding iron. Was it residual fear, or anger?

Madison was still dazed by the experience herself, and all the questions she might have asked piled up in the back of her throat, like a physical logjam.

"I need to get the kids home," he said, in the voice of a stranger. A *cold* stranger.

He finally put Keely down, and she wobbled beside him, clung to his hand for balance. "We have things to talk about."

"I *am too* a McKettrick!" Cavan burst out, glaring at his sister.

Liam turned to the boy, rested a hand on his head. "You sure are, buddy. And no matter what anybody says, I *am* your dad, and you are my son."

Madison felt strangely helpless as she watched this exchange.

She was definitely on the outside looking in, she realized, and that wasn't likely to change.

"Thank you, Madison, for whatever it was you did," Liam said, and his tone was so flat, so grave, that Madison didn't know if he was actually grateful, or if he was furious with her.

With that, and nothing more, he turned, took his children by the hand, both silent now, and left Madison and Charlie behind.

Madison watched until they were out of sight, her arms wrapped around herself, shivering even though it was a hot day.

When Charlie whined despondently after a minute or so, Madison lifted him into her arms and took one step, then another, not quite trusting her balance.

The headache and the nausea had subsided, but she still felt as though she'd been wrung out like a wet dishcloth, and the confusion was overwhelming.

Had she just seen Bliss Morgan, all grown up?

Or had she suffered a psychotic break?

Unfortunately, the latter seemed a lot more likely than the former.

People were born and lived and finally died, but they didn't travel through time. They didn't go back and forth between one reality and another.

Did they?

History was full of impossible, inexplicable disappearances. Had at least *some* of those lost people slipped away into some unseen dimension, where the rules of time and space didn't apply?

That was a terrible thought, so terrible that Madison raised her fingers to her temples and tried to rub some sanity back into her brain. If she tried to explain the experience she and Keely had just shared to Liam, he wouldn't believe her. How could he? And yet he *would* want answers. That was a given.

And what would Keely be able to tell him?

Surely she was too young to even begin to comprehend such a crazy anomaly.

Would the girl think Madison had somehow caused it? That she'd meant her harm?

Would Liam listen to his daughter's account and come to a similar conclusion?

Madison knew she wouldn't be able to bear that.

She'd realized, that morning in the hardware store, that as much as she loved Bettencourt Hall and Painted Pony Creek, they would be meaningless without Liam McKettrick. Somehow, in just a few short weeks, he'd imprinted himself on Madison's very being, like an invisible tattoo that could never be removed.

There would be no point in staying here at Bettencourt Hall if he turned his back on her.

And he would do just that if he believed for one moment that she presented a danger to his children.

What would she do if she lost this man she wasn't sure she'd had in the first place?

Go back to Boca Raton and take up her old life? Build another business from the ground up? Have babies with someone else's sperm and raise them alone?

None of those options held any appeal, not now that she'd faced the fact that she *loved* Liam, loved him in ways she hadn't guessed were possible, and she had from the moment she'd stormed into the Hard Luck Saloon and set eyes on him for the first time.

She'd been too distracted by her own umbrage in the moment to realize that her life had turned in an entirely new direction when he grinned at her.

These thoughts and others like them careened and collided in Madison's head like carnival rides run amok as she headed for home.

By the time she'd gotten as far as the cemetery and begun gathering up the various tools Liam had left behind, Madison's face was wet with tears.

Sympathetic, Charlie whined in commiseration as he accompanied her to the house, where she dumped the tools on the floor of the sunporch and took refuge in the kitchen, always the most comfortable, convivial part of Bettencourt Hall.

She splashed her face with cold water at the sink, reassured Charlie, and then headed for the library.

It was time to read Katherine's journals.

She gathered the stack from the end table, balanced them on her lap, and sorted through them until she'd put them in chronological order.

The earliest volume outlined Katherine's early years of marriage, and there were no marks in the margins.

It was ordinary stuff, mostly—the sewing of a dress, the baking of bread, things she'd planted or harvested in the garden, assorted weddings, funerals and christenings. Katherine described her love for her husband, Charles, and her sorrow over his death, sometimes in prose, sometimes in poetry. Charles had died of pneumonia when their son, Jack, was three years old, and Katherine had made it clear that she had no intention of marrying again.

She'd known she couldn't replace her husband, for there wasn't another man on earth like him, though it was possible, Madison conceded numbly as she read, that Katherine might have changed her mind later on.

Madison hoped so, but she had her doubts, because Katherine's musings reminded her of herself. Once she'd made up her mind about something, she rarely changed it.

Had she married a man like Liam, for instance, and then lost him to death, she wouldn't be able to bury her love with him. She'd have loved—and mourned—him forever.

Presently, she moved on to the second volume, and again, the notes Caroline had promised were absent. Katherine wrote beautifully of cherished memories, of her lively son, of their strange and magical home.

Magical. What had the woman meant by that?

Madison sat up very straight, intrigued, when the descriptions began.

Sometimes, in beams of dust-flecked sunlight pouring through the library windows, I see my beloved Charles. I see others who have lived and loved and, yes, died in this house, too. I've mentioned these experiences to precisely no one, of course, because who would credit such tales as truth? I would most likely wind up in one of those dreadful asylums, where they hide the insane away, out of sight. Those poor, bothersome souls! They are prisoners, both of their own minds, and the doers of well-intentioned evil... No, I cannot tell anyone that there are rooms in this house, secret hiding places, where improbable things happen, where items appear and disappear, where mirrors reflect other times, other people, even other places...but I can record them here.

Madison sighed, closed the journal for a minute or so, trying to absorb what she'd read before going on.

There were more instances of impossible occurrences to follow, and Madison felt a rush of uneasiness, pondering them. It seemed as though Bettencourt Hall was a vortex of some kind, the hub of a wheel, mostly still, but occasionally spun by some unseen force, moving faster and faster, throwing sparks.

Sparks of magic.

She stopped reading long enough to brew a pot of strong tea—she needed steadying, bracing up—and to feed Charlie, but her mind was whirling, striking sparks of its own.

When she thought she could handle more incomprehensible revelations, she read on.

Most of Katherine's accounts were mundane after that second volume, but in the fourth journal, she found what she'd been waiting for and, at the same time, dreading.

Katherine wrote of a "little visitor" who called herself Bliss.

Katherine's son, Jack, had found her sitting beside the creek, looking lost.

Her clothes were odd, unsuitable for a little girl, revealing her arms and legs the way they did, and her shoes left Katherine thoroughly baffled. The soles were formed of a grass-stained, pliable substance she'd never seen before. She'd wondered, not once but many, many times, if this was another trick of that mischievous house.

Despite these and other misgivings, she'd cared for the little girl, seeing that as her Christian duty, at least in the beginning, and soon enough she'd come to love little Bliss as the daughter she'd never had.

Bliss's margin notes began to appear three quarters of the way through the fourth journal, which bulged with recipes and plans for the vegetable garden and a moderate amount of local gossip.

I'm hoping you'll find my words one day, read her first entry, scrawled in a childish hand. *Maybe you'll come across Katherine's books sometime, and you'll read my message and know I'm here.*

Then, further along, *Do you remember me, Madison? When you knew me, I was called Bliss, but when I married Jack, I changed my name to Caroline, because I wanted everything to be fresh and new.*

Madison's eyes smarted, and her heart tripped over a beat or two. "Bliss," she whispered. "Of course I remember you."

She read on, and with each scribbled addition to Katherine's entries, she became more convinced that Bliss's story was true.

It wasn't one she intended to share, except, perhaps, with Liam.

Clearly, Keely, probably running away from Cavan after delivering the news that he wasn't Liam's child, out there in the woods behind the cemetery, had somehow been pulled into that other place. The place where Bliss had grown up, married, and changed her name to Caroline.

And now she was surely dead, on this side of reality anyway.

That saddened Madison deeply.

She'd seen Bliss—*Caroline*—that very day, still young, visibly pregnant, earnest.

As Madison—and the rest of the world—measured time, not only would Caroline have grown old and died years ago, so would the child she was carrying.

Because it was too painful to explore the implications of that, Madison turned her mind back to the messages of the journal.

Caroline's decision to change her name must have been a way of adapting to the life she found herself in, a way of leaving behind her hardscrabble childhood with her modern-day parents. It was, to Madison, also a symbol of the courage it would have taken, in such a situation, just to move forward in the simplest, most basic ways. To make the most of who she was, where she was, and *with whom* she was.

Today—or more than a century ago—Keely had been pulled into another time, and miraculously, Caroline had somehow found the child soon after she made the transition, and, recognizing her modern clothing, was determined to return her to her rightful world, to her father and her brother.

Keely belonged *here*, with the people who loved her, and Caroline had been wise enough, compassionate enough to risk not only her own well-being—perhaps even her very life—but that of her unborn baby, to turn a frightened child around, pointing her toward home.

Intermittently tearful, Madison read on, stopping only to consume a cheese stick for protein and down a tall glass of water.

Charlie had found his way onto her lap the moment she sat down again on the library sofa, and he remained there until long after night had fallen.

Even without the time travel element, Katherine's thoughts and observations were fascinating, simply because they described another era so vividly that Madison almost believed she was there with her ancestress, experiencing it all, but it was Bliss's notes, coming thicker and faster as time passed, that seeded themselves in her mind and began to grow.

Bliss/Caroline wrote of an early twentieth-century childhood—she'd gone to a one-room school, where she'd learned to love words, both written and read.

She'd made friends, good ones.

She'd worked side by side with Katherine, hoeing in the garden, watering, harvesting when the time came. She'd picked apples and pears, cherries and peaches in the orchard with Jack, some to be preserved in jars, others to be dried and stored away in the pantry, or simply devoured at their juicy best, and he'd taught her useful things, like how to fish for trout and bass, how to chop wood, how to dig for wild onions and other tubers down by the creek.

Madison bit her lip, imagining the orchard, now neglected and overgrown, when it was alive and productive, and made up her mind to restore that forgotten acre of dead, gnarled trees, and plant new ones that would bear fruit.

It was on the last page of the last journal that Caroline had written the words that both chilled and restored Madison.

Five years ago to the day, Madison, I saw you again. I was down by the creek when the little girl appeared, and I knew I had to get her back to where she belonged. I'm so glad you were there to receive her. I write this to assure you that the passageway, at least the one between my time and yours, has closed. I've tried, just to be sure, and I've never been able to go back.

I believe the woods and the cemetery are safe places now. You need have no fear, for yourself or for the children, that such a journey could happen again.

I'm convinced it won't.

Also, because you might be wondering, my baby was born healthy and strong. Her name is Adelaide. Her brother,

Gideon, came along three years later, and he, too, is a sturdy and happy child.

Alas, Katherine has been "gathered to her people," as she would have put it, but she died gladly and gratefully, having lived a full life and seen two grandchildren come into the world.

Be well, Madison. I wish we could have known each other longer.

That was the last of it.

Madison pressed herself into a corner of the sofa and sat up very straight, crying many tears, with many emotions behind them.

When she eventually set aside the final journal, she was immediately sleepy.

She took Charlie outside briefly, and then the two of them climbed the stairs.

Reaching her bathroom, Madison removed her clothes—she'd been so caught up in the aftermath of the incident with Keely and Caroline and the contents of Katherine's journals that she hadn't realized she was filthy—took a quick shower, pulled on a nightshirt, brushed her teeth and toppled onto her bed, not even bothering to crawl under the coverlet.

Hours later, after a deep and blessedly dreamless sleep, she awakened to bright sunshine streaming through the windows and to Audra, who was standing in her bedroom doorway.

"I brought you coffee," Audra said, crossing the space to set a steaming, fragrant cup of brew on Madison's nightstand.

"When did you get back?" Madison asked, yawning as she sat up.

"About half an hour ago," Audra replied, frowning as she perched on the edge of a nearby chair. "Charlie about barked his brains out, greeting me. You didn't hear him?"

"Nope." Madison shook her head, feeling mildly ill as memories of the day before crawled back into her mind. She wished she could write the whole thing off as a crazy dream, but she couldn't. The incident in the woods had been all too real—how else could she explain Bliss's notes in the margins of Katherine's journals?—and she had no earthly idea how to process the implications.

This was something she would have to be with, to walk alongside.

And it was entirely possible, even probable, that she would never understand.

"You look terrible, Mads," Audra observed regretfully. "I wish I could tell you to stay in bed all day and get over whatever it is that's got you tied up in knots, but your grandmother's memorial is today, and the catering crew is due in—" she paused to check her watch "—two hours."

Madison groaned. She tried to come up with ways to tell Audra what was bothering her, but she knew her friend would be more than skeptical, and she couldn't deal with that on top of managing Coralee's celebration.

"I'll make breakfast," Audra went on when Madison didn't speak, "while you get dressed and ready for the day."

Grateful, Madison nodded.

Half an hour later, she was wearing her favorite sundress, a pink-and-magenta floral with spaghetti straps and a hem ruffle. She'd pinned up her hair and applied light makeup, and when she looked into the full-length mirror in her bedroom, she saw a normal woman, someone sensible and competent. Sure of herself.

Inside, however, she felt like a ghost haunting her own life.

Alone.

26

They'd just left Madison, driving away in the truck, and Liam was already regretting the way he'd handled the goodbye.

Because he'd been terrified for his daughter, he'd acted like a real asshole, behaved as though he thought Madison had done something wrong, when she clearly hadn't. The fact that he'd almost lost Keely to a situation he couldn't begin to understand was no excuse.

He had some apologizing to do.

And some groveling.

"What happened out there, Keely?" he asked, gripping the steering wheel so hard his knuckles hurt. He'd noticed that Cavan was asleep in his booster seat, which meant he could speak freely.

The boy's face was still red, damp with perspiration and tear-stained, and his eyelids trembled as he dreamed.

"Tell me," Liam reiterated.

"I don't know," Keely whispered.

"You do know." The contradiction was mild, but it was firm, too.

Keely sighed. "I was so mean to Cavan, and I couldn't take back what I said." She swallowed, sniffled. "I guess I wanted to run away from myself, so I wouldn't have to be me anymore."

Liam's battle-weary heart ached, but he was asking a different question.

"We'll get to that," Liam replied. They'd reached the ranch, and he drew the truck to a stop in front of the garage. Then he turned in the seat to look directly into his daughter's face. "What you did was wrong, Keely. *Very* wrong. But right now, I want to know what happened out there, to you and to Madison."

Keely squeezed her eyes shut, and a single tear trickled down her right cheek. "I thought I was dying," she said, meeting his gaze again. "I thought I was so bad that God killed me, because I had this terrible pain in my head, and then I saw the lady."

"What lady?" Liam asked evenly.

Cavan stirred, but thankfully he didn't wake up. The poor kid was exhausted.

"I've never seen her before. She wore funny, old-time clothes, like some of the women who work at Bitter Gulch, and she had a big baby bump. She was fishing in the creek, but when she saw me, she looked really upset, and she said, 'Oh, no!' and that scared me really bad, because I knew I was someplace I wasn't supposed to be. She put down her fishing pole—it was weird, Dad, more like a stick with a string instead of the kind you and Papa use—and then she came over to me and grabbed my hand. She said, 'You must go back, quickly!' I wanted to ask who she was, and what was going on, because my head hurt so badly, and I felt like I was really far away from you and Cavan and Madison and Charlie. And like maybe I wouldn't be able to get back. There was more pain, and this *explosion* of light, and then Madison was there, and she looked as scared as I was. She and the lady talked—I don't remember what they said—and then Madison was hugging me really tight, and the lady just—disappeared."

Liam took a few moments to digest her words, but he couldn't break them down into anything that made sense. Surely Keely had imagined all this, and yet he believed her.

"I was so glad to see Madison," the girl said. "I was so scared, but she held on to me, and I knew that light wouldn't be strong enough to suck me back in, 'cause it had mostly faded away by then. And because Madison wouldn't have let me go."

Liam closed his eyes briefly.

Madison.

He'd treated her like an axe murderer, not the woman he loved. The woman who'd been there for his daughter and quite possibly saved her—from what, he couldn't say.

He needed to talk to her, but that would have to wait, because his kids needed him now, and probably more than ever before.

He wouldn't, couldn't let them down.

So he unfastened Cavan from the booster seat and carried him inside the house. The motion stirred the boy partially awake.

Courtney was standing in the kitchen, stirring a pot of soup.

Keely ran to her, threw her arms around her aunt's trim waist.

Courtney stroked Keely's hair with her free hand and gave Liam a questioning look.

"Later," he said. He was still carrying Cavan, letting him ride on one hip.

Cavan woke all the way up then, and he started to cry again, making a pitiful, whimpering sound that tore his father's heart from its moorings.

Liam carried the child into the living room, where they could be alone for a little while.

"Keely said—" Cavan began, but couldn't continue.

"I know what Keely said," Liam replied quietly into the silence. "And we're going to talk about that, you and me. And Keely, too, when the time is right."

"Do I have to go live with somebody else?" Cavan fretted as Liam set him down on the couch and then took a seat next to him. "Because I'm not yours, I mean? I don't want to leave you!"

"You're not going anywhere, son. We're your family, Keely and me, and you belong with us."

"But Keely hates me!"

Liam mussed the boy's damp hair. "Keely *doesn't* hate you, bud. It might seem that way, but she didn't mean what she said."

"Why is she so mad at me?" The question was small, uncertain.

"I don't think she is, buckaroo. I think Keely is a little mad at herself and a whole lot mad at me. You got caught in the crossfire, and that was wrong. Really wrong. But she's your sister, and she'd probably defend you to the death."

Cavan's eyes widened. "I don't want Keely to die!"

Liam sighed. He wasn't handling this well, obviously. "She won't. I just meant she wouldn't let anybody else hurt you, even though she's hurt you herself."

Cavan sniffled again and tried to look brave. "Did she lie? Is it true that you're not my dad?"

Liam offered up a silent prayer. How was he supposed to explain reproductive biology to a distraught seven-year-old?

"No," he said. "She didn't exactly lie. Do you know how babies are made, buckaroo?"

Cavan shook his head.

Liam couldn't put this off, couldn't say, *You'll understand when you're older.*

Even though that was true.

"I'm your dad in every way that really matters," Liam told his son. "And you are *definitely* a McKettrick."

"You've said that before," Cavan pointed out. "But what did Keely mean?"

Liam suppressed a deep sigh, and even though it was silent, he felt it in every part of himself. "Your mother and I didn't always get along very well, Cav," he began. "She had a friend, and they made a baby together."

"Me?" Cavan asked. His eyes were huge, and he seemed to be holding his breath. "Was I the baby they made?"

"Yes."

"Then he's my dad? Mom's friend?"

Liam's eyes burned, and his voice was a husky rasp when he answered, "In one way, he is." Cavan's biological father, a race car driver, had died in a fiery crash when Cavan was two, and before that, as far as Liam knew, he'd wanted nothing to do with his son. Or Waverly. "In the most important ways, though, I'm your dad."

"You can't both be my dad!"

Liam gave the boy a one-armed hug, a tight one. "You're right. I'm your dad, Cavan. And that's not gonna change."

"Am I adopted then?" The kid was going to grow up to be a lawyer, for sure. Or a journalist. A man who wouldn't stop asking until he got answers he could accept as true.

Liam gave a raw chuckle, ruffled Cavan's dark hair again. "No, buddy. You've been a McKettrick from day one. The first time I laid eyes on you, in the hospital after you were born, you were in a little bed, behind a thick glass window. There were other babies all around you, dozens of them, but I knew you were mine with just one look. My heart opened up then, and you snuggled right into it. You've been there ever since."

At last, Cavan relaxed a little. He huddled close against Liam's side. "I like being in your heart, Dad," he said, his voice muffled by the fabric of his father's T-shirt. In the next moment, the boy reared back and looked up at Liam in consternation. "Dad?"

"What?"

"You don't smell very good."

Liam threw back his head and laughed. Laughed 'til he cried.

Cavan shifted to his knees and tried to brush the tears from Liam's eyes.

"Don't cry, Dad. I'm right here."

Liam made a strangled sound, took the boy into his arms, and shuffled him onto his lap. Then he buried his face in Cavan's sweaty little neck and blew a raspberry.

The peal of childish laughter that followed mended Liam's heart.

As the hours passed, a welcome sense of calm settled over the ranch house.

Keely stayed in her room, and Liam left her alone, though his first instinct had been to wade into troubled waters and sort things out.

Fortunately, Courtney had dissuaded him from that idea.

Liam saw to the evening chores, taking extra time with the horses, not because their presence was reassuring, though it was, but because his heart was swelling with emotion, and he needed a place to put it. If he held it in, he would burst.

That night was long and, for the most part, sleepless.

He woke at dawn, pulled on jeans, a T-shirt and boots, and headed for the barn.

Once the horses had been fed, watered and turned out to graze, he returned to the house.

Courtney was back in the kitchen, sitting slump-shouldered at the table, a cup of coffee growing cold in front of her.

"Are the kids all right, Liam?" she asked without preamble. "Are you?"

"We're dealing with some things, but, yeah, we'll be fine."

"Promise?"

He poured himself a cup of coffee, leaned against the counter to sip at it. No way he'd let it go cold; he needed the zip it always gave him. "I promise," he replied.

"I take it Keely told Cavan about Waverly and the race car driver," Courtney ventured, apparently in need of some convincing that all of them really would be okay.

"Not in graphic detail," Liam answered after a slight sigh.

"But he knows he's not biologically mine, yes. I'm not sure he understands what that means—it's hard to explain that kind of stuff to a little kid."

Courtney closed her eyes, swayed slightly in her chair. She was wearing faded gray sweats and sneakers, and her dark hair was pulled up into a messy bun on top of her head. When she met Liam's gaze again, her face was full of concern. "Did you try?"

"Yes." He choked up for a moment, remembering how Cavan had attempted to dry his tears the day before. "He'll have a lot more questions as time goes on, of course. For now, though, we're good."

"Thank heaven," Courtney breathed. Then, sitting up a little straighter, she added, "What happens now, Liam? Seems to me there's a lot of unfinished business to attend to."

"You're right," Liam said. "I'll take Keely out for a horseback ride later today, just the two of us, if she's ready for that, and talk things through."

Courtney leaned forward just slightly, and her expression was earnest. "Don't be too hard on her, Liam," she said. "Between them, Mom and Waverly did a number on that poor child. Keely isn't cruel, she's scared. And she's confused."

"She's told you all that?"

Courtney nodded. "Yes. Let her come to you, okay? She'll do that when she's ready. I know she will."

Liam set his half-finished coffee aside and folded his arms. "All right," he said. "I'll wait. There's been a lot to muddy the waters lately, and we all need time to let things settle to the bottom." He paused, thought for a moment, then went on. "There's something I need to do in town. Is there any possibility you can look after the kids for a few hours?"

"I'd be glad to," Courtney replied quickly, smiling now. "I believe this situation calls for my famous chocolate chip and cherry waffles. You do own a waffle iron, right?"

"No," Liam answered with a grin and a shake of his head. "I'm sure you'll figure something out, though, culinary genius that you are. That soup you made for supper last night was ambrosia."

Courtney laughed. "Get out of here," she said. "And don't you dare come back without a waffle iron. The fun kind shaped like Mickey Mouse, if you can find one."

Mentally, Liam added a stop at Walmart to his list.

If he got around to it, that is.

He had barely stepped outside when Keely called to him. "Dad, wait!"

Liam stopped, watched as she approached. "What's up?" he asked, his voice a little hoarse as a variety of emotions welled up inside him.

Reaching his side, Keely gripped him by the forearm and stage-whispered, "I really need to talk to you."

With that, she pulled the door shut behind them.

Liam sucked in a deep dose of fresh country air and rested a hand between Keely's shoulder blades, giving her a light push away from the doorstep.

Then he crouched in order to look directly into his daughter's eyes, which were now welling up with tears that glistened in the sunshine. "Talk to me, Keely," he urged quietly.

Keely trembled, bit her lower lip. Now tears were flowing down her cheeks. "I need to know you still love me," she said. And those words rocked Liam's very soul.

"Of course I still love you," he said, his voice husky.

He stood and lifted Keely in the curve of one arm, the way he had when she was little.

Keely sniffled. "I did something really bad, though. I shouldn't have told Cavan he wasn't your son." A sob escaped her, and she buried her face in Liam's shoulder. "I'm so sorry, Dad!"

Liam squeezed her close, then planted a big kiss on her left temple. "What you did was mean, Keely. Really mean. You apologized to Cavan, right?"

Keely nodded and uttered a small, despairing sob. "He called me a meanie-weenie," she said, laughing even as she cried. "Then he told me that if I was nice to him from now on, he'd be nice to me."

Liam gave a gruff chuckle. Cavan. Ever the optimist. But his kids were young, with a lot of growing up to do, and it was unlikely they'd get through the coming years without butting heads occasionally.

Now Keely drew back a little to look directly into her father's face. "I said I couldn't promise I'd never be mean again, because I'm going to be a teenager pretty soon, but that I'd always remember that he *is* your son, and my brother."

Liam blinked hard, but a single tear escaped, and Keely promptly wiped it away with her index finger. "We'll all have to work hard in therapy," he said, "because we've been through a lot, especially you and Cavan, but we're going to make it, Keely. I need you to know that. We're a family, and we always will be."

"Really?"

Liam set his daughter on her sneakered feet. "Really," he confirmed.

"You won't send me back to Gambie's house, or to boarding school?"

"That is never gonna happen," Liam said, swiping a forearm across his wet eyes.

"You promise?" There was so much hope in Keely's shining eyes that Liam thought his knees might buckle, what with all the feelings he was having all at once.

"I promise," he said, meaning it. Then he bent, kissed the top of her head. "I have some things to do in town," he told her. "You going to be all right?"

Keely nodded vigorously, turned, and went back inside the house.

Soon enough, though still shaken, Liam was on the road, headed for Painted Pony Creek.

It was too early to knock on Madison's door, so he'd have to kill some time in town. Plus, she'd be extra-busy today because of Coralee's big send-off, but he had things to say to her, and he was going to say them, even if it was awkward.

He had a leisurely breakfast at Bailey's, keeping to himself, though he responded to every greeting—of which there were many—with a smile and a nod.

Painted Pony Creek was his home now, and it was his kids' home, too. Therefore, no matter how distracted he might be by his immediate plans, he wanted to be friendly.

He ate—ham and eggs and hash browns, with a side of Texas toast—very slowly.

He watched the sun climb higher and higher in the eastern sky.

He read an abandoned newspaper and drank about ten cups of coffee.

Finally, at nine o'clock, he paid up, left a generous tip for the waitress, and headed for his truck. He'd parked it over on the other side of Bitter Gulch.

After a quick stop at Walmart, where he purchased a Mickey Mouse waffle maker, he drove to Bettencourt Hall, and parked a ways back from the house, since the driveway was full of caterers' and florists' vans. It was definitely an action scene, with people hurrying back and forth, carrying pans and bowls and bouquets, and Liam moved politely through the jostle on his way to the back door.

He ran into Audra on the sunporch.

"Mornin'," he said.

She watched him, mouth slightly open, eyes wide, but she didn't say a word.

Liam crossed the sunporch, sidestepping Audra, and knocked lightly on the back door, which was partially open.

Through the gap, he saw Madison.

She was wearing a sundress.

Her hair was up, and her fancy sandals had the same effect

as high heels—i.e., they did things for her long, silky legs that twisted things in Liam he rarely thought about.

She turned at the sound of his knock, looked worried for a moment, then baked him alive with her smile. "Come in," she said.

He came in. Stood face-to-face with her, bedazzled by the soft lavender-and-spice scent of her skin.

Without preamble, he made his announcement. "I love you, Madison Bettencourt."

She looked stunned, but then a look of mischievous triumph came into her magical hazel eyes. "Seriously?"

"Yes. I know this is going to take a while, but I didn't want to let another day—another *hour* go by without telling you."

Madison was still for a long time, so long that Liam started to think she was going to show him the road, once and for all.

Instead, she slipped her arms around his neck.

He felt the warm firmness of her lush breasts through the thin cloth of his T-shirt, and outside, the noise of busy preparation receded.

They kissed, deeply and for a long time.

"Oops," said a woman's voice just before the back door closed.

Madison smiled and looked up into his eyes. "You love me—seriously?" she asked, her tone almost teasing.

"Absolutely," Liam replied.

"Well," Madison responded to his great relief, "I love you, too, Liam McKettrick."

He planted a light kiss on the tip of her nose. "I know Coralee's memorial service is today, but—well, we need to talk, soon. I want to marry you, Madison."

Madison's eyes were still sparkling. "And I want to marry you, too," she agreed. "But we have a lot to discuss. For instance, I need to know if you're willing to have more children. And there will definitely be no big, splashy wedding this time. I don't have the best track record in that area, if you recall."

Liam laughed, though quietly. After all, Madison had lost her only living relative, and today marked the final goodbye.

"I definitely want more kids. With you. And as long as you're willing to say 'I do' and sign the marriage license after the ceremony, I don't care if we get married in the barn."

Now it was Madison who laughed.

And Liam relished the note of delight he heard in her voice. He kissed her again then. Thoroughly.

"Are you coming to the memorial this afternoon?" Madison asked. "You and Cavan and Keely?"

"Do you want us here?" Liam's tone was serious now.

"Yes," Madison said. "I want you here, all three of you. And Courtney, too, of course, if she wants to join us."

Liam's heart shot skyward like fireworks. They were going to build a real family, he and Madison, Cavan and Keely, and the other little McKettricks who were bound to come along in time.

"We'll be here," he promised. He hadn't forgotten, after all, that Madison was grieving, and he wanted to be there to support her in whatever way she needed.

With that decision made, he hugged her close, and she cried a little, and when she'd recovered, Liam headed home to shower and dig through his closet for a suit.

He was well out of town when he pulled to the side of the road, rolled down the window, and yelled for joy.

★ ★ ★ ★ ★